Mary Bernadette:
SECRETS OF A DALLAS MOON

Mary Bernadette: SECRETS OF A DALLAS MOON

A YOUNG VIETNAMESE GIRL'S TALE
from the GRAVE *about the* KILLING OF JFK

JOHN F. BRONZO

Copyright © 2015 John F. Bronzo.

All rights reserved. No part of this book may be used or reproduced by any means, graphic, electronic, or mechanical, including photocopying, recording, taping or by any information storage retrieval system without the written permission of the author except in the case of brief quotations embodied in critical articles and reviews.

Archway Publishing books may be ordered through booksellers or by contacting:

Archway Publishing
1663 Liberty Drive
Bloomington, IN 47403
www.archwaypublishing.com
1 (888) 242-5904

Because of the dynamic nature of the Internet, any web addresses or links contained in this book may have changed since publication and may no longer be valid. The views expressed in this work are solely those of the author and do not necessarily reflect the views of the publisher, and the publisher hereby disclaims any responsibility for them.

Any people depicted in stock imagery provided by Thinkstock are models, and such images are being used for illustrative purposes only. Certain stock imagery © Thinkstock.

ISBN: 978-1-4808-1904-7 (sc)
ISBN: 978-1-4808-1905-4 (hc)
ISBN: 978-1-4808-1906-1 (e)

Library of Congress Control Number: 2015910155

Print information available on the last page.

Archway Publishing rev. date: 8/26/2015

Rooted in the 1963 assassination of John Fitzgerald Kennedy (JFK) and taking place during the Vietnam War in 1971, this is an epic tale of patriotism and sacrifice and of love and intrigue, as seen by the backward glance of a young Vietnamese girl named Mary Bernadette, who was born on the day President Kennedy was assassinated and lived just long enough to see his other assassin—the second gunman on the grassy knoll—be captured.

This book is a work of fiction. Names, characters, places, and incidents are either products of the author's imagination or used fictitiously. Any resemblance to actual events or locales or persons living or dead is entirely coincidental.

Dedication

This book is dedicated to all who have worn the uniform in the defense of this great country of ours—especially my uncle and godfather, who served in the Army Airborne; my three brothers-in-law and nephew, who served in the marines and the navy; and my niece, who currently is serving as a navy surgeon. It also is dedicated to the memory of two friends, one who died when the helicopter he was piloting was shot down in Vietnam and the other who left the seminary to join the marines and fight in Vietnam before returning to law school and a career cut short in the FBI.

In addition, this book is dedicated to four very important people in my life: my father, who helped me with some of the initial research, but died before I could finish; my two sons, who died before their time (if there is such a thing in the Almighty's plan for us); and my grandson, who is said to be a special needs child, but whom I prefer to view as simply special.

I want to thank my family – my mother, Gloria, wife, Carole, children Sandra and husband John J. LePino Jr., John, Christine, and Joseph. Without their help and support this book would not have been possible.

Prologue: The Move On

The sun was beginning to rise over Stockton, California, when the weary driver and his car pulled into the parking lot of the nondescript motel on a chilly morning in May of 1982. The voice on the radio was promising another sunny day. However, the driver, fighting back the fatigue of three days of virtually nonstop driving across the country from New York, was paying little attention. More important to him was the flashing vacancy sign outside the motel office.

As he stepped from the vehicle, he paused for a moment. For even in the vague first light of the morning, he could see what he had done to his trusted companion. This was no ordinary car, after all, but a most special charge with which the driver had been entrusted and which he had named Mary Bernadette. The normally shiny silver 1979 Mercedes-Benz 450 SL that he had so meticulously maintained for the last three years was now in uncharacteristic form. She was covered in road dust, her headlights and windshield were littered with the remains of dead bugs, her brilliant wheels were dull black with brake soot, and her rich red interior was cluttered with empty coffee cups and fast food wrappers from the trip. Much like a husband might look upon his wife with love and gratitude after she had endured the ordeal of childbirth to give him a beautiful baby, the driver gazed with affection and gratitude upon his cherished friend, which had gotten him there safely, and asked himself what had he done to that magnificent machine that was so dear to him. However, the driver knew in his heart that if the car could understand, it too would agree that their mission warranted all that had been endured by both man and automobile.

Opening the trunk, he took out a small gray suitcase and proceeded toward the office door. A few minutes later, he emerged again, with a key to room 38. Once in the room, he fell fast asleep on top of the bed, his clothes still on him. When the alarm went off a mere three hours later, he awoke with a jolt, momentarily forgetting where he was, but quickly regaining his orientation. Showering and shaving for the first time since leaving New York three days earlier, he put on the newly pressed suit he so carefully had packed in the suitcase. As he knotted his tie he looked at himself in the mirror to see if the apprehension he was feeling was apparent to the naked eye. Relieved that it was not, he quickly packed his belongings and walked out of the room to the car.

Following the directions the motel clerk had given to him, he soon spotted the car wash, which was called the Car Spa. According to the clerk, they were known for their meticulous attention to detail and were even rumored to use a toothbrush to clean the most intractable parts often ignored by others. While he waited for the car to undergo its makeover, as they called it, he walked to the flower shop next door to buy a single yellow rose. As he did, he contemplated what he would say later that day when he visited the grave site that had brought him across the country. He knew that no matter how much he prepared, it would not be easy. The last time he had seen the young woman was in 1971, when she was still very much alive, vibrant, and beautiful.

When the car emerged, it was shiny and clean again, and it glistened in the sunlight. The top now was down, revealing the clean, bright red interior. Putting on his sunglasses, the driver got in and set off for the cemetery. Both car and driver were crisp and clean, a far cry from the way they had looked earlier that morning, when they first had arrived in Stockton.

As they drove into the cemetery and pulled up to the grave site, the young man exited from the car. Walking over to the hallowed ground, he knelt, made the sign of the cross, and began to pray quietly.

When he was finished praying, he said softly, "Hello, Claire. I am sorry to have been so slow in coming to see you, but it has been too hard for me, and I always have been able to find an excuse for not coming. Well, that is, until now.

"Please understand that my love for you was so strong and the void in my life left by your loss so great, that it has taken me this long to be able to move on. But I now think, after eleven long years, I have met the soul mate you were so sure that I would meet.

"She is a lovely person, of whom I know you would approve. Not since I first set eyes on you, back in 1971, have I felt this happy and this completely at peace. She, too, is a package deal and comes with a little girl, or as you liked to kid, 'Buy one, and get one free.' She has a daughter, who is as cute as Mary Bernadette and to whom I also have become attached. My only prayer is that the good Lord will allow us to raise a family and grow old together. It seems such a modest request, but it was a bridge too far for you and me.

"I am returning your scarf, as you asked me to do, for I no longer can be your dragon slayer. However, I want you to know that there always will be a special place in my heart that belongs to you alone."

As he spoke, he had been digging a small hole in which he buried the scarf, having gently kissed it before placing it in the ground. Covering the hole, he then placed the single yellow rose on it and stood up. Putting his hand on the headstone, he bent over and kissed it as he continued to speak.

"When I promised you that I would come back for a kiss, I never dreamt it would be like this. Once I get back to New York, I intend to ask her to marry me. I can do that only if I'm free to give her my undivided love. This is the reason for my visit—to say good-bye. I finally have found someone new. Please wish us a long, productive, healthy, and happy life together."

With that, he turned and began to walk away. Not going far, he stopped, and with a backward glance that revealed the smile on his face and the twinkle in his eye, he conceded aloud to her, "I know, you knew it would happen all along—didn't you?"

He then drove to the home of Claire's family to visit with her parents and her brother, John, a fellow Boston College alumnus. They insisted that he stay for dinner, and he did.

Afterward, he got into the 450 SL and drove into the California night. Chasing first the beams of his headlights and then the rising sun, he motored east. Three days later he was back in New York, the trip across the country having been a safe and uneventful one.

On the following Saturday night, May 22, 1982, he became engaged.

— Book One: —
E PLURIBUS UNUM

– 1 –

My name was Mary Bernadette. I say *was* because I am dead. I was buried alive before the age of eight, in June of 1971, by Captain Ton That Dam, a member of the 325th Division of the North Vietnamese Army. Born in the jungles of Vietnam on the day that President John F. Kennedy was assassinated in Dallas, Texas, I lived just long enough to see his true assassin apprehended by the man Captain Dam called the Devil Priest.

The crime of which I was accused and of which I was guilty was that I knew this Devil Priest. Captain John Joseph Chrisandra, or JJ as people liked to call him, was a US Army chaplain assigned to the 101st Airborne Division in Vietnam. He was an Episcopal priest in civilian life and one of the kindest persons I ever met.

I never knew my father or my mother, and if I had a Vietnamese name, I never knew that, either. The name Mary Bernadette was given to me by an American missionary. She was a Catholic nun by the name of Katherine Sullivan, and she was running a small orphanage for girls, named the Orphanage of Saint Francis Xavier, near Binh Gia, a Catholic village only forty miles southeast of the city of Saigon, in the coastal province of Phuoc Tuy. The orphanage originally had been started by the French and had been affiliated with a French mission church in Saigon's Chinese district of Cholon, named Saint Francis Xavier. Hence, the name of the orphanage was derived from that of the mission church.

According to Sister Kate, as she liked us to call her, I was brought to her on November 22, 1963, by a US Army adviser. He found me that day abandoned in the jungle, not far from the orphanage, while he was on patrol with the Vietnamese soldiers he was training. Apparently, my mother was living alone in the jungle to hide her pregnancy until after I was born and actually may have been scared away, only hours after giving birth to me, by the very patrol that found me.

When I was old enough to understand, I asked Sister Kate why my mother would have wanted to abandon me. Sister Kate smiled at me and gently stroked my head. She said to me with a sigh, "I have been expecting that question for a while now, my love. Sit down, please. I will try to explain.

"Many years ago I was born here in Vietnam the way that you were. My father apparently was a Chinese worker, and my mother was a Vietnamese woman from Ha Long Bay in the north. I was left at the door of the mission church of Saint Francis Xavier in Cholon with a note that explained that my father had left to return to China and my mother had no way to provide for me. I was brought to this orphanage, and I lived here until I was adopted by the Sullivan family in 1945.

"Mary Bernadette, you have more than a Western name; you have Western blood flowing in your veins as well. Your mother may have been Vietnamese, but your father was a Western man who I suspect left Vietnam before you were born. Your mother and her family most likely feared reprisal from your village or from the Vietcong once it was known that you were the product of such a relationship. I am sure that your mother thought that the soldiers would bring you here and that you would have a better life at the orphanage.

"My own background as an abandoned baby, as well as my gratitude to my adopted family and nation, formed the inspiration for my desire to become a Franciscan nun and return to Vietnam to continue the work of this orphanage. I wanted to be Hesperidean in my protection of little souls like you. I hope you understand what I am telling you."

"Well, I think I do. But what does that *hesper* thing mean?"

"I'm sorry, love, I got carried away. In Greek mythology, the

Hesperides were daughters of Atlas, a very strong man. They, too, were very strong. They guarded valuable trees and the fruit of those trees the way I guard you and the other girls here at the orphanage."

Sister's explanation didn't help me very much, but I got the general idea and decided to let it go. After all, Sister Kate was like a mother to me, and no one could possibly love me more than she did. Little did I know at the time, it would not be long before I would see proof of that love in a way that even now is too painful to remember.

– 2 –

One afternoon a stranger with a dark complexion staggered incoherently into the front yard of the orphanage. Suddenly, he collapsed in front of the tree where Sister Kate and I often sat when she read to me from the Bible or works of American literature, two of her favorite instruction tools. In response to my cries for help, Sister Kate came running and immediately took charge, ordering me and the other girls to help her get the stranger inside and on a bed.

As we struggled to move the man, he started to mumble in a language that I didn't recognize but which Sister Kate said was Russian. When we laid him on the bed, Sister Kate began to examine him and immediately noticed the snakebite on the fleshy part of his arm. She gave him an injection of some antivenom that she had. Over the next few hours, Sister Kate worked hard to try and nurse the stranger back to health as he continued to murmur deliriously in Russian.

The next morning, he finally began to show some signs of improving, and Sister Kate relaxed enough that I felt comfortable to ask her what he was saying in this foreign language. She responded, "Love, I have been too busy to pay any attention to his gibberish. But what do you say we go in there now and take a listen?"

As we entered the room, I asked Sister Kate where she had learned to speak this strange language. She told me that she had studied Russian in college for four years while she was a student at the University of California at Berkeley. With that we took our places by the stranger's bed and began to listen. Initially Sister Kate looked bored and only superficially interested in what the stranger was saying, but as time progressed I could see from the expression on her face that she was listening far more intently to his words. At one point she got visibly upset with what she was hearing. I didn't dare ask any questions for fear of disturbing her concentration. When I heard him say what I thought was the word *Kennedy*, I no longer could contain myself; I had to ask what he was saying. For Sister Kate had told us many stories about the American president she had loved and admired so much. "Sister," I said, but before I could finish my sentence, she told me to be quiet and go outside to play with the other girls. Reluctantly, I did as I was told. Sister remained alone with the sick man the rest of that day and night, barely taking time to feed us and put us to bed. The next day was more of the same.

It was not long into the third day when my curiosity drove me to peek inside. To my surprise, Sister Kate was speaking on a portable radio similar to the ones that the American army soldiers used. I didn't know that the orphanage had such a radio. Sister Kate had never so much as mentioned that it existed. The door to the medical supplies closet was open, and the back shelf of the closet was moved away from the wall, revealing a secret compartment in which she must have hidden the radio.

I heard Sister Kate state her name as Le Xuan and ask in Vietnamese to speak with Mr. Matt Kerr. Le Xuan is Madame Nhu's name, and it is a name that Sister Kate sometimes called me. It means "beautiful spring" in my language. I can only guess that Sister Kate was speaking Vietnamese and using this name to conceal her true identity from anyone that might be listening.

In any event, after a short pause, the voice on the other end said in Vietnamese, "Matt Kerr here. What is so important that you would risk calling me in this way?" Sister responded with a question of her own and asked, "Is this line secure?" to which Mr. Kerr replied, "Yes." With that, the floodgates opened, and Sister Kate began to speak in a hurried and excited manner.

"You are not going to believe what I am about to tell you." But before Mr. Kerr could say a word, she continued, "A few days ago, a stranger stumbled into the orphanage—the victim of a poisonous snake bite—and collapsed in a delirious state. He may be hallucinating, but he is ranting in Russian about having been a part of the Kennedy assassination in Dallas in 1963.

"I have been probing him for the last three days. He seems to be blaming our democratic form of government for having made it possible for a young and inexperienced leader such as John F. Kennedy to have been elected to such an important office. He claims that President Kennedy's poor showing in his first meeting with Premier Nikita Khrushchev in Vienna in 1961 caused Khrushchev to underestimate Kennedy's true measure as a leader. This miscalculation, in turn, supposedly resulted in the Soviet adventurism that led to the 1962 Cuban missile crisis and the embarrassing need to withdraw Soviet weapons from Cuba."

"Is he saying that Khrushchev had Kennedy assassinated because of the Cuban Missile Crisis?" asked Mr. Kerr.

"No," replied Sister, "he appears to be saying that both Kennedy and Khrushchev were done in as a result of the way they handled that crisis. He claims that rogue elements of the US military industrial complex had Kennedy assassinated in 1963 because they were upset with him for agreeing to forgo invasion of Cuba, which they viewed as the first 'domino' in Latin America." Sister then continued after taking a moment in an attempt to catch her breath, "They were concerned that he would not commit combat troops to fight in Vietnam, which they viewed, along with Korea, as the first two dominoes in Asia. According to the Russian, these rogue elements thought that Lyndon Johnson would be more apt to commit such troops when they were needed in Vietnam."

At this point Mr. Kerr interrupted Sister and asked, "Even if what he is saying is true, and I am not saying that it is, what is the reason that the Soviets and this fellow became involved?"

Sister replied, "This is where it gets really strange. He claims that an ultraconservative and influential element within the Soviet party had become concerned at what they viewed as an emboldened and possibly out-of-control US military."

"What?" asked Mr. Kerr incredulously. "Where the hell did they get that idea?"

Without showing any reaction to Mr. Kerr's outburst, Sister continued in a calm voice, "He claims that during the height of the Cuban Missile Crisis, Anatoly Dobrynin, the Soviet ambassador to Washington, reported that Robert F. Kennedy came to plead with him for a resolution to the crisis because his brother, the president, was under great pressure from the military to use force against Cuba, and that if the situation didn't get resolved soon, the president was worried that the military would overthrow him and take over.

To this, Mr. Kerr, appearing almost to be talking to himself out loud, said, "I was involved, and I don't remember any signs that the president had any such fears. Robert Kennedy must have been using the military as the bad guys in his negotiations with Dobrynin."

"Well, the president's brother must have been very convincing. The Russian claims that this conservative element within the Soviet party, which had been growing increasingly unhappy with Khrushchev for favoring a reduction in conventional Soviet forces and for being what they viewed as too conciliatory to the West, now became alarmed. The prospect of an out-of-control US military, emboldened by Khrushchev's misguided and embarrassing actions, was more than they were willing to accept. He said that they decided to use their influence to remedy the situation."

"Did he elaborate on what he means by 'remedy the situation'?" asked Mr. Kerr.

"Yes," answered Sister. "Apparently, when he was being recruited to be a part of the assassination attempt, this element kept the information from reaching Khrushchev and gave him the green light to become involved, as long as the Soviet Union remained in a position to be able to deny any knowledge of his involvement. He was told that he was a great patriot and must assure that the assassination was successfully carried out, because it was a critical first step in a tripod plan to regain the upper hand for the Soviet Union. A plan that he was told also would see the ouster of the overly conciliatory Khrushchev and the US military bogged down in a long, drawn-out struggle in Vietnam, having been committed to that struggle by a strong and meddlesome President Lyndon Johnson. The same Lyndon Johnson, who in 1961, as vice president, had praised Ngo Dinh Diem as the 'Winston Churchill of Asia'."

"Well," sighed Mr. Kerr, "Kennedy has been assassinated, and until now there is no evidence of which I am aware of Soviet involvement, and Khrushchev has been ousted, and we certainly are embroiled in Vietnam. I cannot argue with any of that. However, I am not sure it would have been any different regardless of who was president in March of 1965, when the decision was made to commit the first American combat troops to Vietnam to guard an airbase."

Without waiting to see if Mr. Kerr was done musing, Sister continued, "According to the Russian, he is the best sniper the Soviets have. He was the 'second gunman' placed on the grassy knoll in Dallas that fateful November day to make certain that the mission was accomplished and fired the shot that sealed the young American president's fate."

"Does he give a reason for casting his lot with this so-called conservative element and not remaining loyal to Khrushchev?"

"Yes," replied Sister, "they convinced him that the Americans had been allowed to surround the Soviet Union with military bases, missiles, and other nuclear weapons, with impunity, in places such as Turkey and Italy. And when the Soviet Union tried to give them a taste of their own medicine, the Soviet Union was humiliated on the world stage by Khrushchev's withdrawal of the missiles from Cuba."

"If what he is saying is true, and I hope it is not, it is a terrible shame because I have always thought that both Khrushchev and Kennedy and their two teams performed brilliantly. Khrushchev got the assurances from Kennedy that he wanted—namely, that Cuba would not be invaded, and that the missiles would be withdrawn later from Turkey, and both men brought the world back from the brink of disaster. What more could one ask for?"

"I agree."

"Did he identify who it was on the US side that recruited him?"

"No, he fell into a deep sleep before I could coax anything more out of him, and I'm reluctant to try to awaken him. His fever appears to be breaking, and he seems to be recovering."

"Did he have any identification on him?"

"No, he has nothing on him and is wearing plain, nondescript clothing, similar to what you might find on a Vietcong guerrilla."

"We know there are Soviet advisers operating in North Vietnam, especially near Hanoi, but we didn't think there were any in the South and certainly not as far south as where you are located."

"What would you like me to do?" asked Sister.

"We need to take precautions. If you have any ink and a camera, please try to get his fingerprints and some pictures of him, especially of any distinguishing features such as tattoos. I will organize a contingent to come and take him off of your hands, but it will take a little time to arrange it so as not to arouse unwanted attention. However, do not try to stop him if he recovers and wants to leave before we can get to you. Under those circumstances, we will settle for the pictures and the fingerprints, as well as any observations you may note. Good work! You really got a great deal of information out of him under the circumstances."

"Thanks, it wasn't easy."

Realizing that the conversation was coming to a close, I scurried to get back to the other girls and their games. I didn't want Sister to know that I had heard her speaking with Mr. Kerr. Not long thereafter, the Russian's fever broke, and he began to recover. He started to speak in English to Sister Kate, with what Sister Kate called a perfect Texan accent. He told her that he was an American civilian from Dallas and was named Billy Bob Duxbury. He claimed that he was working for the South Vietnamese government doing water quality testing work on the canal between Ap Bac and Ap Tan Thoi when he was ambushed and taken captive by the Vietcong. He supposedly had managed to escape from his captors and was making his way back to Saigon when he had been bitten by a snake. Sister never let on that we knew otherwise, and he left before dawn the next morning.

After he was gone, I asked Sister Kate if she would finish reading the *Adventures of Huckleberry Finn* to me. She agreed, noting that we didn't have that much more to go, went inside, and got her heavily worn and dog-eared copy of the book. Once we were seated in our favorite place under the big tree in the front yard, Sister began to read. I settled in, enjoying the sense of normalcy that seemed to be returning to our lives.

An hour later, when she was finished with the story, she asked me what impressed me the most about the tale. I told her that I didn't understand why things appeared to be reversed in America.

"What do you mean?" she asked.

"Why would Jim, a grown man, be taking directions from Huck Finn, a kid, when in Vietnam the young are taught to respect and listen to their elders?"

Sister smiled at me in a way that told me she was impressed by my question and its underlying observation. She then answered, "Because of the pigmentation of his skin, love, because of the pigmentation of his skin. Jim's skin was black and Huck's skin was white. For no better reason than that one, I'm afraid."

When I told her that it still made no sense to me, she answered that it also had not made any sense to presidents, such as Abraham Lincoln, John F. Kennedy, and Lyndon B. Johnson, as well as to civil rights leaders like Martin Luther King, and that they all had worked hard to bring change to the way America looked at things. "In fact," she sighed, "Abraham Lincoln and Martin Luther King gave their lives trying to bring about this change, which remains a work in progress. But I continue to have hope, my love, because I have faith in my fellow Americans to eventually do the right thing." With that, she closed the book.

As she did so, she noticed for the first time the ink on her hands from having fingerprinted the Russian and immediately remembered that she had forgotten to remove the ink from his fingers as well. She knew it only was a matter of time before he noticed and realized what had been done to him. With a new sense of urgency, she took me inside the orphanage and gave me an envelope containing the film she had used to take pictures of the Russian, his fingerprints, and the notes she had made about his claimed American identity. She told me to take them and go hide in the jungle with the other girls. She told us that no matter what happened, we were to remain quietly hidden until the Americans arrived. We did as we were told.

Not long after we had hidden in the jungle, some North Vietnamese soldiers came, led by the man I would come to know as Captain Ton That Dam. They ransacked the orphanage, yelled at Sister, and beat her so hard that her head piece flew off. Finally, the Captain put a rope around Sister's exposed neck and pulled it taut with his left hand as he took her behind the big tree in the front yard, where we had been sitting and reading a few hours earlier. We no longer could see her, but we heard him tell her to kneel. We saw him take out his pistol with his right hand, while still holding the rope taut in his left hand, before he too moved behind the tree. Then, we gasped as we heard the shot ring out.

– 3 –

Captain Dam hadn't bothered to cover Sister Kate's eyes, which now were beginning to bulge from the tightness of the rope around her neck. As she knelt there in that special place where she had so often read to me and the others, her mind began to play tricks on her. At first she allowed herself to gaze on a butterfly that had landed on a blade of grass in front of her. She followed its every movement as it wandered about and marveled at how free it seemed to be. She remarked to herself at what a cherished gift freedom is. If only she could be so free.

She then shut her eyes to help focus her mind on Jesus Christ, on her family back home in Stockton, California, and on us, who were hiding in the nearby jungle. She prayed for the strength to remain faithful to her beliefs to the end and tried hard to draw inspiration from the suffering and death of Christ. She had been so fortunate because she'd been abandoned at birth in a hostile environment, only to be given a wonderful life of warmth and love by the Sullivan family and the chance to return to her roots to try and do the same for us, her "loves." She told herself she had to be Hesperidean to the end in her protection of us, her little souls.

Distracting her from her thoughts was a noise that she normally would not have noticed but now could not silence nor quite make out. *Clang ... clang ... clang* it went, steadily, but not regularly. She could not help but wonder what it was and where it was coming from. Soon she found herself anticipating each clang with increasing dread. The silence between them became torturous to her as she agonized over the increasingly sharp pain to her ears that each new clang brought about. She feared that she would cry out from the hurt and cause us to come running to her from the safety of our hiding place. What she was hearing was nothing more than the sound of the crucifix and beads on her habit being gently blown against each other by the afternoon breeze.

She opened her eyes and began to think that if she could jerk her head at the last second, she might suffer only a glancing wound from the bullet. If she could then pretend to be dead until the soldiers left, she could retrieve us and wait for help to arrive. As these thoughts were going through her head, Captain Dam took out his pistol, put it to the back of her head, and pulled the trigger.

When she saw the shadow on the ground in front of her of his finger pressing on the trigger, she jerked her head as she had planned. She told herself that her timing had been perfect. The bullet had glanced her scalp, causing a mere superficial, but profusely bloody, wound. She fell over and lay still in the pool of her own blood. The sound of the approaching American helicopters carrying Mr. Kerr's men caused the North Vietnamese to scatter quickly and brought us out of hiding. As she struggled to stand up in her weakened state, she could not help but wonder if those same helicopter sounds had distracted her executioner just enough to help him miss.

After what seemed to her like an interminable length of time, she was finally able to stand, albeit in a wobbling way. The pain in her head was excruciating, shooting from side to side like bolts of lightning. Her brain felt like it was going to explode, and her heart was pounding. Her senses seemed to be heightened to a point she had never before experienced. The mild breeze caressing her face felt more like an Arizona sandstorm, and her eyes seemed to see details they had not noticed before. The late afternoon sun felt like an inferno on her skin, and her mind was vigorously processing information at speeds normally reserved for computers. She could not understand why all of this was so, but she told herself she must go on.

Her attention turned to us, who were gathered at the edge of the clearing. She wasn't sure if she was beginning to hallucinate as a result of the blood she'd lost, but we seemed to be talking to a woman dressed in a habit similar to hers, only far more beautiful and colorful. It was blue and white and remarkably clean and crisp for someone travelling in the Vietnamese jungle. She labored to walk toward us, with each step requiring all the strength she could muster. She was becoming increasingly fatigued and thirsty from her efforts, but the sight of us spurred her on. As she approached the gathering, the woman in blue and white turned toward her with the grace and majesty of a queen and reached out to her with a warm and pleasant smile and a familiarity that made her become overwhelmed with excitement. Sister Kate was about to reach out when she felt a momentary staggering blow to the back of her head, and all went quiet. (Her mind was now powerless to play any tricks on her.)

Sister Kate was dead, shot squarely in the back of the head. When her tormentor let go of the rope, her body fell over on its side from its kneeling position and lay motionless in that special place where she so often had read to me and the others, under the big tree in the front yard of the orphanage. The shadow covering her limp form was that of Captain Dam standing over her as he methodically put his pistol away. The date was December 8, 1969.

The North Vietnamese soldiers gathered up their things unceremoniously and lazily disappeared into the jungle from where they had come. We remained in hiding, sobbing uncontrollably, but too scared to cry loudly, until the American helicopters carrying Mr. Kerr's men finally arrived several hours later. They were too late to catch the North Vietnamese or to save Sister Kate, but they gathered us up and took us to safety with them. Once in the helicopter, I turned over the envelope for which Sister Kate had died. The envelope simply read "To M. Kerr from K. Sullivan." There was nothing more to say, and nothing more was said.

– 4 –

John Sullivan Sr., at the age of forty-nine, remained an imposing figure. A former Boston College football star, the six foot five Sully, as he was known within the Central Intelligence Agency, was no stranger to hardship. The eldest of eleven children, he was the only one to be born in Ireland before his parents migrated to the United States in the bowels of an old transatlantic steamer. He remembered firsthand the hardships his mother and father had to endure, starting over in America, especially when the Depression hit. As an ex-marine who had distinguished himself in the Pacific during World War II, earning him a Bronze Star and a Purple Heart, he had seen his share of death and carnage. Still fresh in his memory was the capacity of mankind for cruelty to one another. But nothing could have prepared him for this, the most painful task of his life, having to bury his eldest daughter, the child he had brought home with him from Asia after the war.

In his eulogy of Katherine Sullivan, he recalled the day in 1945 when he first had seen her as a child at the Orphanage of Saint Francis Xavier in Vietnam. He spoke of how he called his wife to see if they could adopt her and the joy that came from that adoption. He described his pride when she graduated from the University of California at Berkeley and decided to become a nun. But most of all, he extolled her courage and determination for having followed her lifelong passion and forged into harm's way, returning to Vietnam to run the orphanage that had been her first home.

It was no accident that the one point of pride that he did not mention was that Kate had chosen to follow in his footsteps and serve her adopted country in the dangerous and shadowy world in which the CIA operates. He finished the eulogy by paraphrasing in English the words of the sailor aboard Tristan's ship in Wagner's opera *Tristan und Isolde*:

> Fresh blows the wind to the homeland;
> My ... child, where are you waiting?

"In heaven, I am sure," he added.

When he was finished, there was not a dry eye in the church, including the eyes behind the sunglasses on the tall, fit gentleman sitting quietly by himself in the last pew. Matt Kerr, known to the outside world as deputy chief of security at the US embassy in Vietnam, and John Sullivan went back a long way, having both joined the CIA together after having been discharged from the marines at the close of World War II.

The fact that one was an Irish Catholic and the other was a WASP and Episcopalian had long since ceased to be a true bone of contention, if it ever really had been, and the opportunity for razzing that the issue afforded both men now proved to be the glue that made their bond ever stronger. Matt Kerr had once saved John Sullivan's life on Iwo Jima, but he had not been able to do the same for Katherine Sullivan, and that was a cross he knew he was destined to bear for the rest of his life—a cross that was made that much more painful by his close ties to the Sullivan family. Mary and John had named their second son Matthew after him. Having no wife or offspring of his own, he had developed a very special relationship with all six of the Sullivan children as he had with his sister's children. They could not have meant more to him if they had been his own. As he sat there quietly and alone in the last pew, his mind went over and over the events of December 8, in an intense struggle with itself as he agonized over the guilt he felt for her untimely death—a budding young life filled with so much idealism and promise yet to be realized and now never to be fulfilled. If only it could have been him instead.

When the service was over, he was one of the last to leave. Walking out of the church, Mary's sister, Katherine Quinn, for whom Kate had been named, and herself a nun, came up to Matt. Putting her arm around his waist, she whispered to him, "I hope you are not blaming yourself for this. Kate would have none of that." It never ceased to amaze him how he and she seemed to be able to read each other's mind.

After the burial, as the mourners began to leave the cemetery, the two men met and had a chance to talk freely for the first time.

"What the hell happened out there, Matt?"

"Kate stumbled on to something big."

"How big?"

"As big as it gets, Sully."

"What do you mean?"

"She stumbled on to someone who claims to be the second gunman who shot John F. Kennedy."

"What the hell are you talking about?"

"A Russian adviser to the Vietcong, delirious with fever from a snakebite, staggered into the orphanage for help and collapsed. While Kate was treating him, he began to rant about what happened in Dallas. When she contacted me, I asked her to get his fingerprints and his picture. I knew she would not be able to hold him there if his fever broke and he recovered enough to want to leave before we could get to her."

"Well, then what?"

"Kate got the prints and the picture, but she must have been distracted by something and forgot to wipe the ink off his fingers. She noticed her mistake only after he had gone."

"How do you know that?"

"After he left, she noticed the ink on her hands while she was reading to Mary Bernadette, one of the children, and realized that she also had forgotten to remove it from his fingers."

"I see. We know of Mary Bernadette because Kate has written

to us about her. She was talking to us about adopting her. Was she killed too?"

"No, none of the children were hurt. When Kate realized the danger, she put the prints and the film in an envelope that she gave to Mary Bernadette for safekeeping. She then had the girls hide in the jungle. The Vietcong shot Kate when she refused to turn over the information."

"That's my girl!"

"Sully, you and Mary know how sorry I am about this, don't you? You have got to believe that I was doing everything I could. I didn't know about the mistake with the ink. It just happened so fast. There was nothing else I could do."

"Please don't beat yourself up, Matt. Mary and I know that you did all that was possible. We don't blame you in any way for this. Kate would not have lived her life any other way, even if she had it all to do over again."

"Thanks, it means a lot to me to hear it from you."

"The important thing is not to have her death be in vain. What have you been able to find out about this Russian, and what do you think the Soviets suspect we know?"

"We don't know the Russian's true identity yet, but we are working on it. However, we have been able to confirm his false American credentials, and they do place him in Dallas on November 22, 1963."

"And what do you think the Soviets suspect we know?"

"They must suspect that we think he is not who he claims to be, since we took steps to try and identify him. They also must be figuring that by now we have checked out his American credentials and know they are bogus. However, we don't think they have any inkling of the fact that we might be aware of his purported connection to the Kennedy assassination."

"Good. Let's hope we can keep it that way until we get to the bottom of this. We don't need any more international incidents."

"I couldn't agree more."

"What are your next steps?"

"Plans are underway to interdict this Russian while he still is in a combat role in Vietnam so as to minimize the chances of any fallout from our actions."

"Sounds good. Please keep me in the loop."

"You got it."

"One more thing."

"Yes."

"Claire is about to graduate from the novitiate and become a nun. She wants to go to Vietnam and carry on her sister's work at the orphanage."

"Sully, how does Mary feel about this?"

"Let's just say that she's not crazy about the idea."

"I can't say that I blame her, Sully. The poor woman just lost her eldest daughter there. Her eldest son is in the thick of combat in that war as a marine. And now you want to send Claire to the very place where her sister was senselessly slaughtered."

"I don't want to send Claire anywhere. Claire is the one that is insisting on doing this, to honor the memory of her sister. These Sullivan women are a tough and determined breed. I'd rather have to fight the Japanese on Iwo Jima all over again, than have to go up against them."

"I understand, but maybe you can slow her down a bit, and in time she will change her mind."

"You don't really believe that do you?"

"No, but it can't hurt to give it a try."

"Listen, Matt, Claire does not know about Kate's CIA involvement, and if she does decide to go, I don't want her involved in any way. Okay?"

"Agreed."

With that, the two men parted company. They would not meet again in person, until the mission to interdict the Russian was in the final stages of preparation.

– 5 –

Matthew Kerr, the only son of Paul Kerr, a prominent New York lawyer, and Edyth Wainwright, was born in New York City on June 9, 1921. He attended a local private day school until he was of age to follow in his father's footsteps and attended the Kent School, an Episcopal boarding school, situated in the quaint Connecticut town of the same name, on the picturesque banks of the Housatonic River.

Paul Kerr personified the Protestant work ethic and took to heart the school's motto: "Simplicity of life, directness of purpose, and self-reliance." Deeming it important to begin developing his son's character at an early age, he read to young Matt from select works of American literature. For example, to teach him the value of hard work, frugality, fear of God, and charity, he read to him from Benjamin Franklin's "The Way to Wealth." The story is told that one time when Matt was called upon in class by his American literature teacher to discuss the views of Poor Richard, he stood up and in answering was able to recite at length selected excerpts from memory, ending with the often quoted phrase "Early to bed and early to rise, makes a man healthy, wealthy and wise."

What Matt's teacher and classmates did not realize was that as a result of his father's tutelage, he could have done the same with many other works. One of his favorites was "Self-Reliance" by Ralph Waldo Emerson.

By the time Matt Kerr entered Yale, he knew that he was interested in a life of service. From a young age, he had been active in his local church, St. Ann's Episcopal Church in the town of Bridgehampton in

New York. His family had a summer home in the neighboring hamlet of Sagaponack, and he had spent his summers on Long Island, working on the nearby Dean family farm. When he was young, he worked at the farm stand with Merilee and Jamie, and when he was older he worked in the fields with Alex and Ian Dean. At Saint Ann's he was a crucifer and later a member of the choir. He long had contemplated entering the ministry and was looking forward to the study of theology at the divinity school.

During his time at Yale, the all-Ivy split end saw his focus shifting more to the service of his country. With the hot winds of war being fanned in Europe by what he strongly viewed as misguided policies of appeasement, he found himself increasingly at odds with the Marxist and Communist views gaining popularity on the college campus and the isolationist sentiment gaining favor on the national scene. As he had so often done on numerous other occasions in his life, he sought guidance from the teachings his father had bestowed upon him in his early years. This time, he turned to the writings of Thomas Paine in *The American Crisis*.

> These are the times that try men's souls. The summer soldier and the sunshine patriot will, in this crisis, shrink from service of their country; but he that stands it now, deserves the love and thanks of man and woman. Tyranny, like hell, is not easily conquered; yet we have this consolation with us, that the harder the conflict, the more glorious the triumph. What we obtain too cheap, we esteem too lightly: it is dearness only that gives everything its value. Heaven knows how to put a proper price upon its goods; and it would be strange indeed if so celestial an article as freedom should not be highly rated.

Upon graduating from Yale one year ahead of schedule, in the spring of 1942, and shortly after the attack on Pearl Harbor the prior

December, Matt Kerr decided to forsake an opportunity to play football professionally. Instead, he chose to join the US Marines that summer. The recruit in the bunk next to his at basic training was John Sullivan.

Paul and Edyth Kerr, along with Matt's twin sister, Dorothy Kerr Kelly, who was married and expecting the elder Kerr's first grandchild, came to San Francisco to see Matt off at the troop ship, the *SS Wharton*, in August of 1943. It was on that occasion that they met Matt's new friend and fellow marine, John Sullivan, for the first time. The Kerrs were immediately attracted to John and his warm outgoing personality. They took comfort in knowing that these two men would have the benefit of their mutual friendship in what they were about to face.

Paul Kerr, not usually one to show emotion, gave his son a big hug and, with tears in his eyes, said, "I am scared for you, but ever so proud, son."

Edyth Kerr added, "Please be careful, son," and gave him a kiss as she quickly turned and walked away with Dorothy, so that he would not see her crying. Dorothy looked over her shoulder and into her twin brother's eyes as she and her mother were walking away. Nothing was said by either brother or sister. It did not have to be. It was understood.

After his mother and sister were gone, Matt turned to his father and said, "Let's hope that by our doing this, the next generation—your grandchild, John's newborn son, and many others—will not have to face war. As you taught me, and Thomas Paine said about 'duty' in *The American Crisis*, 'If there must be trouble, let it be in my day, that my child may have peace.'"

Paul Kerr allowed himself a brief and bittersweet smile in reaction to his son's quote for indeed it was one that he had taught him so long ago. But now it was different, very human and personal, and not an abstract ideal, for it was his son that was the one going off to war. In any event, as time would tell, such a peace was not to be, and two Sullivan children, as well as countless more, would fall victim to a future war in a place called Vietnam.

– 6 –

On March 4, 1865, when the Civil War was in its final throes, Abraham Lincoln beseeched his fellow Americans in his second inaugural address.

> With malice toward none; with charity for all; with firmness in the right, as God gives us to see the right, let us strive on to finish the work we are in; to bind up the nation's wounds; to care for him who shall have borne the battle, and for his widow, and his orphan—to do all which may achieve and cherish a just and lasting peace, among ourselves, and with all nations.

After the end of World War II, the nation set out on a similar mission. John Sullivan and Matt Kerr were a part of this endeavor in their new government roles. When the Soviet Union exploded a nuclear weapon in 1948, the situation became more complicated. A "hot" war, like World War II, was no longer feasible and gave way to the concept of a "cold" war. This concept started as a mainly European effort with the North Atlantic Treaty Organization, also known as NATO, attempting to contain the spread of the Soviet Union in Europe. The goal of NATO was not to let the Soviets spread beyond what British Prime Minister Winston Churchill termed the "Iron Curtin" that had descended on Eastern Europe.

However, the Cold War became global in scale the next year, when the Communists took over mainland China.

During the Eisenhower era of the 1950s, the containment effort resulted in the United States becoming allied with some questionable leaders simply because they were opposing Communist or Marxist movements in their countries or nearby regions. These so-called "dominoes" in the Cold War allowed both sides to spar and occasionally bloody each other's noses; contain their opponent or expand their position, as the case may be; and test their conventional weaponry, tactics, and general readiness—all without incurring the devastating consequences of an all-out hot war. In some cases the fighting was between surrogates. In others, like Korea, one side or the other would commit their own troops. Muddling the water for American foreign policy was the fact that for many of these so-called dominoes, communist leanings often were inextricably interwoven with a strong sense of nationalism and the drive for independence from colonial rule. This would prove to be the case in Vietnam.

In August of 1945, soon after Japan's surrender, John Sullivan had been part of a group that arrived in Vietnam to search for and rescue Allied POWs. He recalled from his visit to Hanoi how impressed he had been by Ho Chi Minh's intelligence network and by the dedication of his fighters and their ability to quickly learn and apply what they had been taught. He also had developed an appreciation for the intricate nationalistic differences that existed in Southeast Asia. From before the time of Christ, the Vietnamese had been fighting to be independent, first from the Chinese, and more recently from the French, and in both cases had shown great patience and a willingness to accept tremendous hardships and casualties.

As part of this same trip, John Sullivan also had visited Saigon in the South and had been surprised and disappointed by the contrast. There he had found nothing but disarray and infighting. He also had found that many of the South Vietnamese army officers still had a *mentalité de colonisé* from their involvement with the French military presence.

When the Soviet Union and China recognized Ho Chi Minh's

regime in 1950, the United States and its Allies reacted by categorizing the Democratic Republic of Vietnam as a "puppet" regime or Soviet satellite. By 1961, when the United States was sending small numbers of advisers into the Republic of South Vietnam to help them resist the Communist threat from the North, John Sullivan and Matt Kerr had risen to senior positions within the CIA. French President Charles de Gaulle, among others, had attempted to warn the United States not to become involved, but the advice was not being heeded. Both John Sullivan and Matt Kerr had been following the developments with concerns of their own. On his 1945 trip to Vietnam, John had seen firsthand the obsession Ho Chi Minh and his followers had for reuniting an independent Vietnam under their control, and he had told Matt that Ho Chi Minh was nobody's puppet. He also had impressed upon Matt that if a war were to be won, America would have to take over the fight and risk being called a colonialist, or the South would have to develop the same nationalistic fervor as the North had. From his experience in 1945, he didn't think they were capable of doing so.

The fight, in his opinion, would have to be taken to the Communists on their home turf in the North, where everyone was the enemy. Furthermore, the North would have to be dealt a devastating, if not mortal blow. This, in turn, had raised fears in both men that America's involvement might backfire and cause the North Vietnamese and the Chinese, as well as their common ally, the Soviets, to put aside their traditional differences and unite in a marriage of convenience to fight the United States and its ally in the South. For these and other reasons, the two men were of the view that the United States should stay out of the fight in Southeast Asia.

However, as 1961 progressed, Matt and John saw their views being swayed, not by their better judgment, nor by the insights John had gained from his 1945 trip to Vietnam, but by a contagious spirit of optimism that was permeating Washington. This optimism was engendered by inspirational rhetoric and being carried out with a missionary zeal. America would rebuild nations like Vietnam in its image by winning the hearts and minds of its people. And while some warned that this nation-building was arrogant and naive and would end badly, it nevertheless persisted and grew stronger as time went on.

Both men had attended the inauguration of John F. Kennedy in January of that year and had heard the poet Robert Frost read his poem "The Gift Outright," a powerful depiction of America's own struggle for freedom from colonial rule. They found themselves haunted by its impassioned words. They also had heard the young president promise in his inaugural address that the United States would "pay any price, bear any burden, meet any hardship, support any friend, oppose any foe, to assure the survival and the success of liberty." The prospect of a free and independent Vietnam, unified under a democratic form of government, crafted from the American vision, on the doorstep of Communist China seduced them and many more.

In the years that followed, the two men, along with others in Washington, ultimately convinced themselves that the Vietnamese would see America as America saw itself—a liberator and not a colonialist. They were wrong, and more than fifty thousand Americans and countless more Vietnamese would die proving them wrong, including two Sullivan children, one of whom was a daughter of Vietnam herself.

– 7 –

The summer of 1965 was coming to a close, and the new school year was about to begin. The weather in New York was hot and getting hotter, as was the opposition to the war in Vietnam. Nowhere was this truer than on the campus of Columbia University.

The three incoming students assigned to room 308, one of the few dormitory rooms considered sufficiently large to be made into a triple, appeared to have nothing in common with each other. One couldn't help but wonder if room assignments were done purely on a random basis and without any regard for common interests or compatibilities. The rhyme and reason became clear to the three roommates, however, as they began to talk with each other. They each had expressed an interest in joining a local US Army ROTC, an officers training program that was offered at a nearby college.

In the days that followed, they completed the enrollment process and were issued crisp, clean dress uniforms to wear to class. As they polished their new black shoes until their reflections were clear in the shine, they anxiously anticipated the new experience.

It was not at all to be what they had expected. Walking to their first class, they were pelted with various projectiles and insults. Some threw rolled-up pieces of paper that they had pulled from their newly purchased notebooks and made into tightly squeezed balls. Others chose to spit on them or throw eggs and other food items. Still others decided to fling insults their way and called them "fascist pigs," "imperialists," "baby killers," and the like. Nevertheless, they soldiered on to class as the chants got louder and more threatening, their uniforms no longer crisp and clean and their shoes no longer perfectly shiny.

Ironically, for Samuel Lerner, one of the three, his first class was English, and the professor chose to discuss "Storm Warnings" by Adrienne Rich. Samuel's life had been a life in transition, even before this most recent event, and he could not help but identify with her work. He too felt the unpredictable nature of the "weather," both within him and outside; but he found himself reading, rereading, contemplating, and then struggling with the line "We can only close the shutters." For he did not want to close the shutters. He wanted to slam them open with all of his might and hold them there so he could absorb the full fury of the weather, both in his heart and outside in his surroundings. And that was what he would try to do.

At the time, Samuel's father, Jacob Lerner, was a colonel in the Israeli Air Force. Born in Brooklyn, New York, in 1927, Jacob had attended Lincoln High School and Columbia University with his first and only high school sweetheart, Jeanette Auerbach. After having skipped a year in high school and finishing college in three years under an accelerated program, Jacob and Jeanette married at the young age of twenty in the summer of 1947. In 1948, Samuel was born, and in 1949, the Lerners moved to Israel.

Having been born too late to be of age to serve his country and stem the tide of Nazism in World War II, he was determined to help protect the nascent Jewish state that would be a refuge for Jews everywhere. With an unabashed love of flying and a grasping ambition, Jacob Lerner quickly proved himself a formidable fighter pilot and just as swiftly rose in rank. He gained a reputation as a fair but tough officer, whose bravery and leadership won him the full respect and admiration of both the pilots that served under him and his superiors. His one weakness was a good cigar, which often doubled as a pointer when he wanted to make something perfectly clear.

The demands of his career kept Jacob away often and left the burden of raising Samuel on a day-to-day basis to his mother, Jeanette. She, in turn, rose to the occasion and did a wonderful job of supplementing the schooling Samuel was receiving in the local Israeli schools. She instilled a strong set of values in young Samuel, who aspired to someday follow in his father's footsteps and enter the military. In Israel the military was a highly respected institution and a source of pride and admiration to the Israeli people, who were deeply appreciative of the protection being provided by it. Consequently, it was not at all unusual for Samuel to have the aspirations that he did.

As Samuel approached his teenage years, he sensed a difference growing between him and many of his friends. While they became very interested in the opposite sex, he found his inclinations to be somewhat different. At first, he denied and suppressed his urges and desires, pretending to be in conformity with the interests espoused by his companions. He even attempted dating a young girl that lived nearby. However, the values his mother had instilled in him and which his father exemplified for him began to cause a degree of discomfort that he simply could not tolerate and he decided to confront the lie that he was living. But how could he tell his mother, let alone his father? Feeling very alone, he began to withdraw and turn inward for support. His schoolwork began to suffer and his mother grew concerned that he might be depressed.

Jacob Lerner was too busy to notice at first. As time passed, he became convinced that his wife's concerns were an overreaction to normal teenage insecurities, exacerbated by the moves and uprooting that Samuel had had to endure. Perhaps the thought of his son suffering from mental illness, as he viewed depression, was inconceivable in his macho world, and he simply was in denial. Then again, maybe he really did believe what he was saying about teenage insecurities. Nevertheless, he loved his wife dearly and could not bear to see her anguish. When his wife's sister, Frances Auerback, suggested that Samuel come to the United States and live with her while he attended Lincoln High School, Jacob reluctantly acquiesced.

Frances Auerback was a beautiful and intelligent woman, who had been popular in school and at no loss for suitors. However, she had never married for one reason or another. Instead, after graduating from college, she had returned to Lincoln High School as a teacher. She had totally immersed herself in her profession and was beloved by her students, who often came to her for advice and help, especially with respect to matters they were embarrassed to raise with their parents. She was considered non-judgmental and a trusted confidante, who somehow never seemed shocked by anything she was told. Calm and steady, she always seemed to have the right solutions for every problem.

Samuel had not been living with his aunt very long when she succeeded in drawing him out of his self-imposed shell and engaged him in an open discussion of his sexual preference. He was surprised and much relieved to see his aunt's accepting demeanor and muted reaction to the news. She assured him that he was not as unusual as he had assumed, that there were many people in the world with the same preference, and that a military career was still possible if he did not openly acknowledge his homosexuality. They also agreed, at his behest, that this was a message best delivered in person and that it would be left to him to choose the time and place to tell his parents.

He would never have the opportunity to tell his father, for they would not see each other again. Jacob Lerner was killed in the 1967 War, at the age of forty. A decorated war hero, Jacob remained in death an inspiration for his son, who mustered the courage to tell his mother of his homosexuality at his father's funeral. Jeanette, like her sister before her, accepted her son unconditionally.

Samuel knew then that he had been thrown into challenging circumstances. He was a determined young man, filled with ambition and aspiring to meet the standard set for him by his father. These aspirations nevertheless scared him, for he had a sober appreciation for his own weaknesses and for the difficulty of the task he was undertaking. Totally consumed by his passion, he vowed then and there to "shutter" his homosexual tendencies forever behind a commitment to celibacy and a single-minded devotion to succeeding in his father's world. Knowing that he could trust his mother and his aunt to keep his secret, he never told another human being of his homosexuality until years later when he lay dying.

– 8 –

By September of 1968, Jacob Lerner had been deceased for approximately one year, and Samuel Lerner was starting his final year at Columbia University and a decision point with respect to his future in the military. Jeanette Lerner, knowing her son as she did, sensed the currents of concern running quietly in the depths of his mind. At her suggestion, they had agreed to meet in Manhattan and take an excursion to the Statue of Liberty.

It was a beautiful day as the boat approached the majestic lady and the island that served as her throne. When they had walked the final distance to the base of the statue, she led him inside the pedestal and asked him to read the engraved bronze tablet affixed to the interior wall. He obliged and began to read the poem, "The New Colossus," by Emma Lazarus.

> Not like the brazen giant of Greek fame,
> With conquering limbs astride from land to land;
> Here at our sea-washed, sunset gates shall stand
> A mighty woman with a torch, whose flame
> Is the imprisoned lightning, and her name
> Mother of Exiles. From her beacon-hand
> Glows world-wide welcome; her mild eyes command
> The air-bridged harbor that twin cities frame.
> "Keep, ancient lands, your storied pomp!" cries she

With silent lips. "Give me your tired, your poor,
Your huddled masses yearning to breathe free,
The wretched refuse of your teeming shore.
Send these, the homeless, tempest-tost to me,
I lift my lamp beside the golden door!"

When Samuel was finished, Jeanette Lerner felt the need to reread the last five lines for him, to emphasize the point that she was preparing to make to him.

"Give me your tired, your poor,
Your huddled masses yearning to breathe free,
The wretched refuse of your teeming shore.
Send these, the homeless, tempest-tost to me,
I lift my lamp beside the golden door!"

She then turned to her son and said, "Emma Lazarus was a Jew like us, and when she wrote this poem in the 1880s, she knew firsthand the plight of Jews trying to find refuge in America after having fled Russia. This country, like Israel, has been a refuge for Jews. If your father had been old enough, he would have fought in the US Army Air Corps during World War II. The birth of Israel after that war was his challenge—his adventure. This country and its fight against Communism is yours."

"Do you really believe that, Mom?"

"I do. Why would you think that I don't?"

"In Israel the people respect and admire their military. Here they think I am a fool and a fascist, and they spit and throw things at me. They have grown soft and take for granted the freedom that they have. They shrink from the service of their country, hiding behind bogus deferments, and leave the fighting to those without the connections or the means to avoid serving."

Jeanette interrupted her son, to say, "I want to make it clear that I don't condone spitting or their throwing anything on you, but I do think that you are being a little too hard on your antagonists. Their views may be genuine and as deeply held as yours are. You have a different perspective than they do, one which comes from having lived in two different cultures. But you also must remember that we all have our roles to play in a free society. You see all the good that America has done and you want to protect that progress. They see all the good that America has yet to do, and they want to prod along that progress. Their right to protest and challenge authority is part of what you will be fighting for. And their protests and challenges may someday win for you and others like you a nation that accepts homosexuality without discrimination."

Samuel was visibly taken aback by his mother's comment. He asked, "Do you really believe that someday there will be equality for gay people like me—that homosexuals and heterosexuals will be accepted and treated equally under the law?"

Jeanette Lerner responded, "Absolutely." She then smiled at her son, and with a tweak of her eyebrow that gave her face a mischievous look, she quoted Winston Churchill's saying for him: "You can always count on Americans to do the right thing—after they've tried everything else." Putting her arm on his shoulder and drawing him closer to her, she told him, "We will get there eventually, I really believe that."

She immediately knew in her heart that the mission she had set out to accomplish that day with the trip to the Statue of Liberty had been a success. Her son was at peace with his decision to serve his country in its military. Her husband Jacob would be proud of her, she told herself. However, as the initial joy at her success started to recede, the void it left behind began to fill with a degree of remorse and a growing doubt. Her intuition began to nag at her, and no matter how hard she tried to suppress it, it persisted, getting louder and louder, until she could no longer deny it a say, a say that tugged at her very worst and deepest fear—that she would live to bury her son as she had her husband—a hero.

Her thoughts were interrupted when her son asked, "Mom, there are tears running down your cheek. Are you crying?" As he instinctively reached to wipe away the tears, he questioned, "Is something the matter?"

"No, son, all is fine. They are simply tears of joy. I am happy for you."

"Good! Because I must tell you, I've never felt so free in my entire life."

His remarks caused her to remember more poignantly than ever before her mother's words to her when she, as a young girl, had nursed an injured bird back to health, "If you truly love that bird, you will set it free." She had then, and she would again.

She truly loved her son as she had truly loved her husband, and she now had set her son free, as she had set her husband free so many years before, knowing in both cases that she had to share them with that jealous mistress—Emma's "Mother of Exiles."

– 9 –

When Samuel Lerner bid his mother good-bye on that beautiful September day in 1968 and returned to his dormitory room at Columbia University, he found his two roommates in the midst of an animated discussion. It was surprising that the discussion had not taken place sooner and that it had taken them until senior year to feel comfortable enough to broach the subject with one another. But it had. And now was as good a time as any to have it.

Jon Trueblood was an American Indian, an Apache, who had kept a picture of the great warrior Cochise on the wall of their room for the last three years. Joaquin Arango was a Chicano who claimed to be a distant relative of Poncho Villa, whose exploits were made famous in *corridos*, such as *"La cucaracha."* The discussion centered on the wrongs that had been done to their respective peoples by the dominant North American culture.

Jon Trueblood had been speaking first and reiterated for Samuel what he had been saying.

"I watched my grandfather die a sad and broken man at the age of 107, in the summer of 1961. He would sit in the same place every day on the reservation near Apache Pass in Arizona. It was by a collection of abandoned cars and an old, forgotten Winnebago, on the bed of his long since defunct pickup truck, which was parked under a shade tree, and he would smoke his pipe and watch helplessly as urban sprawl engulfed the land that he had once roamed freely. This onslaught brought with it highways, small cities with their attendant suburbs, local industries with their accompanying pollution and congestion, and a relentless growth in population. Nevertheless, unemployment and alcoholism remained widespread and continued to be a destructive force on the reservation. Grandfather would brood that his spirit felt trapped by the impinging progress and the simultaneous disintegration of his people.

"When Grandfather was born in 1854, the Apache were living in the twilight of our great history. He would reminisce about his youth, when at the age of sixteen, he fought the white man—the pony soldiers of the US Cavalry—with the great Cochise. He was young, loud, and impetuous then, so he was given the name Screaming Eagle, which he grew to like very much. Cochise initially had success against the US Cavalry, when the main focus of the US Army was on fighting the Civil War. However, in the years following the end of that war, more troops led by experienced Indian fighters were able to bring Cochise to the negotiating table, and in 1872 an agreement was reached. My father and I, because we were born much later, were spared the humiliation of defeat that my grandfather was forced to accept at the impressionable age of eighteen. With almost ninety years of life left to live, my grandfather was never able to adapt completely to the new reality. Rather, he forced himself to tolerate it, and I mean barely tolerate it, for my grandmother's sake."

Samuel interrupted to ask Jon, "If you feel this way, why are you now preparing to join the very army that did this to your grandfather?" But Jon had the answer and continued.

"I am expressing my grandfather's views and not mine nor my father's. My grandmother was determined not to see her son self-destruct and impressed upon my father when he was at an early age the value of a bicultural education that exposed him to the future that America offered, without depriving him of his rich Native American heritage. She taught him that the Apache always had been an adaptive people, moving from hunting ground to hunting ground, as needed. She felt that the progress that the white man brought was not his alone, but belonged to everyone. We identified it with the North Americans, in her view, because that was our only frame of reference. These changes were impacting the entire world to one extent or another, and she believed the Apache must once again adapt.

"She enrolled my father in a mission school, where he learned to read and write in English, as well as to add, subtract, multiply, and divide. It was at this school that he met his future wife, my mother, a young white girl named Mary Hurd, whose mother was a teacher at the school. Needless to say, not everyone was happy with their dating and growing serious with one another. Nevertheless, they were married when my father returned from Europe after serving with the 101st Airborne Division in World War II. He told me that he was determined to serve with the 101st because they were known as the Screaming Eagles, and it was his way of honoring my grandfather and his traditional tribal warrior heritage. Ironically, my father never let on that he was Native American, and the army thought he was white because his skin was so fair.

"My dad never had the opportunity to attend college because he was forced to go to work after the war to support his new wife, his two sisters, and my grandparents. He went to work for one of the very industries that my grandfather so loathed. He never told my grandfather where he worked and my grandfather never asked. I know it had to be hard for my father not to be able to share his accomplishments with my grandfather. But as they say, old habits die hard.

"Even though my dad didn't attend college, like so many of his generation, he impressed upon me the need to attend. I know he is very much looking forward to coming to New York next year to attend my graduation in person. I hope to use my education to improve the plight of my people. I believe, like Dr. Martin Luther King, that change should come peacefully through the system. America is far from perfect, and our government certainly could do better by Native Americans. Under our system, the squeaky wheel gets the grease, and I intend to be a squeaky wheel for my people. Many of my fellow Apache may view me as a half-breed and, along with my father, as a traitor. But some day, if I am successful in my endeavors, they may be appreciative of any improvements I can bring to them."

When Jon was finished, you could have heard a pin drop in the room. The silence was deafening. After a few seconds that felt more like minutes, Samuel simply exclaimed, "Wow!"

Joaquin said, "Jon, you're going to be a tough act to follow." But follow he did and in grand form. After taking a moment to gather his thoughts, Joaquin began to speak in a soft voice.

"As I think that you know, I am a Chicano, or Mexican-American. All Chicanos are mixed-breeds, about 75 percent Indian and 25 percent Spanish. I don't think that we realized that we were a distinct group of people until about four years ago, when Cesar Chavez, a union organizer, and the farm workers united to form the United Farm Workers party in Texas. I read 'I Am Joaquin' when it was published, and it made a huge impression on me. I am Joaquin.

"Many of my fellow Chicanos may view me as a 'pocho,' or cultural traitor, because I speak English or I speak Spanish in an anglicized manner. I want to use my education to help my people, and like you, Jon, I think it is best to work peacefully within the system. I believe in the importance of a bicultural education, as your grandmother did, so that my people have a chance to succeed in the future, while cherishing their past without being imprisoned by it. I want to serve in the military because there is no greater equalizer than the military, and I want to establish my bona fide credentials by fighting for the United States. In doing so, I feel I will have earned the right to criticize America when it becomes necessary, as an agent of change for my people.

"My uncle, like your father, Jon, also served with the 101st Airborne in World War II, and I have been to some of his reunions with him. There is a brotherhood among those men that transcends any differences they may have, and that only possibly could come from having been to hell and back together. The only time I've seen my uncle cry, Sammy, was when he described the horror at one of the concentration camps they liberated. These jerks we go to school with can call us fascist, but they have no clue of what a real fascist is. If they did, they would not use the term so lightly."

Again, there was silence. Then, after a time, Samuel Lerner began to speak in a serious tone.

"I, too, am from a tribe, Jon. I am from the tribe of David. Until 1948, when the state of Israel was formed, we didn't have our homeland and were forced to exist where we could, sometimes in extremely hostile environments. I want to join the 101st Airborne Division of the US Army because, as you alluded to Joaquin when you were discussing your uncle, they liberated the actual concentration camp where my great-aunt and uncle were slaughtered. From what my mother has told me, my relatives very well may have had their remains made into lamp shades or bars of soap and their gold fillings melted down and used for wagering in card games. Man's capacity to be cruel to one another is too great not to remain ever vigilant. I just came back from visiting the Statue of Liberty with my mother. She wanted me to see that America is the one beacon of hope for the oppressed everywhere and must not be allowed to falter. We who have been lucky enough to find a welcome refuge here must protect that opportunity for those that will come after us."

For the first time, the three roommates truly understood the bond they shared and the reason they had been placed together in dormitory room 308 at Columbia University three years earlier. They had a common destiny, and at Jon Trueblood's suggestion, they decided to become "blood brothers" in the Apache tradition and go forward together.

The following year, after graduating from Columbia University and basic training, the three blood brothers reported together to Fort Campbell, Kentucky, the home of the Screaming Eagles of the 101st Airborne Division. Thereafter, they would be deployed together in Vietnam. Only two of them would come home alive. And only one of them would live to realize his dream and become a force of change for his people. Jon Trueblood would become a member of the United States Senate and an advocate for Native Americans in his home state of Arizona.

– 10 –

J. Hector St. John de Crèvecœur offers one of the best definitions of what it means to be an American in *Letters From An American Farmer*.

> He is an American, who leaving behind him all his ancient prejudices and manners, receives new ones from the new mode of life he holds. He becomes an American by being received in the broad lap of our great *Alma Mater*. Here individuals of all nations are melted into a new race of men, whose labors and posterity will one day cause great changes in the world.

Beauregard Hicket, who was the black sheep of his family (and in a certain way, reveled in the distinction, wearing it as a badge of honor rather than a mark of shame), would come to understand the meaning of that definition first hand. The Hickets were an old, aristocratic Charleston, South Carolina, family. A Hicket had been a personal aid to General Robert E. Lee and had been with the general in April of 1865, when Lee and his Confederate troops were surrounded and badly outnumbered by General Ulysses S. Grant and his Union troops at Appomattox Courthouse and were forced to surrender in the McLean house. The Hicket family, under its centenarian matriarch, Hester Ann Hicket, produced several state senators and one governor of the state of South Carolina. Hickets had graduated with distinction for generations from the University of Virginia, the Citadel, the Naval Academy, and West Point. Beauregard's oldest brother, Frederick Hicket, had graduated first in his class from Annapolis and was an officer in the marine corps during World War II. He had fought the Japanese on Iwo Jima with John Sullivan and Matt Kerr, although the men didn't know one another personally. Even the Hickets' family dogs, Ruby and Lilly, two beautiful golden retrievers, had distinguished themselves by winning honors at local State Fairs. And of course then there was Bo, as his friends liked to call him. As much as the family would like to forget that he existed, they could not.

Bo lived in a modest home on John's Island, South Carolina, not far from downtown Charleston and the center of the Hicket family's aristocratic world. An avid sportsman, Bo kept his guns on a rack in his old pickup truck and would slip away at every chance to hunt and fish with his two most trusted companions, his black Lab, Linus, and a bottle of Jack Daniel's Tennessee Whiskey. When the Korean War broke out in 1950, Bo decided to join the army.

Bo didn't know that in 1949 President Truman had ordered the US military to be integrated and was most unhappy when he was assigned in 1951 to one of the first units to comply with that mandate. Bo and the "colored boy from Mississippi," as Bo liked to refer to Jim Perkins, did not have much use for each other and made that abundantly clear from the beginning.

Jim Perkins was a big man, who would have distinguished himself as an athlete if he'd been given the chance. Instead, he dropped out of high school after three years and married his first and only love, the girl who lived down the road, Judy Rivers. When Judy became pregnant and gave birth in 1950 to their daughter, Ashley, Jim decided to join the army to advance himself and earn better money to send home to his wife and new daughter.

By 1952, Bo and Jim, along with the rest of their unit, had been deployed to Korea. Bo and Jim barely were able to contain their contempt for one another, and one day, just as their company was about to be moved up to the front lines, their feuding reached the boiling point and became a source of distraction to everyone. Their sergeant, a fellow named Chipman, knew that he had no choice but to take swift and drastic action to end this turmoil before it resulted in lives being lost—action that never would have been tolerated back home in peacetime.

He ordered two trucks backed up to each other. The distance between the backs of the two trucks was enough so that neither man, when placed in the rear of each truck, could reach the center point of the space between the trucks. He then ordered two broomsticks and had a spoon affixed to one end of each broomstick. The other end of each broomstick was tied to each man's right hand. Next he had each man's ankle and left hand shackled to the inside of their truck. Finally, he ordered a bucket of soup placed on a table in the space between the two trucks.

The only way the two men would be able to eat was if they each used their spoon to feed the other. Neither man could physically feed himself with his own spoon and broomstick. The sergeant informed them that they would stay there until they started to feed each other or one of them dropped dead from starvation. The sergeant then turned and walked away, hoping that they would not call his bluff.

The first day the two men stared at each other silently and with defiant glares until they eventually fell asleep. When they awoke, they were cold and hungry, and wet from their own urine, but neither Jim nor Bo wanted to be the one to make the first move. However, both knew that their resolve was not as strong as the day before and began to look for a face-saving way out. As fate would have it, after about three hours into the second day, the sergeant's dog, Jake, somehow got loose, came upon the scene, and tried to jump up on the table in an attempt to reach the soup. Both men used their sticks to shoo the animal away.

Then Bo said to Jim, "Do you think this would work if we wanted it to?" Jim replied, "I don't know. Should we give it a try to see?" Bo answered, "Why not, what do we have to lose?" as he attempted to reach for the soup with his spoon. Jim did the same.

And so, after one day, three hours, and eighteen minutes, the two men began to feed each other the cold soup. Nobody was more relieved than the sergeant, who had not eaten a thing himself for the same one day, three hours, and eighteen minutes. He would not ask his men to endure anything he was not prepared to endure himself. However, he did make sure that Jake ate well that night. It never was determined how the dog managed to get loose.

One week later the unit was in the thick of battle on the front lines. Two weeks after that the sergeant was killed, shot between the eyes while leading his men up a ridge. Not long thereafter, Bo was wounded while on patrol. Jim stayed with Bo until help could arrive, while the rest of the patrol moved on. A sudden snowstorm and nightfall prevented rescue until the next day. That night Jim lay on top of Bo to keep him warm until the MASH helicopter arrived the next morning to evacuate them. With the amount of blood Bo lost, he wouldn't have survived to be evacuated if it were not for Jim's actions.

Several weeks later, Jim had the opportunity to visit Bo at the MASH hospital before Bo was scheduled to be transferred to a hospital in Hawaii. Bo asked Jim why he had risked his own life to save him. Jim smiled and told Bo that he did it because he thought it would be a fate worse than death for a high and mighty South Carolina Hicket to have to live with the fact that he owed his life to the descendent of a lowly slave. Bo winked at Jim and said, "Good, I'm glad that it was nothing more than that." The two men shook hands and exchanged pictures, trying not to betray the sadness they felt as the orderlies came to take Bo away on his stretcher. They would never see each other again.

Both were discharged from the army after the Korean War ended in 1953 and returned to their separate lives back home, where they drank from different water fountains, used segregated bathrooms, and rode on opposite ends of the bus. In 1954, Jim was killed by a drunk driver. In 1955, Bo decided to reenlist and this time was assigned to the 101st Airborne Division, where he eventually made a career as a jump instructor.

In 1968, Ashley Perkins, to her surprise, was accepted at the University of Virginia on a full scholarship received from an anonymous donor. She assumed her benefactor was one of the university's many successful, magnanimous, and more liberal-minded alumni from the North. She was wrong. The check had come from a small bank on Main Road located on John's Island, South Carolina.

———

In late 1969, on a beautiful Kentucky fall day when Bo was waiting for his next batch of fresh recruits to arrive at Fort Campbell, he allowed his mind to wander back in time almost twenty years to when he and Jim were fresh recruits. He was in an uncharacteristically sentimental mood, because this would be his last batch of recruits. He was planning to retire. Bo smiled to himself when he thought about how difficult he and Jim had made life for their sergeant and thanked God that he had never been so challenged by any of his new recruits. Little did he know what the next busload had in store for him.

When the bus arrived and the door opened, Bo instructed the recruits to announce their number starting with one as they disembarked. He then told one to pair with two and three to pair with four, and so on, as he had done so many times before without incident.

The first four people off the bus that day were Jon Trueblood, Joaquin Arango, Samuel Lerner, and Nadim Haddad. When Samuel and Nadim realized that they had been paired together, they let their mutual displeasure be known. Bo chose to ignore it as he also had done with such complaints so many times before. But like Bo and Jim before them, Samuel and Nadim had no use for each other and made that abundantly clear at every opportunity.

Nadim's family had migrated to America from Syria in 1958, when Nadim was only eleven years old. They settled on Atlantic Avenue in Brooklyn, New York, where they had some relatives and Nadim's father started a small but successful taxicab company. His first cab was a red and white 1958 Ford. With long hours of hard work, the business had grown to include more than thirteen taxis by the time Nadim left to join the army.

Nadim wanted to broaden his horizons and become more American by joining the army. Instead, he found himself paired with a Brooklyn Jew. Samuel Lerner and Nadim Haddad had not crossed paths in Brooklyn, and they were not happy with the prospect of having to do it in Kentucky.

One day, not too much later, the feuding between Samuel and Nadim reached the boiling point, creating an incident that became a distraction to the others. Bo knew what had to be done. He knew he would pay a high price for his actions. But he also knew that these men would soon be seeing action in Vietnam and that he had no other choice if he was going to have them prepared.

He ordered Samuel and Nadim to meet him at the top of the jump tower. When the two men arrived, they were surprised to see that Bo had what looked like an inverted L–shaped pole rigged to the top of the platform. The upper part was horizontal and had a round eye through which Bo had inserted a thick chain. He then attached shackles to both ends of the chain and shackled each man's left hand to the chain. Finally, Bo gave each man a key to the shackles, when to their shock and sheer terror; he swung the pole out over the tower, leaving them dangling high above the ground without a parachute.

They were in disbelief and for the moment put their differences aside to commiserate with each other. Neither could understand what would drive Bo to be so thickheaded and reckless with their lives over this pairing issue. After all, he had been graciously willing to make exceptions so that both of them could worship according to their beliefs. Samuel had been excused from his duties on Friday evenings to attend the local synagogue, and Nadim had been allowed time for his prayers. Why was their request any different? They were about to have their answer.

Bo shouted to the men, "Do you see that American flag flying there?" (There was an American flag flying from the top of the platform where Bo was standing.) Before the men could answer, he proceeded, "When you become an American, you leave all your ancient prejudices behind. In this country and in this army, we all salute the same flag. Do you understand?"

Both men answered yes. Bo then proceeded to speak, but in a calmer voice, "Now we will find out how important it is to the two of you not to be paired together. Either of you can release yourself with the key that I gave you."

Samuel interrupted to say, "But Sergeant, if we do, we will both fall to our deaths." Bo, with a wry smile, responded, "I will be back in a little while. If the two of you are still here, I will know that being paired together is not a fate worse than death for you."

As Bo began to turn away, the men yelled, "Wait!" to which Bo replied, "What?" Both men relented and agreed that they were okay with remaining paired together.

"Good. I knew you would come around," said Bo as he breathed a sigh of relief and swung the men back onto the platform. As the men went to unshackle themselves, they quickly realized that their keys did not work. Bo simply smiled and said, "You didn't really think I was going to let two of my best men kill themselves, did you? I have the real key. I am trying to keep you alive, not kill you. Hold on to that passion and conviction the two of you have, and use it against the Communists instead of yourselves."

Samuel and Nadim now understood, but it was too late for Bo. As soon as the incident came to the attention of Bo's superiors, he was brought up on charges. He quietly agreed to a reduction in rank and a dishonorable discharge.

Back home in Charleston, South Carolina, the Hicket family was not completely surprised by the fact that Bo had become the first Hicket in the history of the family to receive a dishonorable discharge. But Bo didn't mind. He had just repaid a much overdue debt to another sergeant, a fellow named Chipman, who had been shot between the eyes, leading his men up a long since forgotten ridge in Korea many years ago.

To all outward appearances, Bo contentedly returned to John's Island, South Carolina, and the life he loved hunting and fishing. It was not long thereafter in 1970 that Jon Trueblood, Joaquin Arango, Samuel Lerner, and Nadim Haddad, along with the rest of their contingent, boarded a chartered flight for Vietnam. Confident in their training and ready for action, Nadim and Samuel sat next to each other on the flight. One of them would eventually posthumously win his country's highest honor, the Congressional Medal of Honor, for his valor and sacrifice. But Bo would not live to see it happen, for he would be killed only days before in what the local authorities ruled a hunting accident.

Because he was a Hicket, Bo's death was reported in the newspaper at the University of Virginia. Ashley Perkins saw it and sent a copy to her mother because she knew her daddy had known him. When Judy studied the picture in the paper, she noticed something nobody else was likely to notice.

In her late husband's effects, she had found the picture Bo had given him, when Bo was on the stretcher in Korea. It was a picture of Bo in front of his old pickup truck with his black Lab, Linus. The rear window of the truck, through which could be seen the gun rack, had a Confederate flag stickered to it. In the picture in the newspaper, Bo's body lay covered next to his shiny new pickup truck. The gun rack was still in the same place, but this time the flag stickered to the rear window was the American flag.

Judy Perkins took a degree of comfort in knowing that the two soldiers would finally be reunited with each other and their beloved sergeant—three men sharing a common bond of duty and honor in a place where they all could drink from the same fountain of eternal life.

– 11 –

Claire Sullivan was a handful from the beginning. John Sullivan nicknamed her Mother's Worry, but if he were honest with himself he just as well might have called her his worst nightmare. She was stunningly pretty, but oblivious to the fact. With a magnetic personality that caused people of all ages to quickly grow fond of her, she lived life to the fullest with a refreshing sense of excitement and seemingly limitless supply of energy. Her laughter was contagious, as was her optimism. Sensitive and idealistic, she attracted the attention of the boys, from the moment their senses had been awakened through maturity, to her feminine charms.

Mary Sullivan had been a beauty herself and still could command attention upon entering a room. John Sullivan, always the proud husband, never tired of the phenomenon and enjoyed watching it play out at CIA functions. So she knew from experience that her daughter would be pursued early, often, and relentlessly. She worried that Claire would be betrayed by her charm and beauty and fall prey to the temptation to experience the joys of womanhood before her maturity and judgment could properly guide her.

As time passed, she struggled more and more with the idea of introducing Claire to birth control. As a devout Catholic, she knew her religion did not condone it, and as a mother she worried that she would be sending her daughter the wrong message. But haunting her ever more disturbingly was the "what if" of an unwanted and unintended pregnancy. Abortion was out of the question, for she truly believed that life begins at conception, and there were certain lines a Sullivan simply would not cross. And single motherhood or an ill-conceived shotgun wedding would change drastically the trajectory of Claire's life before she ever had a chance to experience all the new opportunities that were being opened to women in society.

She allowed herself a brief smile as she thought back to the time when she and John were grappling with the idea of using birth control themselves. It was right after Lorraine, their youngest daughter, was born. She was a welcome but very much unexpected gift from God—and living testament to the fact that rhythm doesn't always work. John had been able to persuade her to start on the pill with a combination of his silver-tongued blarney, Sullivan charm, and that mischievous twinkle he could get in his eye on such occasions, which she'd never been able to resist. Her smile was in part due to his antics, but in part because she now was willing to admit to herself her secret willingness to be persuaded in the first place.

John had argued that if a nun were to take birth control pills, it wouldn't be in violation of Catholic teaching because she already was being celibate and therefore was not taking the pill to prevent getting pregnant. Similarly, if they practiced rhythm to prevent getting pregnant, it would not be in violation of Catholic teaching to take the pill because the practice of rhythm, not the pill, was being used to prevent pregnancy. The pill was merely a little bit of insurance. Furthermore, he argued, many of the church's rules were aspirational in nature, and modern Catholics were what he liked to call "cafeteria Catholics," picking and choosing from the menu of aspirations according to their conscience and with the hope that they would catch the Lord in a good mood on Judgment Day.

Nuns, Mary thought. I will go and see my sister Katherine. She is a Franciscan nun and will help me decide on the right thing to do.

Sister Katherine Quinn had an uncanny way of always knowing when her younger sister was troubled. Almost immediately after Mary had arrived, she asked her sister what was the matter. But only after the two talked for a while did Mary muster the courage to ask her older sister for the advice she'd come to seek.

For lack of a better approach, Mary simply blurted it out. "Should I be putting young Claire on birth control now that she has blossomed into womanhood?"

She felt herself flinch as she finished, in anticipation of her sister's rebuke. Instead, after a few moments of quiet reflection, the reply she got in a soft-spoken voice from her sister was, "I think it is a marvelous idea."

Mary could hardly believe her ears and said out loud, "Did I hear you correctly?" But hear her correctly she did. For almost in an effort to emphasize the point, Katherine continued, "All things considered, and under the circumstances, I think that you should."

"But why?" Mary asked.

"The church is a wonderful institution that does a tremendous amount of good. And I love it dearly. So much so, I might add, that I have chosen to dedicate my life to its service. But sometimes it is a little slow to react to the changes taking place in the world. Believe me when I tell you that the young girls today know and experience more by the age of fifteen than we did at twenty-one or later.

"At our inner-city mission, I work with unwed teenage mothers. These mothers still are children themselves in many ways. For all practical purposes, their lives as they knew them are over before they have had a chance to begin. While it is true that many of these girls place their baby up for adoption with our help, and you and John similarly could take in Claire's child and raise it as your own, these are less than ideal situations. Many of these young mothers spend the rest of their lives wondering what might have been.

"Abortion is not an option, nor should it be, unless Claire's life is in danger. And I would not want to see Claire marry of necessity or become a single mother in this way. These rules may have been fine when we were an agrarian society and young girls were married off at the age of twelve or fourteen. But today, with school and the other pressures life places on the young, many will not marry until they are in their twenties or thirties. That is an awful long time to wait."

"What about you, how do you do it?"

"It's hard, Mary. Your feelings as a woman don't go away when you put on this habit. I pray a great deal to remain true to my convictions."

"I am sorry. I had no business asking you such a personal question."

"It isn't a problem. But let's turn back to Claire, shall we? You wouldn't let her walk a tightrope without a safety net under her, would you?"

"Of course not."

"Well, then?"

Mary said good-bye to her sister and left the convent, very much at peace with the idea of speaking to her daughter about the pill. She would have her talk with Claire the following week, when she took her for her gynecological appointment.

– 12 –

In the spring of 1965, the entire Sullivan family, with the exception of Kate, who was in Vietnam, set out for Chestnut Hill, Massachusetts, and the graduation of John Sullivan Jr. from Boston College. Joining the family were Matt Kerr and Sister Katherine Quinn, Mary's older sister—the one she had consulted on the question of birth control for Claire.

When the group took their seats at the graduation, the two sisters sat next to each other. As so often happened when Mary saw her sister and Matt together, she could not help but think what a wonderful couple they would have made had they met before Katherine decided to become a nun. Mary was convinced that the same chemistry existed between Matt and Katherine that had brought her and John together. In her view, they easily could have been "soul mates," an expression she liked to use in describing her relationship with her husband, John.

Katherine, knowing her younger sister as well as she did, immediately sensed that Mary's thoughts were somewhere else and not on the graduation.

"Mary," she asked, "what are you thinking?"

"Oh, nothing."

"That's exactly what I feared. The 'nothings' are usually the worst. Come on—out with it, Sis."

"If you must know, I was thinking what a wonderful couple you and Matt would've made if you had met under different circumstances."

"Mary!"

"Oh come on, Katherine, are you telling me that you have never thought about it too?"

Katherine was silent.

"Katherine, I am waiting for an answer."

"Okay, maybe I have."

"Maybe?"

"Okay, okay, yes I have, but I don't see where it is any business of yours."

"Ohhhhh, I seeeee, so you *have* thought about it that much, have you?"

Katherine could feel her sister getting to her in the way that only a younger sister can and sought to end the conversation before it went too far. "I seem to recall that I told you once before, Mary, that your feelings as a woman don't go away when you put on the habit. Now can we please change the subject?"

Feeling bad that she may have pushed her sister too far, Mary said, "Sure. Sorry, Sis."

Katherine leaned over and gave her younger sister a hug and gently explained to her, "It's hard enough having to deal with the temptations of life as a nun on your own, without having someone repeatedly drawing them to your attention for you. Becoming a nun is not for the weak - kneed. I often struggle with my decision, but I pray daily that my vocation will remain strong, because I still am in love with being a nun and all that it entails. This ring on my finger bears witness to the fact that I am married to Jesus Christ and doing His work here on earth."

Mary felt somewhat ashamed at her actions and promised herself that she would never broach the subject with her sister again. But she would, and much sooner than she possibly could have imagined. For unknown to her, her daughter Claire was having thoughts about becoming a nun and already had secretly come to discuss it with her aunt.

The procession of graduates began to enter Alumni Stadium, the hallowed ground on which many a football legend had been born, and the site on which numerous great Eagle victories had been won. On this cool and clear day in May of 1965, however, as happened every year around this time, the stadium would serve as a graduation hall and bear witness to the academic achievements of the class of 1965.

Everyone rose from their seats to watch the procession as the music played. When Mary Sullivan's eyes finally found her son in the line of black gowns and gazed on him dressed in his marine dress uniform, the reality hit her and hit her hard for the first time. She found herself taken back by her reaction. After all, her son had been in ROTC, and both his father and his godfather, Matt Kerr, there in attendance, had been decorated marine veterans of World War II. So why the reaction? she wondered. Then the reason for her concern came to her. She had read that on March 8 of that year, two marine battalions had been sent by President Johnson to Vietnam to guard the US airfield at Da Nang. They represented the first combat troops to be committed to Vietnam. She knew in her heart that more would follow, and her intuition told her that her son would be among them.

Katherine could see that her sister Mary appeared distant and distracted instead of her usual vivacious self. Leaning over and placing her hand over her mouth in a gesture of secrecy, she asked, "You aren't still brooding over our discussion, are you?"

"No, Katherine. I guess it's hitting me for the first time that John may be sent to Vietnam and the prospect is worrying me."

Trying to ease her sister's concerns, Katherine noted that John would have his sister Kate and his godfather, Matt Kerr, there with him. But the reaction Katherine got from her sister was the opposite of what she had expected. Mary began to cry, something she didn't do often. John Sullivan Sr. and Matt Kerr were wrapped up in the moment and discounted Mary's tears as tears of joy. But they were not.

Mary leaned over to her sister Katherine and told her in a very somber voice that she had been having terrible premonitions lately. And that as she saw her son John walking into the stadium in his uniform, she felt an ill wind on the back of her neck and had a chill run down her spine.

"Is there anything more specific about these premonitions that you can tell me?" Katherine asked.

"Well, only that they involve coffins returning from Vietnam."

"Coffins. There are more than one?"

"Yes, twin coffins."

"I think that you're stressed out right now by all that you have going on in your life, with Kate in Vietnam and John going into the marines, and that you're allowing your imagination to get the better of you. You will feel much more at ease this summer when Kate comes home on leave and you see for yourself that she is fine."

"Do you really believe that?"

"Yes. Now let's enjoy the graduation."

As the two sisters turned their attention to the activities on the field, Katherine told herself that this wasn't the time to broach the subject of Claire's desire to become a nun with her sister, Mary. It would have to wait until later in the summer, when Kate was safely home on leave. And it did.

August 3, 1965, was a day like any other. At least that is how it had begun. Around noon, Sister Katherine, her sister, Mary her nieces, Kate and Claire, set out to have a quiet lunch together with the Stockton, California, lunch crowd at Sophie's Salad Connection, a trendy new downtown spot that was located in an old warehouse building on Sandpiper Street near Eugenia Boulevard. The proprietor, Giovanni Caruccio, was a good friend of Sister Katherine, and he'd saved her a secluded table in a private corner of the restaurant. Sister Katherine had impressed upon him ahead of time that the lunch would be the occasion of a special family announcement, and she wanted a nice quiet spot. But quiet it would not be.

As they waited for their salads to be served, Claire announced that she had decided to enter the convent. Mary was in shock and couldn't conceal her feelings. As much as she tried to regain her composure, she couldn't. Finally, she simply stood up, excused herself, and left the restaurant.

Claire was terribly disappointed and very much confused by her mother's actions. She had waited patiently for her sister to come home on leave so she could share her news with her mother and her sister at the same time. She had been anxiously anticipating this moment for months, but this was not how she envisioned her mother reacting. She was sure her mother would be happy for her and full of encouragement and joy. Instead, she seemed angry and resentful.

The three women sat there for a few minutes in silence, looking almost in disbelief at Mary's empty seat. Finally, Sister Katherine spoke and told her nieces, "Let me go talk to your mother. I'm sure that she simply is overwhelmed and will be fine. You two enjoy your lunch and have ours wrapped up to go. If Mr. Caruccio asks, please tell him something unexpected came up and I'll see him next week." With that, she too got up and left.

Claire turned to her sister Kate and said, "I don't understand Mom."

Kate replied, "I'm no longer sure that I do either. When I told her and Dad that I wanted to become a nun and return to the orphanage in Vietnam, they were happy for me and extremely supportive and encouraging. I don't know what has changed to bring about this kind of reaction."

When the food finally came, the two sisters told the waiter that they no longer were hungry and asked him to please wrap everything up to go. They then asked for the check, paid it, spoke briefly to a visibly concerned Mr. Caruccio and left.

Sister Katherine found her sister Mary sitting on a nearby park bench and sat down with her. The two sisters sat there for what seemed an eternity without saying a word. Finally, Mary started to cry, and Katherine cradled her younger sister in her arms and let Mary get it out of her system.

When Mary began to regain her composure, she turned to her

sister, still sobbing, and said, "I know this will sound very selfish of me, but I don't want to lose Claire to the church. Please don't take offense, but Claire has too much going for her to become a nun. She deserves to experience the joys of having a family, seeing the smiles on her children's faces, sharing life with a husband like mine, who is a true soul mate. I don't want to see her growing old alone, in an unnatural and lonely life of celibacy, praying as you do for the strength to endure."

Katherine easily could have taken offense at what her sister said, but she was too consumed by the depth of the hurt Mary was exhibiting to be angry with her.

"It's true, Mary, that I don't have a soul mate like your John, and it also is true that I pray for the strength to endure. But make no mistake about it—I get a great deal of joy and satisfaction from what I do, not the least of which are the smiles and hugs of the young girls that I help at the mission."

"I know, Katherine, but it's not the same, and you know it."

Katherine realized quickly that this line of discussion had played itself out and decided to get right to the point with her younger sister. "Mary," she asked, "if you feel so strongly in this regard, why did you not voice any of this when young Kate decided to enter the convent?"

"When Kate was thinking of entering the convent, she explained to me that she was very grateful to John and me and to the Franciscan nuns at the orphanage for all that had been done for her and that she wanted to give back by devoting her life to doing the same for other orphaned or abandoned young girls like herself. To do this, she decided to become a Franciscan nun and return to the orphanage that had been there for her. In her case, I understood the deep conviction she had to the Franciscans and the orphanage and the somewhat unique set of circumstances that formed the underpinning of her motivation. She had so much enthusiasm when she told me about the Hesperides in Greek mythology and proclaimed that she too wanted to be Hesperidean. I simply couldn't deny her. And so I gave her my blessing. But now I must confess I have some self-doubt.

"Sitting here before you came, I have been asking myself if I have a double standard, one for my adopted daughter and the other for my own flesh and blood. I am scared of the answer, Katherine, because it goes right to what I consider to be the essence of my being, my motherhood. I have striven to love all my children in the same way, without any favoritism or preference. Now I'm not so sure that I do."

"You do, Mary. Every child is different, so what you want for each child is influenced by those differences. If you were as convinced of the soundness of Claire's decision as you are of Kate's, you would not deny Claire. Claire has caught you off guard, because her life up until now has offered you no clue of her calling. Whereas Kate's life leading up to her decision to enter the convent had many signposts that served to prepare you for her vocation. Pray for the strength to keep an open mind, and you will come to understand and appreciate the soundness of Claire's decision."

"How have you come to be so convinced?"

"I've been talking with Claire for several months about her reasons for wanting to enter the convent. She came to see me in confidence last April, and we've been working together ever since. I can assure you that she has thought this out carefully."

"And why have you waited so long to tell me?"

"We had planned to speak with you in May, but when you told me of your premonitions at John's graduation, we thought it might be better to wait until young Kate was safely home on leave from Vietnam. We thought that you might be more at ease and receptive to the idea."

"I see. Well, I'll pray for the strength to keep an open mind, as you suggest, and I'll do my best to understand and appreciate the wisdom of Claire's choice."

"Don't underestimate the power of prayer. As you have noted, it has enabled me to muddle along and endure my lonely and unnatural life of celibacy."

"Ouch! I guess I had that one coming."

Sister Katherine grabbed her younger sister in a heartfelt hug. Kissing her on the top of the head, she said, "A sister's love knows no bounds."

On September 3, 1965, Claire Sullivan entered the novitiate with the blessing of her parents. Before leaving, she returned to her mother, unopened, the birth control pills she had been given. It was the sign for which her mother had been praying and provided Mary with the peace of mind that her daughter indeed had a calling.

– 13 –

John Sullivan Jr. was deployed to Vietnam in early 1968, shortly after the Tet Offensive had taken place. He was assigned to an elite team responsible for guarding the US embassy in Saigon.

In June of 1970, following the murder of her sister Kate that previous December, Sister Claire left for Vietnam, to continue the work her sister had been doing at the orphanage. On May 1, 1971, she returned home to Stockton, California, for a short leave before continuing on to New York, on her way to Paris for meetings with her order.

On Monday night, May 17, 1971, she boarded an Icelandic Airlines jet, at John F. Kennedy Airport in New York, for the flight to Luxembourg, where she was scheduled to catch a train to Paris the next day. Sitting next to her on the plane was a young recent graduate of Boston College by the name of George B. Angelson. The encounter would change Claire's young life forever.

— *Book Two:* —
THE HYPHENATED AMERICAN

– 1 –

The morning of Friday, July 2, 1971, was a beautiful, clear morning in New York City. As I emerged from Grand Central Station, Aurora was peaking over the eastern horizon. The air was clear and remarkably free of humidity, as it usually is after a severe thunderstorm—the same storm that the evening before had prevented my transatlantic European flight from landing on schedule in New York. Because our plane was low on fuel, we were diverted to Boston.

The pilots of the Icelandic flight, unfamiliar with Logan Airport in Boston, had skidded off the runway and mired the plane's right landing gear in the mud. Panic erupted on the plane, which caused the Boston police to be called on board. The police finally allowed those passengers who did not want to continue to New York to disembark without their luggage. Eventually, we were towed from the mud. The plane was inspected and given a clean bill of health, refueled, and sent on its way to New York without further incident.

By the time that we finally landed at John F. Kennedy airport in New York, it was in the early hours of the morning. The only transportation that was available was a bus that ran all night between the airport and Grand Central Station. The first train of the day to Westchester County, where I lived, was still hours away from leaving. A young soldier named Bill Fisher, who had just finished basic training and was coming home on leave to Connecticut before being sent to Vietnam, was the one other passenger on the bus with me. Finding ourselves in the same predicament, we joined forces at Grand Central Station, sat on the floor with our backs to the wall, and took turns napping. When it was time for the first train to Connecticut to leave, I accompanied Bill to his train, bid him farewell, and walked outside to meet my parents, Ralph and Rita Angelson, who had insisted on coming from Westchester to get me. And oh yes—please excuse me for having neglected to introduce myself sooner. My name is George B. Angelson. The B stands for Brian.

As I waited for my parents to come around the corner at Forty-Second Street from Lexington Avenue in my trusty friend, my 1967 Pontiac GTO, my mind began to drift. It drifted back to the last time in my life when I was returning to the United States from a foreign land—Brazil—and the promise I had made then and now had broken, which was never to leave the United States again.

It was early in the summer of 1958, and I was ten years old. We were returning from six years in Brazil, where my father had been working as an executive for an American company. Fluent in several languages, including Portuguese and Spanish, his assignment had been to help the company expand into Latin America, particularly Brazil.

When our ship passed by the Statue of Liberty, my father recited for us the now famous lines written by Emma Lazarus in the late 1880s that are engraved on a bronze tablet that is affixed to the inside wall of the base of the statute. Emma's "Mother of Exiles" with her mighty torch was a welcome sight for me. Leaning over the railing of the colossal ship, I watched small boats, pleasure craft, fishing trawlers, tugboats, and more sailing out of the harbor as we were heading in. As hard as I tried, I could not understand why anyone would want to leave such a wonderful place, the USA, even for a day. I vowed to myself that once I set foot on American soil, I never would leave again. For it was not until I had left and been away that I realized how much I loved and missed the United States.

As the ship docked, the commotion on the pier reached a crescendo, as did the excitement of the huddled masses on the deck. My parents saw our relatives on the pier and began to call out to them, but the noise was deafening to my young ears. Somehow they made contact, as did the others around us, with their loved ones. Tears were flowing, confetti was flying, and pom-poms were being waved in a frenzy of joy and anticipation of long-awaited reunions.

Soon the health inspectors came around to confirm that we all had been properly vaccinated—the last hurdle before we could set foot on our homeland. I barely could contain myself when I was cleared to go, and I pushed ahead of my parents and of annoyed strangers down the gangplank. There to catch me as I came hurdling off were my grandfather and grandmother and several aunts and uncles. All I could say about the fuss that was being made over our arrival was, *"Puxa vida."* Loosely translated it means "Oh my." Yes, I still was thinking and speaking in Portuguese. It would take me a while before my mind fully adjusted to English.

Soon I found myself in my uncle's car, a two-tone green Mercury hardtop. In the 1950s, after enduring the shortages and drab choices of the Depression and the war years, Americans went crazy for a rainbow of colors. Nowhere was this more evident than in the colors of their cars. There were turquoise and white cars, pink and gray cars, yellow and white cars, and I could go on and on. Once I even saw a multicolored car. It was black, hot pink, and white. The colors were discreetly separated by thin pieces of chrome, so that everything looked neat and orderly. Sometimes the separation was more formal and elaborate, with several pieces of chrome and gold metal inserts. Then again, on rare occasions the colors were permitted to freely and openly make contact with each other.

After thirty minutes or so, we arrived at my grandmother's house, where the festivities would begin in earnest. I have no doubt that my grandmother had prepared some of her best dishes for the occasion, but I was interested only in a hot dog right off the grill and a seat in front of the television. We did not have any of the modern conveniences in Brazil, and I could not get enough of American culture.

The summer passed quickly and uneventfully. We were able to move into our new house just in time for my sister and me to start school that September at the local Catholic grammar school. Saint Eugene's was its name, and it was run by the Franciscan nuns.

I basically had been home schooled by my mother in Brazil, so the first day of the term, with more than thirty other students in my fifth grade class, was daunting. I could hardly wait for lunch and a chance to get out in the fresh air and play on the playground.

When lunch came and I finally made it outside, another major surprise awaited me. I had not taken more than three steps onto the playground when a group of kids led by a boy named Mark approached me and asked me my name. When I told him, he asked what kind of name it was. I said American, and everyone laughed.

Another boy in the group, Neal (I think his name was), jumped in to say, "We're all Americans around here, what kind of an American are you?"

I had to tell them I didn't know what he was talking about. Fortunately, Paul Scott, who had sat next to me that morning in class, came over and told the group to leave me alone, and they did. However, I was determined to find out what kind of an American I was, and that night at dinner, I mustered the courage to ask my father.

It was then that I learned that I was an American of Italian descent, or an Italian–American. All the years that I had lived in Brazil, I had been an American. When people wanted to call me a pejorative name, they called me a gringo. Now I had returned to America to learn that I really was not an American. Rather, I was a "hyphenated" American. Suddenly, in my young mind, I felt cheated, somehow betrayed and less than complete. Hyphenation was the price I'd had to pay to come home, and I was powerless to do anything about it.

The next day I went to see my teacher, Sister Nancy, about my predicament. She explained that I would have to wait for the "melting pot" to further heat the emulsion that is America and for all these hyphens to marry one another and have children, who so blended these various heritages, that keeping track of them would become too complicated and unimportant. She then kiddingly referred to herself as being of fifty-seven different varieties, a takeoff on a popular ketchup company slogan and assured me that it would eventually become far more commonplace. She also cautioned me to cherish my heritage and to respect the heritage of others, because it was from the melding of these heritages in all of us, that we truly would become Americans. Then she reached for a book on American literature and read to me the quote by J. Hector St. John de Crèvecœur on what it means to be an American.

Sister Nancy had taught me an important lesson that I soon would be called upon to put to good use, namely, that being an American is a work in progress, and we all must work tirelessly at continuously improving that for which it stands. I felt a renewed sense of energy, because it was far more exciting to be striving for a goal not yet achieved than struggling to hold on to a misconception that never really was. From that day forward, I never had anything but the utmost respect and admiration for Sister Nancy.

In Brazil I had defended my "Americanhood" at great length and sometimes at even greater cost, not the least of which had been several black eyes. It reminded me of the time not that long before when I had defended Santa Claus's honor and returned home bruised but proud, only to be sat down and told Santa Claus doesn't really exist. Now, having stood proud in defense of my Americanhood, outnumbered in a foreign land, I had come home only to be sat down and told there really is no such thing as Americanhood. We were all hyphenated Americans.

What else didn't I know? I soon would find out.

– 2 –

While the upper echelons of society in Brazil still were pure Caucasian and very much European, the average Brazilian was a mixture of African and white. As a result, I did not learn in earnest of the divide between the two races until I returned to the United States. To me the separation between the races in America was analogous to that which I had observed with respect to the cars. In the North, the colors were separated by discreet norms that made everything look neat and orderly. The races gravitated toward their own neighborhoods and tended to marry only among themselves. In the South, the separation was more formal and pronounced, with segregated schools, bathrooms, drinking fountains, designated seating areas on buses, and more. Then again, on rare occasions, mostly in sports and in show business, the colors were permitted to freely and openly make contact with each other.

As the 1950s were coming to a close, the post-war exuberance that had given us all the color and innovation, was giving way to a more somber mood. Sputnik had told us that the time had come to roll up our sleeves and get back to work. The voices of unrest, long quieted, were beginning to grow loud, and it was only a matter of time before they erupted in riots and bloodshed. African–Americans had risked their lives in defense of America during World War II, and now they were demanding to be treated equally. Furthermore, the Supreme Court had ruled that "separate but equal," was not equal. The chrome was being stripped from the cars by American manufacturers, and the color barriers were being stripped from American society by the forces of social change.

Saint Eugene's and the area of Yonkers where we lived were basically white enclaves. It would not be until I started high school at the Iona Preparatory School in New Rochelle, in September of 1962, that I would have any substantial personal interaction with African-Americans. It would come on the very first day of high school as I stepped off the public bus and onto the sidewalk along North Avenue, across from the school.

I accidentally bumped into a young black woman, knocking her school books from her hands and onto the sidewalk. She had been exiting the diner that was in front of the bus stop and talking with her friends when the incident happened. Before I could say that I was sorry, she went into a tirade, carrying on in a way that caught me by surprise. She accused me of having done it on purpose. I was wearing a madras sport jacket, a white dress shirt, and a black knit tie, along with light tan slacks, white socks, and loafers—the unofficial uniform of Iona Prep in those days. She punctuated her ranting by calling me a "madras asshole" and letting me know that her boyfriend would be coming by to teach me some manners. I picked up her books, handed them to her with one last futile attempt at an apology, and crossed the street to go to school. The day was filled with so many new experiences for me that I soon forgot the incident.

In 1962, hazing still was very much in vogue, and Iona Prep was no exception. Seniors took great delight in embarrassing and humiliating freshmen. One of their favorite pranks was to make a freshman get down on one knee and propose marriage to the driver on the usually crowded North Avenue public bus that stopped in front of the school.

On this first day of school, my tormentors were a group of seniors led by a red-headed boy named Jack. Jack made me put my madras jacket on backwards as we waited at the stop for the North Avenue bus to arrive. The plan, of course, was to have me propose marriage to the driver. As if this was not enough, I looked up to see the young black woman from that morning, walking toward us with a group of black males.

The black in the lead came up to me and, sticking his face in mine, shouted, "Hey, Madras, I hear you pushed my girl Michelle around this morning. Would you like to try to do the same with me?" Michelle had not bothered to learn my name, having chosen instead to simply call me Madras, and now this guy had done the same.

I reached inward for strength and with all the conviction that I could gather, replied, "My name is George, not Madras. And that's not true, it was an accident."

Choosing either to ignore me or refusing to acknowledge my name, he barked back, "Are you calling my girl a liar, Madras?"

I hesitated for a moment because there was no good answer. I would either be admitting to shoving her or calling her a liar. Neither answer was likely to result in a good outcome for me. In the ensuing moment of silence, as I thought how to respond, the two groups began to push and shove and shout expletives at each other. In the commotion, I thought I heard someone say that the bus was coming and turned to look. My move must have looked threatening, because the next thing I knew, I felt a crushing blow to my face. A split second later, the pain was registering in my brain, and I could taste my own blood in my mouth. My body was reeling counterclockwise and I was falling to the curb. The sidewalk was rushing up to meet me, or so it seemed, and the best that I could do was to extend my arm to brake my fall.

As I tried to get up, I sensed the shadow of the arriving bus pass over me. My left eye was swelling and now partially closed, but I nevertheless could make out the imposing figure of the bus driver in his familiar blue uniform, stepping off the bus. He was a black man who stood well over six feet, six inches tall and spoke with a commanding voice. I guessed he was a former military guy and World War II veteran.

Looking directly at my attacker, he demanded to know, "What the hell is going on here, Chris?"

"I am evening a score, Mr. Crawford."

"Evening a score for what?"

"This guy shoved Michelle around this morning and knocked her books out of her hands."

"The hell he did. I saw the whole thing. He tripped getting off my bus."

Turning to Michelle, he asked, "Michelle, why you stirring things up like this? Nothing good can come of it."

I expected Michelle to respond by carrying on loudly again, as she had that morning. Instead, she quietly answered, "Sorry, Uncle Dick. I guess something snapped in me. I thought he had shoved me on purpose."

The two groups, those led by Chris Carter and those led by Jack Werner, were silent, and I began to wonder who was this Mr. Crawford that he commanded so much respect from everyone. As I did, he reached down, and putting his right hand under my left armpit, helped me up. He introduced himself to me as Dick Crawford and asked me my name. I replied that it was George B. Angelson.

"Well, George, are you here to propose to me?"

"Yes, sir."

"Well then, let's get on with it; I have a schedule to keep."

While I was getting down on my knee, with my jacket still on backwards, I could feel the tension begin to evaporate from the crowd as the two groups enjoyed a laugh at my expense.

When I was done proposing, Mr. Crawford gave me the same answer he had given so many times before, "I'll have to think about it. Now go take a seat, please."

As I climbed onto the bus, I heard Mr. Crawford telling Jack Werner and the other seniors that he remembered when they had been put through the same nonsense as freshmen, and he was disappointed in them for now continuing to perpetuate it. Unfortunately, I didn't hear their response because the passengers on the bus, who had been patiently following the antics, began to applaud and cheer me as I walked down the aisle, still looking like a fool with my jacket on backwards. The only available seats were in the back of the bus, and that walk felt like it would never end.

It had been a long day, and I still was in pain from the punch when we got to the final stop at Mill Street. I was the last to disembark. As I passed by Mr. Crawford, he stopped me and asked if I had a moment, which I did. He proceeded to tell me that Michelle was his niece and that she'd had a difficult life. Her father had abandoned her mother, who was his younger sister, shortly after Michelle was born. Her mother had become bitter and angry. She felt deprived and cheated by life and had started going out drinking and dancing late into the night several times a week, leaving Michelle to fend for herself. He also told me that several of the kids from the Prep could be condescending to the New Rochelle kids and that wearing that madras jacket was like wearing red in front of a bull. Then he asked me to try and break the hazing tradition when I became a senior and attempt to help the freshman instead. I promised him that I would do my best to end it and stepped off the bus.

Mr. Crawford retired to Naples, Florida, before my senior year. But I kept my promise, and our class replaced the hazing with a Big Brother program. Every freshman was assigned a senior to help him and advocate for him. I don't know if the program was continued after we graduated.

———

The next time Christian Carter and I met was on the football field, later in the year, when Iona Prep played New Rochelle High School on Thanksgiving morning. Michelle was a New Rochelle cheerleader, and her distinct voice rang out over the din of the crowd. New Rochelle won the contest, and Christian sought me out afterward to say hello.

During that first winter, Christian and I met often at various track meets. Slowly, a mutual respect began to develop between us. Eventually, over the ensuing years, our relationship would blossom into a close friendship, and Michelle's frigid attitude toward me would thaw. We often would joke about the circumstances under which we originally had met. However, one thing never changed—both Christian and Michelle always called me Madras, even long after I stopped wearing the damn jacket.

At the time of our graduation in 1966, Christian went off to Fordham

University, and I set out for Boston College. Michelle's situation was more uncertain and complicated, made so mainly by her mother, who still was bitter and disappointed at her lot in life, but now was battling the ravages of alcoholism, diabetes, and depression.

Christian's mother, Vanessa, had died giving birth to Christian. His father, Victor, never remarried, choosing instead to devote himself to Christian's upbringing. A simple man with little more than a grammar school education, his dream was to see his son graduate from Fordham University.

Why Fordham, you might ask? Well, as a boy Victor Carter had peddled hot dogs at Fordham football games, games in which the famous Blocks of Granite had thrilled their fans with legendary exploits. Later, as a married man and then a single dad, he had worked on the grounds and maintenance crew at the Rose Hill campus, a place he liked to call "a little bit of heaven in the middle of the Bronx." As he rode the big mowers on the parade grounds, surrounded by the magnificent Gothic structures, he could envision his son walking up to receive his diploma someday. Or at least he thought that he could.

On September 18, 1968, Victor Carter's hard life caught up with him. Having worked as many as three jobs at a time to support Christian and himself, and having been deprived for so many years of Vanessa's companionship, care, and good cooking, it finally happened. The crazy hours, the chain smoking, the constant coffee drinking, the bad eating habits, and the ever increasing loneliness as Christian became more involved with Michelle extracted its toll. At 1:38 p.m. on that September day, as he worked mowing his beloved parade grounds on the Rose Hill campus, Victor Carter succumbed to a massive heart attack. He was dead before his body had a chance to hit the ground, at that place he liked to call a little bit of heaven in the middle of the Bronx.

Christian was devastated. His rock was gone. For so long the mainstay of his life, the father he foolishly had taken for granted was no more. Christian took to remembering all the cold winter mornings his father had gotten up extra early to make him a hearty breakfast and have clean pressed clothing ready for him, and he had rushed out the door without so much as saying thank you. Then there were all those times that his father had wanted him to stay home so they could watch a Giants football game together, a Knicks basketball game, or a Rangers hockey game. He had always had an excuse why he couldn't and left his father to watch those events alone. Now he wished he could have him back for just one game.

Victor Carter, I am certain, would not have agreed with his son's harsh self-assessments. He had always taken great pride in witnessing Christian's journey into manhood and the character and values he had displayed. Victor was very fond of Michelle and happy to share his son with her. I know he looked beyond his own loneliness to the day she would become Christian's wife and possibly provide him with a grandchild to spoil. But Christian was deep in mourning and would hear none of it.

Left with a broken heart and mounting debts, Christian decided to drop out of Fordham at the start of his junior year and join the marines. Father Patrick Collins, his friend and Jesuit adviser at Fordham, tried in vain to convince him to stay and finish his education. But Christian was determined to become self-sufficient. He felt it was time for him to begin earning a living and paying his own way. It was his way of dealing with his grief. He promised Father Collins that he would return to finish his education, but it was not to be.

When he finished his basic training at Quantico, Virginia, and before he was deployed to Vietnam in 1969, he made it official by proposing to Michelle, and she accepted.

By the time Michelle's mother died in late 1970 from complications caused by her uncontrolled diabetes, Christian had returned from his tour of duty in Vietnam and was temporarily stationed at the marine base in Quantico, Virginia. He was allowed to come home for the funeral and used the occasion to convince Michelle that he should re-up in the marines. Before he was redeployed to Vietnam in early 1971, he and Michelle were married by Father Collins at the Fordham Chapel on Saturday, January 16, 1971. I was the best man and wore no madras.

It was not long thereafter that Michelle learned that she was pregnant and that the baby would be a boy.

– 3 –

My four years at Boston College were transformational. I entered a naïve and self-absorbed individual, and I left with a healthy dose of skepticism and a strong sense of the need to serve others, especially those less fortunate.

My first lesson came before the initial semester even had a chance to begin and taught me to be wary of statistics. The time was a beautiful Saturday afternoon in early September, and the place was the first freshman track meet against our crosstown rival, Boston University. The meet was at the track that in 1966 still surrounded the football field inside Alumni Stadium at Boston College. As we took our positions in the blocks to run the 100 yard dash, on one side of me was my teammate, Donald Noonan, whom everyone called Donny, and on the other side of me was a fellow from Boston University named Butch Maurer.

The gun sounded and we were off. A little more than ten seconds later it was over. Butch Maurer had come in first with a time of 10.1 seconds, I had come in second with a time of 10.3 seconds, and Donny had come in third with a time of 10.8 seconds. Later, when Donny and I were leaving Alumni Stadium after the meet, we ran into Donny's girlfriend, Rose, who had come to meet us.

Rose, in an attempt to actually appear interested, asked Donny how things had gone, and he responded, "I did great! I came in third. But poor George, he didn't have such a great day; he came in second to last." Rose never bothered to ask how many runners there had been, and I was too dumbfounded by Donny's response to say anything and rain on his parade. And so it was.

Two days later, on Monday of the new week, Donny and I had our first political science class together. The teacher, Professor Brooks, entered the classroom wearing an old, worn-out, tweed sport jacket and proceeded to fumble about for his glasses, not realizing that they were where they belonged—on his face. His clothes looked like he had slept in them and for more than one night. His shoes thirsted for a polishing, and his socks were close, but not an exact match. His fingers and his teeth were stained from years of smoking and drinking strong coffee. His papers were a mess and littered with burn marks from the ashes of his cigarettes, or "ciggies," as he preferred to call them.

Donny and I became distracted by his appearance and obsessed with the fact that he might actually be sleeping in his clothes. We decided to keep track of what he wore to class over the next few weeks, and we placed a wager on the outcome. Donny chose what he thought was a sure thing and bet that Professor Brooks didn't change for days at a time. I bet that he did change on a daily basis.

Later that day, while we were at lunch in the Eagles Nest, as the school's snack bar was called, we met Rose, who was coming from her class. When we told Rose of our undertaking, she passed a wisecrack to the effect that our parents weren't spending all this money to send us to college so that we could become haberdashers. However, it wasn't long before Rose became drawn into our ill-conceived endeavor, and she, too, was studying the dressing habits of Professor Brooks.

After three weeks of painstaking research, we concluded that Professor Brooks did indeed change his clothing on a daily basis, with the exception of his tweed sport coat, of course, which was a mainstay of his wardrobe. The evidence showed that everything he wore was a variation on the same theme and could be used interchangeably. It also revealed that he was a widower and that his unkempt look was more likely the product of indifference and benign neglect on his part than it was an indictment of his personal hygiene.

Not long thereafter, I collected on my bet from Donny. He had lost, and now he was required to come clean and admit to Rose that he had come in last at that first track meet against Butch Maurer and Boston University. He did so, albeit reluctantly, and Rose, ever the good sport, pretended that she cared. However, the track meet and the foray into haberdashery soon would be all but forgotten as we became totally consumed by a project Professor Brooks had assigned to us.

Apparently, Professor Brooks had been a policy analyst in the Kennedy administration and had been present at a gathering where President John F. Kennedy, pressed by his advisers to deploy combat troops to Vietnam, had confided to Arthur Schlesinger that sending in troops is similar to having a drink. Soon the thirst is back, and you need to have another.

After writing the comment on the blackboard at the front of the classroom and reading it to us for emphasis, Professor Brooks gave us our assignment, as follows.

> As you may know, in March of last year, President Johnson committed the first combat troops to Vietnam, when US Marines were sent to guard an air base. Now he is being told that he needs to send in more troops. A Washington attorney, one of President Johnson's most trusted advisers, remembers the price the world paid for appeasing Hitler in World War II, and is among those counseling the president to escalate our troop involvement. Another Washington lawyer and good friend of the president is warning the president in private against dramatically escalating our troop presence because he thinks that Vietnam might be a quagmire, without a real chance of victory. The US ambassador to South Vietnam has long been against any US ground war in Asia, but he has begun to change his opinion as a result of peer pressures.

The president has turned to you for advice, and he would like to know:

1. Should we "Americanize" the war by taking control of the fighting ourselves and commit substantial amounts of troops and equipment to the cause?
2. Should we limit our involvement to the extent possible, escalate only where absolutely necessary to prevent losing the war and try to involve other nations or the UN in the fight?
3. Should we find a graceful way to exit Vietnam completely at this time?

I will play the role of the president. I would like you to break up into small groups and research the topic over the next few days. When we meet next week, I would like each group to have designated a spokesperson, to tell me which of these options your group thinks that I should adopt, or if your group should come up with a different option of its own, why I should adopt that option. At some point, when I think it is appropriate, I will ask all the groups that have chosen a particular option, to designate a spokesperson to speak for that option.

This is a very complex subject, and at this stage, I am looking only for a preliminary response from you. I expect that we will develop our understanding of the matter and our views on the subject in more depth over the coming weeks. Try and have a nice weekend, but do not forget that the fate of the free world is resting on your shoulders.

With that, he pushed his hair back from his forehead with his right hand, as he often did, smiled with a sense of contentment, revealing once again his stained yellow teeth, and walked out of the room.

Of course, Donny and I would partner together, but could we solicit Rose's help? We ran after Professor Brooks, who was moving quickly to get outside so that he could light up a smoke. We debated stopping him in the hall to ask our question, or waiting until he was outside and able to indulge his habit. Rather than chance it, we called out to the professor, who turned and stopped.

"Yes?"

"May we involve other students who are not in the class in our research?"

"You may involve anyone you please, for the decision ultimately is mine and mine alone.

"Keep in mind that there may not be any one right answer. Ah, it is great to be king, don't you think? Oh, sorry, I meant to say president. I forgot that we no longer are a British colony."

He laughed and started once again for the door to the outside, holding his matches and his cigarette in his hand. Donny and I looked at each other in bewilderment. While he may have thought that he was being funny, we were convinced that he simply was crazy. He then surprised us by looking back and saying, "That was a hint, so pay special heed to it."

Donny turned to me and asked what the hell he had been talking about. I told him that I really didn't know, but that I didn't think it was worth worrying about at the moment. It was a beautiful day outside, and I wanted to take full advantage of it. Donny agreed, and we walked out into the crisp September afternoon.

In presenting the assignment to us, Professor Brooks had employed an old bureaucratic trick that he had learned in Washington known as the *Goldilocks principle*. By having one option be too weak and another too heavy-handed, he was confident that the class would opt for the middle ground as being the right way to go. He was in for a surprise of his own.

Two thirds of the groups in the class chose option one. Having grown up on a steady diet of World War II movies, starring the likes of John Wayne, Jimmy Stewart, and Henry Fonda, to name a few, they were convinced of the righteousness of America's position and of the purity of its intentions to simply liberate the Vietnamese people from Communist oppression and leave them to govern themselves independently. They noted that on September 2, 1945, Ho Chi Minh, in declaring Vietnam's independence, had quoted from the United States Declaration of Independence. Prior to that, after World War I, he had sought the assistance of President Wilson. In their view, such actions were proof that Ho Chi Minh was a patriot at heart and a communist by convenience. Swift, decisive, and overwhelming action on the part of the United States, they argued, would bring Ho Chi Minh around before the American public had a chance to grow tired of the war.

"And what if the Chinese enter the conflict the way that they did in Korea?" Professor Brooks asked. The spokesperson responded that the groups that had chosen option one were unanimous in their belief that Ho Chi Minh would side with the United States and fight the Chinese. They supported this belief by noting that the Japanese invasion of Indochina at the start of World War II had destroyed the invincible image of white colonialism, and Ho Chi Minh had been one of the first to recognize and take advantage of that fact. They pointed out that in 1946, Ho Chi Minh had worked out a deal with the French in which France would recognize Vietnam's independence, and Ho Chi Minh would allow a designated number of French troops to reenter North Vietnam for five years. This arrangement would have the added effect of removing the Chinese presence from Vietnam. When Ho Chi Minh's critics attacked him for this arrangement, he was quoted as telling them:

> You fools! Don't you realize what it means if the Chinese remain? Don't you remember your history? The last time the Chinese came, they stayed a thousand years. The French are foreigners. They are weak. Colonialism is dying. The white man is finished in Asia. But if the Chinese stay now, they will never go. As for me, I prefer to sniff French shit for five years than eat Chinese shit for the rest of my life.

"In short, Professor Brooks," the spokesperson concluded, "we think Ho Chi Minh would rather sniff American shit for a time than risk letting the Chinese come in again and not leave, thereby forcing him to eat Chinese shit for the rest of his life."

Professor Brooks thanked the speaker and indicated to the class that he would save any further questions or comments until he had heard from the spokespersons for the other two options. With that, he turned to the representative for the groups that had chosen option two. The remaining one third of the groups, with the exception of our group, had chosen option two.

The spokesperson for the option two groups began by noting that they had a different goal in mind than did the option one groups. They had taken a literal reading of the containment doctrine and the domino theory and were merely trying to contain Communism to North Vietnam and prevent the domino of South Vietnam from falling to the Communists. In contrast, they had seen the option one groups looking to unite an independent Vietnam under a democratic form of government. Professor Brooks responded that at this point it was fine for the two groups to have different goals and that he purposely had been ambiguous as to the goal to be achieved.

With that matter settled, the representative for the option two groups began to speak. Citing President Eisenhower as precedent for their position, the spokesperson noted that they would not commit the United States without the involvement of its allies or the United Nations. The South Vietnamese people, in their view, did not exhibit the same passion for independence or the same nationalistic fervor that Ho Chi Minh and his followers in the North did. Rather, the South Vietnamese seemed preoccupied with bickering among themselves for wealth and power, having convinced themselves that the United States had too much at stake to allow them to fail.

According to the spokesperson, the United States, in acting alone, and constrained by the fear of being called colonialist, would be forced to cede control of the fighting to the South Vietnamese, which they viewed as a formula for disaster. The best course of action would be to do the least necessary to buy time, while the involvement of our allies or the UN could be brokered so that when the time inevitably came to fight in earnest, the United States would not be acting alone. The plan would be to arrive at a solution similar to that which was reached in Korea.

Reiterating that he was saving his questions and comments for the end, Professor Brooks did note that America was receiving token help in Vietnam from allies that were potential dominoes themselves, such as Thailand, the Philippines, Australia, and New Zealand. Conceding, nevertheless, that the war was viewed as predominately a US endeavor, Professor Brooks turned to Donny and me and asked which one of us would be the spokesperson for our group. Donny pointed to me and I agreed to do it.

I began by stating that while we appreciated the wisdom of the containment doctrine and the domino theory, we had concluded that, at least in the case of Vietnam, these rules of engagement were being misapplied. In our view, the containment doctrine rested on the erroneous premise that Communism represented a monolithic threat and failed to take into account the very real differences that existed among the North Vietnamese, the Chinese, and the Soviets. History showed that the Vietnamese and the Chinese had been foes for centuries. From our standpoint, US involvement would have the opposite effect of that which was intended; it would serve as a catalyst for the Chinese, the North Vietnamese, and the Soviets to put their traditional differences aside and cooperate in their effort against us. The better course of action would be to disengage from Vietnam and allow these long-standing issues or conflicts to play themselves out. Even if all of Vietnam were to become Communist under a Ho Chi Minh regime, Ho Chi Minh and his followers would never stand for Soviet or Chinese intervention in their affairs. And if need be, we always could intervene at that time upon the request of Ho Chi Minh or his successors.

I then proceeded to explain that from our perspective, Vietnam represented an emulsion in which the desire for independence and freedom from colonial rule was suspended in the misbegotten solution of Communism. Whether that Communism flourished as a result of the fervor witnessed in the North or came about by default due to the indifference seen in the South did not matter. In our view, the dilemma for the United States was whether or not to support self-determination, when the choice of the people, whether by affirmative action or by default due to inaction or indifference, was a Communist form of government. We concluded that America must acquiesce to the presence of such a government if we are to remain true to our founding beliefs. In the absence of an overriding threat to our national interest, any attempt to change such determination must be done through peaceful means and in compliance with international law.

Professor Brooks stopped me at this point to ask if we had found any recent precedent for this conclusion. He was taken back and somewhat surprised when I answered in the affirmative and cited for him President Kennedy's handling of the Cuban Bay of Pigs incident.

Before Professor Brooks could again interrupt me, I proceeded with the explanation of our position. It was the observation of our group that when the Cuban people failed to rise up against Castro and join forces with the Cuban–American exiles trying to liberate them, President Kennedy made the decision not to commit further American assets to the effort, whether those assets were in the form of United States military troops, equipment, or quasi-military American civilian volunteers. For, I continued, the president had read the inaction of the Cuban population as tacit approval on their part of the Castro regime. While he may have been criticized for his decision, in the opinion of our group, he had saved many lives by preventing the country from becoming bogged down in a drawn-out guerrilla conflict in which American forces would be unable to tell friend from foe. Rather, I emphasized, the president resorted to a peaceful economic embargo being placed on Cuba, with the hope that the Cuban people would be moved to rise up against their Communist leader. I concluded by saying that our group felt that if President Kennedy had lived, he would have reached the same conclusions about Vietnam that he had reached concerning Cuba and would have acted in a similar manner. In short, we do not think he would have committed combat troops to Vietnam.

"Mr. Angelson," broke in Professor Brooks, "you do recall that you are advising President Johnson, and you appear to be telling the president that he has made a mistake in committing combat troops to Vietnam, a mistake that his predecessor would not have made had his predecessor been allowed to live."

"It gets worse, Professor," I replied.

"I do not think it can, Mr. Angelson," barked Professor Brooks. "By now you and Mr. Noonan would have been fired, and the guards would be escorting you out of the building."

Amused by our reprimand, the class began to laugh. Content with the reaction of his audience, Professor Brooks once again pushed his hair back, smiled in his usual way, and commanded me to proceed.

To extricate our troops from Vietnam, we would recommend a two-step process. First, we would need to train South Vietnamese forces to replace our US combat troops and take up the fight while we are withdrawing. Second, we would need to assure that the North Vietnamese allow us to withdraw in an orderly and honorable way and that they don't try to "bloody our noses," so to speak, on the way out. This second step, in turn, can be accomplished in one of two ways. One way would be to bluff the North Vietnamese into believing that we would be crazy enough to use nuclear weapons in North Vietnam if they were to push us too far. The other way would be to convince them that we could be trusted to leave peacefully once internationally monitored elections were held in the South, even if the outcome of those elections were to produce a Communist government that asked us to leave.

The problem we were having, we told Professor Brooks, was that we saw President Johnson as a "Goldilocks" of sorts, in that he was too reasonable and moderate to be taken seriously as a crazy, out-of-control hawk, but sufficiently hawkish not to be trusted as a true dove. For example, we thought that Senator Goldwater's pedigree as a hawk would enable him to scare the North into thinking that he might be capable of resorting to nuclear arms and that Senator McCarthy's credentials as a dove would allow him to garner the trust of the North Vietnamese that he would withdraw following fair elections.

"Professor Brooks," I asked, "how do you advise a sitting president that the best course of action he could take is not to stand for reelection in 1968?"

"Gingerly," replied Professor Brooks. "If the president is an intelligent man, as he is, he initially will challenge you, but he eventually will come to see it for himself and act accordingly."

Over the remaining months of the school year, we could sense our understanding of the subject matter becoming far more in-depth and our ability to analyze complex political situations growing in sophistication. In May of 1967, when the course was finished, Donny and I were grateful to Professor Brooks for the grade of A that we each received, but we were far more indebted to him for the education that he bestowed on us and all that we had learned. We had come a long way in a short time, from the frivolous days spent wondering if he slept in his clothes. Indeed, many a night we had fallen asleep in ours, too engrossed in the project to stop.

In 1968, Senator Eugene McCarthy almost defeated President Johnson in the New Hampshire primary. On March 16, 1968, having seen Senator McCarthy's showing in New Hampshire, Senator Robert F. Kennedy announced his candidacy for president of the United States.

The next day, St. Patrick's Day, March 17, 1968, Professor Brooks called Donny and me into his office on the third floor of Carney Hall. As we climbed the stairs, we tried to think of why he would want to see us. After all, it was almost a year since we had completed the course with him. As we entered his office and took a seat, he told us that Robert F. Kennedy had called him to ask him to join a team that would advise his campaign on formulating a policy on Vietnam. He wanted us to know that he would be recommending a variation of our option three to the team.

On March 31, 1968, President Johnson announced, "I shall not seek and I will not accept the nomination of my party for another term as your president." He gave many reasons, and much speculation surrounded his decision not to run. Some cited health concerns, and others said that he had worn out his welcome on Capitol Hill, getting some of the most sweeping and progressive social legislation in decades passed. Regardless of the reasons, he had stepped aside in the best interests of his country, and for that, Donny and I had a new-found respect for the man.

On June 5, 1968, Senator Robert F. Kennedy was assassinated in Los Angeles after having won the California primary.

Donny and I found ourselves wondering what might have been if the Kennedy brothers had been allowed to live out their lives.

> What might have been is an abstraction
> Remaining a perpetual possibility
> Only in a world of speculation.
> —T.S. Eliot, "Burnt Norton"

– 4 –

As Ash Wednesday of 1967 approached, I found myself thinking about what I might give up or do for Lent. I decided that I would attend Mass every day. Donny had told me that there was an early morning service in St. Mary's Chapel that was housed in the beautiful Gothic hall where the Jesuits lived on campus. Apparently, Rose was friendly with two of the Jesuits, and she would attend there when they were saying Mass. I decided that I would start by going for ashes on Wednesday, and I would continue going until the semester ended.

My reasons for attending daily Mass went beyond Lent. Since my sophomore year at Iona Prep, I had been considering the idea of becoming a priest. Then I met Kelly Dougherty in the spring of that year, and she swept me off my feet. We dated through most of our remaining high school years and enjoyed a wonderful relationship. She truly was my best friend, and there was nothing that we couldn't share with one another. We were soul mates, as she liked to say, an expression she had learned from her mother. However, our relationship, like so many high school romances, began to falter as college approached. The pressures of being separated while still bound to one another, in a future full of new temptations and freedoms, began to take its toll, and we eventually broke up.

As I've told you, when I was returning from Brazil in 1958, I had vowed to myself that once I set foot on American soil, I never again would leave. It was not until I had left the United States for a time that

I realized how much I loved and missed America. Well, it wasn't until I'd been separated from Kelly for a time that I realized how much I loved and missed her. But too much time had gone by, and we both now were very different people than we'd been in high school. No, I merely was left to hope that someday I could meet another woman, another soul mate, with whom I could have such a close and wonderful relationship.

Nevertheless, there was one thing that had remained with me from my relationship with Kelly Dougherty—the realization that having a wife and family was very important to me, and I didn't think I could forgo them for a life of celibacy. Now, years later, I was beginning to hear the calling again. At first it was a mere whisper, barely distinguishable from the background breeze, a faint noise on the periphery of my consciousness. But then it became more pronounced, resembling the steady gong of a church bell. The struggle within me was becoming a distraction, and my concentration in class was slipping. I needed to pray for guidance.

Entering St. Mary's Chapel, I saw Father Arthur Phillips, my Comparative Theology professor, giving out ashes. The look on his face telegraphed the fact that he was surprised to see me there. The next morning, when I arrived, he was on the altar, preparing to say Mass. The scene repeated itself each morning for several weeks. On one Monday morning many weeks later, we were the only two people in the chapel, but Father Phillips chose not to acknowledge my presence until after Mass was finished. Then he asked me if I had time to join him for a cup of coffee. When I said yes, I had no idea that he would be the answer to my prayers.

Comparative Theology was an interesting course, made more so by Father Phillips's dynamic teaching style. In it we were learning the differences among the various Christian faiths as well as studying the common traditions shared by our Judeo-Christian heritage. As the class progressed, we came to realize that Father Phillips had certain sayings that he liked to use over and over again. One of his favorite sayings was that we had acquired our religion by accident of birth, and that college was a time to question, investigate, and reflect, as well as to learn and reaffirm our beliefs for ourselves.

The class was made up predominately of Catholics, but there were several Episcopalians, one of whom, Walter J. Rather III, had become a friend of mine. In addition, there was one Presbyterian, Johnson M. Eastmore, and two Jewish brothers, Abraham and Sanford Fox. Their parents, Jack Fox and Adele Lebow, had met while attending Boston College Law School, where they had acquired a respect for the Jesuit tradition of teaching. They had married after graduating from the law school and started a successful law practice together in downtown Boston, a firm by the name of Fox and Fox. They now lived in nearby Newton and had decided to have their children educated by the Jesuits at Boston College. Abe and Sandy lived at home with their parents and worshiped at the local synagogue in Newton.

Father Phillips arranged for some of the classes to be taught off-site by guest lecturers from other faiths. There had been two rabbis, three protestant ministers, and even a Muslim cleric. We also were expected to take "weekend road trips" to attend at least one service in each other's faiths. "Where there is knowledge and understanding," went another of Father Phillips's favorite sayings, "tolerance will surely follow."

One of my weekend road trips took place in late April and was to Bridgehampton, Long Island, to attend an Episcopal service. That Monday morning after Mass, while we were having our usual cup of coffee together, Father Phillips asked me, "Didn't you go with Walter Rather to his home in Bridgehampton, New York, this past weekend to attend an Episcopal service?"

"Yes," I said, "Wally and I drove in his MG-B to New London, Connecticut, where we caught the ferry across Long Island Sound to Orient Point on the North Fork of Long Island. We then cut across Shelter Island with the help of two more ferries and landed in Sag Harbor, a quaint old whaling village. From there it was a short drive to Bridgehampton. I must tell you that I fell in love with Bridgehampton the moment that I set eyes on it and made myself a promise that I would return some day."

As Father added his predictable two packs of sugar and a half a cup of cream to his coffee and began to stir the mixture, he said, "I suspect it is my good fortune to continue to hear more of your weekend exploits before I am to be told of the Episcopal service that brought you there in the first place."

Ignoring his facetious remark completely, I continued undaunted, "Friday night after dinner, Wally and I went to his favorite watering hole, where we were able to hear some live piano music. Later that evening, we got into a big discussion at the bar with a local writer and a friend of his over the Vietnam War, and we still were arguing our respective points when the bar closed.

Saturday morning I got up early and borrowed one of the Rathers' bicycles to ride into town, where I came upon an ice cream parlor and sandwich shop that made its own ice cream the old-fashioned way. The owners had been able to successfully defy the march of time and preserve the atmosphere that still had its original early twentieth-century charm. After having some breakfast there, I walked the bike through town, passing first the Presbyterian church, with its stately white façade, and then St. Ann's Episcopal Church, where we would be attending Sunday service, on my way to the Bridgehampton Library. I spent most of the afternoon researching the Episcopal religion in the library.

Saturday night the Rathers took everyone out to dinner, and I was introduced to crispy Long Island duckling, with orange sauce and wild rice, a most delicious meal. Afterward, Wally and I took a few beers down to the beach, where we made a fire to keep warm while we sat around talking. The next morning we went to the service at St. Ann's.

"What did you think?" Father Phillips asked me.

"I was surprised at how similar it is to our Catholic Mass. If it were not for the fact that the priest was married, and his wife was sitting next to us, I might have mistaken it for a Catholic service. At the coffee hour afterward, I had a chance to speak with Father Thompson and his wife."

There was a pregnant pause as Father took another sip of his coffee. When he was finished, he said, "Yes, would you like to tell me more?"

It was as if he had put his hand down my throat, reached into my very soul, and was pulling it out of me.

"Why won't the Catholic church allow priests to marry?" I asked.

He smiled and in a soft voice said to me, "So that is the issue that you have been struggling with."

"How did you know?"

"When students come to my early morning weekday masses the way you have been coming, it has been my experience that they are grappling with an issue of great importance to them. It may be the failing health or death of a loved one; on occasion it may involve a possible vocation; or it may entail a parental divorce, an unwanted pregnancy, or a brush with the law. But it always is an issue of great magnitude.

"Is there anything in particular about being a priest that is calling you? Because a great deal of what we do can also be done by a lay person."

I explained, "My calling goes to the very essence of the priesthood. It goes to the doctrine of transubstantiation itself. I am driven by the desire to bring spiritual nourishment to my fellow man through the miracle of the consecration of the bread and the wine into the substance of Christ's body and blood.

"When I was a very young boy, we lived in Brazil. My father had many friends who had become Maryknoll priests and nuns. As a result, very often when Maryknoll priests were heading into the interior of Brazil to work among the indigenous Indian populations in the Amazon, they would visit with us before they traveled inland. I remember two young priests in particular because they had played basketball with me in our driveway while they were visiting with us. About a year after they had left us to journey to their mission in the interior, I learned that the Indians had cut off and eaten both of their thumbs and their index fingers. My father explained to me that the priests had been reassigned and were preparing to move to another mission after having spent almost a year there administering to the sick and addressing other health issues, with modern medicines and basic surgical procedures, and teaching everything from simple hygiene to the Scriptures, as well as saying daily Mass. Before the Indians would allow the two priests to leave, they cut off their fingers because they had been attending daily Mass and witnessing the consecration of the host and the wine and thought that the magical healing powers they had attributed to the priests must be contained in those four fingers.

"My father used the incident to drive home a point, and it has had a lasting impression on me. As a child I had fought having to go to church on Sundays. Once there, I had been restless and rambunctious, rarely paying attention to what was going on. He emphasized for me that I was witnessing a miracle every Sunday when the priest consecrated the bread and wine. These two priests that I had come to know had risked their lives and well-being to bring the fruits of that miracle to the outer reaches of civilization and had paid a high price in the process. He told me that I had been taking for granted the gift the Lord had given us at the Last Supper, on the night before he suffered death.

"The incident had a profound effect on my young psyche. From that day forward, I have cherished the consecration and the communion that follows it at Mass, so much so that in high school I began to think about becoming a priest so that I could bring that gift of spiritual nourishment to others."

"And then what happened?" asked Father.

"I met Kelly Dougherty," I replied.

"Ah yes," said Father, "we all have had a Kelly Dougherty in our lives, haven't we?"

"Father, this issue really is starting to become a distraction for me and is affecting my studies."

"Let me give your situation some thought," said Father, "and we can reconvene to resume our discussion again tomorrow morning after Mass. In the meantime, I would like you to put this issue out of your mind and concentrate on your courses. Let me be the one to do the worrying on this matter."

"Okay," I said and started to prepare to leave.

But Father reached out and, putting his hand on my arm, said, "Wait! I still have a sip of coffee left. Aren't you going to tell me about the rest of your road trip?"

While Father may have had some interest in hearing more about the trip, I think his primary concern was to distract me from my weighty thoughts. Nevertheless, I sat back down and obliged him by continuing to recount my weekend adventure.

"Sunday afternoon Wally and his mother went shopping for some things Wally needed in the nearby village of Southampton, and I tagged along for the ride. While they were shopping, I wandered down to the War Memorial in the park at the far end of the village. The memorial was a Roman styled structure at the base of a large pond. I found an inviting place under a weeping willow tree, where the waters of the pond quietly lapped against the banks. I sat down and started to read a book that I had borrowed from the library the day before. However, it didn't take long for me to become distracted by the ducks that I thought had swum over to investigate my presence. But I soon learned they were mainly interested in the cucumber sandwiches Mrs. Rather had insisted that I take with me. Snow white with orange beaks, my newfound friends quickly made me feel guilty for having dined on Long Island duckling with orange sauce the previous night. In an attempt to ease my conscience, I began to feed them the sandwiches. That is, until a local police car pulled up and the officer inside told me it was illegal to feed the ducks. He had been Wally's classmate in grammar school and let me go with a warning, since I was a newcomer to the area.

"Later that afternoon, Wally and I climbed into his MG-B and started the trek back to Boston. On the ferry crossing Long Island Sound, Wally ran into some old friends, and I went out on deck to watch the sun that was setting behind us in the west. Alone with my thoughts, I began to think of the folly that had caused the rock on which Jesus Christ had built His church to shatter asunder in protest. It was all man-made differences and had nothing to do with Christ's basic teachings. Much like the child of divorcing parents, I found myself fantasizing about the possibility of Christendom putting their differences aside and once again uniting in the ecumenical spirit that had been started at Vatican II. Then again, I told myself maybe that too was folly."

Father stopped me at this point to say, "I knew your weekend would be a wonderful adventure, but now I know from your reflections that it also has been the spiritual journey for you that I had hoped it would be. I must go now because I have a class to teach, but I look forward to seeing you again tomorrow."

As I, too, prepared to leave, I was glad that I had mustered the courage to speak with Father Phillips about my vocation. And I felt a great sense of relief. It was as if the weight of the world had been lifted from my shoulders.

The next morning started out like all the others, and after Mass, Father and I went for our usual coffee. But it would end differently, with my life changing direction.

"What is your major?" Father asked me to start with.

"Political science," I replied.

"I have an idea. Why don't you think about becoming a double major and also majoring in philosophy or theology? Doing this will allow you to begin taking a concentration of courses that will be useful to you should you later decide to pursue a vocation. In addition, if you are willing, I am prepared to meet with you one-on-one in my free time to instruct you in more advanced theological studies. I am talking about the type of material that you would be required to take in the seminary. I caution you, however, that I will be expecting a great deal from you, that the work will be extensive, and that your free time will be substantially reduced. On the other hand, if you do well, I will do what I can when the time comes to have you given credit by the seminary for these studies."

I was genuinely moved by what this man was willing to do for me and without hesitation answered yes, thanking him profusely in the process. Then I asked, "Will they let me be a double major, or would it be better for me to drop political science?"

Father Phillips smiled and answered, "Yes, I can assure you that you will be able to take a double major. After all, we Jesuits still are running this place last I checked. And no, it would not be wise for you to drop your original major, because we must continue to prepare you for a career in law or politics so that if you decide to be a husband and father, you have a means of supporting your family."

With a wink, Father added, "We must continue the task of preparing you to be able to render to Caesar that which is Caesar's as we begin to ready you to render to the Lord the things that are the Lord's."

– 5 –

In the days that followed, I was able to register as a double major. However, the semester and my freshman year were quickly coming to a close. My one-on-one study program with Father Phillips would have to wait until my sophomore year to begin.

My second and final weekend road trip for my comparative theology course took place two weeks later. It started with Johnson Eastmore (or Jon as he preferred to be called), Wally, and me accompanying Abe and Sandy Fox to their synagogue for the Friday night service. Sitting among the congregation, I found myself thinking about the Pharisees in the time of Jesus and of their teachings to the Jewish people, at least as I had learned them through my Catholic education. Schooled by the Pharisees to expect a powerful and imposing Messiah that would set them free from oppression, they struggled to adjust to the humble Jesus and His teachings of restraint and of a Kingdom not of this world and came to see Him merely as a holy man and prophet. I had to admit to myself that under the circumstances, I doubt that I would have seen things any differently. Nevertheless, if they had, today there would be no Judeo-Christian tradition, only a Judeo tradition, and we all would be worshiping in synagogues. Then again, perhaps that idea, too, was folly on my part.

After the service, Mr. and Mrs. Fox took all of us out for dinner. While we ate, they explained to us what we had observed and patiently answered all of our questions.

On Saturday morning, Donny and I had a track meet at the College of the Holy Cross, and we rode the team bus to the meet. Mrs. Fox lent Abe her station wagon, a white wagon with wood on the side. Abe, Sandy, Wally, and Jon picked me up in it at Holy Cross after the track meet, and we set out for Scarsdale, New York, where Jon and his family lived. Stopping on the way for something to eat, we arrived at the Eastmore residence around three thirty in the afternoon. We decided to attend the five o'clock Mass at the Catholic church in nearby Bronxville, New York. Afterward, we walked over to Pete's Tavern for burgers and a few beers. Abe and Sandy had the most questions about the Catholic service, but Jon, too, drilled me with inquiries about the Mass we had just attended. Wally was surprised at the similarity to the Episcopal service and understood better the reaction I'd had after attending St. Ann's. We closed out the evening by catching a movie at a theater next door.

The next morning we all went with the Eastmores to the Sunday service at their Presbyterian church. Father Phillips had explained to me that the Presbyterians, along with most protestants, believe in consubstantiation, rather than the Catholic belief in transubstantiation. Consubstantiation, unlike transubstantiation, does not hold that the bread and wine are changed into the substance of Christ's body and blood at the consecration. Rather, consubstantiation holds that for the faithful, the bread and wine are symbols of Christ's presence among us. Nevertheless, I found this part of the service very hard to witness, because unlike in the Episcopal service, the language used was very different from what I was accustomed to hearing.

After the service, the Eastmores took all of us to lunch at their yacht club. As I sat on the veranda watching the boats tied to their moorings on the Long Island Sound, I became curious to know whether the Episcopalians believe in transubstantiation or consubstantiation, for the language I had heard Father Thompson use in Bridgehampton was the same language as I had heard Father Phillips and every other Catholic priest use. I made a mental note to ask Father Phillips the next day when we met for coffee. The answer I got was that it could vary within the

Episcopal church and that the beliefs of the high Episcopalians were the closest to the Catholic beliefs.

My next three years at Boston College went quickly. Father Phillips, true to his word, worked me hard in our one-on-one sessions, but I didn't mind, because I appreciated all that he was doing for me.

In one of our sessions, Father Phillips confided in me that he had been raised an Episcopalian and had converted to Catholicism as a young man. While I found myself attracted to the more progressive policies I had experienced at St. Ann's in Bridgehampton, he had been drawn to the Catholic church by what he viewed as the more conservative and orthodox posture of its teachings.

In my sophomore year, I expressed an interest in learning more about Episcopalian teaching. Father Phillips introduced me to his good friend the Reverend Lewis Pratt, who was the head of the divinity school at Yale University in New Haven, Connecticut. That summer I read the teachings of several Episcopal theologians under the watchful eye of Lewis Pratt himself. Periodically, I would make the trip to Yale in my GTO to confer with Reverend Pratt. It was a practice that I continued the next summer between my junior and senior year at Boston College.

I found myself being increasingly drawn to the Episcopal faith and would drive to Bridgehampton on occasion to attend the Sunday service at St. Ann's. Yet when I was at home or at Boston College, I continued to attend Catholic Mass. In fact, I went to Father Phillips's Mass every weekday morning that I could until I graduated. If someone were to ask me if I was a Catholic or an Episcopalian, the only honest answer that I could give them was that I wasn't really sure, for in a way I had come to consider myself to be both.

However, deep down I knew that if I wanted to become a priest, I would have to choose between the two faiths. As a result, I continued to straddle the fence while I struggled with my conscience.

When I graduated from Boston College in 1970, I already had been accepted by Boston College Law School. However, I'd requested and had been granted permission to defer my starting date until September of 1971. My lottery number in the draft was 228. I expected to be called in a matter of months, and there was no deferment for attending law school. When President Nixon subsequently froze the lottery at 195, I was spared that fate.

– 6 –

With the draft now behind me as an issue, law school still a year away, and no money in my pocket, I decided that it was time to find a job. The family was down to one car, my 1967 Pontiac, since the old family station wagon had died. So at the expense of my dignity, I dusted off my old bicycle and rode into nearby White Plains, New York, to begin my search. Going door to door along Westchester Avenue, asking one business after another if they could use an eager young college graduate with a stellar work ethic, one door after another slammed in my face until one did not. The local Ford dealer offered me a job as a sales person. I parked the bike and called my mother to tell her that I had found a job and would not be home until dinner because they wanted me to start immediately. Selling cars was to prove very lucrative for me, as well as being a great educational experience in the "lessons of life," as my new sales manager liked to say.

One such lesson in life came when I had been on the job only a matter of weeks. Two young men about my age, one black and the other white, walked into the showroom. Neither of them looked like they had much more money than I did. No one wanted to waste a turn waiting on them, so as low man on the totem pole, I reluctantly did. We all had been wrong in our assessment of them. As Sister Nancy had taught me in the fifth grade, you should never judge a book by its cover.

Andy Jefferson and Jimmy Winston had recently been honorably discharged from the US Army and had been awarded Purple Hearts as a result of having been wounded in Vietnam. Both had rolls of one hundred dollar bills in their pockets, neatly held together by ordinary rubber bands, money that they had saved while in Vietnam. Both wanted to buy cars they had dreamed of owning while fighting in the jungles of Southeast Asia, and both were willing to pay in full for the cars with the cash.

Andy had the easier of the two requests. He wanted a brand new Thunderbird, and we had the perfect car in stock for him. It was a dark green model with a black vinyl roof and a black interior.

Jimmy, on the other hand, wanted a car that no longer was being manufactured. He wanted a new Shelby GT500 Mustang. While in Vietnam, Jimmy had been the recipient of a "Dear John" letter from a fiancée who had been too fickle and impatient to await his return, so my heart went out to him. I promised to search for one, and as much as I wanted to make this young hero's dream come true for him, I didn't hold out much hope of finding any new ones still remaining unsold. They simply had been too popular an item. Fortunately, I would be proven wrong.

Due to an inventory glitch, one bright yellow Shelby GT500 Mustang had been unaccounted for at the large Ford Preparation Center in the Port of Newark. The error had been uncovered in a subsequent audit of the inventory at the center, which only recently had been completed. The yellow GT500, now all alone, ignored, and covered in soot and pollution, had watched each one of its siblings be sold one by one, prepared for delivery, and claimed by its new owner. Yet it had steadfastly braved the elements, the wear having begun to show on its fading paint and tarnished chrome, to patiently await the return of its wounded hero from Vietnam—something a fickle and inpatient fiancée had not been prepared to do.

While driving in the new Thunderbird with Andy and Jimmy to the Ford Preparation Center in Newark, New Jersey, to pick up Jimmy's new GT500 Mustang, the two veterans told me of their experience in Vietnam, especially of how they had come to be Purple Heart recipients.

The morning of the day that Andy and Jimmy were wounded

had not been very different from the mornings that preceded it—hot and muggy. On patrol approximately forty miles southwest of Saigon, plodding through the rice fields near the canal that ran from Ap Bac to another hamlet named Ap Tan Thoi, approximately a mile away, the sun was getting extremely hot as the morning marched toward noon. Some of the men began having trouble breathing in the punishing heat and began to chew salt tablets to help them cope. Andy and Jimmy, along with the others, attempted to cover the metal on their weapons so that they would not become too hot to handle.

Andy was walking point, the lead position as the patrol advanced single file along the narrow dikes. As the patrol approached several Vietnamese peasants working in the rice fields in the distance, Andy noticed that the peasants, three women—one of whom appeared to be pregnant—and an old man, had moved a short distance away from where they were working and taken up their toil in a new location. He thought this to be strange, because they had not finished what they were doing in the first location. He turned to report his observation to his commanding officer, Lt. Michael Pastor, who in turn dismissed the concern as delirium resulting from too much sun. The step-by-step decisions of walking point, one of the most dangerous positions, had been weighing on Andy's mind as he sweated profusely in his flak vest, and he had begun to wonder if the lieutenant was right.

Lieutenant Pastor was a recent Virginia Military Institute or VMI graduate and a new arrival to Vietnam. He was a zealot and a patriot who saw himself as a fearless liberator of the Vietnamese people, and he was anxious to get in on the action before the war ended. In the life of the war, time was beginning to cast a long shadow, and Lieutenant Pastor perceived it with a near sense of panic. Buck Jones, a grizzly character who was bringing up the rear of the patrol, often said of Lieutenant Pastor that he was a hero looking for a place to win his medals. It was one of the few things on which Andy had found himself in agreement with Buck.

Lieutenant Pastor had an unnerving tendency to show compassion and kindness to the peasants that he encountered on patrol, especially if they were elderly, women, or children, and that day appeared to be no exception. Andy didn't necessarily object to this empathy on the part of the lieutenant, but he had grown weary of what he thought was a dangerously naïve showing of trust. The Vietnamese all looked and dressed alike, and Andy couldn't tell with certainty who was a friend and who was a foe.

Andy was a draftee and as such was nearing the end of his one-year rotation schedule in Vietnam. Counting the days, his overriding concern had become getting home alive and in one piece. Until Jimmy Winston had been transferred to the unit, a recent event, Vietnam had been a lonely experience for Andy. He was sent over as an individual replacement and not as part of a unit. When he arrived at one of the division headquarters in Vietnam, they randomly assigned him to a company where even his fellow soldiers hadn't taken much interest in him or his well-being. Their biggest concern was that his inexperience might get them killed. Drug use was rampant, morale was low, and relations among racial and ethnic groups were deteriorating. Andy, being black, and Buck, being Buck, were living illustrations of that rising tension.

Robert "Buck" Jones was raised in Detroit, Michigan, in a depressed area that had been turning more and more into a "black" neighborhood. In high school, Buck had been in and out of trouble, more in than out, and got his nickname from a frustrated teacher who told Buck that he was destined to spend his life bucking the system. The high school psychologist told Buck that he suffered from low self-esteem, but he dismissed her advice, calling her a dumb bitch.

As irony would have it, he decided after high school to join the very police department that had been his main antagonist while he was in school. In good physical shape and with no serious criminal record, he passed the physical and other requirements and became a police officer.

Buck did not like blacks; in fact, he did not like many people who were not like him. He liked to say that he was not prejudiced because he hated everyone equally. It might have been funny, if it had not been true.

The problem was that Buck patrolled a predominately black neighborhood—a situation that was bound to end badly and did several months later, when Buck accidentally shot and killed a black youth that he mistakenly thought was pulling a gun on him. The incident occurred in a dark alley late on a moonless night, and it was later determined that the youth had been high on pot and most likely had been reaching into his pocket to dispose of the remaining joints that he had before they were found on him in a search.

Buck carried an unregistered weapon for just such occasions. To his credit, however, he didn't use it. Rather, he called EMS and tried to keep the victim alive, but to no avail. Buck may have acquired prejudices as a result of what he perceived to be the ruination of his neighborhood, but he was not a murderer, at least not yet.

The Detroit press, in publicizing the Buck Jones incident, whether intentionally or unintentionally, had fanned local tensions. Several civil rights leaders became involved and demanded that Buck be dismissed from the police force. It was hard not to agree with them, especially when Buck's history of racial slurs, high school incidents, and short temper came to light, and the police department was left with little choice but to dismiss him.

No longer a police officer, an embittered Buck had become eligible to be drafted. He welcomed the notice from the local draft board when it came almost immediately thereafter. His parents had been deceased for several years, and he had no brothers or sisters or other family to speak of. Nobody, including Buck's "dumb bitch" high school psychologist, was remotely sorry to see him go.

Unfortunately, on that day in Vietnam, Buck had been too far back in the patrol to hear the exchange between Andy and the lieutenant. Several new replacements, along with Jimmy, were walking single file on the dike in between them. But if he had heard, he would have agreed with Andy's concern. Also unfortunately, in deciding between walking on the dike or in the water of the paddies, Andy had chosen to stay on the dikes, thinking that perhaps the peasants had been moving away from a device in the water.

As they reached the peasants, the lieutenant ordered the patrol to stop while he bent down to offer the pregnant woman a salt tablet, which she gladly took. Satisfied that he had done his part to win their hearts and minds, the lieutenant ordered Andy to proceed. A few steps later, Andy unwittingly tripped a wire and set off a claymore device designed to explode behind him. Following close enough behind, the lieutenant had been spared, but four of the new replacements behind him had not been as lucky. The claymore killed two and seriously wounded the other two. The rest of the patrol stayed with the bodies of the dead and tried to help the wounded while they waited for the "dust-off," as the medical evacuation helicopters were called, to come and take the dead and wounded away. As they waited, Andy told Buck what he had observed before the incident. Realizing that the peasants clearly knew of the claymore and failed to warn the patrol, Buck decided to take matters into his own hands.

Buck stood up and prepared to commence shooting the peasants, beginning with the pregnant woman. She started to scream and pleaded for her life in Vietnamese. The sudden commotion caught Lieutenant Pastor's attention, and he immediately ordered Buck to stand down. To everyone's surprise, Buck did. Buck may have had his issues with the Vietnamese, but he was still not a murderer, at least not yet.

Buck had no special feelings for the wounded and killed replacements. He had not so much as bothered to learn their full names or backgrounds, preferring instead to call them by generic names, such as "asshole" or "shithead." His reaction had been for more general reasons and was rooted in his experiences leading up to his involvement with the war. Buck's late father, Daniel Jones, served in the US Army during World War II and helped to liberate Italy. He told Buck of the experience of how beautiful Italian girls had lined the streets of the towns as they marched through, waving little American flags and giving the men kisses and flowers. Here he and the rest of his miserable unit were, with the same American flag sewed on their uniforms that had adorned his father's uniform, trying to liberate these bastards, and they stood by—not on the side of the road, welcoming them with kisses and flowers—but silently, with the kiss of death in their hearts.

Buck's emotions had been in turmoil since arriving in Vietnam. He found that he had jumped from the frying pan to the fire, so to speak. As a Detroit police officer, he had sworn to protect a people he had not particularly liked and who had not had much use for him and his fellow police officers, never willing to give them the benefit of the doubt, but viewing them as a necessary evil to be kept at bay. In part as an escape from that situation, he welcomed the draft, only to find himself trying to liberate a people he had grown to distrust and dislike and who did not have much use for him and his fellow soldiers.

Andy had not seen things the same way as Buck, and the two men had several heated discussions over their differences. Andy told Buck that the black Detroit neighborhood had viewed Buck and his fellow police officers as being there not so much to protect them, but to "contain" them in their squalor, thereby protecting others in the more affluent and mostly white neighborhoods from them. Similarly, he had speculated that many Vietnamese may have viewed Buck and him and their fellow American soldiers as being there not so much to protect and liberate them, but to protect others by "containing" them from becoming Communist. Buck's only response had been short and to the point. "Fuck this containment bullshit!"

Unknown to Andy and Buck and the others, Lieutenant Pastor had studied Vietnamese and understood a large part of what the woman was yelling. She had been trying to explain that the Vietcong were hiding in the lush green mountains that rose in the distance from the rice paddies and would have returned that night to kill her and the others if she had warned them. She told of an incident a few weeks earlier when two men in her village warned an American patrol of a booby trap, only to be dragged from their huts that night by the Vietcong. After being forced to kneel, they were beheaded in front of their wives and children and the rest of the village. The Vietcong then placed signs that had been prepared in advance on their headless torsos that said they had been found to be traitors. It had been traumatic to witness, especially for the families of the victims, and she understandably didn't want the same fate to befall her and her family.

Andy explained to me that it made little difference which ideology prevailed for many of the Vietnamese peasants living in rural areas, who had found themselves, through no fault of their own, caught in this crossfire between the Communist independence movement of the North and the containment policies of the West. They simply wanted to be left alone to grow their rice and raise their families. Instead, they found themselves harassed by the South Vietnamese and US troops during the day and by the Vietcong at night. Rightly or wrongly, Andy felt that the black American soldiers identified more with the Vietnamese peasants than their white brethren because their people also had once been helpless and oppressed and fought over.

After the dust-offs removed the wounded and the dead, Lieutenant Pastor ordered the patrol to head toward the mountains where the Vietcong were said to be hiding. The patrol resumed walking single file along the dikes, with Andy at point and Buck bringing up the rear. The Lieutenant found himself thinking as he walked about how he had narrowly averted the massacre of the peasants, a tragic incident that would have been an embarrassment for him, the army, and America. Buck and Andy, who still were barely able to tolerate each other, continued to find themselves in the unlikely position of being in agreement that the patrol, which had been smaller in number than usual to begin with, had grown dangerously undermanned to be moving further into harm's way to attempt to engage an elusive enemy of unknown size in the dense jungle ahead.

As they left the rice paddies behind and moved into the dark, tangled, mountainous jungle terrain, they were trading the relentless beating sun of the rice fields for the suffocating oven-like heat, leeches, and thick growth of the jungle. With the sweat pouring from his brow, Andy shouldered his weapon and pulled the vines apart with his bare hands. Scratched and bleeding, he inched forward. As he did, one of the nameless replacement soldiers behind the lieutenant rubbed against a vine, setting off a grenade that "blew off part of the poor bastard's chest and head," to quote Buck. Jimmy Winston attempted to stop the mangled soldier's bleeding with limited success, and Andy and Buck pulled the ill-fated newcomer from the tangle. Again they called for a dust-off and moved to a clearing to wait for it to arrive. The unconscious soldier, barely still alive, had been unceremoniously evacuated by the dust-off, and no one had even bothered to learn the "poor bastard's" name. Further reduced by the loss of one more, the patrol nevertheless moved on. However, Andy and Buck were joined by Jimmy, and all three had serious concerns as to the wisdom of what they were doing.

That night as they camped, Buck was smoking marijuana and had an empty stare on his face. The irony of the scene was not lost on Andy, who recalled the fate of the black youth at the center of Buck's Detroit saga who died for doing the same. When Buck volunteered to take the first watch, everyone else, exhausted both mentally and physically from the day's events, had been happy to overlook his marijuana smoking and oblige him. Lieutenant Pastor, as he often did, chose a spot slightly away from the rest of the men so he could read by flashlight without disturbing the others.

Andy and Jimmy had fallen into a deep sleep when the explosion occurred. Everyone jumped up and grabbed for their weapons, when the last remaining replacement began shooting. It was not long before everyone, including Andy and Jimmy, began to discharge their weapons into the darkness. When the shooting stopped, the lieutenant was dead, blown apart by what appeared to have been a grenade. Andy and Jimmy were wounded in the commotion, Jimmy more seriously than Andy, for Jimmy was hit in the back and thigh, accidentally shot by the last remaining replacement. Andy took a bullet in his right leg.

Buck claimed they had been ambushed by Vietcong guerrillas, but Andy had his doubts. Buck had three days remaining before he was due to be rotated out. Andy believed that Buck, perhaps having become paranoid from smoking the pot, decided to resort to "fragging" to take out the lieutenant, murdering him with a fragmentation grenade before he got anyone else "wasted," which was Buck-speak for killed. No one could know for sure, because the virtue of the fragmentation grenade was that it left no fingerprints.

The rest of the night passed without further incident. In the morning Buck called for an extraction, and the remnants of the patrol, along with the lieutenant's remains, were removed aboard a UH1-B, or "Huey" helicopter. Buck's report stated, and the rest of the soldiers corroborated as best they could under the circumstances, that the lieutenant had been killed defending his men in an enemy guerrilla ambush, and Andy and Jimmy had been wounded in the same incident. The lieutenant was awarded the Bronze Star and the Purple Heart posthumously, and both Andy and Jimmy were awarded Purple Hearts. Three days later, Buck went home from Vietnam, alive and in one piece.

Having been punished in Detroit, not so much for a crime he had not committed, but for a prejudice he had blatantly flaunted, Buck now appeared to have gone unpunished for a crime he very well may have committed, with a contempt for the victim that he had barely been able to conceal.

For the lieutenant, a dedicated and compassionate soldier and patriot, *all had been lost save his honor*, to paraphrase Francis I, King of France. And somewhere in Vietnam, a baby was born to a nameless peasant mother who had survived containment and the domino theory through the intercession of that man of honor.

Andy Jefferson at last had the car of his dreams, and Jimmy Winston, forsaken by a Dear John letter from a fickle fiancée, had been united with the car he so had longed for and which had steadfastly and faithfully awaited his return.

As for me, besides once again learning not to judge a book by its cover, I had come to understand the meaning of Buck's slang expression, *wasted*, in all its profound significance. Five replacements (the three wounded also died) were sent home from Vietnam to their waiting mothers—in body bags, their lives having been wasted in a place where hardly anyone even knew their names.

– 7 –

Because it sat for so long in the harsh conditions at the Port of Newark, Jimmy's Shelby required more preparation than originally had been thought necessary and was returned to the preparation center for a major overhaul. Leaks had appeared in places where leaks should not exist on a new car, requiring seals and weather stripping to be replaced. Parts that could not be restored had to be replaced, which added time ordering and waiting for delivery before they could be installed. When the day finally arrived that the Shelby was ready, Andy, Jimmy, and I decided to once again drive to Newark in Andy's Thunderbird and pick up the Shelby ourselves. I had to drive the Shelby back, because we were using the company's transporter plates to get the car to the dealership in White Plains. We agreed that Jimmy would ride back with me in the Shelby, in case he had any issues or questions, and Andy would follow along behind us in his Thunderbird.

The trip to the New Jersey facility was uneventful. The Shelby had been ready to go when we arrived, and the two-car caravan departed from the Port of Newark site almost immediately once the transporter plates had been installed. All was going according to plan. That is, until we got on the New Jersey Turnpike. Having traveled only a few miles, we passed a New Jersey State Police car on the side of the highway. No sooner had we gone by, than the lights went on and the siren began to sound. As the police cruiser leaped into action, sending loose gravel shooting from its spinning rear tires, I expected that it would go flying by us, but it did not. It pulled up alongside Andy's Thunderbird and ordered him to pull over. When we pulled over as well and started to back up on the shoulder to where the Thunderbird had stopped, we must have raised some concern in the police officer's mind, and he must have called for backup. In what seemed like a matter of moments, another police cruiser came racing down the highway toward us with its lights flashing and its siren blaring. It pulled up on the shoulder behind the first cruiser, and the officer got out and stood behind his open driver's door with his weapon drawn. The first officer then exited his car with his weapon drawn and ordered Andy to get out of the Thunderbird with his hands in clear view and without any sudden movements. Before Andy could obey, I tried to exit the Shelby and was told immediately to get back into the car and keep both my hands outside the driver's window, where they could be seen. Jimmy was ordered to do the same on the passenger side of the Mustang.

As the first officer approached the Thunderbird, Andy began to slowly open the door and carefully exit the car. Once he was out and his hands were raised above his head, the officer asked him to turn, spread his legs, and place his hands on the roof of the car. The officer then checked for a weapon, and finding none on Andy, asked Andy for his license and registration. Andy handed them to the police officer.

The officer then asked Andy, "Do you know why I have stopped you?"

Andy wanted to reply, "Yes, for driving while black," but thought the better of it, and simply said no.

The officer then began to explain that they had been having problems with a drug smuggling ring along this route and that when he had run a routine check on Andy's plates, the Thunderbird did not show up as registered.

The Thunderbird had been newly registered, and it was conceivable that the records had not yet been properly updated. However, Andy could not help but think that seeing a young black man driving an expensive new car must have precipitated the check in the first place. Before the first officer could begin checking the license and registration, the second officer recognized Andy and called off the first officer.

Shutting the door of the second police cruiser and holstering his weapon, Officer Robert "Buck" Jones walked toward Andy and told the first officer, "I know this guy. I served in 'Nam with him. He's okay." The first officer then holstered his weapon and told Andy he was free to move about. Jimmy and I exited from the Mustang. Buck, who clearly had been surprised to see Andy, now was even more shocked to see Jimmy. The first police officer then excused himself, got back in his cruiser, turned off the still flashing lights, and drove away.

Totally ignored by the three veterans as they became consumed in their reunion ritual, I found myself studying Buck. I was intrigued by the way he appeared to be so normal, so regular, and genuinely happy to see both Andy and Jimmy. No matter how much I tried, I could not envision him as a murderer, either of a black youth from Detroit or of a young army lieutenant. Flawed in many ways, yes; but murderer, no.

After that day, I would not see Andy again until I returned from the trip I had been planning to Europe. Jimmy I would continue to see from time to time, when the Shelby needed attention because of continuing problems from its long wait on the lot in Newark. On one of those occasions when Jimmy brought the Shelby in for service, he stopped by the showroom to tell me that he had been to visit Lieutenant Pastor's parents, and they had shown him the lieutenant's VMI college ring inscribed with his name, which had recently been returned to them in the mail. Apparently a marine patrol had captured a Vietcong with the ring on him, and the guerrilla had admitted to killing the lieutenant with a grenade. Buck may still have had his issues, but he was not a murderer, at least not yet and maybe never would be.

―――――

By the spring of 1971, I was growing restless and impatient to get on with my life. As successful and lucrative as selling cars had been for me, I was anxious to go back to law school and start my law career.

In March, I traveled to Massachusetts to attend Donny and Rose's wedding. They had been inseparable at Boston College and I never doubted that they would one day get married. But at their wedding, they truly seemed to have become one in their happiness and their shared dreams for the future. Rose had found a wonderful job as a school teacher in Natick, and Donny had settled nicely into a role at his father's construction business. He showed me the plans for the house he was preparing to build for them. They were excitedly moving forward with their lives, and I felt as if I simply had been treading water with mine.

Before that had happened, Christian Carter re-upped with the marines after coming home and getting married. Now Michelle was with child. I knew both of them since high school and was Christian's best man. I got to witness firsthand and up close the joy and contentment that had come to Christian from finding a good woman who agreed to become his wife and then bear his child. And I saw the peace of mind and purpose that entered his life when he found success and a career in the US Marine Corps. I was genuinely happy for both couples, but I couldn't help but wonder if I ever would find such happiness. Had I missed my one chance in this life at such bliss with Kelly Dougherty, or was there another soul mate out there for me? Then again, had my destiny been clear all along—a life of celibacy in the service of the Lord and my fellow man as a priest—and I simply had chosen to repeatedly glance away in the hope that it wasn't so? I would be less than honest if I didn't admit that those fears had been gnawing at me, even more so lately.

Christian Carter's first tour of duty was much different from that which Andy and Jimmy experienced. Having volunteered for the marines, Christian had trained with and traveled to Vietnam as part of an elite Special Forces unit comprised of both army and marine personnel. This unit was focused, disciplined, highly professional, and committed to its mission. In his first deployment, he had been part of the Phoenix Program, a CIA-devised initiative that trained Vietnamese operatives to infiltrate the peasant population to obtain information and to identify and destroy Communist cadres. The Vietcong had been effective in adapting the Chinese Communist cadre system as part of their strategy for fighting in the South. Small cells headed by a Communist-trained veteran who acted as a big brother and confidant kept close tabs on the cell members and reinforced their commitment to the cause. These cadres had been relying on the local peasant population for food and other supplies as well as cover.

The Phoenix Program, which had been loosely named after a mythical Vietnamese bird with special powers, known as *phung hoang*, came under attack by the antiwar movement in the United States as nothing more than the large-scale slaughter of innocent Vietnamese civilians. However, Christian told me that it had been ruthlessly effective in wiping out thousands of Communist cadres and destroying many of their bases of operation in the South. Christian had become a double agent. He was effective in convincing the Vietcong, with the help of the South Vietnamese infiltrators, that he could be trusted by them. He had persuaded them that he was a disenfranchised black American, bitter at having been forced by a predominately white-controlled government to fight a war against another oppressed people, with whom he could identify and certainly had no quarrel.

So effective had Christian been that he caught the eye of a young marine lieutenant named John Sullivan Jr. at the American embassy in Saigon. Lieutenant Sullivan offered Christian a promotion to lance corporal if he would re-up and join his elite team, responsible for guarding the US embassy. Christian, after consulting with Michelle and convincing her of the merits of the move, re-upped, received his promotion as promised, and redeployed to Vietnam as part of Lieutenant Sullivan's command. He still was viewed by the Vietcong as an agent of theirs, a view that would continue to cost them dearly.

Lance Corporal Christian Carter was a United States Marine, and nothing but a United States Marine, loyal to the great tradition of the corps and the nation that corps had faithfully served since its inception. *Semper Fi.*

– 8 –

As the vestiges of winter began to give way in 1971 to the signs of spring—the nascent buds on the cherry trees, the greening of the blades of grass, the chirping of the birds, and the lengthening of the days—the trip to Europe that I had been planning with my father's help began to become a reality for me. For almost seven weeks I would be roaming through Europe on my own, visiting great museums, magnificent cathedrals, and beautiful cities and experiencing cultures that had existed for hundreds of years before the United States came into existence. The growing excitement of my excursion helped to push to the side, at least for a time, the restlessness in me to get back to my schooling and on with my life.

The planning of the trip with my father had been a wonderful bonding experience. He had traveled throughout Europe for years, and he had made the many brochures come alive for me as he told me of his experiences in several of the places being pictured on the pages of the various booklets. He hoped to meet me in Paris so that we could explore the Louvre and Notre Dame together, but business commitments forced him to change his plans, and we now were scheduled to meet when I would be in Amsterdam.

Much to my surprise, my sales manager had agreed to my seven week leave of absence with only a token protest that faintly veiled the true enthusiasm he felt for what I was doing. Many times he told me that I reminded him of himself when he had been younger, and now he confided in me that he wished he had taken such a trip to Greece, his ancestral homeland, when he was single and carefree at my age.

With the coming dawn on Monday morning May 17, 1971, Aurora had promised that a beautiful day would lie ahead, a promise that had been kept, but which I'd been too busy to appreciate, having been consumed by last-minute preparations for my departure that evening for Europe. My father came home from work early that afternoon because he and my mother had decided that they would drive me to John F. Kennedy Airport, where I would catch my Icelandic Airlines flight to Luxembourg. As we said our good-byes, I worried that they may have sensed the touch of concern about leaving that had been growing within me. I realized there was a chance I might never see them again, at least not in this world. I wasn't alone. When I hugged my mother one last time, I noticed the tears swelling in her eyes. I was her eldest, and never before had I been so far away from her for so long. In contrast, for my dad, it was the usual curt handshake, punctuated on this occasion with, "See you in Amsterdam."

Nevertheless, the inevitable had to take place. So with a long, silent glance back, a wistful smile, and a short wave, I turned and walked out of sight, through the doorway of the entrance gate, down the enclosed ramp, and on to the Super DC-8. As I made my way along the narrow isle of the plane to my seat, it happened to me once again. I couldn't believe my good fortune. Not since the first time that I set eyes on Kelly Dougherty so many years before had I been as smitten by the sight of a woman. Her charm permeated every facet of her appearance, plain and understated as it was, a natural and wholesome beauty that couldn't be denied by her lack of makeup and plain dress. She was a treasure of femininity, and her femininity was her greatest treasure. And she was seated in the seat next to mine.

As I stored my carry-on bag in the overhead compartment and prepared to take my seat, our eyes met. For a brief moment in eternity, we were alone, all else around us frozen in time and place, quietly awaiting our command to resume, or so it seemed. Her beauty had taken my breath away; her charm had completely disarmed me. And now her gaze had stolen my very heart from within me. Immobilized and totally captivated by her, I had been rendered helpless to stop my emotions from streaming through my eyes and into hers. She had peered into my soul before I even had a chance to sit.

Her smile told me that she was a woman who knew well of her powers and had learned with maturity to use them with restraint and compassion. "Hi," she said, "I'm Sister Claire Sullivan."

It was then that I noticed the crucifix hanging from her neck. She was dressed in jeans and a white blouse that was buttoned to the collar. The crucifix was resting between her petite, exquisitely proportioned breasts. Not since the fifth grade, with the awakening of my sexual awareness, when I had a crush on Sister Nancy, had I felt so conflicted by my natural appreciation as a man for the attractiveness of her feminine attributes and my reverence as a Christian for the vocation of the sisterhood. The harder I tried to see Claire as a nun and not as a woman the more my feelings for her intensified and my attraction to her grew. Her lips, her eyes, the lobes of her ears, the gentle movement of her hair, all became magnified for me. What came to mind was the poem "I Knew a Woman" by Theodore Roethke—only Claire was a nun that I knew to be lovely in her habit, and felt:

> Of her choice virtues only [God] should speak,
> Or English poets who grew up on Greek

She truly was a Greek goddess, with all the charms of a siren but none of the guile. As I wrestled myself free from Claire's angelic spell long enough to regain my composure and respond to her, I said, "Hi, I'm George, George B. Angelson."

"George B. Angelson, what does the B stand for?"

"Brian," I said. And then, wishing I had stopped myself almost from the moment I heard the words start to leave my mouth, I continued by asking, "Are you really a nun?"

"Well, I haven't taken my final vows yet," she replied, as she showed me the silver ring on her finger. "When I do, I will get a gold ring to replace it. The reason for the gold wedding ring is that a Catholic nun is deemed to be married to Jesus."

"I see. And what order of nuns are you joining?"

"The order of Saint Francis, but we're more commonly known as the Franciscans."

"Oh, I had the Franciscan nuns in grammar school. No offense, but it would take nothing less than divine patience to be married to them. Well, let me correct that—all of them except Sister Nancy. I was crazy about her. She was one of the best teachers I've ever had."

"You didn't like any of the others?"

"Let's just say that they didn't think that much of me, and I didn't think that much of them. Do you know that one of them, Sister Gabriel, told my father at a sixth or seventh grade parent-teacher meeting not to waste his money on sending me to Iona Preparatory School, because I was not college material?"

"And?"

"I not only graduated from Iona Prep, but I graduated last year from Boston College, and I am scheduled to start Boston College Law School in September. It shows you how much she knew!"

"So you are a Catholic, and an irreverent and ungrateful one at that."

"What do you mean?"

"Sister Gabriel must have done an awful lot of praying for you to have so overachieved the obvious deficit in your God-given abilities. And to think that you aren't even smart enough to be grateful to her. It's a thankless task we Franciscans must undertake."

"Wow! I don't think I'm doing too well here. Can I have a do-over? May I stand up and come back and sit down again, and we start this meeting anew?"

"Do you think you could do it this time without ogling me?"

I was so embarrassed and instinctively asked, "Was I that obvious?"

"A woman always knows when she is being looked at by a man, and as difficult as you may find it to believe, I am still a living, breathing woman behind this crucifix."

I wanted to respond and tell her just how well aware I was of that fact, but thought the better of it. Fortunately, our conversation was interrupted at that point when the pilot came on the intercom to ask the cabin crew to take their seats for takeoff as we turned into position, stopped for a minute or so, and then started down the runway with all four engines screaming in glorious harmony.

Our seats were over the wing, and after we took off, there was a jolt and a noise as the pilot raised the landing gear and it retracted into the airframe. Claire grabbed my hand on the armrest between our seats and buried her face in my shoulder. I bent my head down to hers and whispered that it was merely the landing gear retracting, and there was no need to be concerned. She sat up in her seat, looked at me, and softly said, "Thanks. Flying makes me nervous." She then proceeded to tell me that both her father and her brother had graduated from Boston College, her father in 1942, and her brother in 1965.

I began to tell her about my experiences at Boston College, starting with Donny and Rose, and Professor Brooks, and when I got to Father Phillips, she stopped me. It truly was a small world, for Father Phillips, a good friend of her father, had baptized her.

We settled into relaxed conversation as the stewardess served the dinner. I confided in her about my quandary with the priesthood, as well as my exposure and attraction to the teachings of the Episcopal faith, first through Father Phillips's comparative theology course, and later under his rigorous tutelage and that of the Reverend Pratt at Yale. Claire knew of Reverend Pratt through her father's good friend and CIA colleague, Matt Kerr. She also knew that Father Phillips had been raised an Episcopalian.

When dinner was finished, the trays had been cleared and stowed, and the cabin lights had been dimmed, Claire drifted into a sound sleep, and her head came to rest on my shoulder. I sat there as still as I could, listening to her heartbeat, feeling her warm, sweet breath on my exposed arm, fighting sleep, cherishing every waking moment, for I knew that in the morning the woman of my dreams, so near but yet so far, would be gone from my life as quickly as she had entered it.

And I would be left with nothing more than my memories to console me. Eventually, however, my battle with sleep would be lost as I, too, drifted into sweet slumber.

The next day, when we landed in Luxembourg, the weather was beautiful. I escorted Claire to her hotel, for her train to Paris was not scheduled to leave until the next day. I found myself a room in the same hotel and convinced Claire to meet me for dinner that evening after we both had taken an afternoon nap. As I climbed into my bed, I thanked the Lord for sharing Claire with me for a little while longer. If He could read my thoughts, as I believed that He could, He must have known the fear I was feeling of falling prey to temptation. Like a moth drawn to fire, I could not help myself. As foolish as it may sound, I had fallen hopelessly in love with Claire Sullivan.

Anxious to see Claire again, I had awakened, showered, dressed, and made my way to the lobby at five o'clock as planned, but Claire had not yet come down. Having taken a seat in a chair that faced the elevator, I saw her as she stepped out. The few seconds before she saw me were wonderful as I stared unabashedly at her angelic face, beautiful petite figure, and graceful movements. I knew that no matter what else happened, I would remember those few seconds forever. When she saw me, a smile came to her lips, and I could feel my heart yearn.

As we walked out of the hotel, my hand found hers. Holding hands, we walked to the bus that would take us through the pretty countryside to the quaint village of Echternach. There we would buy a stick of salami, a chunk of cheese, a loaf of bread, and a bottle of wine and picnic on a blanket under an old tree on the outskirts of the village.

All alone, one thing led to another, and we quickly became lost in our own world. The twilight gave way to night, the stars began to twinkle in the heavens, and the moon rose majestically, all without our notice. With a magnetic attraction that neither of us had fully anticipated, we began to kiss, at first innocently and then more passionately as she let me touch her breasts. I could sense her panting as well as my own. I gently undid her blouse and scooped her left breast from her soft, lacey bra. It sat high and perky on her chest—soft, white, and firm, with a pink nipple that had stiffened from my loving caresses and sweet kisses. My right leg straddled her right leg, leaving our bodies to brush up against each other, so I knew that she was aware of the effect that she was having on me.

I reached up to gently stroke her hair and kiss her forehead, and I saw the tears in her eyes that glistened in the moonlight. I desperately wanted to tell her that I loved her, but I was afraid to say it. I didn't have to. She could tell, I knew.

"Are you okay," I asked?

"It's been a long time since I've been touched and kissed by a man in the loving way that you are touching and kissing me, and I guess I'm feeling a little overwhelmed by it."

"I'm in love with you, Claire. I didn't plan for this to happen. Honestly, I didn't."

"I know you love me. I could see it from the start. A woman knows these things instinctively."

"I feel guilty."

"Don't. I wanted you to do what you did, and I let you do it because I too have developed feelings for you. But now we must stop."

I knew that my desire for her had become unbearable, from the longing in my heart to the very real pain in my groin. However, the moment had passed, and regardless of how insatiable my feelings may have become, if I truly loved her as I knew I did, I would have to honor her wishes.

I rolled my body off of hers and lay on my back alongside her, staring up at the moon and stars I had been too involved to notice earlier. It was a beautiful night—outside and in my heart. I was so grateful to have been able to share both with her. I would treasure the memory of the favor of these brief intimacies that she had bestowed upon me for the rest of my life, bittersweet though these recollections always would be, for I couldn't deny the sorrow that I knew would be left by an unrequited love.

So engrossed in my thoughts had I become, that I had not noticed Claire fixing her clothing. When she was finished, she turned onto her side to face me, propped herself up on her right elbow, and began to gently stroke my head with her left hand. So soft was her touch that it took a moment or two to break me from my stare and draw me from my introspection.

"Penny for your thoughts," she whispered.

"I was looking up at the stars and thinking about us, and then I began to think about Vincent Van Gogh and *The Starry Night*. I see in the stars above us tonight the beauty he was attempting to capture, but I also feel within me some of the turmoil he was depicting in his work. I bet you didn't know that in a letter to his brother he wrote, 'That does not keep me from having a terrible need of—shall I say the word—religion. Then I go out at night to paint the stars.'"

"George, I hope you don't think I've been toying with your emotions. I, too, have feelings for you. I felt differently tonight than I ever have before. I wanted to give you the full expression of my love. I gave you all that I could and perhaps more than I should have. I have no regrets about what took place. It was beautiful. I always will cherish tonight as I always will have a special place in my heart for you. But I have chosen a different way of life and made a commitment I must keep. You, I am sure, will find another who, as my mother likes to say, will be your soul mate in this life."

Caught off guard by her use of the expression *soul mate*, I smiled to myself, for it had to be more than a coincidence that Kelly Dougherty's mother had favored the same expression. In the game of life, I was not sure how many chances I would be given at finding a soul mate, but I now had two strikes, or at least I was well at work on my second strike.

Suddenly, I felt ashamed for being so self-absorbed, so full of self-pity. My emotions, as well as my body, had begun to calm, and thinking more clearly, I realized that this encounter had not been easy for Claire either. She, too, had been conflicted, and I should have been more understanding and sensitive to her struggles.

I reached up with my right hand and gently put my index finger perpendicularly across her sweet, quivering lips, and whispered "hush" to her. Then I told her that she had made me truly appreciate for the first time in my life what Ralph Waldo Emerson had meant in his essay, "Nature," when he wrote "Beauty is the mark God sets upon virtue."

She protested that she hardly would call herself or her actions virtuous, but her tears betrayed her and told me otherwise. I knew I had put her mind at ease, for her tears were a window to her soul, and their glistening in the moonlight on her soft, white face bore witness to the fact.

Seizing the moment, since the time seemed right, I suggested that perhaps we had better be getting back. My heart, of course, was not in it, but I feigned conviction and hoped that my calm and deliberate voice would sound convincing. Claire must have sensed my equivocalness, or perhaps it was her intuition, but she stopped me and said let's first lie here for a few more minutes and look up at that beautiful moon together. As she reached for my left hand and held it with her right hand, she told me that if I ever wanted to think or talk to her, I should look up at the moon and do it, and she would do the same, and in that way we always would be in touch. I realized it was her way of gently saying good-bye while we were still alone, for probably neither of us would ever see the other again after tomorrow. It was a sweet and intimate gesture that I knew I would cling to.

The ride back on the bus was a quiet one. Neither of us spoke much. She leaned against my shoulder, and I from time to time stroked her head with my other hand until she had fallen asleep.

The next morning I was up, packed, and checked out of my room early, so I would have time to go to the store and buy some film. In all the commotion of leaving, I had forgotten mine at home and wanted to have pictures of Claire.

When I returned to the lobby of the hotel, Claire was in the process of checking out. She was dressed in her habit, and the reality of the fact that she indeed was a nun hit me and hit me hard. Stunned, though I wasn't sure why, I stood there in silence for a moment. My inaction lasted long enough for me to hear the clerk tell her that I already had checked out and left the hotel and to see her body droop in sadness. Witnessing her disappointment gave me a moment of selfish pleasure that quickly gave way to guilt at taking joy in her distress.

"Claire," I called and snapped a picture as she turned to look in my direction, thereby catching her joyous smile of relief at seeing me. The picture would prove to be unnecessary, for the image of her smiling face had been captured—in all its glory—in my mind's eye forever.

She ran to me, and giving me a hug, confided that she thought I had left without her. I promised her that it never would be I who abandoned her. I did not know then that those words would come back to haunt me.

The train ride to Paris was magnificently ordinary. We talked, we sang, and we took in the beautiful French landscape, all along knowing that our time together was coming to an end. Once in Paris, I escorted her to the convent, a lovely structure not far from Notre Dame. On the way she told me that when she was a little girl, her mother would tell her a story about Prince George the dragon slayer.

At the door to the convent, she winked and told me that I would be her Prince George until I met my soul mate, and that I should go forth and slay dragons. She then removed a red and silver scarf from her things and gave it to me, saying, "Here is my banner for you to tie on your lance, but I want it back when you meet your soul mate and pledge your love and devotion to her alone." I took the scarf, I nodded, and I turned and walked away before she could see me behaving in a manner unbefitting of a prince and dragon slayer.

I consoled myself with the promise that I would stop by the convent on that Saturday before I left Paris, but to my regret I never did. Having to say good-bye again had proven to be too daunting a task, and I had let the chance slip away from me.

– 9 –

I would spend five hours walking around Paris looking for a hotel room. The air show was going on, and all the hotel rooms had been taken. Finally, I found a room in an old hotel near the Arch of Triumph.

The next day, Thursday, May 20, was Ascension Thursday, and after going to Mass at Notre Dame, I spent the rest of the day in the Louvre. That night I went to Montmartre, to the Place de la Bastille, and took a boat ride on the Seine. The following day, Friday, it rained, but I didn't care. Paris was beautiful, even in the rain. After eating lunch at the restaurant in the Eiffel Tower, I went back to the Louvre.

On Saturday, May 22, 1971, I left Paris for the Scandinavian countries without first stopping at the convent to say one last good-bye to Claire. More coward than dragon slayer, her Prince George had not the nerve.

From the Scandinavian countries, I traveled on the following Saturday, May 29, to Amsterdam to meet my father. I must confess that it was nice to see my father and to enjoy the luxury and comfort of the Krasnapolsky Hotel where he had booked us. We explored the city, went to The Hague and the seashore and enjoyed some wonderful food and drink together. On Tuesday, June 1, we visited the museum to admire the works of Van Gogh and Rembrandt before leaving for the airport.

At the airport, I saw my father off and waited for my flight, which was scheduled to leave for London later that day. From London, I was scheduled to travel by train to Zurich and then through the Alps into Northern Italy. My itinerary called for me to spend the next two weeks meandering southward in Italy, visiting museums and churches, enjoying the magnificent sites and exquisite food, carefree and relaxed, with no one to answer to but myself. On Wednesday, June 23, I would surface in Agropoli, a small resort town south of Naples my father's family had come from and where some still lived.

Italy offered so much to see. In Bologna, at the foot of the Apennines, there was the University; in Pisa there was the leaning tower that leans more than twelve feet from the vertical; and in Florence there were the chapels, palaces, and masterpieces to see, such as the *Last Supper*, and works of art by Picasso, Van Dyck, and the like. Venice had its canals, and Rome had the Vatican, the Spanish Steps, the catacombs, the Appian Way, and the Coliseum. In Assisi there was the famous monastery of Saint Francis. High on a hill was Monte Cassino, where so many Allied soldiers had fought and died in World War II. There were the ruins in Pompeii, the Blue Grotto in Capri, and the scenic but treacherous roads along the Amalfi Coast. Yes, Italy was not a difficult place in which to get lost, wandering through the centuries, witnessing firsthand mankind's journey of enlightenment. As if to bear witness to the struggles that had erupted between religion and science, along that sometimes tumultuous path, there was the tomb of Galileo.

When I got to Agropoli, it was comforting to be back in the bosom of family again. I could not help thinking of Claire. How I wished she could be there to share it all with me. I know she would have liked my relatives, and they would have taken to her immediately.

After Agropoli, my itinerary called for me to turn north and spend some time relaxing on the French and Italian Riviera before returning to Luxembourg for my flight home to the United States, on July 1, 1971. As I gazed out the train window at the Italian countryside on my way to Rome, the first leg of the trip, I could not help but overhear the laughter and gaiety of my European counterparts in the next compartment. While I did not understand everything they were saying, it was clear to me they, too, were relaxed and carefree, like me, with no one to answer to but themselves. I thought about my friends back home in the United States who had not fared as well as I had in the draft lottery and either were fighting in a place called Vietnam, about which they knew little, or were worried that they might be sent there to fight, for reasons they were not sure they understood. Faced with this burden, some chose to relinquish all and flee to Canada; others acquiesced and went, hoping for the best, but expecting much less; and others still believed in their leaders and went willingly and with the conviction that they were fighting for a noble cause, helping free a people from Communist oppression. All were making sacrifices that would forever alter the direction of their lives, while all of us on this northbound train, enjoyed freedom without the price.

On June 30, the time had come to board a train in Nice that would take me back to Paris, where I was scheduled to switch to a train bound for Luxembourg. With some time to spare between trains in Paris, I decided to stop by the convent to see if I could learn how Claire was faring at the orphanage. It was then that I learned the devastating news that she had been killed in Vietnam.

It was a lovely day in Paris. The sun was shining. The birds were chirping and darting about, chasing each other with reckless abandon. Flowers everywhere were in full bloom, their beauty majestic to behold and their sweet fragrances a delight to the senses. Lovers could be seen strolling or sitting in their private worlds, smiling and giggling foolishly as they whispered affectionately to one another and occasionally stole a kiss or a hug when they thought no one was looking. It was springtime in Paris, young fancies clearly had turned to love, and all appeared to be well in a gay and marvelously frivolous world. That is, they were so for everyone else, but no longer for me.

The news of Claire's death sent a shiver down my spine, and I felt cold and very much alone in my shock and disbelief. All color had been drained from my life, and in my grief, I saw only shades of dark and light, as one might see when dusk approaches on a bleak and frigid winter day. Imagining the carnage and destruction in Vietnam that had to be responsible for such a senseless death, I was left to wonder how the worlds of Saigon and Paris could be so far apart and yet still be present on the same spaceship—Earth. While I told myself that time would heal my wound and that I again would one day see in color, I knew in my heart that I would never quite be the same. A part of me had died with Claire.

I tried to convince myself that Claire was in a better place—in the next life with the husband she had chosen to betroth in this life—and that she was happy and would want me to be happy for her. But I could not be; my faith simply was not that strong. Rather, my heart was filled with a cancerous hatred for those who had done this to her, and that cancer was metastasizing rapidly into a thirst for vengeance. But the harsh reality was that I was neither her prince nor a dragon slayer. I was the weak traveler who weeks earlier had cowardly abandoned her—squandering forever one last chance to say good-bye. It now was for me to live with my regrets.

When the time came, I walked to the train station and caught my train to Luxembourg, where on the next day, July 1, I boarded my flight home to the United States. This time there was no Claire in the seat next to mine when I walked down the aisle and took my place.

– 10 –

Finally, I saw the GTO turn the corner onto Forty-Second Street. My parents at long last had arrived. I had lost a great deal of weight, and my mother could not believe how thin I had become. She protested that I was too frail, but my father dismissed her concerns and stated that I looked fine. For my part, I was content to climb into the back seat and fall fast asleep.

Unfortunately, being home provided no refuge from bad news. I was not back in the United States twenty-four hours when the phone rang and my parents told me it was for me. On the line was Michelle Carter, mustering all the strength she had left within her to tell me that her husband, my friend Christian, had been killed in Vietnam the prior month. I immediately put any plans I had aside and set out to be with her, knowing that it would not be easy—and it was not.

When I reached the apartment on North Avenue in New Rochelle where she lived, the afternoon already was growing long in the tooth. I knew that finding a parking spot would be difficult. But as if to deny me any excuse to retreat, there was an empty space right in front of the building. Parking the GTO, I walked up the two flights of stairs to the apartment rather than take the elevator. The extra time would be well used in composing myself.

Knocking on the door, I heard Michelle say it was open in a voice that betrayed the strength she was trying to project. As I entered, the room was dark from the curtains being drawn, and the air was stale from the windows being closed for a long time. When my eyes finally adjusted to the lack of light, I saw Michelle sitting in an armchair with a box of tissues next to her. Her eyes were red and swollen from her crying, and her nose was chafed from being repeatedly blown. The waste can on the floor was overfilled with spent tissues.

I walked over to her and she got up and hugged me. I held her close to me and kissed her on the head as her sobbing gave way to outright weeping. I stood there quietly holding her for what seemed like an eternity and let her get it all out of her system. When she was finally done crying, we both sat down, and I continued to hold her hand as I told her how sorry I was for her loss. And in an effort to be encouraging, I pointed out that soon she would have a part of her husband back with the birth of their child.

The reference to her pregnancy sparked an unexpected response from Michelle that caught me totally off guard and set me back on my feet. Her entire mood changed almost instantaneously from one of uncontrolled grief to one of steely anger and determination. The weeping came to an abrupt halt as she wiped her eyes and blew her nose.

Looking me straight in the eye, she said, "I gave them a fit and healthy man in his prime. I gave them the person who made me laugh—made me happy—made me glad I was born a woman. I gave them the person who kept me warm at night—who gave me hope and made me want to bring new life into this world. I gave them the only man I have ever loved—my first boyfriend in high school. I gave them everything I had in this world. And what did they give me back?

"They gave me back a lifeless body, a neatly folded flag, and a medal. Well, those things don't keep me warm at night. And they don't give me hope and make me want to bring new life into this world. What for? So that life also can someday be wasted on some useless cause? No, those things do not give me love, and they cannot restore the hope and the future that has been ripped from me."

I tried to interrupt, but she refused to let me. Raising her voice to drown me out and pounding my chest to drive home her point, she continued.

"I hate you, Madras, and all the privileged bastards like you who are allowed to go through life unscathed while those like my Christian, with the least to loose, have to sacrifice and pay the ultimate price doing your dirty work. With your college deferments and other connections, you get to sit out the fight, go to college, and take tours of Europe to 'find yourself.'"

She emphasized the words "find yourself" by making quotation marks with her fingers.

"It simply is not fair—not fair at all, Madras, and I hate you for it. I hate, hate, hate you for it."

Michelle didn't really hate me. Nevertheless, those words did hurt. I guess in part I felt some guilt at still being alive when my friend was not. But the important thing was that Michelle's sore finally had been lanced, and the poisonous venom and festering puss had been allowed to pour out and leave her shaking body.

Michelle always had been physically strong, so I was not surprised that my chest hurt from the pounding her fists had given it. I understood the depths of her grief and frustration, and I realized that I was one of the few people she had left with whom she felt comfortable enough to vent her feelings. However, all the understanding in the world could not prepare me for what was to come next.

She stepped back and away from me, and with a look of fierceness and defiance that I had not seen since that day long ago on North Avenue in New Rochelle, when we first had encountered one another; she announced, "I am going to have an abortion!"

I was stunned. That little male fetus was all that my friend Christian had left of himself in this world. If it were swept from her womb, it would be like the waves on a beach washing away footsteps left behind in the sand. Christian and his legacy would be gone without a trace. There would be nobody left behind to remember him—to visit his final resting place on Father's Day or Memorial Day—and to carry on in his footsteps.

I could not help myself and blurted out, "Michelle you can't mean that. How could you do that to Christian? That baby is the personification of the love that existed between you and Christian."

"You got it right, Madras, it is the personification, as you put it, of the love that we *had*, and I mean *had*, between us. Christian chose his country over me and that child, and now I intend to choose my future over him."

"What are you talking about?"

"What am I talking about? I will tell you what I am talking about. I am talking about not having the bitter, disillusioned life that my mother had—a single mom, abandoned by her husband, living the 'dream deferred' Langston Hughes referred to."

The writings of Langston Hughes and Gwendolyn Brooks had resonated with Michelle in high school, because she often had talked of them in the context of her mother's situation. It was true that her mother had been a disillusioned and broken woman, brooding and sedentary by nature in her later years, and ravaged by diabetes, depression, and alcoholism, but I didn't think she would have wanted her daughter to do something like this if she were still alive.

Walking over to the bookcase in her living room to look for *A Street in Bronzeville*, by Gwendolyn Brooks, I said to Michelle, "Abortion does not come without a price. You will have to live with your decision for the rest of your life, haunted by what might have been if your child had been born."

She interrupted me. "That may be true, but it still is better than having to live a 'dream deferred' because of a decision I made when I had the husband I loved and hope for our future. Slavery is the price my ancestors had to pay for me to be here today and have the opportunities that this country now affords me, and I intend to grab my piece of the pie. I plan to have my abortion, go to college, get my degree, and live the American dream."

"Michelle, you are living the American dream right now. Part of it is growing within you as we speak and someday will bring you much love and happiness as well as a great deal of pride."

She stopped me to tell me not to preach to her. I replied that she didn't have to listen to me, but asked if I could read to her from "the mother," by Gwendolyn Brooks. When she agreed, I began to read.

>Abortion will not let you forget.
>You remember the children you got that you did not get, …"

Before I could read more, she stopped me and asked to see it, telling me she had forgotten that piece.

I handed it to her and said, "Michelle, I know that you have always been a strong advocate for a woman's right to choose and that the choice should be between the woman and her conscience. I have no quarrel with that. All I am asking is that you think this out carefully in making your choice. This is the *only chance* you will ever get to have a child from Christian, the one man you ever loved and all that you had.

"Right now you are angry with me because I didn't have to serve, and with Christian because he chose to serve, and with the unfairness and senselessness of the situation, but trust me that you will see things differently in time. Christian did not abandon you the way your father abandoned you and your mother. He did not put anything before you and the baby. He saw this as a path to a better life for all of you. And with the way things were going, it would have come to pass, if he had not been killed. It was you, his baby, and his country all the way. It was all that he had in this world, and now you and the baby are all that he has left.

"You're a beautiful and intelligent woman, with a big heart and a lot to give. I just know that you will accomplish all that you set out to do and that you will find happiness. Please think about it."

When she finished reading "the mother," she looked up at me and said that she would. Relieved and elated, I suggested to her that we get out of that dark apartment and go to Pete's Tavern in Bronxville for a burger and a beer. It would be my treat. She agreed, but told me she couldn't have a beer because she was pregnant.

I smiled, and when she caught me doing so, she said, "Simply a *precaution*, until *I decide* what I'm going to *do*."

I replied that I understood completely.

Four months later, on Saturday, October 30, 1971, Christian Richard Carter was born at 8:01 a.m. at Lawrence Hospital in Bronxville, New York, not far from Pete's Tavern. He was eight pounds, three ounces and named after two marines, his father and his great-uncle, the bus driver to whom I proposed on my first day of high school back in 1962. *Semper Fi.*

Two weeks later, on Sunday, November 14, 1971, Christian Richard Carter was baptized by Father Collins in the same Fordham Chapel where Michelle and Christian had been married earlier that year. Dick Crawford came up from Florida to be with his niece and grand-nephew, and I came down from law school in Boston to be his godfather. In my pocket was a marine tie pin that Christian had given me to hold after the wedding, telling me—more prophetically than he realized—that he would not need it where he was going. I would hold it and give it to his son when the time was right.

> They also serve who only stand and wait.
> —John Milton, "When I Consider How My Light Is Spent"

– 11 –

As often as I made a point of seeing Michelle in those first few days that I was home from Europe, I never found the right time to tell her about Claire. But Claire remained very much on my mind. As the upcoming weekend approached, I decided to get away and spend it in the Hamptons. I was fortunate to be able to rent the same room that I had rented on prior occasions, a small, single room on the second floor of an old Victorian house on Elm Street in Southampton, which held many fond memories for me. It would cost me only ten dollars per night, and I would have to share the hall bath with the two girls that had rented the double room next to mine. I had done it before, and I knew that it would not be a problem. When Friday, July 9 came, I set out for the place I'd come to cherish ever since being introduced to it by Wally Rather, optimistic that the change of venue would help me come to terms with my life.

Once I had checked into my room and unpacked the car, I decided to drive over to that now familiar spot—the War Memorial and park at the base of the pond—where I liked to go and see the ducks and read. It was a quiet oasis, away from the hustle and bustle that permeated the Hamptons on summer weekends.

I parked the GTO partly on the grass beside the road and walked over to the pond. Sitting on the edge of the bank beneath the weeping willow trees, I let my mind wander as I slowly began to feed the ducks. They were such beautiful creatures as they glided effortlessly through the water, barely creating so much as a ripple. I found myself staring at the full moon that had risen and wondering if Claire could see it, too, from where she was. I so much wanted to communicate with her, and I was recalling what she had told me that wonderful night we spent together in Echternach. As I did, I tossed morsels of bread to my friends swimming in the pond, something I knew from prior experience the town did not allow. The reason for the prohibition was clear. Who would be there to feed them in the winter, and what would become of them if they could not fend for themselves? I meant them no harm and merely enjoyed their companionship. Nevertheless, I knew I was wrong to be doing it.

Unbeknownst to me, Officer Debrowski of the Southampton Police Department was making the rounds in his shiny new 1971 Ford police cruiser when he came around the corner and spotted me feeding the ducks. A graduate of Southampton High School, where he distinguished himself as a tri-varsity athlete, he had lived in the town his entire life, with the exception of the time he'd spent in the marine corps.

As he exited the police cruiser, he straightened his gun belt, walked to the front of the Ford, turned, and crossed in front of the car and toward me. I was totally oblivious to his presence and became startled when he tapped me on the shoulder to tell me not to feed the ducks. I jerked around toward him, and as I did, he immediately observed the grief on my face. His entire demeanor changed almost instantaneously from one of annoyance and disapproval, to one of understanding and compassion. Crouching down next to me, he asked me what was wrong. I told him I'd just lost two people in Vietnam who had been very close to me, one a marine that I knew since high school and who was about to become a father for the first time and the other a young woman who was preparing to take her final vows as a nun.

"The nun, did you meet her in Vietnam?"

"No, I met her on a flight to Europe in May."

"And the two of you became that close that quickly?"

"I fell in love with her. I know it sounds crazy, but that's the way it happened."

"It's not crazy. It's love at first sight. The Hollywood guys make movies about that stuff all the time."

"It sure was, the minute I saw her I was struck by her radiant beauty."

"Funny, the nuns I had in Catholic grammar school wore these black and white habits. You couldn't see a thing."

"That's just it, she wasn't wearing her habit. I had no idea that she was a nun. She was tan and naturally beautiful and dressed in a pretty white blouse and tight jeans that accentuated her petite figure."

"Then what happened?"

"We sat next to each other on the flight to Luxembourg, and then on the train the next day to Paris."

"When did you last see her?"

"I last saw her when I said good-bye to her at the convent in Paris."

"Then how did you find out that she had been killed in Vietnam?"

"I went back to Paris and stopped at the convent on my way home from Europe."

"That must have been a shock. Did you even know that she was planning to go to Vietnam?"

"Yes, she had told me she would be heading to Vietnam to work in an orphanage, but I didn't realize it would be that soon or that dangerous. She would've been twenty-three years old today."

"It is a little weird that you knew two people in Vietnam and they died at around the same time. I know it probably was just coincidence, but were they near each other or somehow working together?"

"No, it was just a coincidence."

"And your marine friend, how did you learn about him?"

"When I got home from Europe a week ago, his widow called to tell me."

"So you found out about the two of them only a few days apart? Wow, that had to be devastating for you. What are the odds of something like this happening? I guess they're right when they say that life can be stranger than fiction."

"I know."

"Listen, I'm sorry for your losses. I wish there was more I could say or do. I know you probably don't want to hear it, but only time can heal your wounds."

"How do you explain all this senselessness: a young nun, dead before she could fully realize the joy of her vocation; a young marine, dead before he could know and play with his son; a young pregnant widow, her life turned upside down, before it even had a chance to begin?"

"I don't know. I was a marine in Korea, and now I'm a police officer in a sleepy little town, where I have to deal with big issues, like you feeding the ducks. Yet, I've had to bury many friends, marines and police officers alike, who left behind unfinished business. It is the risk that we all take when we choose to serve. Being a missionary or a marine in a war zone like Vietnam is not for the faint of heart. They both must have been dedicated and courageous people. All you can do now is honor their memories and make sure they're not forgotten."

"I guess you're right."

"Are you going to be okay?"

"Yes, I'll be fine."

With that, Officer Debrowski patted me on the back and returned to his cruiser. Before he got into the car, he shouted, "Don't feed the ducks, at least not until I'm gone." As he drove away, the ducks paddled back toward me, almost as if they had been waiting for him to leave. I rationalized to myself that the world was so damn crazy, what harm could come from one more senseless act? So I threw the remaining bread on the water. I then returned to my car and drove to Bobby Van's in Bridgehampton to see if any of my friends were out for the weekend.

As I drove into town on the Montauk Highway, my parking space of choice at the corner with Hull Lane was available. I liked this spot because it abutted the small historical cemetery with its white picket fence that was framed on the east by St. Ann's Episcopal Church just across Hull Lane and by the magnificent white Presbyterian church to the west. There was a bench there on which I would sometimes sit and muse about the contrast between the north and south sides of the street. The north side belonged to the living, the revelers, and the young night owls, with its endless line of stores, boutiques, bars, and restaurants. In contrast, the south side belonged to the ghosts of lives past, the saintly and the altar guilders, with its churches, its sleepy graveyard, and its weather-beaten and timeworn headstones. One side was full of life and excitement, and the other side was content to quietly sleep in peace, while time and progress marched by daily on the busy Montauk Highway.

That night the white edifice of the Presbyterian church was accentuated by the silver light of the full moon that was standing guard in the heavens over the church's steeple. It gave the structure a comforting glow as a gentle breeze rustled the leaves on the trees, creating for me the sensation of a deep spiritual presence. I stopped for a moment to sit on the bench and take in the beauty of the scene. Before I knew it, my thoughts once again had turned to Claire and that night in Echternach. How much I wished I could communicate with her but one more time.

Resigned that it was not to be, I turned and crossed the street to the north side—the land of the living—and entered Bobby Van's. Once inside, I saw the two women who were renting the double room next to mine. They were Israeli exchange students, and we had a drink together before I left to take a ride to Sagg Main Beach in neighboring Sagaponack. Seeing the moon in a clear sky over the vast expanse of the ocean—watching the moonbeams glistening on the waves while listening to the mesmerizing sounds of the surf—has always been a spiritual catalyst for me. The majesty of the surroundings made me keenly aware of God's hand at work in our lives, and that feeling of closeness often spurred me to talk with Him, intimately baring my thoughts to Him. That night, I very much hoped it would in some way help to start the healing process in me.

As I drove east on the Montauk Highway and turned south onto Sagg Main Street, the song "Be My Baby," by the Ronnetts came on the GTO's radio. It had been preceded by "Don't Worry Baby" by the Beach Boys. Those were two of the last songs Claire had sung as she played her guitar on the train ride to Paris, only a short two months ago, but now an eternity away. I could still see her smiling face, so full of expression as her lips moved so sweetly and gracefully to the sounds of the strumming guitar.

With the turn south, there in front of me, on cue, was the waiting moon—a dominating presence in the clear night sky. Its spell this time was made that much stronger by the melody of the song and the emotions conjured up by the memories of the happier time when I had heard that song last. Soon my mind began to drift, and my thoughts turned once again to Claire. Encouraged by an imagination that had gone wild, the shadows of the moon took on the image of Claire's smiling face, singing the song the radio was playing. As I chased that enchanted moon down Sagg Main, the powerful 6.5 liter engine was running so smoothly and the road was so straight, that I never noticed the increase in my speed.

The windows were open and the wind was whistling by as I sang in harmony with the blaring radio, my eyes all along fixated on the face of that magnificent celestial wonder. I told myself it couldn't be, it just couldn't be. Those shadows, they were nothing more than ordinary lunar shading. But they were, they really were, they had to be—the face of Claire.

"Be my, be my baby …" The louder I sang, the more convinced I became of the magic of Claire etched on the surface of that beautiful moon. So excited, so fixated was I that I had not noticed the speedometer needle as it traversed the increasing numbers on the face of the gauge. Faster and faster the wheels had been turning, faster and faster the road had been disappearing beneath me. First the general store and then the Foster farm had passed by in a blur, and now it was too late.

By the time my attention snapped back, the road was spent; there was only a beach and the Atlantic Ocean in front of me. I could not jam on the brakes. The sand on the surface of the pavement would have sent the car careening out of control. I turned off the engine so sand would not be sucked into the intake, aimed the GTO for the off-road vehicles beach access, and hoped for the best. As the car hit the sandy incline of the access, it went airborne, suspended in space. Time appeared to come to a halt in the utter silence of the moment, broken only by the whisper of the wind and the drone of the surf.

In the vacuum of that instant, the beaming face of Claire that my mind assured me had taken over from the surface of the moon communicated with me *one last time*—not through the spoken word, but through the sounds of silence that only a broken heart can hear—the wind and the surf. My wish had been granted, and now my soul at last hopefully could find some peace.

Suddenly, the car came crashing back to earth, hitting the beach and jarring to a halt, its wheels still spinning and sinking into the soft sand. The GTO had performed flawlessly, doing everything I had asked of it and doing it well. Yet as fast as it was (and it was fast) and as well engineered as it was (and the professionals at the Pontiac division of General Motors were legendary for their high performance creation), I could not outrun my destiny, not even with the help of my mighty GTO.

I would have to come to terms with my fate and learn to accept it. I should have known from that first moment on the plane when I had set eyes on her (and maybe somewhere deep within me I did) that one as special as Claire had been picked by God for Himself and was destined for an eternal place. But I must confess, I would've preferred to marry, raise a family and grow old with her.

That night I slept under the watchful eye of the moon on the hood of the GTO, with my head resting on the windshield. The song of the surf and the twinkling of the stars lulled me into a deep and peaceful slumber. In the morning I was awakened by Aurora, who gently caressed me with her rays. Once awake, I walked up the road to a nearby farm. The moon, ever vigilant, was still vaguely visible in the morning sky. Cliff, a local farmer, who was up early and preparing for the day's chores, took pity on me and came with his GMC truck to tow me out. For his efforts, he only would let me treat him to a cup of coffee at the Candy Kitchen up in town. We then said our good-byes, and I thanked him again as I walked him to his parked truck.

The GTO and I were none the worse for the wear, and we set out to face the new day and the future together.

And so it was in the summer of 1971.

— *Book Three:* —
OPERATION EXCALIBUR

– 1 –

In the late spring and early summer of 1971, while Americans went about their business unaware of any potential danger of a major international incident that might bring their country to the brink of war with the Soviet Union or China, Operation Excalibur was playing itself out in Vietnam. Not since the 1962 Cuban Missile Crisis nine years earlier had such a danger been so ominously present.

Operation Excalibur was the CIA code name for the combined CIA and US military mission to capture alive in Vietnam the Russian who had claimed in Sister Kate's presence at the orphanage, to have been the "second gunman" in the assassination of President John F. Kennedy in Dallas, Texas, on November 22, 1963. It was considered important to interdict the Russian while he still was in a combat role in Vietnam so as to minimize the chances of any fallout from the effort. This in turn lent a sense of urgency to the operation and called for it to be carried out by the middle of 1971 at the latest. There was a growing view in the agency that American involvement in the war would be coming to an end, either before or immediately following the 1972 US presidential election, and that the ensuing de-escalation would begin in late 1971 and would impact the logistics required for a later operation to be a success.

John Sullivan Sr. and Matt Kerr had been placed in charge of Operation Excalibur by the CIA. Sullivan would remain in the United States and lead the effort within the agency. He would be responsible for securing all necessary approvals and funding for the mission as well as for addressing its logistical needs. Only a handful of individuals within the Pentagon and the agency with the need to know were made aware of Operation Excalibur, along with the president of the United States. Financing for the operation's specific and sensitive aspects was to come from a secretly compiled fund, placed under his control. To the extent possible, funding for the supportive roles not specifically dedicated to the mission was to come through normal appropriations for the war effort.

Kerr would be responsible for assembling and training the team and would lead the interdiction effort from within Vietnam under the cover of his position at the American embassy in Saigon. His methods were unorthodox, even by CIA standards, but his achievements were the stuff of legends, so he was given a wide berth. He liked to form teams based on chemistry, believing that high-functioning teams were better than star-studded groups. His instincts were more important to him than resumes and records.

An unintended consequence of Operation Excalibur was the senseless massacre of me, the other girls at the orphanage, and Sister Claire by an errant North Vietnamese captain. As you know, the orphanage was named the Orphanage of Saint Francis Xavier and was located near Binh Gia, a Catholic village only forty miles southeast of Saigon, in the coastal province of Phuoc Tuy. In today's military parlance, our massacre would most likely be termed "collateral damage," but regardless of what you call it, we were dead and ready to meet our Maker. However, through the intercession of Sisters Kate and Claire, I was given time to remain behind to tell this story that otherwise might never have been told.

In Vietnam, the agency gave George B. Angelson the alias Captain John Joseph Chrisandra, an army chaplain assigned to the 101st Airborne Division of the United States Army. The trip to Europe, about which he has told you, was a cover. When he boarded that Icelandic flight in New York, on May 17, 1971, he was embarking on Operation Excalibur.

What are the chances that any two people will randomly be

assigned seats next to each other on a transatlantic flight? What are the chances that these two people will be attracted to each other, unexpectedly meet again a half a world away in Southeast Asia, and fall in love with one another? Not very likely, I am sure you would agree. Well, now you may be able to understand why John Sullivan Sr. and Matt Kerr, with all their meticulous attention to detail, did not think to check who would be seated next to George B. Angelson on his flight to Europe. In an ironic twist of fate, it would be none other than Sister Claire Sullivan, the daughter of John Sullivan Sr. That one oversight led to a doomed love affair that almost compromised Operation Excalibur after it had successfully been completed and could have resulted in an escalation of the war in Vietnam to include the Soviet Union and China.

As I told you previously, the crime for which Sister Claire and I and the others were put to death was no more and no less than the fact that we knew Captain Chrisandra, or the "Devil Priest," as Captain Ton That Dam, a member of the 325th Division of the North Vietnamese Army, called him.

When Captain Dam came looking for Captain Chrisandra at the orphanage, the army chaplain already had left Vietnam. Captain Dam wanted to know from us where Captain Chrisandra was. We couldn't tell him because we didn't know. The official story that had been released by the US embassy at the time was that Captain Chrisandra had been reported missing when he failed to show for an appointment at a proposed building site for a boys' orphanage. However, Captain Dam refused to believe that story and executed us, in part out of frustration and an attempt to lash out at the Devil Priest. But also in part, I am sure, with the hope that if Captain Chrisandra was still alive, our massacre would cause him to reveal himself. Our deaths would indeed cause Captain Chrisandra to return to Vietnam and with unintended results that almost compromised the just successfully completed Operation Excalibur.

There was so much unheralded good, so much valor and selfless dedication that it is important to appreciate the triumph of the human spirit, albeit in small and isolated pockets, in the face of such adversity. If heroics and selflessness are a shining part of the human struggle, so are self-interest and greed a part of its dark underbelly. It is in the context of these deep and treacherous currents that this tragedy unfolded.

– 2 –

To fully understand the way George B. Angelson came to be involved in Operation Excalibur, we must go back in time to when the seeds for this adventure first were sown in the early 1940s. Before World War II broke out in the Pacific with the attack on Pearl Harbor by the Japanese on Sunday morning, December 7, 1941, the countries of Europe had been falling one by one to the German onslaught. Britain was vulnerable and in danger of being invaded.

There was a growing perception in both Britain and the United States that a great deal of Hitler's success was coming from the existence of clandestine operatives engaged in subversive activities, such as propaganda, sabotage, and other forms of irregular warfare. As a result, President Roosevelt called on Colonel William J. Donovan, also known as "Wild Bill" Donovan, one of the most highly decorated military officers in US history, to form a centrally situated intelligence organization to monitor and thwart these shadowy enemies. Wild Bill was a new breed in a new era, with the type of big picture attitude that the assignment would need. His efforts eventually resulted in the formation of the Office of Strategic Services, or OSS, which was the predecessor to the CIA.

Recruiting from all walks of life, Donovan brought together in the OSS some of the best and the brightest that America had to offer. One of those recruits was a young Italian–American kid from Coney Island in Brooklyn, New York, named Ralph Angelson. Angelson was an anglicized derivation of Angelino, the original Italian surname.

Ralph Angelson lost his father when he was a young boy, but refused to give up on his goal of attending college. With discipline and determination that demonstrated a maturity beyond his years, he pulled himself up the ladder of success that is known as the American dream, one rung at a time. He attended Fordham University on a full academic scholarship and graduated ahead of schedule in three years. He possessed an extremely high IQ and an ear for languages that had made him fluent in at least six of them by the time he was twenty years of age. He first caught Colonel Donovan's attention several years earlier, when he had been awarded the French Medal by the French Consulate General. His award had been challenged because it was said his French was too good and that he must have lived and studied in France, giving him an unfair advantage. However, it nevertheless was awarded to him when it was shown that he rarely had ventured outside the borough of Brooklyn and had never been outside the country.

Upon graduation from Fordham University, Ralph Angelson joined the United States Army Air Corps and was sent to Vanderbilt University to become a meteorologist. He then was assigned to an airfield in the Pacific.

While at Vanderbilt, Ralph Angelson also secretly studied Japanese, and in the Pacific he functioned as a meteorologist in the Army Air Corps and as an agent for Colonel Donovan's organization, monitoring and deciphering Japanese communications and codes. He played a particularly important role in assessing the damage done, if any, when the American Magic operation for reading the Japanese codes was threatened by a poorly thought-out OSS break-in that took place in Lisbon, Portugal, in 1943. That close call almost alerted the Japanese to the need to change their codes.

It was critical for Ralph Angelson to maintain his dual role as OSS agent and army meteorologist, because General MacArthur was not inclined to allow Colonel Donovan's operations within his theater of command and might have put a stop to it, if he had known of it. Ralph Angelson was one of only a few successful insertions that Colonel Donovan was able to make in the Pacific, and that success was owed in large part to Ralph Angelson's exemplary performance as a meteorologist.

After World War II, Ralph Angelson was employed by a small Belgian company in New York that was engaged in an import-export business with China. From this position, he was able to monitor Communist Party activities in China for the CIA. Notwithstanding his efforts and those of countless others, China fell to the Communists in 1949.

Ralph Angelson next became an executive with an American company headquartered in New York. In 1952, he was transferred to Brazil to help the company expand its operations into that country and the rest of Latin America.

What George didn't tell you, because he himself didn't know, is that his father had another more critical and clandestine assignment—an assignment from the agency to monitor the growing activities of the communist movement in Brazil. This time his efforts, along with those of countless others, contributed directly to the lack of success of the Communist attempt to take over the Brazilian government in 1964.

Upon returning to the United States from Brazil in 1958, Ralph Angelson continued in the active service of the CIA until he retired in 1964, after the Communist coup in Brazil had been successfully thwarted. His country and its allies had benefited greatly from his efforts. While Sullivan and Kerr never met Angelson, they were aware of his accomplishments and of the high regard in which he was held.

It should be no surprise, therefore, that in early 1970, when Christian Carter raised the name of his high school friend, George B. Angelson, the eldest son of Ralph Angelson, that Matt Kerr would give the reference serious consideration in connection with Operation Excalibur.

In forming the Excalibur team, Kerr decided to have three layers, with only the top layer knowing the full scope and details of the operation. This top layer would consist of himself, two handpicked marines, and a carefully selected civilian. Of grave concern to the agency man was the need to be able to apprehend the Russian in North Vietnam, or possibly even China, if he no longer was in the south. The civilian either would have to be parachuted deep behind enemy lines in North Vietnam or China, or he would be required to feign conscientious objection and desert to the north, seeking asylum on religious grounds. In either case, it was anticipated that this civilian would have the alias of an Army Airborne chaplain. Since the very early days of Colonel Donovan's operations, the CIA and its predecessor had seen value in using civilians in conducting guerrilla type warfare activities, for obvious reasons: the CIA would be in a better position to plausibly deny involvement and do damage control if things went bad. And such civilian assets were less likely to be known to and recognized by enemy counterintelligence operatives.

The first marine to be selected was a foregone conclusion as far as Matt Kerr was concerned. It would be none other than his best friend's son, whom he had known since the young man's birth in 1943. In Matt Kerr's eyes, the apple had not fallen far from the tree. John Sullivan Jr., like his father, was a man of honor and courage. He was a wealth of character. As Henry Clay had said, "Of all the properties which belong to honorable men, not one is so highly prized as that of character." The fact that he had a personal stake in the matter, his sister having been killed as a result of the man they would be hunting, would not overshadow his professionalism. Rather, it would serve to hone his focus and dedication to the mission.

Kerr's second selection of a marine was a young man John Sullivan Jr. had introduced to him. Christian Carter had impressed Matt Kerr from the very first time he met him at the American embassy in Saigon. John F. Kennedy once said that a man must look inside himself for courage. Christian Carter had that inner courage. An African-American raised by his father in humble surroundings, he had been inspired to join the marine corps by its storied past, a past he had learned at the knee of his wife's uncle, Dick Crawford, a World War II marine veteran. The reputation that Christian Carter had earned among those who had served with him was that he, too, was a man of honor and courage.

As George told you, Matt Kerr and John Sullivan Jr. recently had convinced Christian to consider reenlisting and put him in for a promotion. Christian was a man with a deep sense of duty and honor, who possessed the inner courage of which John F. Kennedy spoke, and he would do whatever duty and honor asked of him. Of this, Matt was certain. His instincts told him so.

The next selection was that of the civilian asset and would present a unique challenge. It was essential that this individual have no prior military record and no previous involvement with the CIA. Both the agency and the military had to be in a position to plausibly deny involvement if things went bad with the interdiction of the Russian in Vietnam. It was essential, in that event, that their fingerprints not be found on the mission, so to speak. Yet the role was a demanding one and would require a high level of competency on the part of the civilian selected. Extensive training and preparation would be necessary. Matt Kerr decided to bring the two young marines he already had selected into the decision process to ensure that the candidate had the support of the team and the necessary chemistry to make it work.

The team conducted an extensive search and reviewed several highly qualified candidates, including, as I mentioned, George B. Angelson. After careful deliberation, the team kept coming back to George as the candidate of choice. Finally, following an exhaustive background check, they unanimously selected him. The next challenge for them was to get George to agree to the assignment and all the risks and preparation requirements that it would entail.

Carter and the junior Sullivan would be dispatched to recruit him once Matt Kerr had been given an opportunity to tie up some loose ends involving the alias the agency had chosen for Angelson.

– 3 –

By the time John Sullivan Jr. and Christian Carter had boarded the military transport in Saigon for the trip back to the United States, they had a well-conceived plan for how they would approach George. It would be tricky because they could not reveal anything about Operation Excalibur until George had agreed to participate.

The alias that the agency had conceived for the civilian participant was well suited to George. He would be an army chaplain named Captain John Joseph Chrisandra, assigned to the 101st Airborne Division in Vietnam. George's uncle had served with distinction in the 82nd Airborne during World War II, being awarded the Bronze Star and a Purple Heart for his actions in the Battle of the Bulge, and George already had a strong background in theology and philosophy and a predisposition to the priesthood.

Both men hoped that they could convince George to agree to the assignment. It clearly would involve intensive training, long hours of religious studies, and a very dangerous task for which there would be no public acknowledgment. George's own family would never know of his involvement. If he were injured or killed, they would be told that it happened somewhere in Europe and under different circumstances. Nevertheless, Christian had reason to be confident that his friend George would rise to the challenge and agree to participate. John Sullivan Jr. was not as sanguine, but then again he didn't know George.

The agency had chosen the alias of a chaplain for the reasons I already have mentioned. In addition, should the plans have to be improvised, for example, if the Russian was still in South Vietnam, chaplains had relative freedom of movement to come and go and didn't normaly attract much attention from the North Vietnamese and their spy network in the South. They weren't considered high value targets from which to gather information. George was particularly attractive because he already had completed a vigorous course of theological studies and was in a very good position to be able to finish the remaining requirements to become a priest in the time frame required.

The question that haunted the young Sullivan was why should Angelson be inclined to volunteer for such a mission? He now appeared to be free of the draft as a result of his high lottery number, and his future as an attorney was set with his acceptance to law school.

Christian Carter, on the other hand, was confident that he knew the answer, because he knew his friend still very much wanted to be a priest. George had recently confided in him that he would like to follow in the footsteps of Father Drinan, the Jesuit priest who also was a lawyer and political activist. Limited by time and resources, George had made the difficult decision to first pursue his law degree and defer his decision on the priesthood. Christian was convinced that George, when given an accelerated opportunity to finish his theological studies and be ordained, without delaying further the pursuit of his law degree or increasing the burden on his finances, would seize upon the chance. Time indeed would prove the young marine right.

The CIA and the military were requiring that Captain Chrisandra be an ordained priest. It would not be ethical to do otherwise, especially in combat situations, where their asset might be called upon to minister to the wounded and the dying.

For this reason, Kerr agreed to undertake the task of ascertaining what would be necessary for George to complete the studies required for ordination as an Episcopal priest and whether or not these studies could be accomplished on an expedited basis in the time frame in which they were operating. Not lost on him was the fact that George was engaged in the extensive study of theology and philosophy at Boston

College under his old friend and classmate, Father Arthur Phillips, now a highly respected Jesuit, but formerly an Episcopal priest. In addition, George was being tutored in Episcopal theology at the Yale Divinity School by another of his old friends and classmates, the Reverend Lewis Pratt, now the head of that school. Knowing these facts gave Matt Kerr a degree of hope that the difficult hurdle placed in his path by the agency and the military could be overcome in the time allowed. His hopes would prove to be correct.

He decided to fly to the United States himself and visit with his two old friends, the Reverend Pratt and Father Phillips. No one thought anything of the fact the next week when Kerr left for the airport at Saigon to board a transport for the flight to the United States. He routinely traveled back and forth, so there was no reason to assume that this trip was anything out of the ordinary.

When Matt Kerr arrived in the United States, he first would visit with John Sullivan Sr. at agency headquarters in Langley, Virginia. Then he would rent a car (because he didn't want to use an agency car) to drive up Route 95 to New Haven, Connecticut, to confer with Reverend Pratt. It had been a while since he'd been back to New Haven, and he was looking forward to the return. Finally, he would continue further east to Chestnut Hill and visit Father Phillips at the Jesuit College. He last had seen Father Phillips when they both attended Sister Kate's funeral in Stockton, California.

His trip to New Haven and Chestnut Hill would prove to be most encouraging, and he would convey the positive results to John Sullivan Jr. and Christian Carter in time for their meeting in Boston with George B. Angelson.

– 4 –

George was excited to receive a message from Christian Carter that he would be passing through Boston with a fellow marine and Boston College graduate named John Sullivan Jr. He was anxious to meet them at the Boston Naval Yard, as they had suggested, and to catch up with his old high school friend. He had no idea how his path in life was about to change as he drove down Beacon Street in the GTO to meet them.

Christian recognized the car when it passed through the gate at the Naval Yard. As George was parking, he and John Sullivan Jr. walked toward it. The sun was blazing hot that day, and the two men could feel the heat of the pavement through their highly polished shoes. When George stepped from the automobile, the sun was so bright that he was momentarily blinded by its white light. However, it wasn't long before he and Christian were shaking hands, embracing one another, and catching up. They quickly became lost in reunion talk before they caught themselves and stopped long enough to allow the patiently waiting John Sullivan Jr. to introduce himself to George.

John remembered that there was a park nearby, and Christian suggested that they drive there to find some shade and escape the heat. Climbing into the back seat, Christian left the front seat for his fellow marine and senior ranking officer. As they exited the security gate, John gave George directions to the park.

When talk of the unusually hot Boston weather had been exhausted, the conversation inevitably turned to Boston College football. John had been an all-American guard for Coach Jim Miller and was anxious to know what George thought of his replacement, Coach Joe Yukica, the current head coach. Coach Yukica had given George a chance to join the team as a walk-on when he took over from Jim Miller in 1968, and George had nothing but praise for the new man. In fact, George made it a point to remind the two marines that in his first victory as the Boston College Head Coach on September 28, 1968, Joe Yukica had beaten Navy 49–15 in Annapolis, the Eagles' first football victory over the Midshipmen in forty years. The young marines didn't respond, choosing instead to let the comment simply drift unanswered into the hot still air of that Boston afternoon.

As things progressed, however, George began to realize that this was not simply a friendly visit. Christian, knowing his friend as he did, sensed George's growing suspicions and spoke first. "George, this isn't just a social call. We have something very important to ask you."

"What?"

"John and I have volunteered for a special mission in Vietnam, and we would like you to join us."

"Christian, you know that I've just been accepted into law school. Why would I want to do that? And more importantly, why do you need me?"

Before Christian could answer, John spoke up to ask George a question to which he thought he already knew the answer. "What's your draft status?"

George answered, "My birthday is June 2, which means that my lottery number is 228. The draft board has been going through about thirty numbers a month, so at that rate, I suspect I'll be drafted in September or October of this year."

"And there is no deferment for law school, am I correct?"

"You are correct. I can be drafted out of law school, but I have received permission from Boston College Law School to delay my start by one year until September of 1971."

"I see. But earlier you said that you thought you could be drafted in September or October of this year. Has something changed?"

"There is talk that Nixon may freeze the lottery at 195, which would mean that I am not likely to be drafted. Technically, I guess he could unfreeze it, or I could be drafted in subsequent years if they were to exhaust all the numbers for those years, but neither seems very likely to happen."

"I agree," replied John, "it sounds like you would be home free if the lottery is indeed frozen at that number."

"I think so," admitted George as a silent pause fell over the conversation.

The uncharacteristically hot and muggy Boston weather that afternoon had been taking its toll, especially on George, notwithstanding the fact that the car was in a shady spot under a big old maple tree in the park. As the three men sat talking in the GTO, the warmth of their bodies exacerbated the already intolerable situation. The slight breeze the motion of the car had been generating while driving there now was a distant memory. George could feel the sweat dripping down the back of his neck. His light-colored shirt had dark stains under the arms and now was beginning to stick to his back as a result of having been pressed against the driver's seat. His palms were moist and sticky, and he could feel the beads of perspiration on his scalp as he ran his hands through his thinning hair. George reached into his pocket for a handkerchief, only to realize he had forgotten to bring one.

He could not help but notice the contrast as the two marines sat crisp and dry in their dress uniforms. They appeared to be so at peace with their lot in life, while his seemed to be so unsettled. The demons he thought he had buried when he finally decided to attend law school and become a lawyer were once again rising up to taunt him. Did he want to be a warrior by agreeing to participate in this special mission his friends were undertaking, did he want to be a priest, or did he want to be a lawyer? If he had his druthers he would choose to be all three, but that could not possibly happen. However, he had made the decision to be a lawyer, and now he felt he was being put upon to revisit that decision and consider being a warrior.

From the earliest history of this country, it has been well understood that freedom is not free but must be jealously guarded time and time again. It is said that when Benjamin Franklin signed the Constitution, he warned that we now have a republic and we will have to sacrifice to keep it. In a time-honored tradition, generations of young men have tested their mettle, earning the right to be free, whether it be crossing the Delaware River with George Washington, charging up San Juan Hill with Teddy Roosevelt, going "over there" in World War I, or storming the beaches of Normandy on the D-Day invasion of Europe in World War II. Now it was the turn of George's generation, and they were being called upon to prevent the domino that Vietnam was, from falling into Communist hands in Southeast Asia. John and Christian had answered the call, had shown their courage in combat, and appeared to be the better for it. There was a piece of George that yearned to join them, in being a part of that tradition, and in doing his share for freedom, thereby earning his stripes in those crisp, dry uniforms. Now he was being forced to confront the reality of that choice, and along with the scorching heat, it was making him uncomfortable.

When George was young, he had dreamed of following in his uncle's footsteps and joining the Army Airborne. His father's and his uncle's generation had saved the world from Nazi tyranny and Japanese militarism. They had freed the oppressed and flung open the doors of the concentration camps forever. But as he had grown older, George also had come to respect the message of non-violence exemplified by Jesus Christ, Gandhi, and more recently, Martin Luther King. His interests had turned toward the priesthood and the law, to help the downtrodden through peaceful change to the social justice system. He had come to very much admire and identify with Robert F. Drinan, SJ, the Jesuit priest who had recommended him to Boston College Law School. Father Drinan had been the dean of Boston College Law School since 1956 and at the time was seeking election to the US House of Representatives from the Commonwealth of Massachusetts. In George's eyes Father Drinan was a man who had found a way to render to Caesar that which was Caesar's and to the Lord that which was the Lord's by becoming a priest and a meaningful voice for change.

George hoped to someday do the same with his law degree, only as an Episcopal priest instead.

Having had to choose among the sword, the collar, and the scales of justice, George had chosen the scales first, with the hope, albeit distant, of someday pursuing the collar as well. The sword had not made the previous cut. Now, he was being tempted by the sword once again. He knew the time had come to be decisive, and his indecision, made worse by the sweltering heat, was making him most uneasy.

Christian was unwilling to give up too easily on his friend George and broke the momentary silence that had come over the conversation in the car to say, "The mission we have in mind may take only a few weeks to complete, and should be over by the fourth of July of next year, in plenty of time for you to return to law school in September 1971."

"Why me?" asked George, still somewhat perplexed by the entire situation.

"I am the one that recommended you for the assignment," answered Christian, "and you were ultimately selected for a combination of reasons. First—and I hope you will not take this the wrong way—we need someone with a plain vanilla background. By that I mean no military or other government service record, and no law violations, especially in connection with drug use. You fit the bill. Your record is squeaky clean and completely uneventful. Second, we need someone who will not be missed while they are unexplainably away from their usual surroundings. You told me in a recent letter that you are planning to travel through Europe alone next year in the late spring or early summer, before you return to law school. The timing for that trip fits perfectly with our plans. No one will question your absence. Third, we need a person with the intelligence, intestinal fortitude, and physical strength and stamina to undergo the extensive training and preparation that the mission will require. I think you have what it takes. You're a varsity football player on a Division One team, you run track, and are in great shape. Fourth, John and I want a person we can trust and who will watch our backs for us, and I know you will. There are other reasons even more compelling than these that I can share with you if and when you accept the assignment."

"Oh, great. Basically you're telling me you want me because I'm boring, I won't be missed, and you can trust me. Those are really compelling reasons! And let's cut the crap about me being tough and a Division One football player. Have you forgotten what one punch from your golden glove fist did to me in high school? Furthermore, I'm a walk-on—a tackling dummy on the BC football team. What makes me so special? What is it that I have to do?"

"You have to make the tackle of your life!"

"I have to make the tackle of my life—what the *fuck* are you talking about?"

John interjected, "We cannot reveal any details to you yet."

"I don't understand, why can't you reveal the details yet? When can I know?"

"Only after you have committed to be involved and have been sworn to secrecy," answered Christian.

"How can I agree to something without knowing what the hell I'm agreeing to?"

"I guess I was foolish to think that our friendship was strong enough for you simply to be willing to trust me," replied Christian, knowing that he was unfairly putting his friend on the spot.

"Christian, I trust you like a brother, and I think you know that, but this is going a little too far and asking a hell of a lot of me. Isn't there anything else you can tell me that would make this decision any easier for me? I have to be honest with you—right now I'm having a tough time with this!"

"Yes," answered John, "I think we can tell you what your alias would be. We would be training you to be a chaplain, assigned to the 101st Airborne Division in Vietnam. As a chaplain, you would be a Captain in the United States Army."

George, somewhat perplexed and concerned, responded, "As an Episcopalian, I think I would need to be an ordained priest to be a chaplain. I don't think I would be comfortable with pretending to be a chaplain. In fact, I know I wouldn't!"

"We not only understand, we agree with you," replied John, "and that is why we are prepared to arrange all the necessary steps for you to be ordained as a priest before you are deployed."

"But that would take too long and could not possibly be accomplished in the required time frame!" exclaimed George with a hint of exasperation in his voice.

"As I said, that is what we are prepared to do for you, and you must trust that we can deliver on our promise," John calmly reiterated. And then just as calmly he continued, "What if we could expedite that process for you, so that you could be ordained within the next year? I don't want to sugarcoat it; it will be a very intense year for you, both physically and mentally. But if we can make it happen, what would you say to that?"

"I would jump at it!" exclaimed George as he turned his body in the driver's seat to be able to look the marine directly in the eye, almost as if to be sure that he was not kidding.

The look on John Sullivan's face told George instantly that this was no joke. On the contrary, appearing to be very serious, John began to speak in a deliberate tone, asserting, "Just to be sure that I understand you correctly, is it fair to say that if we can accelerate the process by which you become an ordained Episcopal priest so that you are an ordained priest at the time that you are deployed, you are prepared to volunteer for the mission?"

"Yes," said George, overwhelmed with excitement at the prospect of achieving a dream he thought he had been required to defer indefinitely. So excited was he that momentarily the danger inherent in what he was agreeing to totally escaped him.

Christian, sensing this euphoria on the part of his friend, interrupted the conversation to warn George that their mission was an extremely dangerous one and that there was a very good chance that one or all of them might not come back alive. George understood and turned further in his seat to look directly at his old high school buddy. When he did, Christian could see from the expression on George's face that he had the reassurance that he was seeking. There was no longer any doubt in the young marine's mind that his friend understood and was committed.

The sun had now started to set and a slight breeze began to blow gently through the open window of the car, offering some relief from the day's heat. George noticed for the first time that his shirt no longer was sticking to his back.

Was he scared? Of course he was scared. Was he nervous about the gravity of the choice he had made? Yes, he was. But these were not the overriding feelings he was experiencing. Rather, he was feeling an inner calm come over him, for he now knew that he had made the right decision, and he was at peace with the path he had chosen. And the two young marines had the reassurance they needed that their man was on board and that he was the right man for the job.

At that point, John told George that they would be getting back to him in short order, but that in the interim, he was to go about his business as usual, and he was not to discuss their meeting or its subject matter with anyone, not even his family. When George agreed, John suggested that they head over to Cronin's Pub, a long-time haunt of his Irish-American ancestors, in South Boston, for some burgers and brew.

All three were in favor of the idea, so George started the GTO, turned on the headlights, and followed the light beams out of the park and into the dusk of the approaching evening in the direction of the pub. The chemistry that Matt Kerr so cherished already existed between the two young marines as it did between the two high school buddies. Inside Cronin's Pub, in a dimly lit corner, the incubation process would begin, carefully nourished by burgers and beers that would bring that chemistry to the relationship between the two Boston College Eagles and to the group as a whole. A strong bond eventually would form among the three men, the type of bond that is born of the mutual respect required of men agreeing to face the challenge before them, knowing that their lives and dreams would be unwaveringly entrusted to each other.

Two weeks later, John Sullivan Jr. would meet George B. Angelson outside Alumni Stadium on the Boston College campus. To any passing observer, they might simply look like two former Eagle players recalling their gridiron glory days at the Heights. Quite the contrary, John was revealing the full details of Operation Excalibur to George for the first time.

Their finest hour was still very much ahead of them.

– 5 –

Matt Kerr was very much looking forward to seeing his old friend Lewis Pratt again. It was raining lightly in New Haven when he exited Route 95 and drove toward the Yale campus with its beautiful Gothic buildings. Getting out of the car, he placed the visitor's pass on the dash, opened his umbrella, and walked to the door of the majestic hall. Once upstairs, he entered Lewis Pratt's office. As he did so, the years seemed to melt away, and it felt to him like it was only yesterday that he had been there to interview for admission to the Divinity School. There was a time when he thought he wanted to become an Episcopal priest. It was a long time ago, and much had changed. He now harvested spies instead of souls.

Lewis Pratt was waiting for him when he entered and could not have been warmer in his welcome. The two men sat down and settled into a trip down memory lane. They had not gotten very far when Olivia, his assistant, came in to see if anyone wanted a cup of coffee. Livie, as Lewis Pratt had grown accustomed to calling her, had been working for the reverend for many more years than she cared to admit, and her coming and going from the office pretty much went unnoticed, it was so routine an event. As soon as she left with a mission to bring back two cups of coffee and some cookies, the two men resumed their nostalgic journey. When she returned with the goodies, the men barely noticed because they were so engrossed in their conversation. But soon the aroma of the coffee and the sight of the cookies won out. Livie smiled to herself at the eventual triumph of her offerings. She then bade the men good-bye and prepared to leave the room. As she was about to shut the door, Reverend Pratt asked her to hold his calls and not allow anyone to disturb them.

When the door finally was shut, Lewis Pratt turned to Matt Kerr and said, "I very much am enjoying your visit, but I know something more than a desire to reminisce has brought you here today."

Kerr replied, "Yes, I need a favor—a very big favor."

"What is it?" asked the reverend.

"I need a cover for an asset," answered Matt.

Lewis Pratt, smiling at what he perceived to be a rather silly way to refer to a person, asked, "What kind of cover?"

"I need him to be an army chaplain, an ordained Episcopal priest. He will be functioning in an active combat zone and may be called upon to perform as a chaplain."

"And you want me to train him. I don't think that will be a problem, provided you give me sufficient time."

"We have one year from this coming May to have him ordained. We need for him to go active in May of 1971."

"Where is he now, and how much training has he already undergone?"

"You know him and, as I understand it, you have been working with him. He is about to graduate from Boston College and he has been studying under Art Phillips. Here is a copy of the young man's transcript along with a letter Art sent me outlining the subjects in which he has been tutored by him."

Skimming through the materials, the reverend said, "You're right, a lot of this won't be necessary. I do know this young man, and I have been tutoring him as well. As a matter of fact, it is Art who sent him to me. He is extremely bright and a fast learner. Looking at this transcript I would say he already has the equivalent of two years or more of Divinity School under his belt."

"So you're willing to work with him?"

"Absolutely. It will be a challenge, but it should be doable. And honestly, I think I'm going to enjoy it a great deal. Success will be its own reward, because I know from my dealings with George just how important this is to him and how diligent a student he will be."

"This is great news."

"The only issue I see is that we cannot give him credit for the courses in which he has been privately tutored by Art until he retakes the courses formally and passes the examination required for those credits. While I have no doubt that under Art's tutelage George has mastered the subject matter, he will need to pass the examinations in these subjects to be given official credit."

"Is that something that you can do for me?"

"I can arrange for him to take the necessary examinations. I also think I can work with him to complete the course materials that he still has to study. But it is going to be close time-wise at best. I take it this is very important for you?"

Matt, breathing a little easier, replied, "I wouldn't be imposing on you this way if it wasn't of the utmost importance. Thanks, Lewis. I owe you big time for this one."

"When can I start this work with him?"

"I will arrange it as soon as possible," answered Kerr.

"That would be great. I need all the time I can get."

Lewis Pratt then walked his old friend to the door of his office, opened it, and shook hands with him before Matt turned and left. No elaborate good-byes were necessary, not between men who had been such good friends for so long.

As Matt exited the building and walked toward his rental car, the weather still was gray and dismal, but the rain had stopped. He could make out a pickup truck with South Carolina plates parked near his car and a tall, rough-looking fellow leaning against it, whom he recognized instantly to be Bo Hicket.

As Matt got closer, he said, "Hi, Bo. Thanks for coming up here to see me."

"No problem," replied Bo, "I have plenty of time now that I've been discharged from the army."

"How is your family taking it?"

"Needless to say, they're disappointed in me. But then again, that's nothing new for them. They have come to expect it from me. However, this time was a little harder even for them since it got so much damn publicity back home."

"Well, I appreciate what you're doing for your country."

"Think nothing of it. By the way, I can assure you that Sam Lerner, Jon Trueblood, Joaquin Arango, and Nadim Haddad are ready for anything you might have planned for them. So who is this new fellow you want me to train?"

"His name is George Angelson, and I want you to work with him at a thirty-four-acre abandoned Nike missile site in West Harrison, New York. It is near the Westchester Airport, should you decide to do any night jumps over Long Island Sound or the nearby reservoirs. You have to turn this fellow into Vietnam ready airborne material in the next twelve months."

"Does he have any military training?"

"None at all, he is a piece of raw meat."

"My favorite kind! But I also would like to give him some jungle training. There is a virtually deserted island back home by me called Kiawah Island. I hunt there all the time. It's full of bugs and snake-infested swamps and will prepare him well."

"Fine. But one more thing."

"Yes?"

"You had better do a very good job because I've decided to expand my core team by one additional person, and you will be coming with us—that is if you would like to."

Bo was an old warhorse who was not taking well to being put out to pasture. He longed for one last fight, one more taste of combat, where a man's senses are sharpened by the focus and concentration demanded for survival, where the camaraderie between men who have been to hell and back together, their lives in each other's hands, can form bonds that transcend any possible differences, and where ordinary men can be inspired by their deep friendship for their fellow soldiers, to perform heroic acts at great personal sacrifice to themselves. There was nothing that Bo wouldn't give for one last chance to place his parched lips on the chalice of valor and quench his thirst with the sweet taste of noble sacrifice. This Matt Kerr knew and was only too glad to oblige.

With an uncharacteristic tear in his eye, or perhaps it merely was a raindrop, for it had started to drizzle again, Bo looked at Matt and said, "You would give me that chance after I was drummed out of the army?"

Matt looked the Spartan warrior in the eye and said, "That is precisely why I want you. You put your duty to those young men and your country before your self-interest. You have earned the right to see the fruits of your efforts and to assure the success of the mission for which you trained them."

"God bless you, Matt. When do I start?"

"In June."

The two men then shook hands in the Yale parking lot and went their separate ways, Bo to John's Island in South Carolina and Matt to Chestnut Hill in Massachusetts, where he would confer with Art Phillips about George.

– 6 –

In the three weeks following his meetings with Lewis Pratt and Art Phillips, Matt had a chance to meet George in person and take his measure of the man. He liked what he was seeing.

Starting in June of 1970, shortly after graduating from Boston College, George began to meet on a regular basis with Lewis Pratt in New Haven. They would continue to meet in this manner until the spring of 1971, when George satisfied all the requirements for ordination and was quietly ordained shortly thereafter, and before leaving for Southeast Asia.

It was difficult for George not to be able to share the good news of his ordination with his family and friends. When he performed his first Eucharistic service, the only one he would be permitted to celebrate prior to being deployed to Vietnam, no one was in attendance other than Matt Kerr and Lewis Pratt. Bittersweet indeed, it was to realize a dream, but be denied the joy of sharing that good fortune. George struggled painfully with hiding his joy from his loved ones. It would be but the first of many struggles for the young priest.

At the same time that George began working with Lewis Pratt, he started training with Bo Hicket. Bo was relentless in the demands he placed on the young college graduate. Driving him harder and further than he had ever driven a recruit in the army, he was determined not to lose this, his last charge, to a body bag. They trained first in the steamy heat of the South Carolina summer and then in the bitter temperatures of the New York winter. They jumped over Long Island Sound in the dark cold of the night onto a deserted island. They lived on snakes, alligator, and deer meat as they waded through the Kiawah Island swamps in the early spring that followed. If he survived the training, George would be more prepared than anyone could ever have imagined. To this goal Bo had committed himself.

The training grew more intense and brutal as time went on, and Bo continued to raise the stakes. Methodically, he molded this mild-mannered man into a lethal weapon, teaching him killing techniques that the army shunned in all but the most elite programs, because it made these soldiers dangerous for reentry into society. But George was stable, and Bo knew the limits to which he could take him. After all, this is what he had done for a living, and he was one of the best at what he did. Even the army had never taken issue with his results, only with his methods.

By the spring of 1971, the strain was beginning to take its toll on George. He had been studying for the priesthood with Lewis Pratt, training for combat with Bo Hicket, and working in a local business to earn money for law school. In addition, he had been living a lie, concealing all that he had been doing. When May 17, 1971, finally came, and he was boarding his Icelandic flight to Europe, he was ready for Operation Excalibur. What he was not prepared for was Sister Claire and the spell her charm and beauty would cast upon him. So consumed by her was he that he forgot all else. It would stay that way until they were forced to part company in Paris a short time later.

The poet Robert Frost, who read from his works at John F. Kennedy's inauguration, wrote a poem entitled "The Road Not Taken." In it, a traveler in the woods comes upon a fork in the road and stops to ponder which path to take. Frost's traveler eventually chose the "one less traveled" and comes to find "that has made all the difference."

As with most Americans, George had no interest in becoming embroiled in the Vietnam War, nor did he anticipate being summoned by his country to help right a wrong done to a fallen American president.

But once called upon, he was honored to answer that call. And like Frost's traveler, having undertaken that path, the one less traveled, the one that would make all the difference in his young life, he was prepared to see it through no matter what the hardship.

– 7 –

By early 1971, Matt Kerr was satisfied that his core team, the first layer, was in place. It would consist of Marine Lieutenant John Sullivan Jr.; Marine Lance Corporal Christian Carter; George B. Angelson, aka Army Captain John J. Chrisandra; and Bo Hicket, aka Dan Werner, a private contractor and adviser to Matt Kerr at the US embassy in Saigon.

In addition to his normal duties as a chaplain, the story being disseminated by the embassy was that Captain Chrisandra had been sent to help start an orphanage for boys that would be named the Mount Saint Vincent Orphanage. George had chosen the name in honor of his mother's college in the Bronx. This was intended to allow Captain Chrisandra to spend time at the Orphanage of Saint Francis Xavier near Binh Gia, ostensibly to learn from their experience, but also to place him near the last place that the Russian had been seen.

The second layer, which would directly support the core team, also was taking shape. This layer would be managed by Bo Hicket and would be made up of two HU-1 Huey helicopters, nicknamed *slicks* because they were armed with only two M60D door guns, giving them a clean profile. Their crews would consist of Samuel Lerner, Jon Trueblood, Joaquin Arango, and Nadim Haddad, now all of the 101st Airborne. In addition, two of the transport pilots also could fly the slicks, if necessary, and Captain Chrisandra and a shadowy character known locally as Frenchie were available as extra door gunners.

The story goes that Frenchie had no formal name and was rumored to have been the product of a wild night of too much drinking and unprotected sex between a French soldier and a Vietnamese prostitute. Too Catholic to abort, too poor to care for him, the prostitute had left him for the nuns to handle. They did the best that they could with him until he ran away to live by his wits on the back streets of Saigon. He had survived by becoming expert at living that way, and few knew their way around the shadowy underbelly of South Vietnam better than he did. Not one for strong political convictions of any kind, he had a deep-seated hatred for the Communists ever since he had been tortured by them as a youngster because of the colonial blood that flowed through his veins.

As with most of the world, he had been smitten by the elegant charm and beauty of Jackie Kennedy. Being somewhat of a romantic as a result of the French in him, he liked to tell anyone who would listen about the time he had seen President John F. Kennedy on the embassy television telling the French people, "I am the man who accompanied Jacqueline Kennedy to Paris—and I have enjoyed it!" To him they appeared to be living the fairy tale life he could never hope to have. That is, until a bullet fired by "some silly little Communist," as Jackie is quoted as saying to her mother in *The Death of a President*, by William Manchester, ended it all on November 22, 1963, in Dallas. Frenchie carried with him an article written by Jacqueline Kennedy for the JFK memorial issue of *Look Magazine*, dated November 17, 1964, in which she said she should and probably did know that he was "magic," but now he was a legend when he would have rather been a man.

Conventional thinking would caution not to trust a man like Frenchie, easily swayed by the weaknesses of the flesh, whether they be wine, women, money, or song. He was a man of few principles, yes, but a hopeless romantic nevertheless, whose one shining ideal in this life had been destroyed by a silly little Communist. Matt Kerr knew that he could count on Frenchie, at least for this mission; his instincts told him so, and they would again prove to be right.

Frenchie would carry with him into action an old, worn picture of Jacqueline Kennedy in her famous pink Chanel suit, with her husband's blood on it. The scoundrel with a cause would prove to be a force to be reckoned with, a knight in shining armor out to avenge the blood on the suit of his lady in pink.

The third and final layer, which would provide indirect support for the team, still needed to be put in place. This layer would consist of two all-female crews to fly two air force transports on loan to the CIA. These planes would be two specially modified cargo versions of the Boeing KC-135 Stratotanker, with extra fuel tanks added that would allow them to fly non-stop from Paris to Vietnam and with only one stop from Saigon to Washington. In addition to their primary duty as transports, these craft would serve as flying command centers, airborne hospitals, and reconnaissance assets. Finally, the modified KC-135s would be joined by a small spotter plane and an old C-47 that had been converted into a gunship, should they be needed.

Matt Kerr's desire that the transports be flown by all female crews was another one of his unorthodox ideas. His cousin was a WASP pilot during World War II, ferrying plans to the combat zones. She had flown almost every type of plane in use at the time. And still fresh in his mind was when Jacqueline Cochran had broken the sound barrier in 1953. Yet, the military continued to resist having women pilots. He told himself he wouldn't make that same mistake.

He found six female pilots who had been trained to fly the Boeing 707, which was very similar to the craft they would be required to fly as part of Operation Excalibur. All six of the women had prior affiliations with the agency and high level security clearances. With the help of his good friend Bob Larson, who was a Pan Am captain and flight instructor on the Boeing 707 aircraft, and a former air force pilot, now retired, with experience on the KC-135 aircraft, Matt was satisfied that these women would be able to handle anything that the mission might throw their way. He had full confidence in them, and they were eager to prove him right. They would do that and more.

Three years later, in 1974, when George would earn his law degree, six women finally would earn their wings as navy pilots. In that same momentous year of 1974, the army would begin training female helicopter pilots. They would've been surprised if they had known that three years earlier, in the spring of 1971, as part of Operation Excalibur, two female civilian pilots by the name of Anne Herndon and Jan Tracy already had successfully piloted one of their spotter planes and gunships during a combat mission in Vietnam. Matt Kerr was a person ahead of his time, as were the six women whom he'd entrusted with his mission.

The lead modified KC-135 would be designated Stewball and would be captained by Anne Herndon, with Elizabeth "Beth" Baton as co-pilot and Diane St. Marie as flight officer. The second plane would be designated Coney Island Baby and would be captained by Carole Radcliff, with Jan Tracy as co-pilot and Lori Heatherton as flight officer.

The lead helicopter would be designated Screaming Eagle and would be piloted by Jon Trueblood and Samuel Lerner, with Joaquin Arango as the door gunner. The second helicopter would be designated Headhunter and would be piloted by Nadim Haddad and Anne Herndon, with Frenchie as the door gunner. One of the things Frenchie could do well was handle a machine gun. He had been trained by the French as a young boy, and he was fearless.

Anne Herndon, who would lead the third layer of support, was the only child of Shari and Christopher Herndon. They had been married for more than ten years and had given up on being able to have a child when Anne came along, a gift from God. In a grammar school essay, Anne had written that when she grew up she wanted to learn how to fly so that she could soar like an eagle. Her teacher dismissed it as a child's fanciful dream, but it was more of a harbinger of what was to come.

In high school in rural South Carolina, Anne would help on the farm prior to leaving for school. Thought to be too serious by her teachers, she still was able to maintain a near perfect average, serve as president of the student body, and excel on the tennis court. Later she would graduate with honors from Clemson University, where she was also captain of the tennis team.

Not long after graduation from Clemson, she fulfilled her childhood dream, when she obtained her pilot's license. She quickly became more and more proficient, taking jobs her male colleagues would turn down. Her skills as a pilot became increasingly recognized as she broke into the ranks of commercial aviation. By the late sixties, she had been certified on the Boeing 707 and its sister the 720.

Matt Kerr became acquainted with Anne and the other women when they had obtained their agency security clearances and had taken on flying clandestine missions for the CIA both in Latin America and in Southeast Asia. He had been through some fairly turbulent situations with them and had the utmost confidence in them.

He recalled being with Anne once when they stopped to visit briefly with her parents on the family farm while travelling to business meetings in nearby Charleston, South Carolina. Shari and Christopher Herndon were growing increasingly apprehensive about Anne's long absences and suspected they weren't being told the true reason for her trips. Anne calmly and patiently reassured them that she was doing what she loved most, and that if anything were to happen to her, they should take comfort in the fact that their only child had lived her life to the fullest—soaring like an eagle. The air of confidence and the cheerful smile that she displayed eventually prevailed as the elder Herndons resigned themselves to their fate. It was not what they would have chosen for their only daughter, but they accepted it for her sake. Equally as important, her confidence and smile had impressed Matt and had won him over as a fan for life. Again his instincts would serve him well and not disappoint him.

Like George, Anne and her fellow female aviators found that taking the path less traveled made all the difference.

– 8 –

In 1970, during the months following the encounter between Sister Kate and the Russian at the orphanage in Vietnam, the CIA set about using the fingerprints and other data she had obtained to try to learn more about the mysterious stranger. He proved to be a complex and interesting study.

His true name was Alexei Buzinov. He was born in the mid-1920s in a rural village at the northern reaches of the Volga River. The inhabitants of this farming community were, for the most part, poor and illiterate. Alexei had been fortunate to be able to remain in school longer than most and enjoyed a relatively happy childhood. His parents were traditional and clung to many of their pre-Revolution beliefs.

He learned to support himself as a hunter when many of the local farms, including the one owned by his family, had been collectivized. Often he'd been heard to say that hunting was good because it couldn't be collectivized. Before long he gained a reputation as an outstanding shot. While still a student, he became a member of the Communist Union of Youth. Being a member of this organization enabled him to advance more quickly than he otherwise might have.

He was sent to join the army at the age of eighteen. His education, albeit thin, qualified him as a junior lieutenant. Before the age of twenty, he'd seen combat, been wounded and hospitalized and had made a full recovery. He already had received two promotions and was a senior lieutenant. His humble origins were viewed as proof of his proletarian sympathies, along with his joining the Communist party. As a result, he had been recommended for three years of advanced training at the Frunze Military Academy in Moscow—Russia's equivalent of West Point. At this time Alexei already had met and married his wife, Anya, a quiet woman who taught French in a nearby elementary school. In Moscow they were given one room in which to live privately, but were required to share the kitchen and bath facilities with three other families. After graduating from Frunze, Alexei was sent to the Military–Diplomatic Academy, a training school for Soviet military intelligence officers who were being groomed as subversives and recruiters of espionage agents.

He rose to the rank of a lieutenant colonel, but in the view of the CIA, it appeared to have little to do with patriotism or military skill. Studies done for the agency concluded that Russian peasants were the most oppressed, the worst exploited and by far the greatest disadvantaged group during the post-Revolutionary Soviet period. These peasants had little reason to trust Moscow and obeyed to survive more than out of respect. While Alexei was stationed in Vienna in the early 1950s, he was observed to be a simple man who felt ill at ease in the sophisticated environment in which he'd been placed. He lived with Anya in the Grand Hotel, one of that city's finest hotels, and attended meetings at the offices of the GRU, the Soviet military intelligence service, in the Imperial Hotel, another of the city's great hotels, but didn't appear to be impressed with any of these surroundings. Rather, according to a report filed by the CIA operative charged with shadowing him, he seemed to hide behind the solitary nature of his intelligence gathering to avoid social interactions where possible.

According to CIA experts, Alexei Buzinov was what the Russians liked to refer to as a *careerist*. He learned to pretend that he was that which he was not, since doing so enabled him to survive and even prosper to an extent. These experts were certain that under his crisp officer's uniform breathed a man who considered himself to still be a simple peasant. The military had schooled him well, and he'd been a good student and learned his lessons. Superficially, he had taken on the role of an officer and a gentleman, but deep inside he had little use for the substance of it all.

In the later 1950s, he surfaced for a time in Paris. His presence at first eluded the CIA, because he had been disguised as a Soviet *illegal*, which is intelligence speak for a person who, like Alexei, is highly trained in espionage and who is given a carefully constructed and extensively documented false identity as a citizen of a country other than his own. Alexei Buzinov had been given the false identity of a Mexican businessman.

His being posted in Paris in 1958 was understandable to the agency because the US Armed Forces European Command had just been located at Fontainebleau in the nearby suburbs. What made less sense to the CIA at the time was why their Soviet counterparts, for whom they had the utmost professional respect, would have given an operative with no business experience, who spoke Spanish only moderately well, and with a distinctive Russian accent, the identity of a Mexican businessman. In time the agency would come to realize that Paris had simply been a stop along the way to Alexei's ultimate destination in the Southwestern United States.

Alexei's true identity had only been discovered literally by chance. He had the misfortune to have an automobile accident while in Paris. The French police, in investigating the crash, which attracted a great deal of attention, unraveled the ruse. As John Sullivan would later note, but for the accident, Alexei's illegal identity might never have been discovered.

Once Alexei Buzinov had been exposed, the CIA, as a matter of routine, undertook an investigation of his activities since arriving in Paris. It quickly became clear that he had started to become corrupted by the ways of the West. This time Anya had remained behind in Moscow with their son Dmitri, and Alexei made a female acquaintance with whom he had freely shared his lovemaking, but apparently little else. Her name was Danielle Fabre, and she was the product of a French father and a Vietnamese mother. Her mother had relocated to Paris with her soldier husband-to-be when he had returned from his tour of duty in Vietnam. Strikingly beautiful, with long, silky black hair and the taut body of a dancer, Danielle caught Alexei's eye in a local cabaret where she performed nightly. In the assessment of agency investigators, her physical charms outpaced her cerebral ability to see beyond his fumbling attention and seemingly plentiful cash. They noted that she appeared to have little or no knowledge of who he really was. Time would tell if their assessment had been correct.

The CIA investigation uncovered another contact that Alexei had made since arriving in Paris. Galina Daluda was of Russian ethnicity and was employed as a clerk for the motor pool at the US Armed Forces European Command center in Fontainebleau. After a routine questioning, the agency investigators summarily dismissed Galina as not being of any importance. In their view, however useful she may have been to Alexei as a source of carnal knowledge, she was of no use to him as an intelligence source. In fact, they concluded that Alexei had sought out Galina for much the same reason he sought out Danielle. The inferior mental capabilities of both women made Alexei feel superior. They offered him not only sexual pleasure, but a welcome escape from the highly sophisticated world in which he was required to operate, albeit with great unease. Once again, only time would tell if their assessment had been correct. The question remained: Had Alexei been content to share only the intimacies of love making with them, or had he also busied himself mining the deepest recesses of their minds?

Once Alexei Buzinov was recalled to Russia, it became difficult for the agency to keep tabs on him. The Soviets had an effective counter-espionage organization in place that made the motherland a *denied area* in spy speak. However, the agency was successful in ascertaining that Alexei had some contact with Lee Harvey Oswald while the American former marine was in the Soviet Union between 1959 and 1962. The details surrounding that contact would have to wait for Operation Excalibur to unfold.

By the time Alexei Buzinov surfaced in Dallas, Texas, in 1963 as an illegal with the alias of Billy Bob Duxbury, his cover had been meticulously embroidered by the GRU and his American handlers. Their choreographed moves had created an international chain of bogus credentials, with a labyrinth of forged documents and fake organizations that the busy and overworked customs and immigration officers on the US and Mexican border had neither the time nor the inclination to check out, since there had been no obvious evidence of wrongdoing.

Billy Bob Duxbury had been photographed in the months prior to the assassination in Filthy McNasty's Pub in the Fort Worth, Texas, Stockyards by an FBI surveillance team. He apparently had been there to meet with Pierce Cutler, chairman of Texas Amalgamated Industries, Inc., a major munitions manufacturer. Cutler was being investigated by the FBI for possible bribery and embezzlement charges. It seems that the financial condition of Texas Amalgamated Industries in 1963 had been far worse than its books indicated, and the increase in munitions sales that an escalation of the US involvement in Vietnam would bring offered a quick and attractive fix.

But the cure had not been without its price. With the FBI closing in on him in early 1964, Pierce Cutler apparently took his own life on the night of January 6, 1964. According to the official reports prepared at the time, the evidence indicated that Mr. Cutler put his pistol into his mouth and pulled the trigger while sitting at his desk in the study of his home. This conclusion had been supported by the manner in which his blood was splattered on the study wall behind him, including on the picture hanging on that wall—of Lyndon B. Johnson being sworn in as president of the United States on Air Force One, with Mrs. Kennedy, her dress still stained with her fallen husband's blood, by his side. Mr. Cutler had been a large supporter of Lyndon B. Johnson throughout Johnson's political career.

Further investigation by the CIA determined that Alexei Buzinov, aka Billy Bob Duxbury, while in Texas in 1963, at first lived alone. Later he lived with the relative of a friend who most recently had worked as a clerk at the motor pool at Fort Hood, a 340-square-mile US military installation 160 miles south of Dallas. The friend was none other than Galina Daluda, the simple woman of Russian origin that Alexei had met five years earlier in Paris.

On January 13, 1964, when Alexei Buzinov left the United States by crossing back into Mexico, Galina drove him across the border. The agency would like to have questioned Galina again, but unfortunately, she was found dead two days later in Mexico, apparently murdered. A local examination conducted at the time of the bruised and partially clad body revealed the presence of semen in her vagina and a bullet lodged deep in her brain. Evidently she had served her purpose and been discarded.

– 9 –

By May of 1971, Operation Excalibur was ready to get underway. It was launched officially on Monday, May 17, 1971, when the Angelsons took their son George to John F. Kennedy Airport to catch an Icelandic flight to Luxembourg for what they thought would be a seven-week vacation in Europe. His good-bye to them seemed a little more serious and had an air of finality to it, but they assumed it simply was a touch of homesickness setting in. Little did they know that he was embarking on a delicate and dangerous mission of utmost importance to his country—Operation Excalibur; it would be anything but a vacation.

On Wednesday, May 19, 1971, after George said good-bye to Sister Claire at the convent in Paris, he headed to the US military installation at Fontainebleau to meet the rest of the team. Besides the sorrow that came from being separated from her, he was feeling guilty at having had to lie to her about his true plans. When he failed to return to the convent on Saturday, May 22, 1971, for one last good-bye, it was because he was too busy preparing and could not.

By that Saturday night, May 22, 1971, the team was ready to head to Vietnam and boarded Stewball for the long flight ahead of them. As the modified KC-135 taxied for takeoff, Captain Anne Herndon was at the controls, with Beth Baton in the co-pilot's seat, running through the usual checklist. Diane St. Marie was sitting behind them in the flight officer's seat, making some last-minute calculations. In the cabin, the team was secured in place. There was a sense of apprehension as well as excitement as the large jet roared down the runway and up into the dark sky. When Stewball's lights faded from sight, Captain Carole Radcliff turned Coney Island Baby, which was following behind, loaded with equipment and supplies, into the wind. As co-pilot Jan Tracy awaited clearance from the tower, flight officer Lori Heatherton sat behind them reviewing the flight plan. Once clearance was obtained, Coney Island Baby followed Stewball's lead into the dark abyss that was both the night sky and the mission ahead.

The only members of the team who knew George B. Angelson's true identity were Matt Kerr, John Sullivan Jr., Christian Carter, Bo Hicket and Anne Herndon. In other words, only the first layer of the team and the leads of the other two layers were privy to that information. The rest of the team knew him only as Captain John J. Chrisandra, a chaplain assigned to the 101st Airborne Division in Vietnam. During the flight, George took Matt Kerr and John Sullivan Jr. aside to tell them that he had met Claire on the flight to Europe and that she knew who he was. He neglected to tell them just how well they had gotten to know one another. However, he was scheduled to visit her orphanage once he was in Vietnam, both as part of his cover of starting a similar orphanage for boys, and to pick up the trail of the Russian. She would know immediately who he really was, and he was seeking guidance from them as to how he should handle the situation.

After conferring by secure communication with the senior Sully at Langley, the decision was made that Captain Chrisandra could tell Sister Claire as much as he wanted, as long as he did not reveal the true nature of the mission. The senior Sully had promised Mary Sullivan that their daughter Claire would not be drawn into agency activity in any way. The Sullivans already had lost one daughter to Vietnam, and they had a son in harm's way there, so it was only reasonable for Mary Sullivan to want to protect Claire. Captain Chrisandra would have to think of something—anything—as long as he did not disclose Operation Excalibur to her.

It would not be easy, and Captain Chrisandra was not relishing the task. Claire would be livid at finding out that she had been deceived and would subject him to the full fury of her Irish temper; this he knew. But he also knew that it all would be worth it just to see her again. The excitement was building in him, and the anticipation began to overwhelm him. In the end, he decided to confide in her brother, his new friend, Lieutenant John Sullivan Jr., and ask for his help. John agreed to be of assistance. Once they were securely settled in Vietnam, John accompanied Captain Chrisandra on the forty-mile trip to the orphanage in Binh Gia.

When they arrived at the orphanage, Captain Chrisandra lagged behind to give Lieutenant Sullivan some initial time alone with his sister. She of course was happy to see her brother, but immediately complained to him about his not having been at the airport to meet her. After explaining that he had been called out of Vietnam and was tied up on business, he told her that he had somebody he wanted her to meet. With that Captain Chrisandra stepped forward and out of the shadows. At first Sister Claire simply stood there in stunned silence; her brain could not process what her eyes were reporting. Then, as if a switch had been flicked, she rushed screaming to Captain Chrisandra. Hugging him, she exclaimed, "I can't believe it; I can't believe it really is you! I never thought I was going to see you again! I have missed you so!"

"Me too, me too!" Captain Chrisandra replied as he hugged her back.

Then, pushing back slightly to take a larger measure of him, she asked, "What in the Lord's name are you doing here, and why, may I ask, are you in that uniform, Geo ...?"

Before she could finish saying the name *George*, her brother interjected, "This is Captain John J. Chrisandra, an army chaplain assigned to the 101st Airborne Division," and placed his finger perpendicularly to his lips to indicate that she should remain silent. She decided to honor her brother's wishes, at least for the time being, but now that the initial shock was wearing off, she could feel the anger building in her. She wanted an answer, and she was going to get it one way or another; that she promised herself.

When her brother finally left and she and Captain Chrisandra were alone, with none of the orphanage girls nearby, she saw her chance. No longer able to contain herself, for now all vestiges of self-restraint were gone, she glared at him with her eyes ablaze with fire and her lips taut with anger and demanded, "What is this all about, George ... or John ... or whoever you are?"

Captain Chrisandra stood there in silence as his mind grasped for something—anything to say. Nothing was coming to him, except that the old cliché was true. She really was beautiful, even more beautiful when she was mad. Those fiery eyes, those taut lips—if only he could kiss them and consume some of that passion. Without further thought, he grabbed her and with all the emotion that had been building up in him, kissed her. At first she resisted violently, then not so much so, and then not at all. They were frozen together in time and place like a statue.

When they finally separated, George looked at Claire with an endearing and vulnerable look on his face that totally disarmed her and said, "Claire, I am so sorry for having deceived you, but you must believe me when I tell you that I had no choice in the matter; I had to."

"You had to?" Claire repeated in an inquisitive tone. Then, after a momentary pause to think, she covered her face with her hands and sighed. "Oh no, George, don't tell me that you are one of my father's shadow warriors. You are, aren't you?"

"Please don't ask me any more questions about who I am or why I am here. I don't want to ever have to lie to you again. It is too painful for me. All I am allowed to tell you is what your brother told you: that my name is Captain John J. Chrisandra, that I am an army chaplain, and that I am here to start an orphanage for boys, similar to this one that you run for the girls."

She put her hand on his lips, and gently kissing him on his forehead, whispered, "I will not ask you any more questions about yourself so that you will not have to lie to me. I know all I need to know about you—from your kiss. My feelings for you run far deeper than I had realized, and I have missed you so since we parted company in Paris. I know you love me, too, and that is all that matters."

"I do, Claire. My life has been miserable since I left you at the convent. All I have been able to think about is you—your beautiful smile, your sweet scent, and your contagious laugh. It has been driving me crazy."

"Good, you deserve to be driven crazy for lying to me! Just tell me if you can—are you really a priest, and are you scheduled to go to law school and follow in Father Drinan's footsteps as an advocate for change, the way you told me?"

"Yes, I am an ordained Episcopal priest and I am scheduled to start Boston College Law School in September, and I do hope to follow Father Drinan's example, as I told you. Why do you ask?"

"I want to know if the man I have fallen in love with is a man of peace—a man of the cloth; or if he is a gladiator—a man of armor—like my father and my brother. I am tired of living by the sword. I have seen what it has done to my poor mother. Everything else I can wait to learn about when you are free to tell me."

Captain Chrisandra was ecstatic for Claire had said she was in love with him, something he had longed to hear and had thought he never would. He promised himself and her that when his reason for being there was finished, he never again would bear arms. His promise was well-intentioned, but it was not to be.

In the evening, after the girls were fast asleep in the orphanage, Sister Claire and Captain Chrisandra took a bottle of wine and a blanket and strolled to a graceful old tree at the edge of the clearing of the orphanage. As they sat there on the blanket by the tree, under a beautiful moon, enjoying the wine, Claire told him that she had decided not to take her final vows. Even if nothing else ever became of their encounter, the feelings she had for him had taught her that she was not meant to be a nun. She would see her work at the orphanage to completion, and when a suitable replacement could be found, she planned to return to civilian life in California. He in turn assured her that having won her love, he would never forsake her.

That night under the moon, they finished what they had started in Echternach as they made passionate love to each other. It would be the most memorable night of their young lives. They once again promised each other that whatever the future might bring, they always could look up at the moon and know that the other was doing the same, from wherever they might be, and thinking about what they had shared that night.

Claire did not press George for any more information, as she had agreed. George did not betray his confidence to the CIA and the nation, as he had promised. Yet, without the need for a single spoken word between them, they both understood that their future together remained divided—*divided by the sword in the stone*—at least for a time, a time of unspoken danger. And for that time, their future would be uncertain and would remain so—*until the sword had been removed from the stone*—until the Russian had been removed from Vietnam, removed with the completion of Operation Excalibur.

– 10 –

The next morning began in usual fashion. The girls were having breakfast before the day's classes would begin. Captain Chrisandra had been put to work fixing a loose shutter, and Sister Claire was bringing him a cup of coffee, when a woman emerged from the tree line. As she approached, Sister Claire put down the coffee cup and walked to meet her. Captain Chrisandra remained on the ladder, with hammer in hand.

The woman appeared to be at least partially Vietnamese and spoke English with a French accent. She asked to speak with Sister Kate. Claire was visibly taken back by the request, but regaining her composure, told the woman that Sister Kate was deceased. When the woman seemed lost at the response, Claire explained that Sister Kate had been killed two years earlier and that she was her replacement. By this time, Captain Chrisandra had descended from the ladder, placed the hammer down, and walked over to the two women. Not wanting to alarm the woman or disrupt her conversation with Claire, he simply introduced himself as Father Chrisandra and neglected to mention his military rank.

The woman identified herself to Sister Claire as Danielle Fabre and told her that she had been the product of a marriage between a French soldier and a Vietnamese mother. She had been raised in France where she met a man that had become her lover. They had returned to Vietnam in the 1960s, and he had been bitten by a snake and was nursed back to health by Sister Kate. She seemed genuinely surprised to learn that Sister Kate had been murdered.

When she finally was made to understand that Sister Kate had been the adopted older sister of Sister Claire, she removed a sealed envelope from her pocket and gave it to Sister Claire. She explained that her lover had asked her to deliver this letter to Sister Kate, but that in light of the circumstances, she thought he would want her to give it to Sister Claire. She did not appear to know anything about the content of the envelope and left as quickly and quietly as she had come, once it had been delivered.

Claire handed the letter to Captain Chrisandra, who opened it. As he read it, a clear look of disbelief came over his face. He could not fathom what he was reading. It was too good to be true, but it was true. The letter read

Dear Sister Katherine Sullivan,

I hope that this letter finds you well. I still remember your kindness, when you nursed me back to health. As ill as I was, I am able to picture you sitting there through the night, wiping my brow with a cool, wet cloth, softly encouraging me to fight on, as I went in and out of consciousness, until my fever broke. It is one of the only times in my life when I have been treated like a human being. And for that I will always be grateful.

In addition to being a Catholic missionary, you must be an agent for the Americans or the South Vietnamese; otherwise you would not have bothered to take my fingerprints. Yes, I know that you did, because you forgot to remove the ink from my fingertips. Have no fear, I removed the ink myself, for I did not want one as kind as you to get in trouble.

By now you must have turned my prints over to your superiors, so you likely have confirmed me to be an American named William Duxbury. That is not the case. I am a major in the Soviet military and a former member of the Soviet Secret Police.

I had contact with Lee Harvey Oswald when he was living in Russia. I also was in Dallas, Texas, in 1963, when he assassinated President Kennedy. Furthermore, I have been in North Vietnam since the early to middle 1960s, and I have information on the fate of many of your agents who have vanished in the North.

I am concerned that my life may now be in danger, and I long to be back in the West, especially the Southwestern United States. I would like to defect to the West. I am in possession of information that is of extreme value to the Americans.

I have sat across from the American embassy in Saigon, but have been afraid to present myself because I do not want my intentions to be found out by the North Vietnamese, who will tell my country's secret police. Please deliver this letter to a trusted superior of yours in the American government. I wish President Nixon to know that I have reevaluated my role in life and that I am prepared to devote myself to the goal of an improved world for all mankind.

I ask your President Nixon to consider me as one of his loyal supporters. Going forward, the US Army has an additional soldier, for I want to enlist and join in the struggle for a free and democratic world for all human beings.

Sister Katherine, you should have no reservations about my devotion and steadfastness, or my sincerity in the battle for this ideal, which now also is mine. If you deliver this letter, you will have no regrets and you will always have a good memory of me. This I promise you.

Your loyal servant,
Alexei Buzinov

When Captain Chrisandra was finished reading, he folded the letter without showing it to Sister Claire. Claire did not know about her sister's role in the agency, nor did she know about the incident in question—the Russian, the fingerprints, any of it. It was her mother's wish and her father's promise to his wife that Claire would be spared, and Captain Chrisandra vowed to honor that wish. But what would he tell her that would not raise her curiosity even more?

In response to her inquiries, he told Claire that her sister Kate had nursed a man from the North of Vietnam back to health, and in return, he was providing information on some South Vietnamese agents who had gone missing when they were sent to spy in the North. "My concern," he told Claire, "is that this may be some type of provocation. They may well be trying to see if your sister was a spy—and now you also are one by implication. The embassy staff will know how to tell if this is real or a provocation. In any event, I think it is better for you if you are kept out of it."

Sister Claire seemed to accept the explanation, and the matter was dropped.

The next day, when Captain Chrisandra was back in Saigon, he met privately with Matt Kerr and Lieutenant Sullivan. Matt Kerr had conveniently allowed to leak from the US embassy in Saigon that a Russian citizen with American and Mexican aliases who had been nursed back to health by a Western missionary after being bitten by a poisonous snake now was attempting to defect to the West. The ploy had been unorthodox and a huge gamble, but it had worked. The men could not believe their good fortune. Their quarry had reached out to them before they'd had to seek him out. But the Russian had failed to give them a time and place to rendezvous with him. Hopefully, there no longer would be a need to risk sending Captain Chrisandra into North Vietnam or China to attempt to locate the Russian, either through a dangerous clandestine air drop or as a bogus conscientious objector seeking asylum.

– 11 –

There was instant chemistry between Captain Chrisandra and me that existed from the moment we met. He seemed to be such a gentle yet strong person. He had a calm confidence about him that I found reassuring in the uncertain world to which I had been born.

When Captain Chrisandra had to go into Saigon on business the day after the strange lady visited the orphanage, he let me come with him. While we were walking on Cong Ly Street in Saigon near Gia Long Palace, several blocks from the American embassy, I saw an elegant lady driving a shiny silver sports car with a bright red interior. Captain Chrisandra told me that she was the wife of an important dignitary and that the car was a brand new Mercedes-Benz SL. I gushed to Captain Chrisandra that someday, when I would go to live in the United States with Sister Claire and become a famous movie star, I would buy a car just like that one. He smiled warmly at me and told me that he very much hoped that my dream would come true for me. It would not, but I had no way of knowing that at the time.

Another thing I had no way of knowing at the time was the business that had brought the captain to the American embassy. While I patiently waited outside the office, cutting out paper dolls with Mr. Kerr's assistant, Captain Chrisandra was showing him and Lieutenant Sullivan the letter.

The captain was scheduled to leave shortly for Europe, and the other two men would check out the authenticity of the letter as well as the circumstances surrounding its delivery while he was gone—gone to meet his father in Amsterdam. When the time finally came a few days later for the captain to leave for Europe, Lieutenant Sullivan accompanied him to the airport, where Stewball was fueled and waiting.

On Saturday evening, May 29, 1971, George met his father, Ralph Angelson, in Amsterdam, as planned. After the first really fine meal he had eaten since leaving New York on May 17, he fell fast asleep in the first comfortable bed he had seen in the same time frame. The Krasnapolsky Hotel was a welcome luxury, and seeing his father again truly was priceless.

The next day, as George and his father explored the sights in Amsterdam, the young American could not help but notice how carefree his European peers were, enjoying their youth and life with reckless abandon. Love was free and everywhere, as were drugs. The contrast to what his fellow Americans were enduring in Vietnam was not lost on him. If the domino theory was valid and America was keeping the world safe for democracy, then why was the burden being borne so disproportionally?

George had only been in Vietnam for a little more than a week. Yet his life already had been permanently altered. He never would view things the same again. It would not be long before he would be bidding his father farewell and descending back into that hell called Vietnam. But there was a part of him that could not wait—wait to once again be reunited with Claire. After almost twenty-three years of life, how could so much have happened in a little more than a week?

On June 1, 1971, one day before he was to turn twenty-three years old, he saw his father off for home at the Amsterdam airport. Standing by a large window inside the terminal, he watched his father's plane take off and disappear into the blue afternoon sky, along with life as he had known it. As he did, he thought of the lifetimes he would be living before he saw his father, his family, and his home again—if ever.

When his father's plane finally had been totally absorbed into the peaceful blue heavens, George turned and walked away. It was time to meet his supposed double, the person the agency had found and groomed to impersonate him and travel through Europe in his stead. The young man had earned the nickname "Colorado" as a result of having trained there for the Olympics before an unfortunate injury abruptly ended his hopes of competing. Colorado bore a remarkable resemblance to George and had mastered many of his mannerisms. George felt he would do fine.

With that task behind him, the time had come to board Stewball. The modified KC-135 had been quietly sitting in wait at an inconspicuous spot on the tarmac to take him back—back to hell, back to Claire. As he boarded, Captain Herndon handed him a brown bag with a cheese sandwich, an apple, and a bottle of water in it and told him that Matt Kerr and John Sullivan Jr. were waiting for him inside. He immediately realized that there must have been significant developments while he was away for them to be on board.

– 12 –

By the time Anne Herndon had the big jet rumbling down the runway and defying the laws of gravity as it lifted off the ground, the three men were deep in discussion. Matt Kerr was explaining the latest developments in a raised voice and with a great deal of animation, in part to compensate for the loud roar of the straining engines, but more so because of his excitement. Apparently the letter had not been a provocation, and the Russian was correct in his assessment of his situation—his life was in danger.

From what Matt had been able to gather from the chatter being generated, the South Vietnamese had been able to piece together parts of what was happening, but not the entire story. The South Vietnamese knew from the leaks that the Russian was seeking asylum. They also seemed to have ascertained, notwithstanding the American effort to keep the mission secret, that the Americans were sending an envoy, who would be disguised as a priest, to rendezvous with the Russian in the coming months. They did not appear to know yet when this envoy priest would arrive or what his actual identity would be.

According to Matt, the Russians were searching for their man, who apparently had gone into hiding, but with only halfhearted help from the North Vietnamese, who seemed not to be particularly interested in the matter. More specifically, intercepted communications had indicated that Viktor Martynova, one of the more powerful figures in the Soviet hierarchy, had taken a very strong interest in the matter and was pressing Hanoi to find Alexei Buzinov and bring him back dead or alive. Furthermore, top secret U-2 flights over North Vietnam had photographed the arrival of several large Soviet transports, consistent with the deployment of a fully equipped special forces unit. This degree of attention and activity was unusual for the defection of an ordinary military adviser and was far more consistent with the loss of a high value subject.

Of even more of a surprise was the fact that a contingent in the South Vietnamese government of President Nguyen Van Thieu also was actively trying to locate the Russian before anyone else found him. From what the American embassy was hearing, back in 1963 the Russian had taken money from a rogue element within the South Vietnamese government of President Ngo Dinh Diem, as well as from a wealthy American industrialist, who had been acting in concert with them, to facilitate the assassination of President Kennedy. The South Vietnamese officials and their American cohort had become concerned at the time with rumors of an American pullback and thought that they would have a better chance at obtaining an American escalation of the war effort under a Johnson Presidency than they would under President Kennedy.

The regime of President Nguyen Van Thieu uncovered what had taken place and was searching for the Russian because they were concerned what the reaction of the American public would be if they were to learn of what transpired in 1963. But there was more—far more— that worried President Nguyen Van Thieu.

In October of 1968, only a month before the US presidential elections, there had been a possible breakthrough in the peace negotiations that were underway between the North Vietnamese and President Johnson's envoy in Paris. Richard Nixon, who was aggressively campaigning against Hubert Humphrey to succeed President Johnson in that election, fearing that his campaign might be harmed by just such a last-minute development, had established a secret line of communication with the South Vietnamese ambassador in Washington. The go-between was the widow of one of the Flying Tigers of World War II.

This woman, who had been born in China and had many connections all through Asia, had been made an adviser to the Nixon campaign. When she learned that a deal was in the works at the negotiations and then informed Nixon campaign officials about this, she was told to tell the South Vietnamese to reject the deal because a better one could be had under a Nixon administration. President Nguyen Van Thieu turned down the deal, and Mr. Nixon went on to win a close election victory. Matt Kerr knew it was true that President Nixon had worked to sabotage the peace negotiations in October of 1968 because on instructions from then President Johnson, the US had been wiretapping the telephone lines of the South Vietnamese ambassador and had learned of Mr. Nixon's subversive actions. Even though President Johnson never made public Mr. Nixon's efforts, in part because he did not want to admit to the illegal wiretaps, CIA sources investigated and confirmed the activities in question for Matt.

After he became president, Mr. Nixon instituted a painfully slow withdrawal of American troops while he pushed for Vietnamization of the war effort and sought peace with honor. Under this Vietnamization process, President Thieu had been the beneficiary of a massive build-up that had seen his army grow to more than one million soldiers, trained by the US and equipped with state-of-the-art planes, helicopters, weapons, and ammunition. Furthermore, US bombing of North Vietnam kept the North at bay and allowed Vietnamization to appear to be a success. Understandably, President Thieu was benefiting greatly from this turn of events and did not want to see it end any time soon.

By June of 1971, morale among American troops had dropped dramatically, and drug use had become widespread because many felt they were fighting, not so much to win, but to keep President Thieu's corrupt regime in power. The more cynical saw Vietnamization of the war and seeking peace with honor as nothing more than President Nixon attempting to obfuscate the inevitable loss of the war and to repay President Thieu for helping him win the 1968 election against Mr. Humphrey. It was not inconceivable to Matt Kerr that President Thieu was concerned that these revelations might hasten the time when the gravy train might come to an end, giving him a strong interest in preventing the Russian's defection from succeeding.

Of equal concern to Matt was the fact that Captain Chrisandra's life now also might be in danger. The South Vietnamese contingent was attempting desperately to learn the identity and arrival time of the envoy priest. If they could not stop the Russian, the alternative might be to stop the American envoy. Keeping Captain Chrisandra's identity secret had become an even higher priority in a country where money spoke loudly. The three men on the plane agreed that it would be best to make their move before June 15, 1971, since the South Vietnamese were under the erroneous impression that the envoy would not be arriving in Vietnam until later in the month.

The Russian was thought to be in the vicinity of Ha Long Bay, a beautiful area of Vietnam near the Chinese border, because that appeared to be where the Soviet special forces were concentrating their efforts. While Ha Long Bay was famous for its spectacular volcanic islands, it would be a difficult place from which to extract the Russian, especially if Soviet special forces were in the vicinity. Of even more concern was the fact that the Russian might panic and decide to seek refuge in China, thereby further complicating matters. All three men agreed that regardless of the dangers and difficulties, they had to act immediately, before anyone else got to their quarry.

The team got an unexpected but welcome break the next day when a contingent from COLIAFAM, the Committee of Liaison with Families of Servicemen Detained in North Vietnam, an anti-war organization, was on a visit in the North. One of its members was approached by a man who identified himself as a Soviet citizen and claimed that he was being pursued and in trouble. The COLIAFAM member described the man as being approximately forty-five years old, of medium to large build, and about five feet ten inches tall. He said the Russian begged for help and gave him a sealed envelope addressed to Sister Katherine Sullivan at the Orphanage of Saint Francis Xavier near Binh Gia.

The COLIAFAM member decided instead to bring the sealed envelope to the US embassy because he thought it might be some kind of a trick. Shortly after noon the next day, the member walked into the embassy and up to the Marine Duty Desk and handed the envelope to the marine on duty—Lance Corporal Christian Carter.

Christian immediately brought the envelope to Matt, who upon opening and reading it, called a meeting with Lieutenant Sullivan and Captain Chrisandra. The letter read

> Dear Sister Katherine Sullivan,
>
> I do not know if you got my previous letter, but I desperately need help. I have at my disposal very important information for your government. I wish to provide your government with this information in exchange for asylum in your country. So that they may know that I am genuine, I am enclosing personal material that belonged to the now deceased Mr. Pierce Cutler, the former chairman of Texas Amalgamated Industries, Inc., along with a copy of my US passport in the name of William Duxbury. I also am enclosing a cufflink with a helmet and sword on it. It was a gift to me from Viktor Martynova at the Kremlin and bears the inscription "Dallas Moon." I have the matching one, so that your people will be able to identify me. I will be carrying no other identification with me, other than my watch.
>
> I will travel to the following coordinates [redacted] by 0200h on June 9. It would be desirable to meet your people there at that time. I am actively being pursued and cannot remain in one place too long. To acknowledge this rendezvous, your people should place an advertisement in the Saigon newspaper on Sunday, June 6, offering an award of $300 for a missing West Highland white terrier dog named Pebbles. [Matt Kerr's assistant, Elise Colgate, had a Westie named Pebbles that

the Russian had observed her calling to and walking around by the embassy.]

I ask that in working with me your people observe all the rules of espionage trade craft and security and not permit any slipup. Please ask them to protect me.

A.B.

The decision was made. The mission would take place before first light in the early hours of the morning on Wednesday, June 9, 1971. A small force consisting of two helicopters, a spotter plane, and a C-47 gunship to provide limited air cover would rely on the element of surprise to preemptively snatch the Russian from his pursuers.

Stewball and Coney Island Baby would immediately be flown back to the United States. Stewball would be equipped with a full complement of electronic communication and listening devices and would serve as a flying command center from which Matt Kerr would oversee and direct the mission. It would be staffed by a CIA electronics team that had been handpicked by John Sullivan Sr., or Sully, as Matt liked to call him. Coney Island Baby would be equipped with an operating room, state-of-the-art medical devices, and a staff from the Bethesda Naval Hospital in Maryland that also had been chosen by Sully.

At 2303h on Friday, June 4, 1971, Stewball lifted off the runway in Saigon unnoticed. A tired Captain Herndon was at the controls. She was accompanied as usual by co-pilot Beth Baton and flight officer Diane St. Marie. They would refuel in Hawaii before heading on to the mainland. Five minutes later, at 2308h, Coney Island Baby would do the same, with Captain Carole Radcliff at the controls, accompanied by co-pilot Jan Tracy and first officer Lori Heatherton.

On Sunday, June 6, 1971, the ad for the missing Pebbles would run in the Saigon newspaper as requested. (Pebbles, having been pressed into agency service, went into hiding at an undisclosed location, only to be conveniently found a few days later, none the worse for the wear.) *The game was on.*

At the same time, in Virginia, Sully was dealing with a last minute glitch—there had been a high level objection raised to allowing Captain Chrisandra, as a chaplain, to be a full-fledged combatant. With few exceptions, chaplains traditionally have not been permitted to bear arms and participate as combatants. However, argued Sully, Captain Chrisandra was first and foremost a CIA operative, who had been trained as an airborne soldier and sent to Vietnam to act as such. His cover was that of a chaplain. He was in actual fact an ordained priest and could function as one should the situation dictate. But unlike other chaplains, he had not been sent to Vietnam with serving as a priest as his primary objective. The battle was heated and bloody, but in the end Sully prevailed. The game was on for Captain Chrisandra.

On Tuesday, June 8, 1971, both planes touched down on the runway in Saigon, fully staffed and equipped, in time for Operation Excalibur to begin the next day. John Sullivan Sr. had made it happen. *The game was on—really on.*

– 13 –

Upon his return to Vietnam, Captain Chrisandra came to stay at the orphanage. It was during this stay that I came to know and love this gentle but strong man. He brought with him no weapons in deference to Sister Claire, and he busied himself with repairs around the complex. I helped him paint and clear brush.

As young and as innocent as I was at the time, I could see the deep love and respect that existed between the two of them. Their faces would light up at the mere sight of each other, even if the separation had been only momentary. They would constantly touch and brush against each other, seemingly unconsciously, as they spoke and went about their ways. I do not think that they realized just how much they were telegraphing their feelings for one another.

There was a twinkle in Sister Claire's eye that I had not noticed before, and she sang and hummed as she went about her chores. He in turn beamed with content and whistled while he worked. Those days were short in number, spanning a little more than a week, but they were a wonderful time. I wish they could have lasted forever, but I am grateful for the short time that they did endure.

War has a way of accelerating and intensifying life. At any moment, a seemingly secure and peaceful oasis can be transformed into a living hell, with destruction raining down everywhere and the fog of confusion and chaos shattering what remains of order and tranquility. Where love and hope together with promise once flourished, all that is left is a trail of bloody carnage and twisted wreckage along with broken dreams in the wake of such destruction.

Sister Claire and Captain Chrisandra knew all too well this fragile state of existence—a world that could turn on a dime—and savored every moment of their time together. They were thankful for what they had, but unsure that fate would once again so bless them in the future—*She would not.*

What I had no way of knowing at the time is that Sister Claire and Captain Chrisandra had dared to tempt fate ever so slightly and had begun to plan for their future together—a future that would include me. They had begun to contemplate marriage, to dream of growing old together, of becoming soul mates that finished each other's thoughts for one another. They would adopt me, and I would become Mary Bernadette Angelson. Of course, I did not know Captain Chrisandra's true name at the time and thus knew nothing of the Angelson name. But I did know and love the man.

There was more that I did not know at the time. We were being secretly watched by that contingent of the South Vietnamese government who were betting that the Russian would come to the orphanage to seek asylum. They had managed to learn of the mysterious letter that had been delivered by the COLIAFAM member to the embassy, the one addressed to the deceased nun from the orphanage. Captain Chrisandra's presence with us, unarmed and performing innocuous chores, served to hold their attention while the Russian made his way to the June 9 rendezvous point. While the cat was watching an empty mouse hole, the mouse was far away making his escape. Mr. Kerr's intuition and unorthodox ways had once again proven to be correct. Leaking the arrival of the letter and stationing Captain Chrisandra at the orphanage had served to fool the Russian's pursuers. But more needed to be done in the way of creating a distraction, and Mr. Kerr felt he knew the perfect diversion. It not only would reinforce the Soviet's current thinking—they were convinced their man was in the Ha Long Bay area—it would serve to throw the South Vietnamese contingent (and the North when they inevitably were forced to become involved) off the defector's trail. He would first leak information about and then stage a diversionary naval extraction in the Gulf of Tonkin.

With each passing day, the Soviets increased the pressure they were placing on their proxies, the North Vietnamese, to help them find their man. While the North Vietnamese remained ambivalent on the issue, they finally capitulated to the arm twisting and assigned Captain Dam to hunt down the Russian. Captain Ton That Dam of their 325th Division was considered by Hanoi to be a rising star and one of their best and brightest officers. He'd come through for them once before, about two years earlier, when the Russian had gone missing. Sent to find him, Captain Dam had located the Russian and learned that he'd been bitten by a snake and nursed back to health by a nun at the orphanage. Secretly observing the ink on the Russian's thumb, he'd returned to the orphanage to ascertain that the nun was a CIA operative and eliminated her.

In 1969 Hanoi and the Soviets didn't want the American public to learn there were Russians fighting against their American forces in Vietnam. Knowing of this Russian involvement might hamper the sympathetic coverage Hanoi was hoping for from the liberal American press, a key element of their strategy to undermine American resolve. Russian participation exposed Vietnam as a domino in the global struggle between the super powers over the spread of communism, and worked against the image the North was attempting to foster that America was interfering in the internal struggles of a humble people to free themselves from colonial influence and become independent.

Once again mobilized in 1971 by Hanoi to apprehend the Russian, Captain Dam also dispatched a surveillance team to the orphanage. Ironically placing this team there would end up working to his detriment.

The need for the diversionary action in the Gulf of Tonkin had become more critical with the involvement of the North Vietnamese, and Matt Kerr decided to visit with his old friend Admiral Wheatley on the *USS Midway* to organize the event. It was agreed that on the night of June 8, the destroyer *USS Hollister*, DD–788, under the command of

Commander E. J. Handler, would sail close to Hon Me Island, a North Vietnamese military radar installation located three to four miles inside the twelve mile limit. The purpose would be to provoke a response from the 135th Torpedo Squadron of the North Vietnamese Navy, which provided protection for the island base. Simultaneously, fast patrol boats manned by South Vietnamese sailors would join in and attack the radar installations on the island. During the commotion that ensued, a Navy SEAL team would insert a bloodstained raft with the Russian's US passport in the name of William Duxbury and other identifying material and provisions. In advance of the raid, Mr. Kerr would strategically leak the rumor that the Russian was scheduled to be interdicted at that time and location and that the true purpose for the raid was to provide cover for the interdiction effort. If all went according to plan, the bloodstained raft would be found either by the North or the South Vietnamese patrol boats, and the Russian would be presumed to have been killed and his body lost at sea in the failed attempt to reach him.

When the North Vietnamese patrol boats approached within ten thousand yards of the *USS Hollister*, the destroyer called in air support and opened fire. The fighting was ferocious. Before it was over, the *Hollister* had fired over two hundred three-inch and five-inch shells, and fighter jets from the *Midway* had strafed the North Vietnamese boats, sinking one of them and damaging another. The North Vietnamese shelling was intense and alarmingly accurate, forcing Commander Handler to have to feverishly change course, constantly zigging and zagging to avoid having the *Hollister* be hit. The North Vietnamese rounds were consistently falling where the ship would have been, but for the young commander's evasive maneuvers. As it was, the *Hollister* did sustain minor damage. At one point a North Vietnamese torpedo exploded prematurely so close to the stern of the ship that her fantail momentarily lifted out of the water. The South Vietnamese boats had been able to inflict only minor damage on the radar installation, but more importantly, the Navy SEALs had been able to successfully insert the raft without being detected and with one SEAL suffering merely a superficial injury.

The diversionary attack was a partial success in that the Soviets and the South Vietnamese contingent were convinced by the discovery of the raft that the Russian had died in the failed attempt to rescue him. However, Captain Dam didn't take the bait. He knew better. He knew the Russian well and was aware that he couldn't swim and had a fear of the water. He was convinced that his quarry was further south and would try to return to the orphanage by traveling through Cambodia to avoid detection to meet the envoy priest, who he believed was Captain Chrisandra. He had a good idea of where to pick up the defector's trail, because he knew the route the Russian had taken in 1969. He planned to move quickly, but first he would confirm that his surveillance team was in place at the orphanage to monitor the Devil Priest's movements. It was imperative that he know if Captain Chrisandra left there.

– 12 –

Captain Chrisandra told us that he would be leaving after dinner on the night of Tuesday, June 8 to look at orphanage sites for his boys' orphanage. That afternoon I helped him pack his things. When we were finished, he sat on his bed and asked me to come and sit next to him. I did, and he whispered to me that he had something special for me. He then removed a Bible from his bag and gave it to me. As he did, he made me promise that I would not show it to Sister Claire until after he had left. I opened the cover to see the following inscription inside.

> Dear Mary Bernadette,
>
> I hope the wisdom in this book can bring comfort and hope to you until I return and throughout your life.
>
> Fondly,
> Captain JJ

(Sister Claire allowed us to call him Captain JJ.)

At dinner that night, Captain Chrisandra seemed more quiet and serious than usual. When we were finished eating, he took Sister Claire aside. When they thought we were not listening or watching, he told her that his travels would be taking him through some hostile and dangerous areas and that there was a chance that they could be captured or killed. He then kissed her, first briefly and gently, then more passionately and for what seemed an eternity to me. I did not think their lips ever would part, but eventually they did. Sister looked taken back by the extent of the kiss, but before she could speak, he said to her, "I promise you that nothing will stop me from returning to you for another one of those kisses. Please promise me that no matter what you may hear about me, you will hold true to that belief and not lose faith."

Her voice still somewhat weak from the kiss, she struggled to gather her thoughts and emotions as she attempted to react to his message. But at his insistence, she finally acknowledged his request and quietly said, "I promise."

With that, I decided to scurry back to the others before Sister and the captain saw me and realized that I had been observing them. Undetected, I rejoined my peers who hadn't noticed my being absent from them.

When Captain Chrisandra and Sister Claire rejoined the rest of us in the main room, he told us that the helicopter would be coming for him shortly, and he asked Sister that she and the girls please stay inside. If there were any Vietcong in the tree line, the helicopter would draw their attention and possibly some small arms fire. Sister agreed, and without further ado, Captain Chrisandra stepped out into the night, shutting the door behind him.

A few minutes later we heard the helicopter approaching in the distance, and I decided to show Sister the Bible that Captain Chrisandra had given me. As she read the inscription, it must have caused her to finally process the thoughts and emotions that had been swirling around in her head. The look of concern that came over her face told me that she had begun to realize that this trip that Captain Chrisandra was taking had to be more than to look at orphanage sites. It had to be something far more risky and dangerous. It had to be the mission that had brought him to Vietnam in the first place.

Throwing caution to the wind, she ran to the door and opened it. The blast of wind and noise from the landing helicopter rushed in as fast as she rushed out. Struggling against the elements, she was in time to see Captain Chrisandra run from the shadows and leap onto the helicopter, even before its runners had set down. He must have changed in the nearby shed that he always kept locked, for he was in battle fatigues, his face was camouflaged with dark paint and before he put his helmet on, she saw that he was wearing around his head the red and silver bandanna that she'd given him in Paris. He was armed with an M-16 rife and grenades—not what you would expect of an army chaplain going to look at orphanage sites.

The fears she'd been suppressing resurfaced with a vengeance. The demons that were wreaking havoc in the recesses of her mind, had been right all along. He indeed must have been one of her father's shadow warriors—a gladiator like her father and brother and not a man of the cloth like Father Drinan. But he'd sworn to her that he was a priest and would return to law school in three months to become an advocate for social justice like his role model. He'd told her he didn't want to lie to her again because it had been too painful. Had that, too, been a lie? She couldn't bear to think that it might have been.

Her emotions raged within her oscillating uncontrollably across the full spectrum of possibilities. She was angry—more furious than she'd ever been before, and she wanted to kill him. Yet she was terribly fearful. She was so worried for him and that she would lose him. She longed for one more chance to tell him of her deep love for him and wondered if she'd ever see him again. In the end, she simply fell to her knees, trembling and exhausted. She wept and wept and wept some more. When I came to the door, I saw her kneeling there, crying. Seeing me, she gathered herself, stood up and came to me. The helicopter had managed to drop off a box full of candy, cookies, and soda for us. Trying to be strong, she picked it up, and putting it under one arm, she put her other arm around me and said, "Come on, let's have a little dessert and get you and the others to bed. Tomorrow is another day." *But it would be no ordinary day.*

Captain Chrisandra didn't see Sister Claire outside the orphanage when he ran and jumped on the hovering helicopter. Nor did he have the chance to look back and see her fall down to her knees, weeping. This was fortunate, for if he had, he may have lost his resolve.

As Screaming Eagle sped away with Jon Trueblood and Samuel Lerner at the controls and Joaquin Arango back at his door gunner position, after having tossed out the box of goodies for us, no ground gunfire had been encountered. Inside the noisy, lumbering contraption, Lieutenant Sullivan, Captain Chrisandra, Christian Carter, Bo Hicket and Frenchie set about the business of finalizing their interdiction plans. Once on the ground at the landing zone, they would proceed north to the point of rendezvous with the Russian. Captain Chrisandra would show the Russian the cuff link, as planned, and wait for him to produce the matching one. The team would do a quick physical search and mental evaluation of the Russian, clean him up, and replace his uniform with an American uniform.

Defection can be a traumatic experience, and the concern among the team had been to assess and stabilize the Russian to the extent possible beforehand. Having him blend in with the others would draw less attention to him and help protect him.

Frenchie would don the Russian's clothing in an attempt to take on his appearance and would head west, as the Russian had been doing. The hope was that he would draw the defector's pursuers away from the team that would be heading south with their prize, back to the landing zone. Once he'd traveled a sufficient distance, he would bury the Russian's clothing and backtrack in a southeasterly direction to meet the others at the landing zone.

In the meantime, Christian and Bo would circle around to come up from behind on any North Vietnamese lying in wait to ambush the team upon their return with the Russian to the landing zone. They first would go east, then south, and then west to come up from behind any unsuspecting enemy.

Matt Kerr and the communications team would be high above in Stewball, monitoring the events. Beth Baton would be filling in for Anne Herndon as Captain and Diane St. Marie would be doing double duty as co-pilot and flight officer. The spotter plane (dubbed Sally

Plane), piloted by Anne Herndon, and the C-47 gunship, piloted by Jan Tracy, with Nadim Haddad doing double duty as co-pilot and gunner, would be airborne and available to be called in if needed. Coney Island Baby would remain on the ground in Saigon with its medical team, ready to receive, treat, and evacuate the wounded. Captain Carole Radcliff would be at the controls with Lori Heatherton doing double duty as co-pilot and flight officer. The backup helicopter, Headhunter, also would remain on the ground in Saigon should it be needed. Matt Kerr's lean, mean machine was ready to go.

If all went according to plan, the team, with their Russian prize in hand, would be back on board Screaming Eagle and heading home before the first light of dawn—beating Aurora to the punch.

The mission went as planned, without detection, and the team made contact with their target on schedule. The Russian bore the filth and stench of a man that had been on the run for days, without food or drink, and without any opportunity for even the most basic hygiene. And in his eyes could be seen the fear and paranoia that comes from being hunted like an animal. Dehydrated and starving, he nevertheless appeared to have his wits about him and asked Captain Chrisandra to show him his cuff link as he in turn produced his. When queried about the inscription on the cuff links, he was lucid in explaining that "Moon" was Viktor Martynova's code name for John F. Kennedy, who had promised that America would go to the moon, and "Dallas Moon" was Mr. Martynova's way of referencing the successful assassination attempt in Dallas. Rather than exhibiting any trauma, the defector showed visible relief to be free from the terrible stress he'd been under and to be in the hands of the Americans, protected, cleaned up, and in one of their uniforms, being treated like a human being again.

Frenchie, with great trepidation, put on the repugnant clothing the Russian had been wearing over his. He then set out in the same direction the Russian was previously traveling, leaving a sloppy trail behind him, as the exhausted defector had done. Once he'd gone the desired distance, he stopped by a stream, disrobed, buried the clothing, backtracked over the messy trail he'd been leaving, and disappeared into the night in the direction of the landing zone. Captain Dam's instincts were spot on, and Frenchie could hear the muffled voices and footsteps of his pursuers in the distance as they approached.

Christian and Bo started to circle back as instructed. They already had headed east, made the turn, and were heading south when Christian, who was in the lead, stopped short and started to step back cautiously, his eyes still riveted straight ahead. As Christian stepped back and into Bo, Bo quietly asked him what was wrong. Christian, the fear visible in his eyes, whispered in a shaky voice, "Cobra!"

Having grown up with snakes in South Carolina, Bo smiled to himself at Christian's reaction and took the lead, moving forward carefully with his red-filtered flashlight in one hand and his weapon in the other. He had taken only a few steps when he, too, recoiled in shock. In the red light, a hooded cobra rose out of the foliage a few feet in front of him. Its head stood above his knees, but shy of his belt buckle, and its eyes were fixed on him. Bo immediately recognized the distinctive hissing sound and could see the creature's tongue tasting the moist air between them. He estimated that the snake was approximately twice as long as his M-16 rifle and not to be reckoned with. Carefully retreating, with his weapon still pointed at the cobra's head, its huge fangs visible in the red light of the flashlight, he hoped that he would not be required to use his weapon and give away his position. He would not. Moving out in another direction, the two men resumed walking in combat mode, heel-to-toe, heel-to-toe, giving the nasty snake plenty of respect.

As Christian and Bo approached the landing zone, they moved stealthily, stopping often to listen. They could hear two voices talking quietly in a tree off to their left. Bo signaled to Christian that they would wait for an opportunity to surprise the two North Vietnamese. That opportunity came when one of the men climbed down to move his bowels. As the unsuspecting man squatted, Bo snuck up behind him with his combat knife drawn. He rammed his still very muscular arm around the Communist's head, stifling his mouth, and sliced his throat from ear to ear with the combat knife. There was no sound other than the man's bowels evacuating. A short distance away, Christian was climbing the tree. As the unsuspecting second North Vietnamese laughed and commented on the speed with which his comrade had done his business, Christian did the same to him. So quiet had the deaths been that all that could be heard was the dead man's blood dripping from the tree onto the foliage below.

Their work done, the two Americans would lie hidden and wait for the others to arrive.

– 15 –

Captain Ton That Dam prided himself on being a first class professional soldier. A firm leader of men, he could be ruthless when the situation warranted—a trait he considered to be one of his strengths.

He had come to resent the more than three thousand Russians that were operating within Vietnam. They, like the French and the Americans, were white devils, interlopers on the sacred ground of his ancestors. In his view, once there, they never would leave without a fight. However, he understood the need to tolerate them until their technology and aid no longer were necessary to fight the Americans.

He had especially come to dislike Alexei Buzinov. Having had to clean up after him in December of 1969, when his actions almost exposed the fact that Russians were fighting in Vietnam, he now had been ordered by Hanoi to track the man down and kill him if necessary. He was more than happy to oblige.

As Captain Dam and his men followed the Russian's trail west, they had crossed into Cambodia several hours earlier. Something seemed wrong to Captain Dam. Why was the Russian still heading west and not south toward the orphanage, as he had expected him to do?

He had stationed some men in the tree line near the orphanage to keep watch on Captain Chrisandra, the man he considered to be the Devil Priest and the contact the Russian was trying to reach for asylum. He decided, out of an excess of caution, to radio the surveillance team and confirm that Captain Chrisandra was still at the orphanage. The response he got was, "Yes, the American captain is still here and inside. The only activity in the last twelve hours occurred when a helicopter dropped off a package without actually landing. The nun came out, kneeled down to pick it up, and then went back inside. That incident took place at 2238h last night."

Captain Dam smelled a rat. Notwithstanding what his surveillance team had reported to him, his experience told him the facts were not what they appeared to be. Pulling out his map, he wanted to reconfirm the location of the nearest landing zone. It was behind them to the southeast, as he had thought. His men wanted to continue forward. They had lost the trail at a stream up ahead and were convinced the Russian was walking and wading up the stream. Captain Dam's instincts told him otherwise, and he ordered his men to head southeast with the utmost of haste to the landing zone. He already had sent two men there earlier as a precaution, and now he could not reach them on the radio. He suspected the Americans, those damn white devils, had a hand in it, but he had no concrete evidence of their presence in the area, at least not yet. He knew that if he was wrong and the landing zone was deserted, he would lose face with his men, but it was a chance he was prepared to take.

In the meantime, Lieutenant Sullivan had been keeping his group moving slowly but steadily toward the landing zone. Covering his trail as best he could, he and Captain Chrisandra methodically progressed with the exhausted Russian in tow. Then came a call over the radio from Matt Kerr. They'd intercepted a transmission from Captain Dam to his superiors advising them of his decision and the gamble he'd be taking. He received no response, so the team on Stewball concluded he had reversed course as planned and was now heading for the landing zone.

Matt Kerr's instructions to Lieutenant Sullivan were frank and brief. "Forget about covering your trail or taking other evasive measures. Get to the landing zone ASAP. I've ordered Screaming Eagle back in. That son of a bitch that is pursuing you has figured us out and we are wise not to underestimate him. He is good, and if he catches us with our pants down in Cambodia, it will be a diplomatic nightmare. I can see the newspapers now. 'US Kidnaps Soviet Diplomat and Tortures Him in Secret Camp Illegally Set up in Cambodia before He Is Rescued by North Vietnamese Soldiers.' Repeat, get to the landing zone ASAP."

Lieutenant Sullivan simply replied, "Roger."

He and Captain Chrisandra then put the Russian's arms over their respective shoulders and began carrying the almost limp body of the weakened man, who was virtually dead weight for them as they moved forward with all the speed they could muster. Lieutenant Sullivan estimated that they didn't have far to go, but it would be a challenge to beat the seasoned troops that now were following them to the landing zone. It was a race against time, and he told Captain Chrisandra it would be close—too close to call.

At the landing zone, Christian and Bo allowed themselves a moment to relax and let their guard down. Christian turned to Bo with a nervous laugh and said, "That was one big motherfuckin' snake back there. I came close to needing a change of underwear."

To which Bo answered, also now laughing, "I have killed snakes and gators back home since I was old enough to hunt, but nothing back home could prepare me for that son of a bitch. He reared his head as high as my belt buckle and had his eyes locked in on my balls. All I could think of was shit, what would I tell that sweet thing nurse Dee from Bethesda waiting on Coney Island Baby when she asked me where I was bit?"

Both men laughed as Christian noted, "If that fucker bit you, I don't think you'd need to worry about any of that. The only thing you would ever be in a position to screw again would be the body bag they'd be putting you in!"

As Bo was about to concede to Christian that he thought he was right, both men heard a rustling in the brush and readied their weapons as they shouted, "Who goes there?" It was Frenchie. He had cut the angle on his return and hadn't seen Lieutenant Sullivan and company on the way back.

As Lieutenant Sullivan and Captain Chrisandra were approaching the landing zone with the Russian, they could hear the muffled sound of the helicopter incoming in the distance. Captain Dam and his men had made up the distance between them and also could hear the approaching craft.

Supremely satisfied with himself for having guessed right, Captain Dam knew he had no time to gloat, or he would be left empty-handed as the olive green bird snatched his prize from him. Without hesitation, he ordered his men to attack.

Bo and Christian leaped to their feet and charged without regard for their own safety into harm's way, hopelessly outnumbered by the onslaught of attackers, passing Lieutenant Sullivan and Captain Chrisandra, who were scurrying in the other direction to get the Russian on board the landing helicopter. Bo and Christian knew the peril of their situation. They were facing a much larger force that was now too close to them to call in air cover. There was a pressure point, a narrow spot where the attacking enemy was vulnerable, and if they could hold them at bay there long enough to allow the helicopter to be loaded, they then could make a run for it with fire cover from the chopper. It was a desperate situation, but both men knew it was the best they could hope for and took it at great risk to themselves.

Jon and Samuel brought the Huey in under heavy fire, refusing to be denied. Joaquin was returning fire as best he could, but he didn't want to hit his own guys.

Bo was the first to be shot. He had been badly hit and was bleeding profusely. Frenchie, after helping Lieutenant Sullivan and Captain Chrisandra get the Russian safely on board the helicopter, rushed back to help bring Bo to the Huey. Christian held his position alone, holding Captain Dam and his men back until all were on board the helicopter. Captain Chrisandra called to Christian to break it off and make a run for it, and they would provide cover for him.

Christian ran for the helicopter, but just as he was about to jump on, he was hit in the back. Captain Chrisandra was able to pull him on board as the helicopter lifted off. The craft had taken a barrage of fire and the controls were sluggish, but Jon and Samuel were determined and managed to get the wounded bird airborne and on its way. Joaquin had his door gun blazing, but the real damage would be done by the C-47 gunship that was now swooping in for the kill as Screaming Eagle vacated the area.

Matt had ordered the strike by the gunship, not out of revenge, but in the hope of preventing Captain Dam from communicating with his base of operations. He had assumed correctly that in the heat of the battle, Captain Dam had not had a chance to inform his base that he had been correct, that the Americans were there, that they had retrieved the Russian, and that they had escaped by helicopter. Matt desperately was trying to preserve the element of surprise until the helicopter landed at the airbase near Saigon, and the Russian had been transferred to the waiting Coney Island Baby, for the flight from Vietnam to the United States.

Captain Dam, however, had been too smart to fall into that trap. He had studied the American devils and took great pride in knowing how they thought and behaved. As the helicopter lifted off, he ordered his troops to disengage and scatter for cover, as he, too, sought protection and called in to his superiors. He informed them that he had found the Russian, but not in time to prevent the Americans from retrieving him. He advised that he was planning to organize an attack at the airbase near Saigon. It would be a bold move to penetrate the heavily guarded base and pull off such a guerrilla attack right under the noses of the American Imperialists, but it would leave the Russian dead and no longer of any use to them. He assured them that he had the perfect man for the job and that it was the right time to activate him. If only he could be there to see the white devils' faces as he wiped away their smiles and snatched their victory from them at the very last minute.

The Vietcong had managed to infiltrate the base earlier in the war and had agents in place. The family of the man Captain Dam had in mind had been killed by an errant American bomb. The American devils had apologized and tried to make amends to him, but Lee Tang would have none of that, preferring to patiently wait for the day when he could return the favor. Accepting a job among them at one of their busiest bases, he knew his chance would come. Captain Dam smiled as the American gunship roared overhead, firing at where they had been but now were not, for he knew that Lee Tang's time had arrived and that the lonely, distraught man gladly would accept death to exact his revenge.

– 16 –

The wound Christian received punctured his vital organs and was far more serious than anyone at first realized. The bleeding caused him to lose a critical amount of blood. Despite the team's best efforts, it became clear to all on board the droning bird, including Christian himself, that he was not going to make it. His friend Captain Chrisandra, kneeling on the hard metal floor of the vibrating machine as it undulated with the pulsation of the overhead engines, cradled the stricken warrior's head in his lap, gently wiping his brow. As he did so, warrior now turned chaplain Chrisandra took off his helmet and put down his weapon. He reached into his pocket and removed a stole, which he placed around his neck, as well as a small canister of anointing oil and a pocket Bible, and set about the sad task of administering the last rites to his dying friend.

When he was finished, he reached for his canteen and attempted to give the expiring man a drink, but Christian waved him off and pulled him close to his mouth. Mustering the last breath he had left in his lungs, Christian asked his friend to promise that he would watch after his wife and soon-to-be-born son. Father Chrisandra, fighting back the tears welling in his eyes, made the promise without hesitation. It was an awesome responsibility that he would be undertaking, and he knew it, but it was the least that he could do for his longtime friend, now a true American hero. Leaning down again, George (yes, for it was George that was undertaking the lifelong obligation) whispered to Christian that there would be a condition attached to his promise—that condition being that he could turn young Christian into an Iona preppy and introduce him to the joys of wearing madras. Christian smiled his consent, squeezed his friend's arm with the very last ounce of strength he had left in him, and expired quietly as the first signs of the dawning sun could be seen on the eastern horizon.

A blanket was placed over Christian Carter's body as the remaining members of the team began the task of planning for their arrival at the large airbase. They all understood that the mission had not yet ended. The Russian sat silently as his future was being planned out for him. Bo tried to listen, but he was growing weaker and weaker from his wounds and found concentrating difficult. As his mind wandered and he gazed at the sunrise, he knew that he, too, was dying. He told himself that he would not live to see that same sun set.

Jon Trueblood interrupted to tell Lieutenant Sullivan that they had crossed the border and were back in Vietnamese air space. All on board breathed a sigh of relief, but none more than Lieutenant Sullivan himself. However, he knew that true peace of mind only would come when the Russian was safely out of Vietnamese air space and over the vast blue Pacific Ocean, headed for the good old U S of A.

The drone of the helicopter's blades began to fade into the background as Bo watched the sheer beauty of the dawn through the doorless opening on the fuselage and thought to himself that his demise was of little or no consequence to Mother Nature, who was promising her world, at least this part of it, another gorgeous day. Here he was, a mighty South Carolina Hicket, and yet nature was taking no notice of him and simply going about her business as usual. His blood, along with that of his Negro friend from New York, would be intermingled and indistinguishable on the metal floor of the helicopter, to be unceremoniously washed away, along with the other debris, when the fuselage floor was hosed down upon the craft's return to base.

A smile came to his face as Bo tried to guess where and how

his obituary would recount that he had died. He knew it would not be on a helicopter in Vietnam, and he was right. Bo would die later that day, five hours into the flight home, on Coney Island Baby over the Pacific Ocean. It would happen when the line on the monitor to which he was attached went flat, and the alarm sounded, despite the efforts of Dr. Julie Martin, head nurse Sandra Dee, and the rest of the medical team from Bethesda who had been working feverishly to save him.

Immediately upon his death, a damage control plan was implemented. The medical team replaced the Russian-made bullet that had killed Bo with a spent bullet from a hunting rifle that commonly was used in South Carolina and did their best to have Bo's wounds look consistent with a hunting accident. Once back home in South Carolina, his body was allowed to begin decomposing outside in the elements and to be partially eaten by animals indigenous to the area, so that any autopsy results would be inconclusive. John Sullivan Sr. dispatched an agency team to South Carolina to stage the accident, and their expertise and attention to detail enabled the ruse to be successful. Bo had used as the cover for his extended absence a prolonged hunting, fishing, and camping trip. So no one seemed surprised when his death was found to have been an unfortunate and tragic accident and reported as such in the newspaper.

The day of Bo's funeral was a beautiful day in Charleston, South Carolina; much like that day in Vietnam, when he had been fatally shot. That is, with one exception. At the apex of the ritual, there was a sudden downpour that went as quickly as it had come. There were those from the mission, including John Sullivan Jr., who upon hearing about it, were convinced it had been Mother Nature's way of letting Bo know that she had taken more notice of him than he had thought. Then again, such sudden, short-lived downpours were known to be somewhat common in South Carolina at that time of year.

A true unsung hero, his contribution to his country would be known only by those grateful few who had been with him and had benefited from his selflessness—his band of brothers.

From this day to the ending of the world,
But we in it shall be remember'd; We
few, we happy few, we band of brothers. For
he who today that sheds his blood with me
Shall be my brother ...
—William Shakespeare, Henry V

– 17 –

It had all been meticulously planned out by Matt Kerr. At a designated point over Vietnam, Anne Herndon would feign engine problems with Sally Plane, report her position, and crash land the spotter plane. The Huey with Lieutenant Sullivan, Captain Chrisandra, and the others on board would divert from its flight path back to Saigon and rescue the downed pilot. Jon Trueblood and Samuel Lerner would report encountering ground fire in attempting the rescue. Whatever casualties were incurred in Cambodia as well as any damage to the helicopter that was sustained in Cambodia would be attributed to the rescue in Vietnam and reported as such.

It was a brilliant plan, except for one small surprise. There was a contingent of four Vietcong in the area, unknown to the Americans, and they took Anne Herndon captive. As the rescue helicopter arrived on the scene, the Vietcong were running for the cover of the nearby forest with their catch—an injured Anne Herndon. There was no time to do anything but act and act quickly and decisively. If the Vietcong made it into the protection of the forest's tree canopy, the rescue would become almost impossible.

Jon and Samuel brought Screaming Eagle in low and hard. The battle-scarred Huey, weakened and riddled with bullet holes from the day's earlier encounters in Cambodia, strained and groaned to comply. But it did so and with flying colors, thanks to the dedication and professionalism of the General Dynamics engineers who had overengineered it and their fellow employees who had meticulously constructed it.

As the adrenaline-filled young pilots approached the rear guard of the Vietnamese running for the cover of the trees, they swung the big bird to the right, banking heavily to starboard. At the moment that the helicopter complied and banked away, Captain Chrisandra, with Lieutenant Sullivan behind him, leaped from the port side door opening as the pilots had the screaming beast flying so low that its starboard skid was practically skimming the ground.

As the two Americans hit the ground running, with their left feet first, they swung the butts of their M-16s at the two Vietcong, who had been bringing up the rear and had turned to confront them. Still propelled by the momentum of the helicopter from which they had come, the crushing blows from the rifle butts of the two attacking Americans sent the pair of unfortunate Vietcong straight to the next life. The remaining two Vietcong, looking over their shoulders and struggling to drag the downed American pilot along with them as they fled, were just in time to see the skulls of their two comrades explode from the blows of the rifle butts. Seeing those same M-16s turned around with the business ends now pointed at them caused them to jettison the partially naked and badly bruised pilot and run for the tree cover. One of the Communists had the misfortune of becoming entangled with the American pilot as he tried to make his escape. Not wanting to risk a shot with Anne Herndon so close by, Lieutenant Sullivan used his combat knife to slit the man's throat—no questions asked.

The Vietcong had been beating the downed American pilot to break her will and make her more submissive. They taunted and humiliated her by stripping off her clothing. She was the first female pilot they had seen, and they were planning to have a little fun with her when they were interrupted by the sound of the approaching American helicopter. They had assumed to their detriment that the incoming helicopter was a dust-off, a medical evacuation helicopter, and not one loaded for bear so to speak, as Screaming Eagle had been. And now there were three less Vietcong to show for it. The lone surviving Vietcong was nowhere to be found.

Anne was visibly shaken and trembling from her ordeal. Captain

Chrisandra took off his shirt and gave it to her. It was drenched in sweat and stained with the blood of Christian Carter and Bo Hicket, but she was grateful to have it. Her fingers were swollen from having been stomped upon by her tormentors. Frenchie, who had stayed with the Russian but now had joined the other two men, fumbled to help her button the shirt, apologizing that as a Frenchman his expertise was in romantically disrobing beautiful women, not in unceremoniously dressing them. As much as he tried to be the gentleman, his eyes could not help but notice the cigarette burns on the young woman's milk white breasts.

While Lieutenant Sullivan complimented the chivalry of his two companions, he barked that they all had better get their asses back on the helicopter, clad or unclad. He and Frenchie then put their hands under Anne's arms, being as gentle as the situation would allow, and carried her to the waiting Huey, which Jon Trueblood had set down in the clearing. Captain Chrisandra brought up the rear, walking backwards, his M-16 and his eyes fixed on the tree line. As he did, he thought to himself that that had been what Christian had been doing earlier in the day, when he had been killed. But this time there was no enemy onslaught, and when all were safely on board the aircraft, Jon Trueblood lifted it off and headed for the airbase at Saigon. The helicopter now was dangerously low on fuel, and Jon hoped they could reach their destination. Weary and tired, Screaming Eagle would not let them down, and both man and machine would make it back in one piece.

Once airborne, Samuel Lerner would report to base that they had encountered enemy resistance that they had been able to subdue in rescuing the downed pilot, but that they had suffered one loss in the process. An air strike on the crash site was then ordered to eliminate any remaining Vietcong activity in the area.

Upon his return to Saigon, Lieutenant Sullivan filed a report detailing Lance Corporal Christian Carter's acts of heroism. But the person being rescued was Anne Herndon, not the Russian. And the location given was the crash site of the spotter plane in South Vietnam, not the interdiction site of the Russian in Cambodia. As a result of John

Sullivan's report, corroborated by Jon and Joaquin (Samuel Lerner would not survive long enough to corroborate it), Christian would be awarded the Bronze Star and the Purple Heart posthumously. For obvious reasons, Captain Chrisandra, Bo Hicket, and Frenchie did not corroborate the report, although they would have liked to.

Christian Carter's remains would be flown home to the United States, where they would be interred with full military honors at Arlington National Cemetery. The land ironically had once been part of the estate of General Robert E. Lee, who had led the ill-fated fight for the preservation of the Confederacy and slavery in America. From his final resting place, on a crisp winter day, when the trees are bare, one can see the Washington Monument, the Lincoln Memorial and the Capitol.

– 18 –

Matt Kerr had carefully choreographed the steps to be taken by the team when they reached the airbase. The injured Anne Herndon, along with Christian Carter's body, would be removed first by ambulances. At that point all non-essential personnel would be cleared from the area and Bo Hicket and the Russian would be transferred to the waiting Coney Island Baby. The modified KC-135 would then depart immediately upon completion of the loading process and would receive a fighter escort out of Vietnam. Once it had been confirmed that the big jet transport had cleared Vietnamese air space, he would notify his good friend Sully at CIA headquarters in Langley, Virginia, that Operation Excalibur had been successfully completed.

Captain Dam, unfortunately, had other plans for the team. His man, Lee Tang, was in place and waiting when the helicopter returned. Once the wounded woman and the dead marine had been removed, Lee looked for his chance to strike as all non-essential personnel were asked to leave the area. Having carefully hidden from the watchful gaze of the young MP, his presence went undetected. Captain Chrisandra and Lieutenant Sullivan carried Bo. Frenchie helped the Russian from the helicopter. Jon and Joaquin remained on board. Samuel already had exited the craft and was standing in front and to the right of the cockpit, speaking to Nadim, who had come over from the C-47 gunship. Dressed in a South Vietnamese uniform, Lee Tang saw his chance. Stepping out of hiding and walking to the starboard side of the helicopter, he pulled the pin on the grenade, held it for a moment, and lobbed it into the group. Before anyone else realized what was happening or could react, Samuel threw himself on the grenade just before it exploded, sacrificing his life for his brothers. The force of the explosion caused his torso to momentarily lift from the ground as his blood and flesh were ripped asunder and scattered all around. Nadim was thrown to the ground and visibly dazed.

The Russian, realizing that if not for this heroic act by the young helicopter pilot, he might have been severely maimed or killed, turned to Lieutenant Sullivan to comment on the fact that this young American would have done something like that for him. Lieutenant Sullivan smiled politely and replied to the Russian that Samuel may have saved his life, but he had done it not so much for him as he had for his country, having been charged with the responsibility of returning him safely to America.

The Russian answered simply and humbly, "As one who has rarely been treated as a human being, I nevertheless am most grateful to him."

"Me too," answered John Sullivan with a warmer smile and a pat on the Russian's back. The group then carried Bo and helped the Russian to the waiting transport. Meanwhile, the MPs tackled and arrested Lee Tang and aided the still very much dazed Nadim.

Captain Chrisandra kneeled down and carefully rolled Samuel Lerner's body over. The young airborne soldier appeared to still be alive and semi-conscious, but barely so. Captain Chrisandra leaned forward to see if he still was breathing.

When he did, in a voice so weak that it was barely audible, Samuel asked, "I ... I have a confession to make. I'm ... I'm a homosexual and ... and I'm scared. Do you think ... think God ... God and my father will accept me ... accept me for who I am?"

Kissing the wounded warrior on his bloody forehead, Father Chrisandra whispered, "Do not be afraid. You are one of God's children. I pray He will bless you and receive you into His arms on the day of final judgment." He worded this with respect for Samuel's beliefs as a Jew, as he understood them from his earlier visit to the synagogue in

Newton with the Fox family, rather than his own as a Christian. "Your selfless and heroic act was one of pure love for your brothers. Tonight I know you will break bread with your father Jacob in the hall of heroes, for you have earned your place there beside him. You have made it in his world—you are a hero. My only wish for you is that you can find there the peace and acceptance that has so eluded you here."

A tear swelled in Samuel's eye, but before it could find its way down his cheek, he expired, and the blank stare of death overcame him. Father Chrisandra, with the fingers of his right hand, moist with the anointing oil he carried in his pocket, gently pulled down his fallen brethren's eyelids (or were they the "shutters" of which Adrienne Rich wrote?) as he pondered the life that just had passed, so ravaged by a world still intolerant and unaccepting of sexual preferences—*Sammy Lerner*, a son of Israel who always had given his mother a single yellow rose on Mother's Day.

For his selfless act of love, Samuel Lerner would be posthumously awarded the Congressional Medal of Honor and would be flown to Israel, where he would be buried alongside his father. Mrs. Lerner knew that she had married an exceptional man, and in giving birth to his son, should have known and I suspect did know that she had created another. She was proud of her heroes, and if she would have preferred an ordinary husband that grew old with her or a son that would marry a nice Jewish girl and give her grandchildren (or a rose of another color), she never let it be known.

The words of John's gospel rang true for the young priest. There is no greater love that one man can have for another than to lay down his life for him.

– 19 –

In the days following the successful completion of Operation Excalibur, Captain Chrisandra returned to the orphanage. At first Matt Kerr objected because he was concerned for Captain Chrisandra's safety. However, he relented when an intercepted radio transmission revealed that Captain Dam had been recalled to Hanoi.

Apparently the Soviet special forces had returned the US passport of William Duxbury to Viktor Martynova along with other items found in the bloodstained raft, and they had convinced the Soviet titan that his man—Alexei Buzinov—indeed had perished attempting to defect. However, he was angry that the North Vietnamese had not done more to help his special forces, which might have resulted in the Russian being retrieved alive before he had gotten as far as he did. As a result, Captain Dam apparently was being recalled to explain why he had failed to cooperate more fully with the Soviets and chose instead to go on a wild goose chase into Cambodia. It seems that everyone from the Soviets to the North and South Vietnamese had been convinced that the Russian was killed in the Gulf of Tonkin altercation and that the American helicopter was damaged and its crew injured and killed attempting to rescue the female pilot in South Vietnam. Even Lee Tang, Captain Dam's man, upon being questioned by the MPs and their South Vietnamese counterparts, said he had not seen any disheveled man in a Soviet uniform, but only uniformed American soldiers before he tossed the grenade. The Russian had been extracted from Vietnam and was being brought to the United States without anyone, including Viktor Martynova, knowing that he was still alive and a threat to those trying to keep secret what really had taken place in Dallas on November 22, 1963. Matt Kerr's unorthodox ways once again had produced an outstanding result.

It also became known from that same intercepted radio transmission that the sentries posted by Captain Dam remained under the impression that Captain Chrisandra had not left the orphanage and was still there. Wanting to take advantage of that misimpression, Matt arranged for Captain Chrisandra to be disguised and snuck back into the orphanage late at night. The clever subterfuge had been successful, and the sentries did not notice his return. When queried by Captain Dam in another transmission the next day, they reported that Captain Chrisandra still was at the orphanage and had never left. Of this they were certain, because that very morning they had seen him going about his chores as usual. The fact that they had not actually seen him the prior two days did not concern them, so sure were they of themselves.

It was a bittersweet time for all concerned at the orphanage. Sister Claire had already revealed to us that she had made the decision not to take her final vows and that when her replacement could be arranged, she planned to return to her home in California. On the one hand, I was happy and excited because she had confided in me that she planned to try and adopt me. Sister Kate had wanted her family to adopt me before she was murdered. And Sister Claire took a special liking to me the first time we met. I reminded her of her deceased sister. On the other hand, it was hard to know that I would be leaving the other girls behind and most likely would never see them again. I understood that there was only so much that Sister could do. What made it hard was that I had lived almost my entire life with these girls, and they were like a family to me. But in the short time that I had known her, I had come to love Sister Claire like a mother, and I knew I could not bear to be separated from her. So when she gave me the choice, because she had told me that the choice could only be mine, I chose to be adopted.

Captain Chrisandra and Sister Claire had been like two bees at the end of summer, frantically trying to make the most of their dwindling time together. One night, after we had been put to bed, he and Sister went for a walk. Sitting under the tree where they first made love, he put his right arm around her and gently stroked her hair and face with his left hand. As he did, he said softly to her, "I promised you once that I never would lie to you again. Do you remember?"

"Yes," she answered.

"I have not kept that promise, not because I did not want to, but because I could not."

"I understand. You do not have to explain any further. I know you are one of my father's shadow warriors. I am not happy about it, but I have come to accept it."

"How do you know that?" asked the surprised Captain Chrisandra.

"I saw you leaping onto the helicopter the other night in full combat gear. I don't know where you were going, or what you were doing, but I am sure of one thing, and that is that you were not going to look at orphanage sites."

"Well, for the most part you are right," answered Captain Chrisandra. "I cannot tell you what I was doing, nor can I tell you where I was going, but it was not to look at orphanage sites. However, you are wrong about one thing. I am not one of your father's shadow warriors, as you put it, at least not any longer. The assignment that brought me to this place is now finished, and I will be leaving soon."

"Honest?" asked Sister Claire.

"Honest," replied Captain Chrisandra.

"So, when you leave the day after next, you really are going to look at an orphanage site?"

"No. I have been given permission to explain that my being Captain Chrisandra and searching for orphanage sites has been part of my cover. I will be leaving to return to my travels in Europe as I was doing when we first met and to being whom I really am—George B. Angelson, the guy who fell in love with you the first moment he saw you. Shortly, Captain John J. Chrisandra will go missing, never to be heard from again. Have you been able to follow everything that I have been saying?"

"Yes, I think so."

"Good."

"But wait one minute," she said as she abruptly stood up. "Then what happens to me and my relationship with the man with whom I have fallen in love?"

"That is why I have brought you here in the first place—to ask you to marry me."

Before Sister Claire could say anything, Captain Chrisandra knelt down on one knee, took Sister's hand, and asked, "Claire darling, will you please marry me—George B. Angelson—the hopeful lawyer to be that met you on the flight to Europe last month?"

"Oh, George, of course I will. I love you so much!" she exclaimed as she kissed him and hugged him.

He felt as if he were standing on air. He was so happy as he kissed her and returned the embrace.

Then she interrupted their loving exchange to ask, "Is it okay if we adopt Mary Bernadette?"

"Of course, why not? You know, I have grown extremely fond of that little girl."

"I know. I could tell from the inscription in the Bible that you gave her."

"I tell you, Claire, I think that imp already has me wrapped around her finger. When she went with me to Saigon, we saw a flashy new silver and red Mercedes SL, and she informed me that when she becomes a famous California movie star, she's going to get one. And what is worse is that I found myself saying okay."

Laughing, she resumed hugging and kissing him as she whispered, "You are such a wonderful man. I cannot believe how lucky I am to have met you. If I were to die tomorrow, it would be with a smile, for I already have had a blessed life."

Those words would live in George's mind, haunting him for years to come as he struggled to cope with the blame he placed on himself for having been the cause of her death.

As they walked back to the main building of the orphanage, he told

Sister that he could not wait for the day when he would be reunited with her and me in the United States. He then kissed her with great passion for quite a long time and afterward told her he would be coming to California the first chance he could for another one of those kisses. As she was recovering herself, he once again asked her to promise that she would tell no one, not even me, of what he had told her. She promised him, a promise she would die trying to keep for him.

On Friday morning, June 18, 1971, Captain Chrisandra came into my room, tiptoeing so as not to wake me, and gave me a good-bye peck on the cheek. Not realizing at the time that I never again would see him, I pretended to be asleep. If I had known then what I know now, I would have jumped up and hugged him and never let him go.

At the airbase, Stewball was fueled and ready to leave. Anne Herndon had recovered from her ordeal and was at the controls when the big bird lifted off the runway at 0813h on that Friday morning. The manifest indicated that there were no passengers on board. In reality, Captain Chrisandra was sitting alone, in the back, the only light in the dark, empty cabin coming from the window next to his seat. Saddened to be leaving, he sat alone in his thoughts. What he did not realize was that by special arrangement, Anne had been granted permission to fly over the orphanage as she climbed slowly to her assigned altitude. While she executed a slower and steeper turn than usual, her voice came over the intercom, telling Captain Chrisandra to look out the window. Her special maneuvers afforded him a clear view of the orphanage, and he could see Sister Claire reading to us in the front yard. Too high for us to appear to him as anything more than specks, Captain Chrisandra did not care. His imagination already filled in our features, with all their grace and beauty, just as he had committed them to memory.

As Stewball cleared Vietnamese air space at 0831h, he officially ceased to be Captain Chrisandra and returned to being George B. Angelson. At that time, he thought he would never return to either that identity or that place. But he would return to both, and with a vengeance, sooner than he ever could have imagined.

On Sunday, June 20, 1971, Captain Chrisandra was officially reported missing when he failed to show for his appointment at a proposed building site for the orphanage. A search was conducted, but he was never found. Sister comforted me and told me not to worry, that he most likely was captured and would be returned as a POW after the war was over. She said she wouldn't be surprised if he turned up in California looking for us some day. I suspected that she might know more than what she was telling me, but I was content to leave things alone.

– 20 –

On Wednesday, June 23, 1971, George arrived in Agropoli, Italy, a beautiful Mediterranean seaside community. He was there to visit with relatives on his father's side of the family. He weighed only 135 pounds, considerably less than what he had weighed when he left New York in May.

In the warm bosom of his hosts, George slowly began to adjust to civilian life once again. He viewed pictures of his relatives and visited the house where his grandfather had lived before leaving everything behind for the promise of a better life in America. He frequented the store his relatives owned to pick out a pair of sunglasses, and he ate copious amounts of homemade pasta. The love being showered on him by his relatives helped mitigate the pain he was feeling, but that pain never completely left him.

Ordinary men, peace-loving souls who have had to viciously take human life and who have had to watch it be taken up close and dirty in answering their country's call to duty, unless they are insane to begin with, require time to adjust and regain their peacetime equilibrium. George was no different, and he spent hours swimming alone in the warm, tranquil, blue waters of the Mediterranean, trying to once again find his inner peace. He sat for long stretches on the beach, examining and reliving every last detail of his part in Operation Excalibur: Pulling Christian onto the helicopter as his body was being ripped apart by incoming fire. Cradling his friend's head in his lap as the man died never having known his son. Watching the life slowly slip away from his instructor Bo as the old soldier lay bleeding on the floor of the helicopter. Seeing Sam Lerner's body recoil from the force of the grenade blast and still recalling the feel of his friend's blood and tissue as it splattered his face in a burst of violence. Witnessing an enemy's head explode in front of him from the impact of his rifle butt, the result of his premeditated action. Seeing the precious blood shed by his friends being unceremoniously washed from the floor of the helicopter in which they had suffered and died, by a ground crew using an ordinary garden hose as part of a routine post-op cleanup of the craft. And then there was the hooded cobra—had it been angry? Or had the serpent been trying to warn Christian and Bo—the two to be fatally wounded on its turf in Cambodia during Operation Excalibur—not to upset history by bringing the Russian's involvement in the assassination to light? Tortured so was George's mind.

There in front of him on the beach were beautiful young women and handsome men in their prime, frolicking whimsically and carefree in the bright sunshine, their bodies tan, wet, and glistening, firm and sculptured, not yet having experienced the ravages of time and age. Some of the men looked like they could have posed for Michelangelo when he was sculpting his *David*. Many of the women wore thongs and nothing more, proud to display their charms.

What should have been beautiful to behold and appreciate had been twisted by his experiences and now raised painful images and memories for George. The beautiful tan breasts of the topless young women, while exciting and attractive, brought with them memories of Anne Herndon, standing dazed and helpless, bruised and naked, her womanhood having been scarred by cruel and senseless burns from a cigarette butt. The breathtaking Mediterranean sunset that had been unfolding before his eyes, although magnificent, conjured up thoughts of the dying Bo wondering if he would live to see that day's sunset. Then there was the guilt at having survived when the others had not. Tortured, he wished that those who had been through the mission with him and who would understand what he was experiencing could be there with him. They remained back in Vietnam, still very much living the experience.

Before the sun would have a chance to set three more times, George, too, would be back in Vietnam, living the experience in true gladiator form as Captain Chrisandra, killing more viciously than he had before. The mild-mannered George with the heart of a dragon slayer, having been sufficiently provoked by Captain Dam, would be a force with which to contend as he would slay the vicious North Vietnamese dragon and extract revenge for what he had done to us—for we also were now victims of Operation Excalibur.

After a wonderful lunch with his relatives on the breeze-swept veranda of their magnificent home high on a cliff overlooking the beautiful Mediterranean and the family's olive groves, George bid them farewell. The date was Friday, June 25, 1971, and he would board a train to Battipaglia, where he would switch to a train headed to Rome. From Rome he would travel to Nice and the Rivera.

When George exited the train in Rome, he was surprised to see Anne Herndon there waiting for him. He could not imagine why she would be there. The moment she saw him, she no longer could maintain her composure and began to weep. George knew it couldn't be good, but he had no idea how bad it would be.

While George was enjoying the warm hospitality of his relatives, Captain Dam, upset as a result of being reprimanded by Hanoi and still believing Captain Chrisandra to have had a part in the incident, came looking for him at the orphanage. Not finding Captain Chrisandra there, he tortured, raped, and murdered Sister Claire and buried us girls alive, one by one, with me going last, in an attempt to learn the whereabouts of the Devil Priest.

Captain Chrisandra's exit from Vietnam, like that of the Russian, had successfully gone unnoticed, and Captain Dam's spies had told him that there was no indication that the US Army chaplain had left the country. Angry and skeptical, Captain Dam refused to believe the story of the American's disappearance, the same as he had refused to believe the conclusion that the Russian had been lost in the

Gulf of Tonkin altercation. With an intense desire to capture the troublesome priest and find the true whereabouts of the Russian, Captain Dam had awakened a sleeping dragon slayer, something he would live to regret as he the hunter would become the hunted and be relentlessly pursued.

– 21 –

Sister Claire awoke earlier than usual on the morning of Wednesday, June 23, 1971, the last day of her young life. It was the same day that George arrived into the welcoming arms of his relatives in Agropoli, Italy, a half a world away. She felt an unexplained sense of urgency to get going with her tasks. Stepping outside to begin her day's chores in the yard, she gathered her tools, comprised mostly of shovels and clippers, into the waiting wheelbarrow. She and her loaded apparatus rumbled and clanged along only a short distance when Captain Dam and his men came into view and approached her.

Captain Dam, dispensing with formalities barked, "Where is the Devil Priest?"

"I don't know what you mean," answered Sister, feeling somewhat intimidated by his demeanor.

"I mean Captain Chrisandra; where is he?"

"I don't know."

Grabbing her by the back of the neck, he said in a gruff voice, "I am not one to be trifled with, as you will soon find out if you continue to deny me." Ordering his men to go into the orphanage and gather the girls into the front yard, he smacked Sister across the face with such force that she was knocked down to the ground.

At the time there were thirteen of us at the orphanage. All of us had still been sleeping and were dragged from our beds, confused and scared. He ordered his men to rip off our nightgowns and tie our hands and feet with the remnants. He then had us lined up in a row facing him and Sister in the front yard.

Sister was beside herself when she saw this unfolding and began to shake she was so upset. She shouted at him, "You animal, why are you doing this? Are you crazy?"

Ignoring her, Captain Dam ordered his men to begin digging a long trench behind us with the shovels from the wheelbarrow. Turning his attention to Sister once again, he yelled, "I will ask you one more time, where is Captain Chrisandra?"

Apprehensive for our well-being as we stood there naked in front of her, shivering and whimpering with cold and fear, she broke her promise to her shadow warrior and lover, because she knew in her heart he and her father and his agency would have agreed and told Captain Dam all that she knew. "He has left Vietnam and is in Europe—Italy I believe—with no plans to return here. That is all that I know, I swear!"

"You're a liar. I'm told by my sources that he hasn't left Vietnam. I've had enough. Now you will be taught a lesson." Dragging her with him behind the shed, he smacked her several times until her lips were bleeding and her eye was swollen. Convinced that she now would be submissive, he tore off her clothing and had his men hold her down as he raped her. He then invited each of his men to do the same. Sister Claire tried to pray for strength and to focus attention elsewhere, but the repeated penetrations by the line of men began to tear at her insides, and the pain became unbearable. She screamed with every thrust and looked with dread at the line of remaining soldiers, standing with their pants undone in anticipation of their turn. Bleeding from the damage being done to her and exhausted from the pain and screaming, she finally was rendered unconscious by the ordeal.

Captain Dam then had her limp, naked body dragged back to the front yard, where her wrists were tethered to two trees, leaving her hanging upright by her arms, facing the terrified row of us. Her face was visibly bruised, swollen, and bleeding from the beating she had sustained, her arms bore the marks from being held down by the men, and there was a steady trickle of blood mixed with semen running down her leg from her ravaged vagina. She then was revived and given a salt pill and some water, but nothing more.

The sadistic captain next walked over to the wheelbarrow, picked up a pair of pruning shears, and began to menacingly caress her breasts with the point of the shears as he again asked her where Captain Chrisandra was. Suddenly, Kim, the first girl in the row and the one closest to Sister, tried to run—but because her feet were bound, could only hop—to Sister's protection, yelling, "No! No! No! Don't do that!"

As she struggled desperately to close the distance between her and Sister, she fell on her face before she could get there. Whereupon Captain Dam ordered one of his soldiers to grab her by her long, jet black hair, drag her back to where she had been standing, and throw her in the trench. Kim yelped in agony as her tender body was indiscriminately scratched and punctured from being dragged over the rough terrain. Her scalp burned with pain from being pulled by her hair. When Kim was tossed into the trench, the girl next to her panicked and tried to run, but one of the other soldiers swung his shovel at her, smashing her in the chest and sending her flying backwards into the trench.

Sister Claire, still dazed and only partially conscious, begged for them to please stop. But they would not. One by one, down the line, each girl was pushed into the trench, screaming with fear and the hurt from not being able to break her fall, while Sister continued to plead for Captain Dam to order a stop to the actions of his men. Finally, he did, when I was the last girl standing.

Turning to Sister Claire, with the shears still in his hand, he asked, "Are you ready to tell me where Captain Chrisandra is?"

"Yes! For God's sake please believe me when I tell you that George is in Europe and not here any longer. I think he is in Italy, and he has no plans to return. That is all that I know!"

Captain Dam became increasingly frustrated with Sister Claire's answers. He could not believe that his methods were failing him. He also had begun to think that Sister might be losing her senses, because she was now calling the army chaplain by the strange name of George.

He knew he had one ace left, and that was me, the last girl standing by the trench.

Putting down the shears, he drew the ceremonial sword he wore on his side and walked over to me. Looking at Sister, he said, "This is your last chance before I impale your little girl." I was terrified—so terrified that I could barely stand or see straight, I was trembling so much.

Sister screamed in a distraught voice, "What is the matter with you? I have told you the truth—everything I know. Why won't you listen? George is gone, never to return!"

Captain Dam roared back at her, "I don't care about this George; where is Captain Chrisandra that is what I want to know?"

"He doesn't exist, you fool!"

Angered beyond control, Captain Dam thrust his sword into my unprotected abdomen and lifted me into the air, impaled on the horizontal blade. As he held me over the trench, the weight of my body caused the sharp edge of the sword to rise up my stomach toward my chest as I slid down the sides of the blade. The pain was blinding, and I could no longer see or think clearly. Only blurred images were registering as I struggled, but for what—I knew not.

Not wanting the blade to puncture my heart or lungs and end my deathly journey too quickly, Captain Dam tilted the point of the sword downward and watched me slide off and into the trench below. The pain was excruciating as I lay there face up. I could make out Sister's voice calling for me to be brave and pray. Dirt began to fall on me as Captain Dam's men began to fill in the trench. I and the other girls could hear each other groaning and sobbing, unable to scream or cry, until one by one we went silent.

At that point Sister Claire was totally spent and barely conscious. Her reason for fighting on had been buried with us. She no longer cared what this evil man did to her. When he once again picked up the shears and touched her with them, she hardly flinched. Rather, she mustered all the strength and determination she had left within her, lifted her head to look directly at him, and defiantly proclaimed, "Go ahead and have your sadistic pleasures with me, you pathetic little pervert."

Looking to the image of her Lord, naked and bleeding on the orphanage crucifix for inspiration, she continued, "You may be able to mutilate my chest or puncture my heart, but you never will be able to stop me from giving the love they hold within them to those I choose. Nor will you ever be able to take from me that which truly defines me—my soul! So go ahead and have your fun, but be careful what you seek, for you may get your wish and find your 'Devil Priest'—when my brother and my Prince George come calling. And they will! For they will not be able to let what you have done here today stand unanswered."

Thinking that she had totally lost her mind, Captain Dam put the shears down without using them and told his men to prepare to move out. When the trench finally was filled, they departed the orphanage, leaving Sister Claire to die slowly, tethered to the two trees.

The next day, Thursday, June 24, 1971, when John Sullivan Jr. and a group of his marines came to check on the orphanage, they found the carnage left by Captain Dam. Sister Claire was dead, still tied to the two trees, her body partially eaten by scavenging animals. John Sullivan Jr. wept openly as he cut his younger sister's body down—by far the most difficult thing he had ever had to do.

The marines with him, all of them combat-seasoned and battle-scarred, nevertheless became ill as they dug up the body of one lifeless little girl after another until all thirteen of us had been recovered. The next day, Friday, June 25, 1971, we were given a proper burial in the small graveyard at the orphanage. We had all been dressed in clean, new, white dresses, bought with money donated by the marines who had dug us up.

Earlier that same day, Sister Claire's body had been flown to California for burial beside her sister in the Sullivan family plot. John Sullivan Jr. would not accompany his sister's body home. He had unfinished business to attend to that required his immediate attention. He would be joined by Captain John J. Chrisandra, who would return from Europe on Stewball and slip back into Vietnam unnoticed.

The Devil Priest had come back to harvest Captain Dam's soul—not for God, but for the Devil.

– 22 –

When Alexei Buzinov was brought to CIA Headquarters in Langley, Virginia, he stopped to read the saying enshrined on the lobby floor at the entrance. It read "And ye shall know the truth, and the truth shall make you free." He wondered to himself as he was ushered along if the people he was about to meet would be able to handle the truth of what he was about to tell them. They would, but to varying degrees, some more than others. However, there were several bureaucrats within the agency that were so upset with what he had to say, because it contradicted the advice they had been giving to their government, that they wanted to return him to the Soviets, which surely would have resulted in his demise. Fortunately, John Sullivan Sr. was not one of them. The ex-marine took seriously everything that the Russian had to say, having come to trust him, albeit guardedly.

Alexei had been given a new identity by the CIA. He now was Russell Pulton, or Russ Pulton, and he would remain so for the rest of his life. All involved were instructed to start referring to him as such, and they did.

Russ Pulton provided the CIA with a wealth of information over the next several days. This information covered topics that spanned Captain Dam's whereabouts, Soviet involvement in the Vietnam War, the fate of South Vietnamese spies sent to the North to gather information, the fate of a downed American pilot, and Soviet involvement in the assassination of John F. Kennedy—the first being the most urgent, as far as Lieutenant Sullivan and Captain Chrisandra were concerned, and the last two being of utmost importance to the agency as a whole.

While Russ Pulton was meeting with the senior Sully on Thursday, June 24, 1971, word came from Matt Kerr and John Sullivan Jr. of the massacre at the orphanage. Sully had to excuse himself to be with his wife and family, as they grieved the loss of their second daughter.

John Sullivan Jr. had told his father that Captain Dam left a message at the scene for John Chrisandra, taunting him for having hidden behind a nun's habit, and challenging him to show himself. He told his father that he wouldn't be coming home for the funeral and to please smooth things over with his mother. Intercepted North Vietnamese radio transmissions indicated that Captain Dam had once again been recalled to Hanoi, presumably to explain the basis for his actions, but this time he had failed to show. The North Vietnamese seemed not to be sure of Captain Dam's whereabouts and appeared to be searching for him themselves. The young marine explained to his father that his reason for not coming stateside was because he had pressing unfinished business there. Both men knew the exact nature of that business, and the father ended the conversation by admonishing his son to please be careful, that his mother could not survive having to bury a third child in less than two years.

His son's reply was simple and direct and spoke volumes. *"Semper Fi."*

As the senior Sully hung up the phone, he whispered under his breath, *"Semper Fi."*

As distraught as he was, Sully forced himself to return the next day, Friday, June 25, 1971, to meet once again with Russ Pulton to see if he could shed any light on Captain Dam's motivation and whereabouts. Russ Pulton, after expressing his sympathies, explained that to figure out Captain Dam, the motives underlying his actions, and his possible current location, it would be helpful to first understand certain of his formative experiences and three myths surrounding the origins of Vietnam, and also to become familiar with the Ha Long Bay area from which the Captain had come, especially two grottos in that bay. These experiences, myths and environmental influences all drove his thinking.

Some of the agency questioners who had been working with Russ Pulton while the senior Sully excused himself to be with his family were growing impatient with what they perceived to be ramblings on the part of the Russian. However, Russ Pulton pressed his point, insisting that he had spent a great deal of time with Captain Dam, and that the North Vietnamese Captain was a complex personality that only could be fully appreciated in context. Sully was inclined to agree, but before doing so, commented to Russ Pulton that he was surprised to hear that Captain Dam was from the Ha Long Bay area, that from his experience in Vietnam back in 1945 following World War II, he would not have associated a name like Ton That Dam with that region. The Russian smiled and said, "Precisely my point. Even the man's name is not what it might appear because it is not his true name. He changed it for reasons that I will get into with you." With that, Sully said, "Fine, please proceed."

Turning first to the mythic origins of what now is Vietnam, Russ said that according to ancient teachings, Lac Long Quan, an emperor who is reputed to have descended from the dragons of the sea, married Au Co, a goddess from the mountains. Their union produced one hundred sons, who settled in the mountains and by the sea and had many descendants who became the Vietnamese people and now carry on the blood line. For this reason, the Vietnamese people, including Captain Dam, consider themselves to be the children of dragons and goddesses that continue to aid and protect them.

In 111 BC, the Chinese invaded what is now Vietnam, and their occupation continued for more than one thousand years, until 939 AD, when Ngo Quyen was victorious over them in a battle on the Bach Dang River. Starting in the sixteenth century, merchants and missionaries came to what is now Vietnam from Europe. They were mostly French Catholic missionaries who tried to impose their religion and culture on the Vietnamese. When they encountered resistance, they ultimately were successful in urging the French government to conquer and colonize Vietnam, which the French did in the late 1800s. One of the early heroes of the anti-French movement was Ton That Thuyet.

At this point the CIA staff began to once again grow restless. They didn't need the Russian to give them a lesson in the history of Vietnam. But Sully asked them to please allow the man to continue, so in deference to him they did. Russ then proceeded to tell them that Captain Dam was the product of a Chinese father and a Vietnamese mother who had never married. His mother had come from Ha Long Bay, a beautiful area of spectacular volcanic islands along the coastline of Bai Chay Beach in the Gulf of Tonkin. It was to this place that Captain Dam would return as a young man, become a Communist, and join the People's Army.

Russ then went into the second myth, the one surrounding this magnificent place from which the Captain's mother had come and to which he had returned to find himself.

Russ leaned forward to take a drink from the water glass that had been provided for him. He began to speak as he placed the glass back down. The story is told, he said, that in ancient times, when the forefathers of today's Vietnam were fighting a foreign invasion from their north, the gods had a family of dragons descend on what is now known as Ha Long Bay to help them. These dragons spewed gems, which, upon splashing into the water, became the islands that now act as a defense against attackers. The dragons, it is said, grew to like this tranquil place so much, that they decided to stay and become a permanent part of it. The mother dragon became what is now Ha Long, and her babies became what now is known as Bai Tu Long, with their tails forming the part of Bach Long Vi that today is renowned for long stretches of white sandy beaches.

Turning to Sully, Russ next explained that the union between Captain Dam's Chinese father and Vietnamese mother also had produced a younger daughter, a sister to Captain Dam. She had been left at the door of the mission church of Saint Francis Xavier in Cholon when the Chinese father abandoned them to return to China. The mother had to turn to prostitution to support herself. Captain Dam, being older, was left to fend for himself on the streets. It was then that he eventually found his way back to Ha Long Bay, where he became a Communist and joined the North Vietnamese army.

Russ Pulton asserted that Captain Dam fantasized that his mother was a direct descendant of one of the sons of Lac Long Quan and Au Co and that he, as the offspring of a dragon and a goddess, was being guided and aided by his ancestors in all that he did. He further believed that he possessed the power of a dragon and the cunning of a goddess and that his actions were justified by his destiny.

Captain Dam was a loyal soldier in the army of Ho Chi Minh, but he disagreed with his leader in one fundamental regard. Ho Chi Minh was a fierce proponent of Vietnamese independence, whether that be from the Europeans, the Americans, or the Chinese. Captain Dam saw the issue more in terms of color—the yellow man versus the white man. When he returned to the north of Vietnam and joined the army, he decided to change his name to hide his past. He was ashamed of his mother for having become a prostitute for the French colonialists and did not want to use her name. Because she had never married Captain Dam's father and did not want him to have a Chinese name, she named him Van Le. Instead of keeping the name Van Le, he chose the name Dam and combined it with that of the anti-French hero, Ton That Thuyet, to arrive at his current name of Ton That Dam.

This is where the third myth comes into play, Russ contended. Taking another sip of his water before proceeding, he leaned forward to make the point that it is important at this juncture not only to know this story, but to know the manner in which it has been distorted by Captain Dam. Turning first to a discussion of the myth itself, he stated that it is a story of the Trinh Nu or virgin grotto and the Trong or male grotto. The story goes that a poor fisherman's family was forced by a rich governor of fishing rights to give him their beautiful daughter as a mistress in exchange for the right to fish. The pretty young girl already had a handsome young boyfriend and refused to marry the governor. Angered, the governor had her banished to an island in Ha Long Bay, where she was turned into the stone that comprises Trinh Nu Grotto. Her lover set out to find her in a boat that was sunk in a storm, and he had to swim to a nearby island. A burst of lightning during the storm revealed her to him, but the loud winds drowned out his calls to her, and he, too, eventually was turned into the stone that now makes up Trong Grotto. The two grottos have faced each other ever since and still do today.

According to Russ, Captain Dam distorted this beautiful but tragic myth to suit his needs. Russ contended that Captain Dam interpreted the poor fisherman's beautiful daughter to be Vietnam and her young lover to be China. The governor of fishing rights that wanted her as a concubine in exchange for the right to fish was the white devil French colonialist who controlled and polluted everything. Russ further explained that Captain Dam blamed the French for driving his father away rather than admit that the man simply had abandoned them. Dam accused the French of forcing his mother into their service, instead of conceding that she had chosen prostitution on her own. In addition, he viewed the fact that his father was Chinese as a sign to him that his ancestors wanted the Chinese and the Vietnamese to join together to defeat the white devils. When they do, he claimed, the two lovers will be returned to life and reunited in love and happiness. Russ Pulton punctuated his point by stating, "These are the distorted beliefs that are fueling this man's passion, I tell you!"

"Interesting," commented Sully as he mulled over what the Russian had been saying.

Russ added, "Don't feel too bad. Captain Dam hates us Russians as much as he does you Americans and the French. He has convinced himself that once you Americans are expelled from his country, his people will have to fight to rid themselves of us Russians. He tolerates us because he has been ordered to do so by Hanoi, who needs our help and technology in fighting you. He loathed having to protect me in the past, and I am certain that he was beside himself when he was given instructions to hunt me down and kill me. I know how he thinks because I have spent so much time with him. He brags of having killed Frenchmen and Americans, and I have no doubt he would not miss the opportunity to add a Russian to his list."

Sully noted that Captain Dam seemed to have conveniently forgotten that in the myth about Ha Long Bay, the gods sent the dragons to help fend off a foreign invasion from the north, where China is situated today.

Russ smiled as he replied. "Remember that Captain Dam believes that when the yellow man unites against the white devils and expels them, rather than fighting with each other and trying to oppress one another, the lovers will be returned to life and reunited in love and happiness."

In a manner that indicated that he was more thinking out loud to himself than actually responding to what the Russian said, Sully mentioned, "I often have worried that our involvement in Vietnam may be having the unintended result of driving the Vietnamese closer to their Chinese neighbors and causing them to forget their suffering under one thousand years of Chinese occupation before the victory by Ngo Quyen in the battle on the Bach Dang River drove them out in 939 AD."

Laughing as he spoke, Russ told Sully he had nothing to worry about while Ho Chi Minh was in charge. Letting the Chinese back into Vietnam was one mistake Ho Chi Minh was not about to make. He noted, "That is the reason we Russians are there helping, more so than the Chinese."

After a short break, the meeting resumed. Russ told Sully that there were close to three thousand or more Russians secretly fighting alongside the North Vietnamese, providing them with Soviet technology and teaching them how to use it. Of course, he continued, they are called *advisers*, but in reality they are doing far more than providing advice.

Sully made a note to himself to explore this topic with Russ in more detail at a later point, but first he wanted to get back to the subject of Captain Dam and his possible whereabouts.

What the Russian had to say next sent chills up the spine of the World War II marine veteran. It seems Captain Dam had captured and turned over to the Chinese a downed American navy fighter pilot by the name of Scott Broderick, along with parts from the wreckage of his plane, as well as parts from other crash sites that had been gathered over time. According to the Russian, unless they had moved him, the Chinese were holding and interrogating Lieutenant Broderick at an old airfield in a rural part of China that is both near the coast and just north of the border with Vietnam, not far from Ha Long Bay. The airfield apparently dated back to World War II, when it originally had been built to serve as an emergency landing area for Allied planes fighting the Japanese. The Chinese desperately wanted to learn American technology, strategies, and procedures. They would do whatever they had to do to extract the information from the downed American flier, regardless of how brutal that might be. They were not concerned, because they would deny the existence of the American pilot and kill him once he had outlived his usefulness to them.

Russ elaborated that Captain Dam did not tolerate vodka like a Russian and had told him of this in the not too distant past, when they had gotten drunk together. To collect on a bet, and being proud of his achievement, Captain Dam more recently took the Russian there to see for himself. Russ, trained as a spy to observe, rendered a full account of what he had seen.

Upon hearing this disturbing news, Sully decided to adjourn the meeting until the next day, Saturday, June 26, 1971. He wanted to give the agency staff time to investigate the Lieutenant Broderick story. A subsequent check by the agency staff confirmed that in late April of 1971, a Lieutenant Scott D. Broderick from Tampa, Florida, failed to return to his carrier, the *Midway*, after his F-4B had been launched from Yankee Station on a sortie over North Vietnam that was scheduled to last only a few hours. He officially had been listed as missing in action. At the time, his wife, Karyn, was three months pregnant with twin girls that were due to be born on October 11, 1971. Karyn was waiting for her husband's return to pick their names. Apparently they had been discussing names in the days before he took off on that last mission.

———

Later, upon Scott's safe return to her in July of 1971, Karyn Broderick would agree to name the girls Katherine and Claire at his request. Her husband told her that he thought he'd been rescued by three British special forces commandos and was particularly grateful to two of them—both named John, but one nicknamed Prince George by the other. Scott was so appreciative of his rescuers that he wanted to name his daughters after them, but they prevailed on him to name the girls Katherine and Claire instead, after two women the men had known and admired.

Karyn thought her husband might still be feeling the effects of his ordeal. When she called to thank the British embassy, the British ambassador, Read MacPherson, thinking it was simply a case of the Americans having a little fun twisting the lion's tail once again, politely explained to her that his government had no commandos operating in that area that could have done what she was recounting. Scott also was insisting that he was rescued from the Chinese and not the North Vietnamese. But the US authorities were not able to corroborate that account of events either, other than to confirm that Scott somehow was able to escape and commandeer an old C-47 that he managed to safely land on his American carrier, the *USS Midway*, operating in international waters near the Gulf of Tonkin. The C-47 had been in such disrepair that the crew of the *Midway* simply pushed it overboard into the sea, where it sank without a trace.

In the end however, Karyn didn't care, so happy was she to have her husband back with her and there for the birth of their daughters. She already had grown extremely fond of the two names Katherine and Claire and wondered why she hadn't thought of these names herself.

The Brodericks would go on to have three more children, three sons named Scott Jr., John, and George. From time to time young George would affectionately be called Prince George by his father, who considered him to be spoiled as a result of being the baby of the family.

– 23 –

When the meetings with Russ Pulton resumed the next day, Saturday, June 26, 1971, the senior Sully asked the Russian if he thought Captain Dam had been acting with the knowledge and approval of his superiors when he turned Lieutenant Broderick over to the Chinese. Russ answered that he didn't know for sure, but that he would be surprised if Ho Chi Minh was interested in helping the Chinese develop their military weaponry.

Next Sully asked how Captain Dam could possibly have been operating alone and without at least tacit approval from his superiors. With the soldiers under his command knowing of this activity, it was hard for Sully to believe that word would not get back to Hanoi of Captain Dam's actions.

Sitting up in his seat, leaning toward Sully, and placing his right hand on the marine's left arm to accentuate what he was about to say, the Russian replied, "The answer to that question, my friend, also is the answer to why the South Vietnamese spies you have trained and sent north to gather information have appeared to vanish without a trace." He paused for a moment to allow a degree of anticipation and suspense to build before explaining. "The Communists in Vietnam have succeeded in developing a strong network system that reinforces party doctrine and authority, builds support for its leadership, and fosters loyalty among its followers. The relationship is similar to that seen between a servant and a master, or among the faithful and their religion. This system has produced secular leaders that—either through charisma or close personal relationships similar to that of a big brother or a father figure—have been able to command great loyalty and respect and exact almost blind devotion from their followers. This strong devotion is both to the leader and to the ideology from which that leader derives authority."

The Russian went on to explain that these cadres became like families and that obedience to the leader, endowed with authority from the Communist state, is like that of a child to his father. "Your South Vietnamese spies, once removed from your support network in the South, and alone in the North, were easily absorbed into these cadres or families, and either were converted or were eliminated. Similarly, Captain Dam's men would not think to question the authority under which he had been acting or discuss those actions outside of their unit."

Sully agreed with a great deal of what the Russian said, but like many of the other Americans in the room, he wasn't convinced that Russ Pulton's views were totally correct. Captain Dam's superiors in Hanoi seemed to be well informed of his actions at the orphanage, both in 1969 and at present, so why wouldn't they have been equally informed about their man turning over the American pilot to the Chinese? When they put this apparent contradiction to him, Russ smiled and said that he could only speak to the 1969 incident at the orphanage, since he'd already been removed from the country at the time of the more current event.

Turning in his seat to face Sully, Russ looked directly at his new American friend and said, "What I'm about to tell you is going to be a shock to you. Would you rather we speak in private?"

"No," replied Sully, "I can handle whatever it is you have to say."

"Okay," responded Russ, as he settled back in his seat to begin divulging the full story of what happened at the orphanage in December of 1969. Rubbing his chin several times, in an apparent attempt to first organize his thoughts, he commenced to speak.

"I never told Captain Dam of the ink marks, nor did I realize that he had noticed the ink on my fingers, but he had. When he came to the orphanage that December day in 1969, it was to retrieve the fingerprints and any other materials Sister Kate may have compiled about me and to ascertain exactly what she knew. His concern at the time, being responsible for me, was that you would find out that I was Russian and that Russians were fighting against you in Vietnam alongside the North Vietnamese. Neither he nor I were aware of what I had revealed during my delirium, nor did we have any reason to suspect I had said anything about being involved with the John F. Kennedy assassination. Only more recently did it become apparent that you were aware of my connection to Dallas, and I became concerned for my life and sought asylum from you. At the time, he was more concerned that Sister Kate might be an American spy, because he could not figure out why a nun would be interested in taking a stranger's fingerprints. It was foolish of her to have used ink and not my blood to take my fingerprints. Blood would not have left a clue."

Captain Dam, upon being called to Hanoi, told his superiors that he executed Sister Kate because he had obtained a confession from her that she was a CIA agent. And he was able to produce a confession that he had forced her to sign. However, the true reason he killed her is because when he saw her and the similarity that she bore to the memory he had of his mother and then looked for and found the telltale beauty mark that he knew his sister had on the back of her neck, he realized that she was his sister. He was enraged that she had become the enemy. She was now an American and had taken a Western name and identity. Furthermore, she had become a Catholic Franciscan nun, the very missionaries that he blamed for instigating the French to colonize his country. It was all too much for him, and he became overwhelmed with anger and rage. For this reason and this reason alone, he executed his own sister."

There was total silence in the room when Russ ceased speaking. After a long pause, Sully, looking incredulous, turned to the Russian and asked, "Are you telling me that this animal is the brother of my sweet Kate?"

"Yes," answered Russ.

"I don't believe it!" exclaimed Sully. Neither did Lieutenant Sullivan, when his father told him about it in a subsequent phone conversation. But it was true. Mary Sullivan confirmed for her husband that Kate had the beauty mark on her neck that the Russian mentioned. It also was true that she was a CIA agent, and Sully felt instant guilt at having involved her in his world. He blamed himself for having made her one of his minions. But what he could not know, because the Russian himself did not know, is that she never admitted to being an agent and never signed the confession that had been forged by Captain Dam to cover his tracks and make him a hero with his superiors. It was a strange twist of fate that his lie was in fact true. She indeed was a CIA agent, but it was not for that reason that he killed her.

"Why did you reach out to Kate seeking asylum, if you already knew she was dead?"

"I didn't know anyone else and simply hoped that my requests would be forwarded to you, as they were."

"I see," said Sully, and he thanked Russ for the light he had shed on the circumstances surrounding his eldest daughter's brutal murder. It would not bring her back, nor would it lessen the burden of guilt the ex-marine was shouldering, but it would offer a degree of closure. No one could possibly have foreseen that a brother and a sister, separated early in their lives, could have taken such divergent paths, and yet would have collided so violently, as Kate and her brother did, on a chance encounter in the winter of 1969.

The meeting adjourned, and Russ and Sully were the only two left in the room, the CIA director's private dining room on the top floor, with a picture window that afforded the two men a beautiful view of the lush foliage surrounding the secluded headquarters building. But neither one was taking any note of the view. Russ had known Sully for only a short time, but had nevertheless come to like him. Seeing the trouble still lurking in the American's eyes, he asked if there was anything else that he could do for him.

Sully, desperate to make sense of what happened to Claire and the girls at the orphanage, seized upon the Russian's offer. After acknowledging that Russ already had left Vietnam when the massacre happened, he asked Russ if he nevertheless could think of any explanation for Captain Dam's actions. After all, Claire was not a CIA agent and had not done anything to even suggest that she might be, as Kate had. And she was not a long lost sister to the madman. So—why? Why the carnage?

With the caveat that it was only a guess, Russ answered that they were all simple pawns and deemed expendable in the epic battle Captain Dam saw himself locked into with Captain Chrisandra, a man he viewed as an evil deity and called the Devil Priest.

Sully stopped Russ to ask, "Why Captain Chrisandra, when there are so many other army chaplains in Vietnam? What is so special about Captain Chrisandra?"

Russ paused before answering. He was not sure the American would be able to believe what he was about to tell him. But there was no easy way to explain it, so after thoughtful consideration, he decided to go immediately to the point and work backwards from there to shed more light and give more details on the situation. Taking a deep breath, he began.

"The short answer, which I don't expect to make sense to you—at least at first—is that the other chaplains aren't disguised warriors, and they have not been delivered to Vietnam by goddesses. Before you stop me, let me now try to explain what I mean in more detail."

"Thanks, please do, because I'm lost with what you have said so far," replied Sully.

Seizing the opportunity, Russ jumped into a detailed explanation.

"It is important to realize that while Captain Dam is a brilliant and charismatic military leader, he also is a very twisted individual mentally. For one thing, he has taken the wonderful myths that depict the origins of his people and the beautiful region from which his mother came and through some troublesome and tortured thinking has revised them to justify his existence and provide himself with a mandate of sorts. While most Vietnamese believe they are the children of dragons and goddesses that continue to watch over and protect them, and at one time Captain Dam may have held a similar belief, he now thinks he is the reincarnation of one of these dragons from the sea. According to him, the dragon was slain by a foreign warrior who tricked the dragon by disguising himself as a holy man. In so doing, the foreign warrior was able to come close enough to the dragon to be able to thrust his sword—hidden in his garments—into the dragon's heart. I suspect that in Captain Dam's mind, this is a metaphor for the French Catholic missionaries who, while claiming to have come in good will, instigated the colonization and exploitation of his people by the French. In any event, Captain Dam now is convinced that through him, the dragon will be given a second chance to slay the foreign warrior, who once again will come disguised as a holy man."

Sully interrupted to say that while everything the Russian was saying was fascinating, he still was having trouble making the connection to Captain Chrisandra. The intercepted radio transmissions from Captain Dam's own men told him that Captain Chrisandra never left the orphanage and could not have been involved in the interdiction. The only other person that might have been able to tell Captain Dam of Captain Chrisandra's involvement, Lee Tang, was arrested before he'd had the chance. "In other words," asserted Sully, "there's no reason for Captain Dam to draw a conclusion that Captain Chrisandra's role in Vietnam was anything more than that of a chaplain. Unless there's something I'm missing?"

"There is something you're missing," the Russian told his friend as he took a sip of water to sooth his parched throat. "Captain Dam claims that he was warned in a dream or vision, I am not sure which, that he would know of this warrior's return to Vietnam, notwithstanding his disguise as a holy man, because he would arrive in the arms of winged goddesses from a distant place."

"Winged goddesses from a distant place," repeated Sully. "I still seem to be missing something here!"

"You are," replied Russ. "You see John, Captain Dam reached the conclusion that Captain Chrisandra must be the Devil Priest, not because of anything that did or did not take place at the orphanage, but because of the strange manner in which he arrived at the airbase in Vietnam. Lee Tang, his agent at the base, who is the same person who tried to kill me, as you know, told him that two large US military transports flown by all female crews had arrived empty, except for a few passengers, one of which was Captain Chrisandra, who appeared to be a US Army chaplain. The Vietnamese are not accustomed to seeing female American pilots in their country, let alone all female crews piloting large, sophisticated US Air Force jets. You must have realized that your actions were being carefully watched and that such an unusual event would draw attention. While I am no expert in the ways of your country, I doubt that most chaplains have arrived in Vietnam that way."

"No, you're right," replied the ex-marine. "We meant well and hoped our actions would accelerate the time when female pilots would have a place beside their male brethren in military cockpits, but we never envisioned this consequence. Who could anticipate that some madman would have a dream about winged goddesses? All I can say is this is really crazy shit. I hardly can believe it."

"These people are patient and meticulous in observing your every move," Russ added, "and often they know what you're going to do before you decide to do it, because they have studied your habits and tendencies to predict your actions. Trust me when I tell you they are methodical and thorough and good at what they do. They leave nothing to chance."

Sully wished the Russian hadn't chosen that expression about leaving nothing to chance, because it only served to remind him of his own perceived shortcomings. However, of more concern to him at the moment was whether there was anything else about Captain Dam that he should know. When he put the question to Russ, the Russian was ready with his answer. "Yes!"

"What?" asked the ex-marine.

"I know Captain Dam well enough to assure you that he doesn't accept the common belief that I am missing and dead. He remains convinced that I'm still alive and being kept in hiding by you in Vietnam. If he can find Captain Chrisandra, who he believes was sent to his country to retrieve me, he can be led to me and regain his tarnished reputation by producing me for his superiors and their Soviet friends. Also, he is steadfast in his view that Captain Chrisandra is his nemesis and must be slain by him for his vision of Vietnam to come to pass. These are the reasons why I think he has committed the heinous acts at the orphanage, to taunt Captain Chrisandra into showing himself. Your daughter Claire and the girls at the orphanage were brutally killed because of their importance to Captain Chrisandra. Captain Dam is hoping that their fate will be the bait that will lure Captain Chrisandra out of hiding and in the process reveal my whereabouts, as well as afford him the opportunity to do battle with the Devil Priest and slay him."

Sully acknowledged to Russ that he thought he might be right, because Captain Dam had left a note to that effect at the scene. With a newfound respect for his North Vietnamese opponent, and now realizing more than ever that they would be acting at their peril if they didn't take this despicable lunatic seriously, Sully shared with the Russian the latest developments involving Captain Dam. Intercepted communications indicated that he once again had been recalled to Hanoi, presumably to justify his heinous actions at the orphanage, but on this occasion he apparently failed to show.

Russ surmised that Captain Dam couldn't easily explain away his behavior this time and most likely had fled to China. His men, their hands now equally dirty from having been caught up in the moment at the orphanage, had no choice but to follow him. According to the Russian, there was a place near the abandoned airstrip where the downed American pilot was being held, that Captain Dam often went to meditate and communicate with his ancestors. Russ assured Sully that was most likely where Captain Dam would be found.

The Russian then removed his watch and took a piece of paper from inside it on which he'd been writing and drawing during the interrogation that had taken place earlier and gave it to Sully. Russ said, "Here, these are for you. Your son and Captain Chrisandra will need these when they go to the abandoned airstrip to capture Captain Dam and his men and to retrieve the imprisoned American pilot. This device, which is built into my watch, will activate a magnetic transponder that I attached to the hangar; once you're within a mile or so of it, it will activate and help guide you to the site.

Sully thought the Russian must be losing his mind if he believed his son and Captain Chrisandra were going to attempt a raid inside China. Nevertheless, he thanked Russ and graciously accepted both items. Then, as he was preparing to return to his office, Sully turned to the Russian and asked him why he had planted the device. Russ explained that he planned to recommend to his Soviet leaders that they undertake to blow up the plane's wreckage, because he didn't want the Chinese to obtain its technology.

The piece of paper contained a detailed map of the Chinese complex at the abandoned airstrip, including the size and deployments of the Chinese troops; the routines that they followed in eating, sleeping and patrolling the complex; where the only communications facility was located; and where the American was being kept and how he was being guarded. Sully thought to himself that an advance team of American commandos couldn't have prepared a better scouting report. It was too bad that it never would be used; any sojourn into mainland China was out of the question. At least, that's what he thought.

Walking to his car later that evening, Sully pondered what the odds might be that he would lose two daughters to the same madman, one because she was his long lost sister and the other because a crazy dream about winged goddesses had made the man she was in love with his nemesis, but in both cases because of a chance encounter at an old, broken-down orphanage on a small plot of land in a war-torn country half a world away. He'd devoted his life to a profession where he was paid handsomely to leave nothing to chance—to borrow Russ Pulton's expression. Yet he'd allowed chance to enter the equation, and two of his daughters along with thirteen innocent children had paid the ultimate price for it.

As he drove out of Langley that Saturday night, he told himself that the time had come to hang it up. When he returned to the office on Monday after the funeral, he would ask his secretary to type up his letter of resignation. His wonderful wife, Mary, had told him that he could have the little beach cottage he often talked of getting down in Baja, California, when he gave up being a spook. Yes, the time had come to put the Sullivan family first—before his extended family, the American people; before his jealous mistress, the agency; and before the biggest culprit of them all, his own ambitions to someday head up the house that his hero Wild Bill Donovan had built.

It would not come to pass. Mary Sullivan would hear none of it. The big, handsome, strapping marine she had married had come home from the war only when his work had been finished, with the end of hostilities. His exit from the CIA would be no different. As much as she wanted to see her husband retire from the agency, she knew him too well to allow him to leave while there still was unfinished business. He first must tend to that business. She told him so, and he reluctantly agreed.

With that matter resolved, she suggested that he make himself a drink and relax while she put the finishing touches on a special dinner she had been preparing for him. Claire's murder had taken place only three days before and the wound was still raw. This dinner would be the first step in a long and difficult healing process.

Sully was pouring himself a second drink when the phone rang. It was his son John and his friend Matt inquiring about the funeral arrangements and the interrogation of Russ Pulton. Sully filled them in on both topics in great detail, including mentioning the piece of paper and device that he had been given by the Russian, before being ushered off the line by Mary because dinner was ready.

As he hung up the telephone, he shook his head in amazement, finding it hard to believe that he had allowed the two men to talk him into sending them a copy of the piece of paper and the device. But that would have to wait for an early Sunday morning visit to the office before the funeral that would be held later that day, with special permission from the Cardinal, Mary's brother, who would be saying the funeral Mass for his own niece and goddaughter—*Claire*. He had not been home to have dinner with Mary in months, and tonight he wanted to give her, the only woman he had ever loved, his undivided attention.

They were about to bury their second daughter in less than two years. No parent should have to go through that ordeal once, let alone twice. Mary's faith in God was unwavering, and John knew it would be strong enough to get her through it. It was himself that he worried about. The burden of the blame he had imposed upon himself weighed heavily on him and would require her support to help him work his way through it.

Their pain was unrelenting and insatiable, but you would not have known it, to watch the two of them around the candlelit dining room table. They looked like they did when they were young, carefree lovers, as two students eating lunch in the Eagle's Nest at Boston College. They rediscovered their love for one another over dinner, as their bond grew stronger—seared by the pain of their loss, forged by the adversity and sorrow they were enduring together.

The next day, Sunday, June 27, 1971, would be very difficult and grueling, and they both knew it. They would be boarding a private jet for the flight to the west coast. A Sunday funeral had been specially arranged for them with the help of Mary's brother the Cardinal, Claire's uncle and godfather. They would leave Virginia at 8 a.m., after Sully had stopped by the office to send the device and a copy of Russ Pulton's notes, as he had promised. And they would not be back in Virginia until 11 p.m. that night. Sully had to be at the interrogation on Monday morning to finish the work that had claimed the lives of his two daughters. Their deaths would not be in vain; this he had promised himself and them. Any thoughts of retirement were now a fading memory.

– 24 –

Monday morning, June 28, 1971, was a beautiful day in Langley, Virginia. Sully was up early and out of the house with a renewed sense of purpose. Claire had been buried the day before in Stockton, California, and while he still was grieving deeply, he was determined that her death and that of her sister before her would not be in vain. It was his way of dealing with his loss.

Thoughts of retirement were gone from his thinking as he gave Mary an extra-long kiss good-bye and walked out to the car. Once in the office, he was surprised to see he had received a transmission from Matt. Apparently, it was in response to the Russ Pulton document and device that he had sent to Matt by special pouch early the previous morning. Running late for that morning's scheduled meeting with the Russian and the others, he stuffed the transmission in his pocket to read later. They would be discussing the Kennedy assassination, and he anticipated that they would take all the time allotted and more.

As Sully walked into the room, Russ Pulton saw the renewed spirit in the American's demeanor. It wasn't long before the meeting started and everyone got down to the business at hand. Sully turned on the recording device and Russ began to speak into the microphone. There wasn't a sound in the room as he spoke.

"The assassination of your President Kennedy was part of a tri-part plan that also involved the removal from power of Mr. Khrushchev and the entanglement of the United States in Vietnam. The final months of

1963 were a particularly critical time in the evolution of the Cold War and the nuclear threat that underpinned it and fueled it. The forces that came together on that infamous day, November 22, 1963, were a product of their time and place in history. To comprehend how I came to be involved in this mix, it might be helpful to think of a string of pearls. Each pearl and its place on the strand must be known to fully understand my role.

"The first pearl on the assassination necklace was the Bay of Pigs incident that took place in April of 1961. It started there. The Soviet political advisers to Mr. Khrushchev took away a valuable insight about President Kennedy from the way he responded. Some referred to it as the 'Catholic Doctrine,' and others in my government called it the 'Kennedy Doctrine.'"

"The Catholic Doctrine? What is the Catholic Doctrine?" asked Sully.

"You, too, are a Catholic like your president was, aren't you, Mr. Sullivan?"

"Yes," replied Sully.

"I believe that your religion teaches you that your God helps those who help themselves, am I correct?"

"That's correct," answered Sully, who then added, "But I think it is a broader teaching than that; more of a Judeo-Christian teaching, I would say."

"That may be," replied the Russian, "but the breadth and the origins of that teaching are not as important to understanding my involvement, as is the fact that Mr. Kennedy had adopted and incorporated it into his political thinking."

"Fair enough, but I'm still somewhat confused."

"The insight that the Soviet advisers took from Mr. Kennedy's actions at the Bay of Pigs was that he wasn't likely to commit American ground forces to combat in the aid of another people unless those people were willing to help and fight for themselves."

"But the invasion force was comprised of Cuban-Americans."

"The Soviet advisers saw a distinction between the Cubans still living in Cuba and the Cuban-American exile brigade. When the people of Cuba didn't rise up against Castro in reaction to the invasion by the Cuban exile brigade, President Kennedy refused to commit further American military forces. Whether you wish to call it the Catholic Doctrine or the Kennedy Doctrine isn't important. Regardless of its name, it was profound for us that your president was willing to endure the humiliation of a highly visible failure and incur the wrath of the Cuban-American community and his military rather than spill additional American blood under those circumstances."

"I am sorry, but I still fail to see the connection between the Soviets, the Bay of Pigs, and the assassination."

"If you are patient with me and allow me to continue to string my pearls, you will come to see that it became an imperative for some in my government that the United States be embroiled in a land war in Vietnam. And the Kennedy Doctrine told them that President Kennedy would never allow that to happen. On the other hand, if Lyndon Johnson were president, he was seen as more likely to permit it."

"I see. My apologies; please continue," said Sully somewhat impatiently.

"The second pearl on the necklace was the summit meeting that took place between Mr. Khrushchev and Mr. Kennedy in Vienna in June of 1961. Premier Khrushchev came away from that summit with an impression of President Kennedy as young and inexperienced. He saw him as a far cry from the formidable opponent that he thought Mr. Nixon would have been, had he won the 1960 election in the United States. Our premier saw an opportunity to exploit that perceived weakness on the part of your new president, and he acted quickly. In August and September of 1961, he resumed atmospheric testing of nuclear weapons, and he ordered the erection of the wall between East and West Berlin in Germany."

Russ could sense the impatience growing in his hosts. He was very much aware that the first two pearls that he had strung for them, while critical building blocks, had not yet revealed enough for them to comprehend the chain of events that had led to his being in Dallas on that fateful day in November of 1963. Anticipating their unrest, he again asked for their indulgence, but foreclosed his audience from actually interrupting him by intentionally proceeding without further pause.

"The third pearl," he announced, "was related to the one that preceded it and involved the crisis that took place in Berlin. You may recall that your General Clay provoked a sixteen-hour confrontation in October of 1961 at Checkpoint Charlie, at the center of the newly constructed Berlin Wall, between our tanks and yours. Our intelligence community had been observing the training exercises that preceded this confrontation, which had taken place in a nearby forest where American tanks with bulldozer devices attached to them attacked a mock wall built by your military.

"It quickly became clear to our intelligence people that we knew more about the actions of your retired General Clay than did your young president. While the confrontation was defused when your president—through his brother—informed us that if we withdrew our tanks, he would do the same with yours thirty minutes later, it left lasting concerns with some in the Soviet government. These concerns went to the oversight that your Mr. Kennedy had over the actions of his military. It is true that the military withdrew on his command, but it also appeared to be true that they precipitated the confrontation in the first place, without his knowledge or blessing."

Sully smiled to himself as the Russian spoke, for he and his CIA colleagues were privy to facts concerning the apparent state of Nikita Khrushchev's relationship with his regime, and also with certain actions that the Soviet leader took that were not known to the Russian and most likely had intentionally been kept from the Soviet military and the Soviet Intelligence hierarchy at the Kremlin. At the Vienna Summit, John Kennedy suggested to the Soviet leader that an unofficial channel of communication be established between the two leaders in order to circumvent the usual bureaucratic networks. In September of 1961, during the Berlin crisis, seemingly under pressure from within his government to press the issue with the Americans, Mr. Khrushchev wrote confidentially to John Kennedy. Likening the world to Noah's Ark, he sought the young president's cooperation in reaching a peaceful resolution in Germany that would keep the world ark afloat. Soviet intelligence may have known more about General Clay's actions than did the president, leading them to conclude that the US military might be out of control. But the president and the agency had a far better understanding of the Soviet leader's thinking and strategies for peace and, when necessary, had no problem ordering the US military to stand down and make the peace a reality.

As much as Sully would have liked to tell Russ of Mr. Khrushchev's private correspondence, he knew he mustn't. Instead, he would allow the Russian to continue to string his pearls. Unaware, Russ continued. But now, Sully was sitting up in his chair and taking notice. The misconceptions on the part of some in the Kremlin had put them on a far more dangerous trajectory than the ex-marine at first appreciated.

"The fourth pearl," the Russian proceeded to state, "was the result of a Soviet espionage coup. One of our spies, and I don't know his or her identity, learned that your Mr. Dulles presented a plan to your president during the summer of 1961 calling for a preemptive nuclear attack on our country before the end of 1963."

Sully was shocked to realize that the Soviets knew of the plan that the Joint Chiefs of Staff and the CIA Director presented to the president at a National Security Council meeting in July of 1961. He took a pen from his pocket and made a note to himself on the pad he was holding to speak with his friend Jim Angleton, who was responsible for counterintelligence at the agency.

"The next pearl to be strung now moves the timeline into 1962," Russ continued, as he watched Sully making the notation on his pad to speak with Jim Angleton. "In particular, it brings us to March of 1962, when President Kennedy was quoted in an article as stating that the United States might initiate use of nuclear weapons were vital interests at stake. This apparently was an alarming change from what Mr. Kennedy and other American presidents had always said before that time. That is, they would not be the ones to initiate a nuclear strike. This development convinced everyone in the Kremlin, including Mr. Khrushchev, that the Soviet Union would have to reevaluate its position. It is my understanding that as a result of this review, the decision was made that either Soviet missiles would need to be installed in Cuba—ninety miles from the US mainland—or a way would have to be found to remove US missiles from Turkey."

"Are you saying that John F. Kennedy's comment precipitated the Cuban Missile Crisis?" asked Sully.

"Mr. Castro was very nervous. He was convinced that the president and his brother Robert were attempting to have him killed and that they were considering another assault on his country. Mr. Khrushchev tried to convince Mr. Castro that as long as he could maintain control over his people, he had nothing to fear as a result of the Kennedy Doctrine we discussed earlier. But Mr. Castro would hear none of it. He was sure that the Kennedy administration was out to get him."

"So you are saying that this confluence of events precipitated the placing of the missiles in Cuba?" asked Sully.

"Yes. Along, of course, with the constant goading by the Chinese."

"I see; fine. Please continue," said the American.

"The reason the missile crisis is the next pearl on the necklace is twofold. First, it reconfirmed growing fears within the Soviet intelligence community and the Soviet military, dating back to the Berlin Wall crisis, that the US military had become far too adventuresome and that the control that your commander in chief had over them was tenuous at best. This confirmation came for us when the president's brother once again approached us through a back channel, when he asked Ambassador Anatoly Dobrynin to deliver a confidential message to Mr. Khrushchev. In the message delivered by Robert Kennedy, your president said to our premier that he needed his help once again in resolving the crisis peacefully because he was in danger of being overthrown by his military leaders, who appeared ready to seize power from him."

Sully could not help himself and interrupted Russ to say he thought that such an interpretation of the event might be a bit of an exaggeration. While there may have been legitimate differences of opinion between the commander in chief and the military as to how to handle the situation, there never existed any danger of a coup, or anything approaching it. Now satisfied that he had set the record straight, Sully asked the Russian to please proceed.

"The second part of the reason the missile crisis is the next pearl on the necklace," continued Russ, "is that it added to the growing perception among some in the Kremlin, a perception that also had begun in Berlin, that Premier Khrushchev had embarrassed the Soviet Union by backing down in Berlin and again in Cuba a year later."

"But," interrupted Sully, "I do not understand. In both situations Mr. Khrushchev accomplished what he set out to do. At the Berlin Wall, our tanks never bulldozed the wall. They backed away thirty minutes after your tanks did, leaving the wall intact. Similarly, in Cuba, Mr. Khrushchev obtained a commitment from us not to invade Cuba and to remove our missiles from Turkey."

"Mr. Khrushchev and his supporters in the Soviet Union would agree with you. They believed that the confrontations in Germany and Cuba had been huge successes for them. However, there were others in the Kremlin that were humiliated by what they viewed as capitulation on the part of Mr. Khrushchev. In addition, these perceptions were being reinforced by the reaction of the Chinese, who apparently were taunting us and calling Mr. Khrushchev a coward; and by Castro, who was upset and goading us to stand our ground."

"I see," said Sully. "So are you saying that there were fissures growing in Mr. Khrushchev's regime?"

"Yes," replied Russ, "and they were led by the man that commissioned me for the assassination assignment, Viktor Martynova, chairman of the KGB. After Stalin died, Mr. Khrushchev had been merciless in consolidating his position as the successor. Viktor Martynova viewed himself as far more statesmanlike and deserving of the position than Mr. Khrushchev, who he considered to be a common thug. However, realizing that he had lost, Viktor Martynova then focused his attention on heading up the KGB, a very powerful position, as you know, and waited for the chance to unseat Mr. Khrushchev. That chance came in the early 1960s, and Mr. Khrushchev was unseated in 1964."

"Are you saying that Viktor Martynova led a faction that authorized the assassination of a sitting American president and that faction did so without the knowledge and blessing of Mr. Khrushchev and his supporters in the Kremlin?"

"Yes, that is exactly what I am saying."

"That had to take a set of brass balls," exclaimed Sully!

"I am told he is most popular with the ladies in Moscow," replied Russ with a straight face.

At first there was some muted snickering as some in the room rustled in their seats, and then laughter broke out. Viktor Martynova's womanizing escapades were the stuff of legends and well known to the agency, which had thought of exploiting them for intelligence purposes. But this was no laughing matter. This was the man who had ordered the assassination of John F. Kennedy, and John Sullivan Sr. reminded the group of this solemn fact. The room quieted down and did so quickly.

Embarrassed but also somewhat amused by the response his comments had garnered, Russ asked to be allowed to continue.

"What I am telling you must be viewed in context. In late 1962, we had just removed more than 150 nuclear warheads from Cuba, only ninety miles from the US mainland. These missiles had been ready to fire. The US missiles still were in Turkey, and there was no guarantee that they subsequently would be removed. It was known that your agency and the US military wanted to exploit the window of opportunity that they thought would be closing by December of the next year to end the Cold War by making a preemptive nuclear strike against us. Furthermore, your president had worried everyone, including Mr. Khrushchev, by being quoted as saying that a first nuclear strike was not out of the question. Framing all of this was the perception being fueled by the Chinese and the Cubans that the Premier was losing his nerve. It was in this context that Viktor Martynova called a secret strategy meeting of his faction in December of 1962 that would seal the fate of your president."

Sully was surprised to learn that the Soviets had more than 150 fully operational warheads in Cuba at the height of the crisis. The agency previously had not been aware of that fact, and he once again reached for his pen to make a notation on the pad he was holding. As he did, he asked Russ if it would be possible for him to elaborate on the strategy session that he had just referenced.

"Absolutely," replied Russ, eager to oblige his host. "But may we first take a short recess so that I may use the bathroom?"

"Yes, of course," replied Sully as he called for a ten-minute break and escorted Russ to the men's room.

Ten minutes later, the session resumed on schedule with Russ picking up where he left off.

"You may recall that when I began speaking this morning, I told you that the assassination of your president was part of a tri-part plan that also involved our premier and Vietnam. This plan was conceived in the December 1962 strategy session, and the decision to implement it was taken there as well. The first leg of the tripod involved removing your president. The second leg involved removing Nikita Khrushchev, and the third leg involved embroiling the United States in a drawn-out conflict in Vietnam."

Russ paused to see if there were any questions. When Sully answered for the group that there were not, Russ suggested that he proceed by first discussing Vietnam, the third leg of the tripod. Sully agreed, noting that more than likely there would be no need to cover the second leg or the removal of Mr. Khrushchev in 1964 since the agency was well-versed on that point. With that, Russ again began to speak.

"It quickly became clear to our strategy group that the best way to curtail the adventuresome propensity of your military was to bog them down in a drawn-out conflict—similar to the Korean War—that they could not win without risking all-out war. In our view, South Vietnam and its corrupt leadership under Ngo Dinh Diem were being perpetuated in power solely by the United States. If with our help Ho Chi Minh could do to you Americans what he had done to the French, our goal would be achieved. Should you choose to wage the war too aggressively and become too successful in your efforts, by taking the fight to the North, for example, you would run the risk of the Chinese intervening, as they did in Korea. Should you wage a limited war with your military shackled with unrealistic controls, such as being limited to fighting only in the South, the American public would lose patience with the war. And the loss of prestige that your military would suffer waging such a controlled war would weaken their position at home, making it more difficult for them to be adventuresome."

"Very interesting," interjected Sully. "Am I to assume, Russ, that because of your so-called Kennedy Doctrine, you had concluded that Mr. Kennedy would not commit US combat units to Vietnam and therefore had to be removed from office?"

Sully and Russ had started to confer on a first name basis after the private one-on-one discussion that had taken place a few days earlier in the Director's Dining Room. The friendship and mutual respect clearly was growing between the two former adversaries.

"Yes, John, but the Kennedy Doctrine was only a part of the basis upon which we had reached that conclusion. We knew through our intelligence organization that in 1961 Mr. Kennedy sought and received the advice of General MacArthur not to commit ground forces in Asia. We also learned that in 1962 Defense Secretary McNamara ordered General Harkins, commander of the Military Assistance Command for Vietnam, to compile a strategy for turning the war effort over to the South Vietnamese. Added to that had been the fact that Senator Mansfield, a supporter of Diem in the 1950s, who more recently had become critical of the US Vietnam policy, had been asked by the president to visit Vietnam and report his findings. At the same time that our strategy group was meeting in December of 1962, Mr. Mansfield issued his report cautioning the president against what we were hoping to have him do—become embroiled in Vietnam. It was a well-known fact that Senator Mansfield long had been one of the Diem government's strongest supporters, so it was the consensus opinion of our intelligence strategists that President Kennedy was waiting to get reelected in 1964 and then would turn the effort over to the South Vietnamese and withdraw from Vietnam."

Sully had first met John F. Kennedy when he traveled with him and his brother Robert to visit Vietnam in 1951. The three men had become friends, and Sully could not help but be impressed by the work of the Soviet strategists. He visited with the president in 1963, shortly before he was killed, and the president confided in him that he planned to withdraw from Vietnam after the 1964 elections. They even discussed how he planned to do it, so as to avoid a loss of prestige. The president said he would convince the Diem government to ask him to leave, or he would replace that government with one that would.

"Our opinion was confirmed in early 1963," continued Russ, "when the Diem government began to call for a reduction in the American presence in Vietnam. Mr. Diem and his brother and adviser, Mr. Nhu, were astute individuals and could see what was coming. In addition, the North Vietnamese informed us that they had begun to receive informal feelers from the two South Vietnamese, attempting to reach some mutual understanding."

"Again, very interesting," interrupted Sully, "but why the risky timing for the assassination, in November of 1963, when the so-called US window of opportunity for a first nuclear strike capability still existed?"

"That is an excellent question, John, and it was given extensive consideration at the time. As we saw it, we were dealing with three possible American presidents: Kennedy, Johnson, and Goldwater. It was our view that if Mr. Goldwater were elected in 1964, he would go all out in Vietnam by taking the war to the North, engaging the Chinese when they entered the fighting, and at the very least authorizing the use of tactical nuclear weapons. In short, our strategy would implode on us under a Goldwater administration."

Sully spoke up to say that there were probably many within the agency who would have agreed with that assessment at the time, he among them. He then reached for the pitcher of water on the table and refilled Russ's glass and handed it to him. The Russian was appreciative and took a long drink before proceeding.

"If President Kennedy were reelected, as I already have indicated, we thought he would be true to the title of his book and be a 'profile in courage' by withdrawing from Vietnam, regardless of how unpopular that move might be. He had behaved in a similar manner at the Bay of Pigs, and there was no reason to think that he would not do so again."

"I take it, Russ," interjected Sully, "that this was your so-called Kennedy Doctrine at work again?"

"Yes," replied Russ, "we thought he would be willing to help the South Vietnamese by training them and supplying them, but Kennedy would expect them to help themselves by taking on responsibility for the fighting as the North Vietnamese and the Vietcong had done. The South Vietnamese simply were not a serious fighting force in the way the North Vietnamese and the Vietcong were."

"I can appreciate what you are saying," said Sully, "but what was the sense of urgency that convinced you to risk taking such drastic action in late 1963, when our apparent window of opportunity still was open to strike at you with nuclear weapons and survive?"

"The answer to your question, John, is rooted in our assessment of Mr. Johnson. We viewed him as a president that would be focused primarily on his domestic agenda. However, not wanting to be the president that lost Vietnam or to be perceived as soft on defense, especially with Mr. Goldwater in the background, he would give your generals their war. Still, fearful of escalating the conflict and drawing in the Chinese, as had happened in Korea, he would take control and shackle them, by closely managing their actions and by limiting the fighting to the South of Vietnam. He would not be fighting so much to win, as he would be fighting not to lose. Essentially, he would be the ideal president for our strategy. We thought it was imperative to seize the moment and give him sufficient time in office to assure that he would be able to defeat Mr. Goldwater in the upcoming 1964 election. We were terrified of Mr. Goldwater and a Goldwater win."

"Am I to assume that you and your group led by Viktor Martynova consider your strategy to have been a success?" asked Sully.

"Yes, very much so, John. The Soviet Union never was struck, Mr. Khrushchev has been removed from office, and your country remains bogged down in Vietnam today. Let's be honest. The South still is a corrupt mess and slowly losing the war, and the North still is Communist and slowly winning. Mr. Johnson won the election, defeating the feared Mr. Goldwater, and was successful in passing into law his and Mr. Kennedy's ambitious domestic agenda, an agenda that some of your political scientists argue Mr. Kennedy may not have been as successful in getting passed. And President Johnson was able to leave office without having the war in Vietnam escalate out of control or be lost on his watch."

"You appear to conveniently overlook, Russ, that it is not a coincidence that Mr. Johnson was a one-term president," retorted Sully.

"One term, one year, one month and eight and a third days in 1963 to be exact," replied Russ. "You might say everyone got what they wanted."

Visibly upset, Sully stood up and shouted, "Not Mr. Kennedy! And not the thousands of young Americans that have followed him to their deaths or been wounded in Vietnam, not the least of which are my two daughters!" The loss of his daughters was still a raw issue for the grieving ex-marine.

After a long silence, Russ answered softly and compassionately. "John, you are right, and I apologize for being so insensitive. But please understand that I must weigh that against the millions of innocent Soviet citizens that would have died in an unjustified first nuclear strike against my country."

"I understand," sighed Sully as he sat back down, thinking to himself what a sordid business this whole thing was. Slumping in his chair, with his hands touching each other and his lips in a praying or pensive position, he silently thought for a moment about Kate and Claire, about his old friend Bo Hicket, and the young marine and airborne soldier that had died in Operation Excalibur, about his son still in harm's way and the young man—the young man who had taken his chances in the draft lottery and won a free pass, whose parents thought he was frolicking in Europe, but who had been roped into this hell of a mess by him and his accomplices at the agency. *What in God's name were they doing?* he thought to himself.

The momentary pause caused Russ, still smarting from his insensitivity, to continue to apologize. "Please know, John, that it is not easy for me to sit across from you here and know that two of your daughters have fallen victim to our strategy."

"Thank you, Russ," replied Sully, sitting up in his chair and quickly regaining composure. He told himself he owed it to his daughters and the others to see this matter through, and he would. Turning to Russ, he asked another question.

"I can't help but observe from your responses that you seem to have a deep regard for the man you assassinated, which you must agree is most unusual?"

"Shooting John F. Kennedy was extremely difficult for me. I had grown to have a great deal of respect and admiration for him and for his wife, Jackie. I am still haunted by the image of his face in the sights of my rifle. I took great pains to shoot when Mrs. Kennedy was not looking and was out of harm's way. I am a professional and I did what I had to do. It was not easy, but you must admit, he was the first United States president to say publicly that he might consider a first strike where American interests warranted it, and he had indicated to us during the Cuban Missile Crisis that he was under pressure and in danger of being overthrown by the US military that had been pushing for a first strike while they thought they still had a window of opportunity to do so and survive."

At this point, Sully rose from his chair, thanked Russ without responding further, and said that he thought they had done enough for one day. It was almost 2 p.m. and lunch service was being held open in the dining room for those who were interested. They would plan to reconvene in the morning.

– 25 –

As Sully walked back to his office after having had a long lunch with Russ in the dining room, he couldn't help but think of his freshman year at Boston College and the Sir Walter Scott quote that his Jesuit English professor loved to use over and over again. "Oh what a tangled web we weave, When first we practice to deceive." The Johnson administration and even the Nixon administration, albeit to a lesser extent, had tried to play down the war to the American people, and now the government had lost the trust and support of its constituents. But how could America avoid falling victim to the Chinese proverb "Ch'i 'hu nan hsia pei," which loosely translated means now that the United States has mounted the tiger by having introduced combat troops into Vietnam, how does it dismount without being eaten by the tiger? The old Jesuit was so right, he thought to himself, *What a mess we had gotten ourselves into.*

Then he remembered the transmission from Matt Kerr that he had stuffed in his pocket earlier in the day. Retrieving it, he unfolded and began to read it.

> Sully,
>
> It appears that Captain Chrisandra may have returned to Vietnam to take up Captain Dam's challenge. A person of his likeness was seen near The Yellow Rose of

Texas, the old C-47 gunship that was used in Operation Excalibur. The plane is unique and has a storied past. Before it was used in Operation Excalibur, it had been flown by two bigger-than-life characters, Ty Steere and Tex Jamerson from Fort Worth, Texas, and had been used primarily to train South Vietnamese paratroopers for long-distance missions into hostile territory. It had been specially equipped with extra fuel tanks, lightweight materials, and juiced-up engines to give it an extended range of operation. It also had been well armed.

It was for all these reasons that the C-47 had been picked by Matt for Operation Excalibur after Ty and Tex rotated back to the United States. Tex's favorite song was "The Yellow Rose of Texas," which was based on a legend from the Texas War of Independence about a woman named Emily, who is said to have seduced General Santa Anna, thereby helping Sam Houston defeat the Mexican at the Battle of San Jacinto. Tex had the name of the song painted on the fuselage of the plane beneath the cockpit windows. Matt, too, had liked the song and preserved the name when he requisitioned the plane for the mission. It also had not been lost on Matt that the streets of Dallas had been littered with yellow roses on Friday, November 22, 1963.

The flight plan that was filed for the old plane called for a maintenance flight to Da Nang and back. However, after the plane refueled and took off from Da Nang for the return trip, it climbed out toward the South China Sea and within several minutes dropped off the radar screen. Also unaccounted for and thought to have been on board the C-47 were your son John and Jon Trueblood, the latter presumably being at the controls of the vintage machine.

Please call me as soon as you can.—Matt

When Sully got to his desk, he immediately called Matt. The first question he asked his friend in Vietnam was if he thought they had crashed. Matt answered no. He said he had ruled it out for several reasons. Da Nang had conducted a search and rescue mission in the area and there had been no sign of wreckage. Furthermore, there had been no distress calls or loud explosions.

"Well, Matt, if they didn't crash, what is it that you think they're up to?"

"Sully, I think they may have gone to China to confront Captain Dam and to retrieve the downed American pilot that he is said to have turned over to the Chinese," replied Matt.

"I don't know, that seems a little farfetched don't you think?"

Both men agreed to treat the plane as missing, as had been reported, at least for the time being, and not disclose what they had been speculating might be happening. Another search and rescue mission was being planned, and without further proof to corroborate their thinking, it would only serve to create unnecessary angst to speculate on something as controversial as a possible raid into China.

Nevertheless, they continued to talk and speculate on the phone. Sully commented that even if they had enough fuel to reach China, they would not have enough for their return and most likely would have to ditch at sea. He surmised that they must be flying just above the waves to avoid radar detection. Matt noted that the trip had to be grueling on the pilot, who they assumed was Jon Trueblood. If he flew too high, they would trigger enemy radar and be shot down. If they flew too low and clipped a wave with one of the wings, the plane would cartwheel and most likely explode from all the extra fuel that was on board.

Sully asked Matt what carrier battle group was in the vicinity and who was in command of it. Matt replied that the closest was the *USS Midway*, under the command of their mutual friend, Admiral Cliff Wheatley. Both men agreed that Matt should arrange to be airlifted to the *Midway* immediately to have a private briefing with Cliff Wheatley in case their speculation was correct and The Yellow Rose of Texas had to ditch at sea near the carrier group.

Not long thereafter, Matt had made the necessary arrangements and was en route to the *Midway*. He had arrived and was on board only a short time when the carrier had to scramble its jets to come to the assistance of an American C-47 that was being chased by Chinese fighters. The lumbering old plane had managed to make it into international air space, so the Chinese pilots had no choice but to peel off when they saw the American jets coming. Not to have done so would have made for a very bad day for them, and they knew it. With a welcome fighter escort, Lieutenant Broderick managed to land The Yellow Rose of Texas safely on the *Midway*.

When Admiral Wheatley stepped into the doorway of the old C-47 to be the first to welcome back Lieutenant Broderick, no one on board the carrier paid any attention to the package wrapped in plain brown paper that he was carrying under his arm. No one, that is, except Matt, who watched as the admiral conveniently left the package that contained three navy seaman uniforms behind on the floor of the plane.

In all the commotion of welcoming back their shipmate and with all the clamoring to know what had happened to the downed pilot, no one but the admiral and Matt noticed shortly thereafter when three navy seamen exited the C-47 and quietly climbed into Matt's aircraft.

The admiral, moved by the selfless act of bravery of these men in rescuing their fellow American, asked Matt, "How are we as lucky as we are as a nation, to find young men like these generation after generation? I wish I could ask them what motivates them to do the kind of thing they have done in risking everything to save my downed pilot."

Matt smiled at his friend and said, "If you walk me to my plane later, you can ask them your question, but don't expect to get a serious answer out of them."

"What do you mean?" asked Admiral Wheatley.

"I know these guys, and they will give you a polite but evasive answer—something to the effect that it helps them to impress the women they try to meet. Come on, Cliff, you aren't that old that you can't remember back that far?"

Both men laughed and shook hands as they bet five dollars on what the response might be. On the orders of the admiral, The Yellow Rose of Texas was unceremoniously pushed off the side of the carrier by the crew of the *Midway* and sank quietly into the sea.

Not long thereafter, the admiral walked Matt to his waiting plane. Sticking his head inside, he asked the three men his question. "Why do you volunteer for such dangerous assignments?"

The answer he got caused him to reach into his pocket, take out his wallet and hand his friend a five-dollar bill. "Because chicks dig it, sir!" (Matt knew his men).

By the time Matt's plane returned to Saigon, Stewball was ready and waiting to take off for Europe. As soon as an unscheduled passenger had been loaded onto the modified KC-135, Anne Herndon taxied the big jet into position and immediately took off upon receiving clearance to do so. This time the transition from Captain John J. Chrisandra to George B. Angelson would be permanent and would not be reversed. When the war eventually came to an end in 1975, there would be no record of a Captain John J. Chrisandra ever having served in Vietnam or in the US military—the agency had seen to it.

As Stewball headed away from Vietnam, George took out of his pocket a speech Matt had given him to read. It was a speech that had been delivered by Major Michael Davis O'Donnell at Dak To, Vietnam on New Year's Day of the previous year. In it he had asked the vets, when returning home, to save a place in their hearts for their fallen brethren and admit to themselves that they had loved them. He also had beseeched them to take a "backward glance" for where they no longer could go and store what those deaths had taught them with their own memories so that they could remember these "gentle heroes" when others saw fit to call the war "insane."

As George looked out his window at the blue sky above and the clouds and seemingly endless world below, he could not help but take the major's words to heart and think of all that he was leaving behind. There was his dearest Claire, whose beautiful smiling face would forever be etched in his memory and whose loss he was sure his heart would never completely overcome. There was Claire's sister Kate, who had been the inspiration that had brought Claire to be in the seat next to his on the plane that fateful day in May. There was his high school friend, Christian—recently married to his high school sweetheart and father to a son he never would have the chance to meet—a life with so much promise left unfulfilled. There was his instructor, Bo—so much the unsung hero. There was Sammy, who had laid down his life so that his comrades might live to see their dreams and aspirations come to pass. And of course, there were me and my fellow orphans. As he looked out the same window he had looked out the last time, when Anne Herndon flew over the orphanage on their way out of Vietnam, he still could picture us in his mind's eye, playing. Only now we were playing in our crisp, new, white dresses. And no longer were we orphans, for we were in the loving family of our eternal Father and showered with love from Sisters Kate and Claire, at last forever married to their beloved Lord.

As he thought about the trail of carnage and suffering he had left behind, he could not help but feel a sense of guilt to be alive. The weight of Captain Chrisandra's M-16 had been replaced by the burden of George's guilt at having been spared the fate that had befallen those he now was leaving behind him.

He told himself that he owed it to all of us to live a full and productive life, a life he would be living for us as well as for himself. He vowed that there never would be any room in that life for discrimination, whether it be based on race or skin color, gender or sexual preference, religion or mental or physical disability, but there would always be a special place for children, especially the most vulnerable of them. He took some meager comfort from what had transpired, but I am not sure how much he truly believed it. Christian Carter and Samuel Lerner had died warriors' deaths. Their accomplishments forever would be noted and magnified by their sacrifice, as would their memories always be sanctified by the pure selflessness of their heroic acts. Their youth and vigor would be frozen in time, never to know the ravages of age. Bo Hicket eventually would be given his due—a star on the Wall of Honor at CIA Headquarters—and no longer would be his family's black sheep.

The star added next to his on that solemn occasion would be for Sister Katherine Sullivan.

Of greater comfort to him was the fact that the one human being who either directly or indirectly had been responsible for every one of these losses never again would be in a position to do any harm. The man who thought he was a dragon from the sea had been returned to the sea from whence he thought he had come. Captain Dam had been slain by Claire's Prince George, the dragon slayer. His work now done, he was free to leave. He had not been able to save them from the dragon. However, he had been able to avenge their deaths and save for them, the dragon's victims, a place inside himself and a backward glance when he was leaving for the place they no longer could go—*home*.

– 26 –

George did not realize just how exhausted he was, until they cleared Vietnamese air space and he truly was able to relax for the first time in days. He had barely eaten or slept in the last ninety-six hours. It quickly caught up with him, and he fell into a sound sleep. Hours later, when he awoke, he wolfed down a couple of ham and cheese sandwiches and some soup that Anne brought along for him. Matt had alerted him to the fact that he would be debriefed by John Sullivan Sr. and perhaps others as to what had taken place in China. He would be expected to give the whole story and not the sanitized official version that had been released by Matt Kerr and the admiral. It was time to gather his thoughts and prepare.

As he began to think back over the last several days and weeks, it became clear to him that he no longer was the same person who left New York on May 17, and that no matter how much he might try, he never again truly could be that individual. The rest of his life would be a never-ending struggle to try and recapture who he'd been and not disappoint his loved ones and others, who would be expecting nothing less of him.

In his first visit to Vietnam, he'd killed ruthlessly in the service of his country. And in Europe, on the beaches of Agropoli, he'd successfully begun the process of coming to terms with his actions and finding once again his inner peace. But upon his return to Vietnam, he'd crossed a line, one from which he could never retreat, for he had with premeditation murdered in cold blood. Yes, he could rationalize that the man he killed had been evil and that he'd been avenging the vicious crimes his despicable victim had committed. However, in his heart he knew that he'd acted no differently than the Russian he'd been sent to retrieve—as a cold-blooded killer. While saying good bye, Matt had confided in George that the Russian had rationalized his heinous assassination of President Kennedy by saying he was saving his country from possible unprovoked nuclear annihilation.

George promised himself that upon his return to the United States, he would return his priest's collar to his friend and mentor at Yale, the Reverend Lewis Pratt. He'd chosen to live by the sword and in the process had defiled that collar, the tradition for which it stood, and all the men of peace who had worn it before him. He momentarily allowed his mind to wonder if he would even be given the chance to make the return of the collar, or would he first die by the sword. He was sure there were those within the agency that would frown upon a Young Turk who had taken matters into his own hands and jeopardized a highly sensitive agency mission. It was not inconceivable to him that as a result of what he knew and had done, he would be deemed too great a security risk to be allowed to live and could become the subject of an executive action (CIA speak for a contract on his life). He had the support of Matt Kerr and John Sullivan Sr., but would that be enough to overcome the cries for his head? He didn't know.

He told himself that he would have to convince his handlers of his trustworthiness. It was time to start preparing for his upcoming inquisition in earnest. He would have to account for his actions, especially his unauthorized return to Vietnam and the Chinese raid, step-by-step, from beginning to end. He decided to focus his attention on the raid—first on the planning and then on the execution.

The map that Russ Pulton had given them showed that the abandoned airstrip and barracks were located about thirty-eight miles north of the North Vietnamese border and approximately eighty miles inland from the South China Sea.

The airstrip was about one quarter of a mile north of and at a slightly higher elevation from the barracks and the compound. It ran east and west and on the south side contained an old, unused tower, a small office that was in disrepair, and an abandoned hangar that now contained parts from the wreckage of the American fighter jet. A small, partially overgrown dirt road ran down the hill for the quarter-mile stretch between the field and the compound below.

The compound had a perimeter fence surrounding it and a gate at the northwest corner. At that corner there also was a tower with a searchlight, a machine gun, and a helicopter landing pad. There was a fuel dump next to the landing pad, and the pad usually contained a helicopter with a working radio. Along the south side of the compound, from east to west, there was a barracks, a structure containing a mess hall and communications hut, and a building that housed a makeshift infirmary and jail. The only operating radios were in the helicopter and the communication hut. The surrounding area was mostly rural and unpopulated.

According to the Russian's note, there were thirty-eight military personnel at the compound, including the helicopter crew, also one male nurse, and the commander. Chinese engineers were being shuttled to the site intermittently—mostly at night—by an inconspicuous propeller-driven plane to inspect and take samples of the parts from the wreckage, but they did not appear to be staying there.

The compound was being protected at all times by three guards. One guard remained in the tower and at night operated the searchlight. Another guard stood by the gate and helicopter pad, and a third guard walked the perimeter fence. The trip around the perimeter usually would take the guard about ten minutes. Very often at night, the guard in the tower would follow him with the searchlight as he made his rounds. The guard teams worked in eight three-hour shifts. In contrast, the airstrip, including the hangar with the parts of the wreckage, was unguarded. It had been abandoned for years and had been used only occasionally by small propeller-driven planes bringing supplies to the compound when the helicopters were not available. And the Chinese apparently were content to have it maintain its low profile.

Captain Chrisandra and Lieutenant Sullivan conceived the plan in an office on the second floor of the CIA station in Saigon, which was located across from the American embassy. The two men thought they had kept their plan secret from Matt Kerr, but they should have seen his invisible hand in the ease with which things had gone their way. Matt had been following their every step, content to remain in the background and help facilitate their moves while maintaining the cover of *plausible deniability* for the agency and the government he had sworn to serve and protect. The questions and the hypothetical scenarios in the communications with John Sullivan Sr. had been designed to disguise their true meaning and to protect that cover while keeping Sully informed in a full and timely manner.

The plan was to strike in the overnight hours between Monday, June 28, and Tuesday, June 29. They would be in and out of the Chinese facility in less than two hours and leave no evidence of an American presence. They would use The Yellow Rose of Texas, but they would modify the C-47 by removing all unnecessary weight, including all of its armament. However, they would leave the compact bathroom that had been installed in preparation for Operation Excalibur. It had been intended for use by the female crews, the "winged goddesses" who might be called upon to fly the old plane during that mission. They had a very special purpose in mind for that bathroom. They would add extra fuel cells to the fuselage to give them more range and a trip wire hook on the undercarriage in case they had to land on a carrier. They would recruit Jon Trueblood to fly the plane, but would forgo having a co-pilot to save on the weight. They knew the plane would be a flying bomb, but they had no choice. They needed the extra fuel as part of their exit strategy. And they wanted a plane that would look and sound in the night sky like the planes the Chinese occasionally landed at the airstrip.

Jon Trueblood was an ideal choice to pilot the plane because he had extensive experience flying DC-3s, the civilian version of the C-47, loaded with water or fire retardant liquids, from fighting forest fires in the Rocky Mountains during his summers in college. He often had been required to fly through heavy blinding smoke in the mountainous terrain, managing the sluggish controls of a plane weighed down with water or retardant.

They would file a flight plan for a routine maintenance trip to Da Nang and back. At Da Nang they would refuel and fill the extra fuel cells that they had added. On the return leg, after taking off from Da Nang, they would climb to their assigned altitude over the South China Sea and head south. After a short time, they would drop down to 200 feet, below radar coverage, and disable their tracking mechanisms. Then they would turn around and fly north at a cruising speed of approximately 200 miles per hour. They first would maintain a north-northwest course and then a north-northeast heading as they flew up the center of the Gulf of Tonkin with the waves licking at their fuselage. At the appropriate point, they would turn north-northwest again and head for the Chinese mainland and the abandoned airstrip. As they approached the landing strip, they would cut their engines and glide in for the landing.

After takeoff from Da Nang they would change into North Vietnamese clothing and shoes, apply camouflage to themselves, and rearm themselves with North Vietnamese weapons and ammunition. Everything else would be jettisoned from the aircraft. They could not change the American markings on the outside of the plane, but if all went as planned, they would not be visible in the dark.

Once on the ground in China, they first would secure the airstrip, wire the hangar with timed explosives, and refuel the plane using the fuel cells they had brought with them. Then they would proceed down the dirt road to the compound and take out the three guards.

After the team gained control of the light tower, gate, and perimeter of the compound, Jon Trueblood would disable the communication equipment in the helicopter (if there was one on the pad) and climb the tower to continue operating the light. Captain Chrisandra and Lieutenant Sullivan would proceed to the barracks where the Chinese and presumably their North Vietnamese visitors would be sleeping. If the Russian was correct, they would encounter no resistance because he said there were no other guards posted inside the compound. Once the outside of the barracks was secure, the two Americans would don gas masks and gas the barracks. Then they would proceed to the communications hut and do the same. Finally, they would gas the infirmary and jail building. The gas they would be using was designed to leave no trace of its use and simply would temporarily render its victims unconscious but not kill them.

When the gassing was complete, Jon Trueblood would descend from the tower, don his gas mask, and take up his position outside the communication hut. Once he was in position and the other two were in place outside the infirmary, they would simultaneously enter both buildings and, using their North Vietnamese arms, kill the unconscious Chinese. Captain Chrisandra and Lieutenant Sullivan then would carry the unconscious American prisoner to the helicopter on the pad, if there was one, otherwise they would carry him to the gate.

All three of them would then enter the barracks. They would bind the hands and feet of the unconscious Chinese and, using North Vietnamese weapons, shoot them in the back of the head execution style. All the North Vietnamese would be left unharmed except for Captain Dam, who would be bound and gagged and carried to where the American prisoner had been left.

If there was a helicopter on the pad, they would board it, and Jon Trueblood would fly them the short distance to the airstrip. Once there, the still unconscious American pilot and Captain Dam would be moved to the C-47, and Jon Trueblood would park the helicopter next to the hangar so that it would be destroyed when the hangar blew up. If there was no helicopter, they would have to walk up the hill to the waiting C-47 and carry the two unconscious men. All their Vietnamese weapons and unspent ammunition would be left behind at the airstrip.

The still unconscious American airman would be strapped into the pilot's seat, and the bound and gagged Captain Dam would be locked in the bathroom built for the winged goddesses. Captain Chrisandra, Lieutenant Sullivan, and Jon Trueblood would shed their North Vietnamese uniforms and don makeshift British uniforms to convince Lieutenant Broderick, when he regained consciousness, that he had been rescued by British commandos. Jon Trueblood would fly the plane from the co-pilot's seat until Lieutenant Broderick regained consciousness and could take over the controls and land the C-47 on the deck of the *USS Midway*. All communication with the carrier would be by Lieutenant Broderick.

Before leaving from Saigon, they would leave a letter for Matt in a sealed envelope with Anne Herndon, detailing their plan to rescue Lieutenant Broderick. She would be instructed to give it to him in the event they had problems with the old plane and be reported missing. In the letter, they also would ask Matt to please alert the admiral so that when and if they were fortunate enough to make it to the *USS Midway*, he could help hide them. The official story would be that Lieutenant Broderick had managed to escape from his captors, commandeer the vintage plane, and fly it back to his carrier. Many C-47s had been left behind in Southeast Asia after the end of World War II, and many were still in use. His claim of being rescued by British commandos would be dismissed as hallucinations resulting from his ordeal. And no one would believe that he had been held captive in China and not North Vietnam.

The plan had been designed to convince the Chinese that they had been double-crossed by Captain Dam and his men. The intention was to have the Chinese think that Captain Dam had taken back the US pilot and sold out to the Americans, and his men had been caught in the act of finishing the betrayal. Confused and unable to explain why all the Chinese were dead, Captain Dam's men nevertheless would be executed by the Chinese, who would not believe them, as they had not believed and executed Sister Claire and her innocent orphans. A separate fate would lay in store for Captain Dam, who fancied himself a dragon from the sea.

Gazing out the window of the modified KC-135, as he turned back to his thoughts, George told himself that it had been a very good plan, and its execution had gone flawlessly.

They took off from Saigon late in the afternoon on Monday, June 28, shortly after the Russian device had arrived from the United States.

The flight to Da Nang had been routine and uneventful. At Da Nang, they refueled and filled the extra fuel cells, as planned. By the time they had finished, The Yellow Rose of Texas weighed close to her maximum takeoff weight. Jon Trueblood had to use all of his skills as a pilot to gently coax the old girl to become airborne. She used much more runway than usual in making up her mind. Captain Chrisandra and Lieutenant Sullivan grew more and more nervous quietly watching the runway grow shorter as it disappeared under the nose of the plane. When they finally lifted off, sensing the tension and in an effort to break it, Jon Trueblood looked back at his two comrades with a gleam in his eye and said, "The last time I had to coax a woman that hard, I was fourteen and trying to convince her to let me make love to her."

"Fourteen," laughed Lieutenant Sullivan. "And how old was she?"

"She was twenty-five and my schoolteacher on the reservation. She liked to wear these sheer blouses, and you could see her bra through them. Boy did she have a set of knockers."

"Now I know why the plane was having so much trouble getting off the ground. It's because you're so full of shit. Give me a break, Jon, you wouldn't have known what to do with her," retorted Lieutenant Sullivan.

Captain Chrisandra interjected, "After today, I think we should change his name from Screaming Eagle to Running Eagle, in recognition of the fact that he's too full of shit to get off the ground."

"Hey, kiss my ass. We're in the air, aren't we?"

It was silly and immature banter, the type that men under tremendous pressure and staring death in the face resort to as a means of coping with the tensions of an almost impossible task, their very sanity hanging in the balance.

The tension having been released, the men finally turned back to the business at hand. They were about to drop down to 200 feet, disable their tracking mechanisms, and turn around to head north into harm's way.

As they flew north at 200 feet above the waves, Jon Trueblood maintained such a tight grip on the controls that his knuckles were white. His concentration was intense as his eyes continuously darted between the instruments and the window to check the plane's position. He kept the cockpit window open to better hear and smell the salt water that was so uncomfortably close beneath them. The night was clear, but there was a slight haze over the water. All three men had changed into their North Vietnamese gear and put on their camouflage before the plane descended to this perilous altitude. Now Captain Chrisandra and Lieutenant Sullivan checked the North Vietnamese weapons and cleaned and oiled them. They wore no jewelry and carried no identification. Like ghosts in the night, they went about their tasks, rehearsing their roles in the mission plan and preparing themselves mentally for what lay ahead.

The further north that they went, the worse the weather became. At first the clear skies gave way to increasing clouds and intermittent showers, then to a steady rain, and finally to a wind-driven downpour. The aging Pratt & Whitney R—1830 Twin Wasp radial piston engines, even after having been juiced up, struggled against the punishing headwinds that buffeted the plane and slowed its forward progress. Climbing to 250 feet to give them a slightly greater margin of error, Jon Trueblood calmly managed to keep the plane flying and out of the water. The rain was relentless and pelted the fuselage mercilessly. The strain on the engines became a strain on the men, who knew all too well that any engine failure could make the next moment their last. On and on it went, minute after minute, hour after hour. The pelting of the rain became louder and more ominous, and the buffeting grew more and more intense for what felt like an eternity.

Captain Chrisandra stood up to stretch his legs. Bracing himself by placing his hand on the side of the bouncing and jostling fuselage, he clumsily walked and stumbled his way to the cockpit, where Jon Trueblood was intently at work. He leaned out the open window to glance at the angry sea below. The howling wind drove the rain to sting his exposed face. Beneath them, the furious waves were foaming and white at the crest, mysteriously black like the night itself at the base, and a menacing and uninviting green in between. They gyrated in a cacophony of never-ending loud, thundering claps. The thought that all that stood between them and the hell below was an air frame that was older than the men flying in it and the two seriously overworked engines that were propelling it sickened the young chaplain. He felt the contents of his stomach begin to churn within, rising and then plunging in syncopation with the waves. He pulled his head back in before he gave up the roast beef sandwich he had eaten for lunch and maybe even the eggs from as far back as his breakfast. His face was still stinging as he made his way back to his seat. Surely, he thought to himself, there are no atheists out in that stuff tonight.

When the time finally arrived to change course and head for the landing strip, it was a welcome relief. As they turned and flew toward the Chinese mainland, the rain began to slow and the wind started to taper off. In approaching the coastline, Jon Trueblood was forced to climb, but he hoped that by hugging the terrain they would remain undetected.

At this point, Lieutenant Sullivan turned to Captain Chrisandra and said, "How about a prayer, Padre?" Before Captain Chrisandra was able to respond, Jon Trueblood interjected, "Please keep it short and sweet. We are getting close!" The admonition had not been necessary, for Captain Chrisandra knew exactly the prayer he wanted to say. It was short and to the point. "If it is your will, Lord, please see us safely through this coming danger. And if not, we beg for your forgiveness that our souls be judged ready."

To which Lieutenant Sullivan added, "Amen!"

Suddenly the Russian device began to sound in a loud and brisk reminder that they were within a mile of the airstrip. *Honk, Honk, Honk, Honk, Honk, Honk, Honk, Honk* ... It startled the men for a moment until they remembered what it was and what it portended.

It stopped as abruptly as it began.

Jon Trueblood cut the engines, pushed forward on the controls to start their descent, and shouted, "Hold on, we're goin' in!"

Lieutenant Sullivan and Captain Chrisandra braced themselves, as the sudden silence seemed deafening. All that could be heard was the sound of the wind whistling by the still-open cockpit window, the light rain tapping at the fuselage, and the men breathing in anticipation of what was to come.

The Yellow Rose of Texas introduced herself to China, hitting the primitive airstrip with a sudden loud and rude jolt. She bounced along in modest protest, jostling her passengers like rag dolls to let them know she wasn't entirely pleased with the way she was being treated, then relented and came to a rolling stop in what Jon Trueblood later termed a "controlled crash."

The three men disembarked immediately, but as the Russian had predicted, the airstrip was unguarded and deserted. It had been beyond the comprehension of the Chinese that anyone would have an interest in their remote and abandoned relic of an airfield. They were wrong, and thirty-eight of their countrymen were about to pay the ultimate price for their mistake.

The Americans followed their plan precisely. First they set the explosives around the hangar and timed them to detonate in three hours. Their thinking was that if they were still there at that time, they probably would have been captured or killed. Next, they refueled the plane, being careful to deposit all the empty fuel cells back inside the craft so as not to leave any evidence of an American presence, before descending down the dirt road to the compound. Although it had stopped raining, the rain clouds still hung heavy over them, and the darkness enveloped them. Their clothing, soaked from their perspiration and the rain, clung to them in the damp, humid air. The insects were as relentless and merciless as the rain had been earlier.

The men walked in a single file, carefully placing one foot in front of the other, and stopped regularly to check the terrain and listen. Walking through deep puddles, grassy clumps, and thick mud was difficult. They took great care to secure anything on them that might make any noise and to avoid stepping on any twigs or other debris that might make a sound. It was critical to surprise the three guards and take them out without alerting the rest of the compound.

As they approached the gate, they stepped off the rustic road and into the foreboding, cold, wet brush and crouched down, hoping there were no snakes or other unwelcoming denizens to contend with as they observed their prey—the three Chinese guards. The guard at the gate sought shelter under the tower and had his back to them as he smoked a cigarette. The guard in the tower had been following the guard walking the perimeter with the searchlight. Judging by the placement of the light, the men concluded that they had about three minutes before that guard would make the turn at the northeast corner of the compound fence and start walking toward them and the gate. The time had come to commence their assault, the men told each other through prearranged hand signals.

Captain Chrisandra placed the girlie magazines he had purchased in Saigon inside his shirt for safekeeping and stealthily disappeared east into the brush. The other two men remained where they had been. Two minutes later and thirty yards to the east, Captain Chrisandra crawled out from under the brush and slithered across the path the sentry walked to the perimeter fence. Once there, he removed the magazines from his shirt and shoved them under the fence and up against the inside of the wire mesh to appear to have been blown there from across the compound. As he pushed his body backwards across the path and back into the thick brush, his eyes caught a glimpse of the beautiful bare-chested model that was smiling at him from the page of the magazine pressed against the mesh. She definitely would snag the guard for him, of that he was sure, but he could not help taking pride in the fact that she had nothing on his beloved Claire.

He returned unnoticed to the other men by the time the unsuspecting guard finally rounded the northeast corner. As the guard approached the magazines, the searchlight that had been accompanying him illuminated the provocative pictures to his surprise and delight. Taking the bait, he excitedly called in Chinese to the other two guards in a hushed conspiratorial voice as he ran to the gate. The Americans hadn't understood a word he said, but they nevertheless got the message. The guard that was smoking under the tower flicked away his cigarette and hurried to open the gate and join his comrade. The guard in the tower positioned the light on them and climbed down from his perch to join them.

All three guards either left their weapons behind or put them down in their excitement to grab and view the magazines. With their backs to the Americans, they became totally engrossed in the pictures, as they chatted and laughed loudly. It would prove to be a fatal mistake.

The three Americans sprang into action in unison. Lieutenant Sullivan took the guard on the left. Reaching over the guard's right shoulder from behind with his right hand, he thrust his oversized knife into the unsuspecting man's heart, while he covered the startled soldier's mouth with his left hand. Jon Trueblood chose the sentry, who was standing in the middle buried in his magazine. Having become aware of the sudden commotion to his left, the man turned and looked in that direction. As he did, Jon Trueblood charged into the amazed soldier, ramming his large knife into his victim's chest, killing him instantly. The man and his magazine fell silently to the ground. Captain Chrisandra picked the guard on the right. The doomed sentry started to turn in an attempt to scream for help. Before he had the chance, Captain Chrisandra was on him. With a sudden and powerful swipe of his combat knife, he slit the Chinese soldier's throat from ear to ear, severing everything in the knife's path, in one devastatingly violent act. When the three Americans were finished, the only sound to be heard was the noise of the magazine pages flipping in the wind.

The first phase of the attack accomplished, the three men set about the next step in their plan of assault on the compound. Captain Chrisandra removed the key to the compound's gate from the dead guard's pocket and locked the gate with all inside before returning the key to the pocket where he found it. Seeing that there was a helicopter on the pad, Jon Trueblood disabled the radio in it, before he climbed up the tower, bringing with him a Soviet RPG–7 rocket-propelled grenade launcher. He began to operate the searchlight as Captain Chrisandra and Lieutenant Sullivan donned gas masks and took up their positions outside of the barracks. They shot special gas canisters into the barracks designed to render the sleeping soldiers unconscious for a short period of time without any lasting effects or any trace. In the interim, Jon Trueblood was prepared to use the RPG to blow up the helicopter and the communication hut had the assault turned hot. Both Lieutenant Sullivan and Captain Chrisandra had instructed Jon Trueblood, much to his chagrin, that if things went badly, they were prepared to die in avenging Claire's death, and he should also blow up the barracks with the RPG to assure that Captain Dam didn't get out alive. Fortunately, things went according to plan, and the gas canisters did their job, sparing Jon Trueblood having to face a difficult decision. Lieutenant Sullivan and Captain Chrisandra next repeated their gas canister attacks, first at the communications hut, and then at the infirmary, in both cases with success.

Jon Trueblood came down from the tower, put on his gas mask, and took up his position outside the communication hut. The other two men were already in position outside the infirmary. They simultaneously entered both buildings and proceeded to kill the unconscious Chinese that they found. Jon Trueblood came across the passed out radio operator in the hut, and the other two Americans found three unconscious Chinese that they identified as the base commander, the male nurse, and a guard. They also found Captain Dam and the American prisoner there, unconscious.

They bound and gagged Captain Dam as planned and rescued the American prisoner from the torture he had been undergoing. They carried the unconscious North Vietnamese and the navy flier to the Chinese helicopter on the pad by the compound gate. At that point they ascertained that they had killed a total of seven Chinese and prepared to enter the barracks to kill the remaining thirty-one.

When they first conceived their plan, both Lieutenant Sullivan and Captain Chrisandra were uncomfortable with the notion of killing the Chinese soldiers while they slept in their beds. However, after witnessing what they had been doing to Lieutenant Broderick, their qualms dissipated. They found the prisoner naked, his hands and feet tied to a wooden chair. Soaking wet towels were wrapped around his head and sucked into his mouth and nose as he desperately attempted to breath.

Electrical wires were attached to his genitals. Next to the chair in which the prisoner sat tethered, was a table on which there sat a large container of water and a ladle. Also on the table was a battery to which the electrical wires attached to the prisoner could be connected. The loose end of the wires were found in the hands of the male nurse, who was unconscious and lying across the table. It didn't take the American rescuers long to conclude what had been taking place there—an endless cycle of water torture that took the prisoner to the point of passing out and electrical shocks that brought him painfully back to consciousness for more of the same. It was a miracle that he hadn't been electrocuted yet. He probably would've been, once they were done with him.

When they entered the barracks, Captain Chrisandra remained by the door with a Soviet AK-47 in hand in case any of the unconscious soldiers came to and surprised them. The other two Americans counted the Chinese in their beds and the Vietnamese who were sleeping on the floor. All the Vietnamese soldiers that Russ Pulton had told them to expect were accounted for, but one of the Chinese men was missing from his bed, which understandably raised a concern among the Americans, who immediately began to search for him. It wasn't long before Jon Trueblood found the missing Chinese soldier, unconscious in the barrack's latrine, and put a bullet in the back of his head.

Jon Trueblood and Lieutenant Sullivan gathered all the weapons that they could find and dumped them outside the barracks in a pile. As Captain Chrisandra continued to stand guard at the door with the AK-47, the other two Americans began to bind the hands of the Chinese behind their backs while they lay face down and unconscious on their beds. Next they shot each bound Chinese soldier in the back of the head, execution style, with the North Vietnamese weapons. When they finished, the three Americans exited the barracks, leaving the fifteen still unconscious North Vietnamese soldiers unharmed. Once on board the Chinese helicopter, Jon Trueblood fired it up and flew them the short distance to the airstrip.

When they arrived at the airstrip, Captain Chrisandra picked up the limp body of Captain Dam, carried him to the waiting C-47, locked the still unconscious, bound, and gagged North Vietnamese Captain in the plane's bathroom, and hung an Out of Order sign on the door. He put the key to the lock in his pocket. Lieutenant Sullivan picked up the passed-out American pilot, carried him to the plane, and placed him in the pilot's seat. In the meantime, Jon Trueblood parked the Chinese helicopter near the hangar so that it would be destroyed when the explosives around the hangar detonated.

When Jon Trueblood returned to the C-47, he joined his brethren in changing from his North Vietnamese clothing to the makeshift British uniforms they brought with them, and they dressed Lieutenant Broderick in North Vietnamese clothing and strapped him into his pilot's seat. The rest of the North Vietnamese clothing, as well as the North Vietnamese weapons, they left behind on the field when they closed the door to the aircraft.

When the plane was readied and in position for takeoff, Jon Trueblood gunned the engines and The Yellow Rose of Texas roared down the old runway, bouncing and shaking in protest before finally becoming airborne. It was as if she knew that this would be her last flight.

As they climbed to the east, Aurora was there to greet them with the first signs of the coming dawn. Behind them, back at the airstrip and the compound, they had left not a trace of an American presence, not even a footprint. However, all three men knew well that their mission hadn't ended yet. They still had to clear Chinese air space, find the *USS Midway*, and land on her rolling deck.

Shortly after they crossed over the Chinese coast and turned south to head down the middle of the Gulf of Tonkin, they flew over a Chinese trawler. It had been running without lights, and they hadn't seen it until it was too late. They hoped that they still were shrouded in enough darkness that the Chinese captain didn't recognize the American insignias. Such was not the case, and the Chinese mariner radioed in their position. However, in the darkness he mistook them for a P-3 Orion recon plane, another propeller-driven aircraft.

At about the same time the Chinese were scrambling their jet fighters to intercept what they thought was a sophisticated American electronic surveillance aircraft in their air space, the explosives detonated at the hangar on the old airfield. The explosions were deafening and brutal. They startled the semi-conscious North Vietnamese soldiers at the compound and obliterated the hangar, its contents, and the helicopter. It was beyond the imagination of the Chinese to connect the dots, and they treated the two incidents as unrelated.

Unable to make contact with the compound, the Chinese dispatched a team of helicopters to investigate the unexplained explosion. When the Chinese arrived at the scene, they found the destroyed helicopter and the demolished hangar still in flames. Entering the compound, they found their dead countrymen and the North Vietnamese attempting to escape in a state of panic. Mistaking this panic on the part of the North Vietnamese for guilt, the Chinese quickly became angered and frustrated by the lack of an explanation for what had happened. Convinced that they were being stonewalled by the uncooperative North Vietnamese, they requested and were given permission to use whatever means necessary to extract answers from the North Vietnamese. The resulting interrogation was as agonizing for the North Vietnamese soldiers as our interrogation at their hands on the whereabouts of Captain Chrisandra had been for us. When death finally came for them, they found it a welcome relief.

When the Chinese jet fighters reached their quarry, they were surprised and disappointed to find the old C-47 gunship instead of a sophisticated spy plane. They were joking with one another over their radios that the trawler captain had better get his eyes examined, when they spotted American fighters approaching from the *USS Midway*. When they contacted their base on the Chinese mainland to report that the target was an old gunship—something the Americans called a "puff" or a "puff the magic dragon"—and was not worth fighting over, the Chinese fighters received permission to break off and return home. Little did they realized that this "puff" had a real, self-proclaimed "magic dragon" on board, and that thirty-eight of their countrymen had died trying to break the will of the young American lieutenant piloting her. His secrets and the technological secrets of the wrecked fighter he had been flying had been preserved. He still may have been hurting and sore, but no one questioned his intestinal fortitude.

As The Yellow Rose of Texas was escorted back to the *USS Midway* by her fighters, the only person visible through the cockpit window and heard conversing on the radio was Lieutenant Broderick. He was the one who landed the C-47, and he alone emerged from the craft with the admiral. The three other Americans remained out of sight on board the plane and changed into the seaman uniforms that the admiral brought them in the brown wrapping. Captain Chrisandra was careful to take with him the key to the lock on the bathroom door of the old plane when he changed his clothing. They then inconspicuously boarded Matt Kerr's plane, where they cost the admiral five dollars when they responded to his question of why they had done it, by saying, "Because chicks dig it, sir."

Not long thereafter, the crew of the *Midway* unceremoniously pushed The Yellow Rose of Texas off the side of the carrier at the request of their admiral. Still bound and gagged and locked in her lavatory, but now conscious and aware of the rising water, as the gracious old lady quietly slipped under the waves of the tranquil South China Sea, was the dragon himself—*Captain Ton That Dam*—his thrashing restrained and his screams muted until he went silent and still, as had we in our graves. The self-proclaimed dragon returned from whence he said he came, not by the "winged goddesses," but in one of their airships, slain by Claire's Prince George the Dragon Slayer.

– 27 –

On Tuesday morning, June 29, 1971, the meeting with Russ reconvened in the conference room at Langley. Sully had been the first to arrive and was seated, drinking his second cup of coffee, when Russ was brought into the room. The others filed in randomly, some with coffee, others with coffee and a donut, some alone, and others in groups. Once everyone had a chance to get settled, the microphone was turned on, and Sully invited Russ to begin.

Clearing his throat and saying good morning as he moved his head to survey the room, Russ began to speak.

"Yesterday I explained the reasons behind the decision of our group to assassinate President Kennedy. Today I will explain how we decided to go about doing it and why we chose the method we did.

"You in the CIA have an expression you call *sheep dipping*. As I understand it, American farmers dip their sheep in a liquid to remove the parasites from the sheep's skin. In the intelligence community, I am told you use it to describe the process by which an agent's connection to the agency is removed and a new skin or image is given to that person. Well, you might say that I was put through a sheep dipping to remove my connection to the Soviet government and to give me a new image as a rogue soldier of fortune, so to speak. My records were altered to show that I was given a dishonorable discharge from the Soviet military for insubordination and that I had become a freelance gun for hire. My skills as a sharpshooter were well documented, as was my reputation as a disgruntled loner with violent tendencies. In short, if you needed an assassin, I was your man. I also still had a prior alias as a Mexican businessman from my days in Paris in the 1950s, if I needed it to help me enter and exit the United States."

"We are aware of that alias," interjected Sully, before motioning the Russian to please continue, which Russ gladly did.

"We officially named the endeavor Operation Paladin, after the American TV series from the 1950s called *Have Gun—Will Travel*. Viktor Martynova saw the show when he visited the United States in 1959 with Nikita Khrushchev and liked it. As you know from my earlier discussion concerning the cuff links, Viktor secretly renamed the operation Dallas Moon at a later point in time. Regardless of the name, however, the Soviet government had to be able to maintain plausible deniability for my actions."

"How did Viktor Martynova obtain clearance for such a mission?"

"He procured it from Premier Khrushchev and his lieutenants at the Kremlin, including Mr. Kostikov at the Soviet embassy in Mexico City, by deliberately misrepresenting its purpose to them. He informed them that he had reason to be concerned that an attempt might be being planned to assassinate the American president and blame it on us or Fidel Castro and the Cubans. His worry, of course, was that this might lead to an all-out nuclear confrontation. He told them that under Operation Paladin it would be my mission, undercover as a malcontent soldier of fortune and potential assassin for hire, to try and uncover the facts and to thwart the effort, if necessary. Mr. Kostikov indicated that he had been hearing some faint rumblings to the same effect, although he had not been able to confirm any of them. Viktor Martynova assured them that he and I would keep Mr. Kostikov apprised of our actions, and Premier Khrushchev acquiesced.

"In reality, it was my mission to have myself hired by any persons or groups, other than Fidel Castro, of course, who might want to eliminate your President Kennedy. I was then to carry out the assassination in a way that would deflect blame away from us, including removing any loose ends that might tie me to the event.

Viktor Martynova secretly renamed the mission Dallas Moon, when it later was determined that the assassination would take place in Dallas. He had promised me that if the operation was a success and I remained undetected and anonymous, after a reasonable amount of time, he would arrange a hearing that would vindicate me and restore me to my former military rank."

"And did that happen?" a curious Sully asked.

"Yes. A hearing was convened in 1965, after Premier Khrushchev was removed from power and while I was still in North Vietnam. It was after that hearing and the restoration of my rank that I became an adviser to the North Vietnamese."

"I see. Is this the reason that Viktor Martynova took such an unusual and vigorous interest in having you found after the story leaked about what you'd revealed at the orphanage in 1969?"

"Yes, I had outlived my usefulness and was nothing but a liability to him, so he wanted me dead. It's that simple."

"I understand," said Sully.

Next he asked Russ if he could change gears and elaborate on the clients he had been able to attract and how those relationships had come about. Russ agreed and began to speak again.

"The first client I garnered was the administration of Ngo Dinh Diem. I wish to make it clear that I never actually met with or spoke directly with Mr. Diem or his brother and adviser, Mr. Nhu. My contact was a senior person in the South Vietnamese government who claimed to be representing them. His name was Nguyen Long. I was introduced to this senior person by an undercover North Vietnamese agent by the name of Tran Van Tam, who was working in the Saigon administration of Mr. Diem. As I've said, the two brothers were astute and by 1963 could see what was coming once President Kennedy was reelected. I had no reason to doubt the authenticity of what I was being told. I was to be paid $500,000 in US dollars up front and another $500,000 upon completion of the job. The initial $500,000 was deposited in a Swiss bank account, where it still remains, untouched by me. The other $500,000 was never paid, of course, because Mr. Diem and Mr. Nhu already had been killed, as had Mr. Long, by the time the assassination of Mr. Kennedy took place.

"I went to North Vietnam in early 1963 in my role as a soldier of fortune. Nguyen Long told me that I was attractive to them because their American sponsors wouldn't be aware of me, nor would they think to connect me to the Diem regime.

"It was through Nguyen Long that I was introduced to Pierce Cutler while he was on a business trip to South Vietnam in early 1963. At first, we both danced around the issue that had brought us together. However, as the bourbon flowed, the conversation became far more direct and visceral in nature. He let me know that he was a longtime friend of Mr. and Mrs. Johnson and had been a major contributor to the vice-president's various political campaigns. He felt strongly that President Kennedy had lost his nerve at the Bay of Pigs and was about to do the same in Vietnam. Mr. Cutler then assured me that if his friend Lyndon were the president, things would be very different. He lamented that products such as the munitions his company produced were the best in the world, but that these products were of no value and his company would be ruined without leadership that wasn't afraid to use them when the situation warranted doing so. When he was finished, he offered to pay me an additional one million dollars over and above what Nguyen Long had offered if I would come to the United States and assassinate the president in Dallas later that year.

"I played my soldier of fortune role as we had scripted it. In telling him that I now was for all intents and purposes persona non grata in the Soviet Union, I made a point of letting him know that I considered myself to be a man without a country or any particular ideology. I made it clear to him that the reasons for his request were not as important to me as was the color of his money. I could see that my response was resonating with him. And I finished by stating that I had a gun for hire and would travel to the great state of Texas in the United States to use it.

"He asked for a demonstration of my skills, which we provided the next day when Nguyen Long drove a jeep at approximately eight miles per hour with a garbage can in the back, and I put three shots into the can in under eight seconds from a little less than ninety-eight yards away. He was visibly excited and told me that he would make the necessary arrangements and send me the documentation that I would need. One month later, the documents were delivered to me by Nguyen Long. I was very impressed with their quality and detail and with the comprehensive nature of my new identity. I was a United States citizen, with a US passport, a Texas driver's license, a social security number, a place of employment, and a home address. My name was William Robert Duxbury, my nickname was Billy Bob, and I worked as a security guard at Mr. Cutler's munitions factory outside Dallas. I was licensed to carry firearms and lived in the Oak Cliff section of the city.

"As I have told you, Viktor Martynova's code name for John F. Kennedy was Moon. And it was when I reported to him that I had been hired to assassinate the president in Dallas, Texas, that he secretly renamed the true assignment Dallas Moon. Upon my successful completion of that task and the restoration of my identity, he gave me, as a commemorative gift, the cuff links that I used to identify myself to your interdiction team. He also had a matching set made for himself.

"In September of 1963, I left Vietnam for Bangkok, where I became Billy Bob Duxbury and caught a plane to Paris. From Paris, I flew to Mexico City, where I stopped and visited the Soviet embassy before crossing the border into the USA. My reason for visiting our embassy was to check in with our assassination expert, Mr. Kostikov, as Viktor Martynova had assured Premier Khrushchev that I would. While I was there, I met with Mr. Kostikov and received a briefing from one of his top aides. I was told by the aide that they were aware of Lee Harvey Oswald's recent activities. He also informed me that Mr. Castro remained concerned that the Kennedy administration might be attempting to assassinate him and that a double agent, whom he identified only as a minister in the Cuban government, might be trying to provoke the Kennedy administration by offering to assassinate Mr. Castro for them. If the Americans were to take the bait, he told me that the Cubans were making noise about responding in kind and might be dumb enough to become involved with Oswald. The same aide also told me that with that in mind, they had hired a US counterintelligence agent to kill Oswald, but that on the day before our meeting, the agent had been arrested in El Paso, Texas, attempting to rob a bank. That is the last I heard on the subject, because I had no further contact with our embassy in Mexico until after the assassination of President Kennedy."

Russ stopped to take a drink of water to quench his thirst and sooth his dry throat. As he did, he asked if there were any questions.

After a momentary silence, Sully asked Russ if he had seen any evidence that Pierce Cutler may have been acting with the authorization and knowledge of Lyndon Johnson or any other high profile US government figure. Russ answered that Pierce Cutler was a serial name dropper, who also claimed to know many of the Texas oil aristocracy and Richard Nixon, among others. In fact, he made a point of saying that Mr. Cutler indicated that he would be seeing Mr. Nixon at a corporate event in Dallas in November that was scheduled for around the same time the assassination was being planned. But no, Russ was careful to note that he never had seen any evidence of involvement by Mr. Johnson or any of the others. Smiling, however, he mused that he doubted that he would've been made privy to it by Pierce Cutler, even if Mr. Johnson or any of the others had been involved. When it came to details about the assassination, Russ lamented that Pierce Cutler was all business and operated strictly on a need to know basis.

"So, let me confirm," said Sully, "you're saying that to the best of your knowledge, neither Vice-President Johnson nor Mr. Kostikov had anything to do with the Kennedy assassination."

"Correct," responded Russ, "that's what I'm saying."

"Thank you," replied Sully, before suggesting that the group take a five-minute break.

When they returned, Sully asked Russ if he thought Pierce Cutler had been acting alone. Russ was quick to answer that he didn't think so and was pretty sure of the opposite. However, he had no clear idea who these accomplices might have been, because the Texan had not chosen to share those details with him.

Sully nevertheless pressed the issue by asking the Russian to speculate on who those persons or entities might have been. Visibly uncomfortable with having been asked to do so, Russ reluctantly obliged. Moving nervously in his seat, he began to respond.

"There must have been someone from within your government involved, at least tangentially, because on the day of the assassination I was provided with a Secret Service badge and a revolver to use, and that badge was sufficiently authentic in appearance to satisfy a Dallas police officer who stopped me and asked me for identification immediately following the shooting. It convinced him that I was a Secret Service agent, and he let me proceed.

"I also think that Pierce Cutler may have had some help from your American Mafia. On the morning of the assassination, I was picked up at my home in Oak Cliff and driven to Dealey Plaza by a man I knew as Jake Diamond, who owned a local night club and striptease place. Many mob members, along with local police officers and at least one person from your agency, frequented this establishment. I know because I would go there from time to time, and when I did, Mr. Diamond would introduce them to me while joking and talking with them. I think he enjoyed being able to impress me with his importance."

"Did you ever see Pierce Cutler in the establishment?" asked Sully.

"No, and I don't think he ever went there. Jake Diamond seemed to be more of an assistant to Pierce Cutler. Their relationship was one of business acquaintances, and I don't think that they traveled in the same social circles. As I said, Mr. Diamond is the one who picked me up in his green pickup truck on the morning of November 22, 1963, and drove me. He also is the one who gave me the badge and the service revolver and instructed me on what I was to do. He previously had supplied me with the Italian rifle—a Fucile di Fanteria Modello 91/38 that you refer to as a model 1891/1938 infantry rifle—that he insisted I must use. It had been manufactured in Terni, Italy and was not as reliable a weapon as my own. I had to spend hours practicing with it at a firing range. He also is the person who lent me a red Ford car to use for that purpose and from time to time, when I needed a car. I think the Ford was called a Falcon or a Comet, but I don't really remember."

Sully interrupted Russ once again to ask, "Do you remember the names of the local law enforcement personnel and of the CIA employee you met there?"

"Only the first names of a few of them because that was all that anyone ever used. For example, most people simply knew me as Billy Bob. I doubt this will be of any help to you, but the local police officers whom I met and whose names I still can remember, were John, Dan, and Joe—very common names. There was one fellow that I think was a local policeman, but I'm not sure. His nickname was KJ. The CIA agent was Chris or Christopher.

"I do remember the full name of a retired Dallas police officer that worked there as a bouncer and as an occasional body guard for Mr. Diamond. His name was Richard Albridge, but everyone called him Dick. The reason he sticks out in my mind is that he drove an old Ford that had been a Dallas police car. He bought it earlier in the year from a used car dealer, and it still had the number 107 painted on it. That number registered with me because that was the age my grandfather was when he died, and he was the oldest person I've ever known. I even told that to Dick and he started calling his car Old Jan because my grandfather's name was Jankowsky. He was a nice guy and would give me a ride home sometimes, either in the Ford or on his Harley—he loved that motorcycle."

Sully stopped Russ, to ask, "If people only used first names, how did you know that they were in law enforcement or organized crime?"

"They all seemed to know each other rather well and revealed more than they realized about themselves as they drank and joked with each other. For example, they had nicknamed the CIA employee Secret Agent Man. One of the police officers looked a little like President Kennedy, so they called him Officer Jack or Mr. President. The people that were rumored to be affiliated with organized crime were mostly from out of town and came from places like Miami, Chicago, and New Orleans. I knew who they were because they commonly were referred to as the Crooked Nose Crowd. But Mr. Diamond did not make as much of an effort to introduce me to them. I didn't have much interaction with them or know them very well."

"Were there any other persons or groups that you saw who may have been working with Mr. Cutler and Mr. Diamond?"

"Yes," replied Russ to Sully. "I think Jake Diamond may have recruited some people from the Cuban exile community who were unhappy with President Kennedy because they had lost relatives in the Bay of Pigs fiasco. However, I never saw or met any of them until the day of the assassination."

"What do you mean? Can you elaborate on that?"

"As I've said, John, on the day of the assassination, Jake Diamond drove me to Dealey Plaza in his truck. As we drove there, he instructed me to meet a railroad worker named Martino Gutierrez on the grassy knoll, who turned out to be a husky Cuban. I know he was Cuban because we spoke while we waited for the president's motorcade to arrive. What I don't know is if his name really was Martino Gutierrez or something else. He did refer to himself by that name, but that doesn't mean anything, since I referred to myself as Billy Bob Duxbury.

"Let me back up a little bit and go back to when Jake and I arrived in Dealey Plaza. I got out of the truck, walked to the back, and lifted out my rifle, which was wrapped in paper. I carried it with me as I walked up the slope of the grassy knoll and met Martino, who was standing behind the fence at the top. He had recognized Jake Diamond's truck and knew who I was as I approached. As we waited for the motorcade, he seemed to busy himself doing something with the railroad tracks or a switch. I don't know enough about railroads to know if he really was working or simply acting busy. Nevertheless, we spoke as he worked. He told me that his wife, Isabella, had a sister named Victoria who had lost her boyfriend—I think his name was Sam—in the Bay of Pigs invasion. I told him that I was an American of Russian and Polish descent and that my parents had changed our name when we came to America because nobody could pronounce our Russian name, but that I still could speak a little Russian from listening to them in our house growing up. He laughed and asked me where I came up with Billy Bob Duxbury. He had been expecting a real Texan—a broken-boned, ex-rodeo rider type. I told him Billy Bob was the name of a bar and dance hall in Fort Worth, and Duxbury had been the name of the street on which my parents had lived when they first moved to the United States. They wanted me to have a real local name. He once again laughed loudly and in a jovial and animated manner as he waved his hand to pretend he was lassoing a steer said to me, 'You do, you do, my friend.'

"Martino was dressed like a railroad worker in dirty blue striped overalls and wore thick gloves and a puffy hat. I of course had a suit and tie on, as I had been instructed to wear, so that I would appear to be a Secret Service agent.

"My orders were to wait and not shoot until I first heard a shot from the Book Depository building. Presumably, the reason for waiting was to deflect attention away from me. I waited, and as soon as I heard the shot from the building, I took two shots. I had planned to take a third, but it wasn't necessary because I saw through my gunsight the damage my second shot did to the president's head—I knew a kill shot when I saw it. Instead, I quickly gave the rifle to Martino, who dismantled it and put the pieces into a railroad tool bag he had with him. He walked casually with the bag in hand to a green station wagon that he had parked nearby, and I walked back along the fence. It was at this point that I was confronted by the Dallas police officer, who accepted my credentials as that of a Secret Service agent and let me go. Shortly thereafter, I, too, went over to the green station wagon and got into the passenger side front seat. We drove out of the parking lot along the north side of the Book Depository and turned right onto Houston Street. Next we made another right onto Elm Street, when Martino abruptly pulled to the curb and stopped. A man who had been running down the slope from the direction of the Book Depository jumped into the back seat of the station wagon.

"As we sped away in the direction of Oak Cliff, Martino introduced the man in the back seat to me as Lee Harvey Oswald. I said hello without turning my head because I instantly became alarmed. I met Oswald in Russia, when he was working at the factory in Minsk and when he was in Kiev. I was certain that he would remember me if he saw me and would know immediately that I wasn't who I said I was. It had turned into an extremely tense situation for me, because I already had concerns that I might be eliminated once the assassination took place. It was not inconceivable that they would want to be rid of me as a loose end that could be linked to Pierce Cutler or Jake Diamond. This encounter only made matters worse. I still had my Secret Service sidearm on me, so I reached inside my jacket to loosen the holster in an attempt to be better prepared to defend myself should I need to. It would not be necessary.

"Martino, in an effort to make conversation among us, told the man in the back seat that I spoke a little Russian, which in turn caused the man to try and converse with me in that language. I immediately turned around to look at him because I knew then that he couldn't be Oswald. His Russian was much too poor. The Lee Harvey Oswald I knew in Minsk had been fluent in Russian. I didn't let on that I knew he wasn't who he said he was. However, I did marvel at how much he resembled Oswald—even though he was bigger and stronger than I remembered the ex-marine to be. He didn't recognize me, further confirming for me that he wasn't Lee Harvey Oswald."

"Two questions: Do you know why Oswald was in Kiev? And can you tell me anything more about the green station wagon—its make, license plate, or anything like that?"

"I may be mistaken, but my recollection is that Oswald was in Kiev to speak with Cuban exchange students. As for the wagon, it was a Rambler with Texas plates, but I don't remember the number. I think it was owned or used by a woman because it had a lipstick canister; a small mirror and a frilly box of sweet-smelling tissues on the front seat; and a pair of high heels on the floor under my feet that I don't think belonged to Martino—they clearly weren't his size."

After some momentary laughter by the group in the room, Sully got things back on track, by asking Russ if he had been seriously concerned for his life, or had he just been taking reasonable precautions?

"Oh, no, I had very serious concerns! If these guys had the wherewithal to kill a sitting American president, I didn't think they would have any problem eliminating one loose end, especially an outcast loner as I was pretending to be. I was so concerned that I arranged my own exit strategy and didn't rely on theirs. I also quietly kept my old alias as a Mexican businessman in my back pocket in case I needed it to get out of the US.

"Jake Diamond had told me he would pick me up in the red Ford at my residence in Oak Cliff later that afternoon and would drive me to a dry river basin where a plane would be waiting to fly me to safety. When we arrived at my Oak Cliff apartment, I got out of the green station wagon, said good-bye to Martino and the man in the back seat, and started to walk toward my apartment. As soon as the Rambler was out of sight, I turned and walked quickly in the opposite direction to a parked car in which my friend, Galina Daluda, had been waiting for me. She already had gathered my personal effects from the apartment and placed them in the trunk. So we immediately drove away once I got in the car. I never even took the chance of going back into my apartment. Instead, she took me to a nearby apartment of a relative of hers where I planned to stay in hiding until things settled down."

At this point, Sully rose from his seat and suggested that they take a break for lunch. He told the group that they would reconvene in one hour and asked them to formulate any questions that they might have because he planned to begin the afternoon session with a question and answer period.

When the room had cleared, Sully invited Russ to have lunch with him in his office. His secretary had arranged to have a small table and two chairs brought in and had ordered two hot meals from the Langley dining room for them. They would be dining on a cup of consommé, a small garden salad, Maryland crab cakes, green beans, and wild rice. Dessert would be an assortment of fresh berries and coffee. (She had been acting on instructions from Mary, who was very protective of her husband's diet.) She even managed a chilled bottle of white wine, a vase of flowers, and a white tablecloth for the occasion.

As the two men sat down to lunch, Sully told Russ that he had received a communiqué from Matt Kerr in Vietnam saying that the raid on the abandoned airstrip had been a complete success, in large part due to the information Russ had provided to them. The American airman had been rescued, the wreckage of his plane destroyed, and it did not appear that the Chinese were aware of the American involvement. He added that Captain Dam had been killed, and it was presumed, but not confirmed, that his men also were dead, having been done in by the angry Chinese. No Chinese had survived the interdiction.

The two men toasted the success with their wine glasses, as Russ was eager to learn more about the mission. They became engrossed in their discussion and barely had finished their lunch when it was time to resume the meeting in the conference room. As they walked back, it was clear that a genuine friendship was developing between the two former Cold War warriors—a friendship that would prove to be rocky at best.

When the question and answer period began, the others in the conference room could sense that Sully had some definite queries on his mind and remained silent in anticipation of him asking the first questions. It was as if he were the alpha male and they were going to let him feed on the carcass first, which he did without hesitation.

"Russ, I would like to begin by confirming certain points with you. You have indicated that law enforcement officials, whether local to Dallas or federal in nature, as well as individuals from organized crime in at least three cities, together with some Cuban exiles may have been implicated in the assassination of President Kennedy. Is that correct?"

"Yes, that's correct."

"Yet, with the exception of Martino Gutierrez and Jake Diamond, you place none of them in or about Dealey Plaza on the day of the assassination, nor have you shown that any of them, with the possible exception of Pierce Cutler, had a hand in the planning. The only evidence of their guilt seems to be by association—that they frequented Jake Diamond's establishment in the days, weeks, and months before November 22, 1963. While I am prepared to concede to you that at least in the case of the law enforcement officials, they might have shown better judgment, I will need more proof than you have given me if we are to conclude that they indeed were involved. For example, wouldn't you agree that the Dallas police officer who confronted you on the grassy knoll immediately after the shooting and asked for your identification appears to have been doing his job, as he should?"

"Yes, that certainly is true, but you're overlooking the fact that the badge that I showed that Dallas police officer either was genuine or was a very professional copy, good enough to satisfy him that I was a Secret Service agent. Furthermore, I can tell you that there was no Secret Service presence in Dealey Plaza where Martino and I were operating. Furthermore, the windows of the Depository and presumably the other buildings in the area hadn't been secured as you would've expected them to be!"

"Russ, the points you make are valid ones, but we're not talking here about incompetence or complacency; we're talking about evidence of active involvement."

"No, in that regard you're correct. The only evidence of active involvement that I witnessed was on the part of Jake, Martino, and the man claiming to be Lee Harvey Oswald. As for the latter, I heard the shot from the Book Depository, but I couldn't say who fired it, and the man in the back seat of the Rambler never admitted in my presence to doing anything of the sort. Look, John, I never was told beforehand by Pierce Cutler or Jake Diamond of Lee Harvey Oswald's involvement, nor can I place him in Dealey Plaza that day. The only thing I can tell you for sure is that I was the second gunman, regardless of who was the first gunman, and that I was helped by a man claiming to be a railroad worker who said his name was Martino Gutierrez."

"Speaking of Martino Gutierrez, one man does not a movement make. The fact that he was Cuban does not mean that the Cuban exile community was involved. Did Martino ever indicate to you that he was a member of Alpha 66 or any similar organization?"

"No, the only emotional connection he mentioned, as I told you earlier, was that his wife's sister's boyfriend—Sam I think was his name—had been killed in the Bay of Pigs. I must confess though, that he didn't seem to be making a personal matter of it and simply performed his role as I did mine—professionally."

Russ seemed to be getting a little agitated, and Sully, noticing it, asked him what was wrong.

"Hell, John, as I've told you previously, I don't even have firsthand evidence that Lee Harvey Oswald was the other shooter, let alone that he was in Dealey Plaza that day. Does that mean that he, too, wasn't involved?"

Smiling, Sully reached over, patted the Russian on the back, and said, "He never was convicted of the crime in a court of law and died claiming to have been merely a patsy. Who's to say that he wasn't telling the truth and that the imposter that you encountered is the only one that did the actual shooting from the Depository? After all, both a Depository employee, Carolyn Arnold, who knew Oswald; and a Dallas police officer by the name of M. L. Baker, who was being escorted by Roy Truly, the Depository superintendent, as he investigated the building immediately after the shooting, place Oswald in the Depository's second floor lunch room—one immediately before the shooting and the other right after it."

"You don't really believe that Oswald wasn't involved do you?"

"No, I don't, but you must admit that it's a real possibility, especially in light of what you have told us about there being an imposter at the scene who knew Martino Gutierrez and appeared to be working in concert with him and Jake Diamond. Also, I must confess that it always has bewildered me why Oswald didn't take what I think would've been his best shot—when the limousine carrying the president had to slow to practically a stop as it negotiated the hairpin turn from Houston to Elm Street. Instead, he waited to shoot when the car was picking up speed and driving away from him. Again, however, it makes more sense now in light of what you're telling us, namely, that Oswald or his impersonator merely was providing cover for your shots from the grassy knoll, and he very well may have been set up to ultimately take the blame."

"Everything you say is true. I too can't rule any of it out as a possibility."

Next Sully found himself asking Russ, "Speaking of Oswald, why didn't you try to stop him beforehand? After all, it would've been in line with the reason given to Premier Khrushchev and Mr. Kostikov for your mission in the first place, and it would've justified your trip to America."

The Russian hesitated for a moment and took a deep breath before responding.

"Lee Harvey Oswald represented a delicate and somewhat murky situation for me when I arrived in the United States. In retrospect, it's clear that he was involved to some extent in the assassination of John F. Kennedy in Dallas on November 22, 1963, even if you want to claim that it was merely as a patsy. But the situation wasn't as clear beforehand. When I met with Mr. Kostikov's aide in Mexico, he informed me of several rumors. One had an attempt being made on your president's life in Washington, DC, toward the end of that month, which was September. Another had Mr. Kennedy being shot while on a trip to Chicago at the beginning of November. And the third referenced the assassination being planned for Dallas, for which I'd been recruited. Lee Harvey Oswald's name had surfaced with respect to Washington and Dallas, but not in connection with the rumored attempt in Chicago. Complicating matters for me was the fact that Oswald knew me and my true role within the Soviet system from his days in Russia and was in a position to see through my cover story. Furthermore, Pierce Cutler and Jake Diamond never brought his name up to me, and I was reluctant to raise his involvement with them. After all, what reason would I have to know about him in my role as a malcontent outcast and soldier of fortune who'd been purged from the system?"

Sully stopped Russ to ask a question that had been gnawing at him. "Did Mr. Kostikov's aide give you the name of anyone in connection with the rumored attempt to take place in Chicago, if it wasn't Oswald?

"Yes, he told me that as with Oswald, it was another disgruntled ex-marine. The man's first name was either Thomas or Arthur, and I think the last name was something like Valley."

Sully suggested that the group take a short break. He wanted a chance to check out this name Russ said he had been given by the Soviet embassy in Mexico City. What he found is that an ex-marine named Thomas Arthur Vallee indeed had been arrested on Saturday, November 2, 1963, in Chicago, shortly before President Kennedy was scheduled to arrive and had been questioned by the Secret Service.

When they resumed, Sully reported to the group what he'd been able to find out about Thomas Arthur Vallee. He then asked Russ if he'd been able to obtain any other advance confirmation that Oswald might be involved in Dallas, if not from Pierce Cutler or Jake Diamond. Russ thought for a few seconds, pensively rubbing his chin, and then responded.

"One night when Dick Albridge, the retired Dallas police officer that worked for Jake, was giving me a ride home from the nightclub, I casually mentioned to him that I thought I'd heard one of the guys from the Crooked Nose Crowd talking about a Commie called Lee Harvey Oswald, and I was wondering who he was. Dick simply told me not to worry about Oswald, that he merely was a 'distraction.' Yes, that is the exact word that he used—a 'distraction.' I decided to quickly drop the subject by moving to another completely different topic, because I didn't want to give him the chance to ask me for the name of the person I'd overheard mentioning Oswald's name. I was afraid of having to lie and then run the risk of getting caught should he decide to check my story out. He never did pursue it."

"I see," said Sully. "Is there anything else you want to add?"

"Yes. As a practical matter, by the time I arrived in the United States in September of 1963, it was too late to do anything about the supposed attempt planned for that month in Washington, DC. Furthermore, the rumor that our embassy in Mexico City had been hearing about the Chicago plot scheduled for early November was that an effort would be made to blame it on the South Vietnamese regime of President Diem and not us or the Cubans. Consequently, I decided to concentrate on my role in the Dallas scheme, since it was the one that I knew for a fact was in the works. I told myself I would investigate Oswald privately on my own time, and I did. I made several trips by the Oswald residence on West Neely Street, and then later, after he moved, by the apartment on Beckley Avenue in Dallas. I did this in the days leading up to November 22, 1963, but I never saw anything unusual.

"Nevertheless, I took steps to be in a position to kill Oswald if it became clear to me that he had been involved in the assassination and that his activities might be used to implicate us or the Cubans. However, all that became moot when Jack Ruby murdered Oswald for me."

Stopping Russ, Sully asked, "What steps had you taken?"

"My friend Dick would lend me his car, the former police cruiser he called Old Jan, to use from time to time. He was very relaxed and left some old identification and a gun that had its serial numbers removed in the glove box. He also kept several of his old Dallas police uniforms in the trunk. I made a copy of his keys and his identification, and I took one of his old uniforms that I altered to more or less fit me.

"Following the assassination, Galina picked me up at my apartment in Oak Cliff and took me to her relative's nearby apartment. Then I decided to make an attempt to go after Oswald. I put on the Dallas police uniform and went over to Dick's place, which was nearby, and where I knew the old police car would be parked. Albridge always preferred to ride his Harley on nice days, and it was a beautiful day.

"As soon as I got into Old Jan, I removed the gun from the glove box, checked to make sure it was loaded and placed it on the seat next to me. Then I drove over to Oswald's apartment on Beckley Avenue. I was counting on the fact that Oswald must have known Dick, if Dick knew that Oswald was being set up as a distraction, as he put it; and that Oswald would recognize the car, if he was there. When I pulled up to the curb in front of the apartment, I tapped the horn twice—something Dick had a habit of doing—hoping to prompt Oswald into coming outside, where I could take a shot at him from the car and take off. But he must not have been there or did not recognize the car because he never came out. I didn't want to draw too much attention to myself, so after a short while, I gave up and drove away around the corner. I put the gun back in the glove box, parked the car where I'd found it, and returned to the apartment of Galina's relative to figure out my next move. It wasn't long thereafter that I put on the TV to learn that Officer Tippit had been shot and Oswald had been arrested in a nearby movie theater. By then I began to resign myself to the fact that I might have to attempt to kill

Oswald while he was in police custody, so I decided to hold on to the uniform. Fortunately, the situation took care of itself for me two days later, when Ruby shot Oswald."

"And why did you still feel that you needed to eliminate Oswald after the fact?" Sully inquired of Russ.

"It remained part of the official reason given for my mission by Viktor Martynova to Premier Khrushchev and Mr. Kostikov, and I still had real concerns that Oswald would be used to place the blame on us or Fidel and the Cubans. Whether Oswald had actually been the gunman or not didn't matter. I now knew that the powers that be went through the trouble of having an Oswald impersonator at the scene. Consequently, it must have been important to their plan to have the world think Oswald was there as an active participant. Furthermore, after what I'd been told by Mr. Kostikov's aide about Castro's concerns of being killed by the Kennedy administration and of his apparent attempt to provoke them with a double agent, I couldn't be certain that Castro hadn't hired or been tricked into hiring Oswald in an effort to get to Mr. Kennedy before your president could get to him."

"Were you surprised by Oswald's behavior following the assassination?"

"In what way, John? I'm not sure that I know what you mean."

"I mean that he hid the murder weapon with his fingerprints all over it not far from the sniper's nest at the Depository after having previously photographed himself holding it in his yard. He shot a police officer that had made a routine stop and then hid in a movie theater rather than try to escape. He didn't appear to have any coherent exit strategy following the assassination."

"Well, we can deduce from the existence of the impersonator that Pierce Cutler and Jake Diamond had a role for Oswald in their plan. And we know from Dick that at least beforehand that role was as a distraction. I suspect that Oswald wasn't aware that he was being framed as part of the plan to shift the blame to us or the Cubans until it was too late. His behavior is consistent with a man who thinks he merely is providing a smoke screen, then suddenly realizes that he isn't a diversion, rather he is the fall guy, and panics. I am inclined to think that he was playing some kind of double role as an undercover operative for someone other than us and kept thinking his handlers would come to his rescue. Instead, they let him get shot while in police custody."

Sully asked Russ if he had watched the television coverage of Lee Harvey Oswald being shot, to which he answered yes.

Next he posed a hypothetical question to Russ, "If you didn't know for certain that the person in custody, who got shot, was Lee Harvey Oswald, how sure would you have been that he was the individual you remember meeting in Russia and not the imposter that got into the station wagon with you?"

"Are you asking me to put reality aside and suppose something that isn't true? Because we know for a fact that it was Lee Harvey Oswald, who got shot, right?"

"Right."

"Okay. If I didn't know, it would be hard to say with absolute certainty. They looked so much alike. I think I could only know for sure if I heard them speak in Russian. Although, I must admit that the stature of the man shot on television was smaller and more in line with what I remember."

"Had you ever seen Jack Ruby, the man that shot Lee Harvey Oswald, before you saw him on television after the assassination?"

"The man you call Jack Ruby could have been a brother to the man I knew as Jake Diamond."

"Could they have been one and the same person?"

"No."

"How can you be so sure?"

"Jack Ruby is dead, unless I'm mistaken?"

"No, you're correct; he's dead."

"Well, Jake Diamond is alive and well and living very comfortably under an assumed identity in Costa Rica."

The silence in the room was such that you could have heard a pin drop. After an extended pause, Sully asked Russ how he had come to find that out.

Russ began to explain.

"After Khrushchev was removed from power in 1964 and Viktor Martynova rose in stature under the new regime, I was able to obtain access to many records, including those concerning the Soviet embassy in Mexico City. I learned from these records that Jake Diamond had been a double agent and had been working for us while also working for Pierce Cutler. After the assassination, his death was staged, and he was relocated to Costa Rica under the assumed name of Jack Ruben."

"Jack Ruben!" exclaimed Sully as he made a notation on his pad to investigate and verify the existence of a Jack Ruben living in Costa Rica. "But you confirmed for me earlier, Russ, that Mr. Kostikov had no involvement in the assassination of John F. Kennedy. Which is it now?"

"Mr. Kostikov didn't have any involvement, as I told you. He knew Jake Diamond was a Soviet agent, as he knew of my cover as a soldier of fortune, but didn't know any more about Jake Diamond's part in the assassination plot than he did about mine. Viktor Martynova was the puppeteer, and he kept all the strings to himself. Even I and the rest of the strategy group, at least as far as I can tell, didn't know that Jake Diamond was a double agent until after the fact in 1964."

"I said it before and I'll say it again. This Viktor Martynova has a brass set, wouldn't you agree?"

"I have to admit, it was pretty gutsy of him."

"Did you ever see Jake Diamond or Jack Ruben, as he now apparently is known, after November 22, 1963?"

"No."

"How about Martino Gutierrez, the railroad worker, or the Lee Harvey Oswald impersonator?"

"No."

"Do you have any idea what may have happened to them?"

"Not really, but I wouldn't be surprised to learn that they were given new identities as well. All I know for sure is what I heard them say that day in the green Rambler station wagon. They also were to be picked up by Jake Diamond later that afternoon in the red Ford and driven to the river basin to be flown by a waiting plane to safety. But after they dropped me off, I never saw or heard from them again."

"Were they any more specific about where they were going to be flown to?"

"They seemed to think it was New Mexico, but that made no sense to me. Why would they stay in the United States? I figured they had misunderstood Jake and would be flown out of the US to Mexico. It certainly was my plan to go to Mexico using my alias as William Duxbury or as a Mexican businessman once things settled down."

"Did Jake ever tell you where they were going to fly you?"

"No, he simply said that once I was on the plane, I would receive confirmation that the rest of my fee had been deposited in the Swiss bank account and I would be flown to safety. I hadn't pushed the point, because I knew I had no intention of being on that plane or of collecting my fee."

"Did you ever see Pierce Cutler again after November 22, 1963?"

"Yes, I saw him on the night of January 6, 1964, when I went to his house to kill him, but found him already dead. I had remained in hiding at the apartment of Galina's relative until the start of the New Year. It was my plan to leave the United States and cross into Mexico with Galina on or about January 13, 1964. But before I did, I had decided to kill Pierce Cutler and Jake Diamond so that there would be two less people in the United States that could connect me to the assassination. I couldn't find Martino Gutierrez and had no way of finding the Oswald impersonator. I quickly learned that Jake Diamond had been killed in a fiery car crash on the night of January 3, 1964, and when I got to Pierce's house that night, nobody else was home, and he appeared to have recently shot himself in his study, in what I thought at the time was an apparent suicide."

"You say 'in what I thought at the time was an apparent suicide.' Do you have a different view now?"

"Yes, I suspect that Jake Diamond got to him before me and before he left for his new life in Costa Rica. I now recall a detail that I should have taken notice of then but didn't. Jake Diamond left his calling card on Pierce Cutler's desk—a single yellow rose."

"A single yellow rose?" said Sully. "I don't understand."

"The streets of Dallas were lined with copious amounts of yellow roses on the day we assassinated John F. Kennedy. The yellow rose apparently has a special place in Texas history that you may understand better than me. However, when Jake Diamond dropped me off in Dealey Plaza that day in his green pickup truck, upon seeing the yellow roses, he told me that Pierce Cutler commented that they would have a secondary meaning that day. They would symbolize the death of a president too 'yellow' to use the munitions his company made and do what had to be done in the world."

"I see—very interesting. What did you do after you left Pierce Cutler's house?"

"I went back to the apartment where I had been staying until Galina drove me across the border at Nuevo Laredo, Texas, on January 13, 1964."

One of the other agents in the room asked Russ, "Are you sure you didn't kill Pierce Cutler?"

Somewhat indignantly, Russ replied, "I have just admitted to you that I killed your president. Why would I lie to you about killing Pierce Cutler? If I had killed him, I would tell you. I didn't. I found him dead in his study with a blood-splattered single yellow rose."

"But Russ, you did kill Galina once the two of you got to Mexico, did you not?" asked Sully.

"I had no choice; she had become a loose end. Our business is a ruthless one, as you well know. Lives hang in the balance. We made passionate love and enjoyed a most romantic two days together at the Hotel Comercio in Mexico City before I did what I had to do. I think of her often and long for that time that we had together."

"And what became of the relative at whose apartment you had stayed?"

"She met with a most unfortunate accident while taking a bath. The radio to which she was listening fell into the water and electrocuted her."

"Another one of your loose ends, I suppose?" inquired Sully.

"Yes, but I waited until we were ready to leave and Galina was in the car. She died without ever finding out what had happened to her relative."

Sully was quickly losing his warmth for Russ as he listened to the ruthless and cold, matter-of-fact manner in which he justified his actions. He felt conflicted because Russ had been so helpful in connection with Operation Waccabuc, the China raid to rescue Lieutenant Broderick, and yet he was so ruthless in other ways. Finally, he regained his composure and proceeded to ask Russ what he had done after leaving Mexico.

"I returned to Vietnam via Bangkok—as I had come. Over the intervening years, I lived in Vietnam with Danielle Fabre. I also made several trips between Vietnam and the Soviet Union to meet with Viktor Martynova, who as I have told you eventually held the hearing and restored my reputation, as he had promised to do. Unfortunately, it happened too late for there to be any hope of a reunion with my wife Anya and my son Dmitri. They had been killed in a train crash the year before. So I remained in Vietnam as an adviser right up until the time of my run-in with the snake and my visit to your daughter Kate's orphanage."

"I know we discussed it earlier, but I must reiterate that now I think I finally understand why Viktor Martynova took such an unusual interest in your fate and tried so desperately to have you captured or killed. Up until the present, his actions had been somewhat perplexing to me."

"Make no mistake about it; he wants me dead—so much so that I would not be surprised if he were to come after me here. He has a very good chance of becoming the next Soviet premier. That is, of course, unless he was to become implicated in the scandal that would come to light by the revelation of my involvement in the assassination of your president."

"Well, you have nothing to worry about, Russ. He appears to have bought into our ruse and thinks you were killed during a melee in the Gulf of Tonkin while trying to defect."

"You say melee in the Gulf of Tonkin. What melee, John? What are you talking about? Do you not know that I was rescued in Cambodia?"

"What you don't know is that we staged a diversionary interdiction in the Gulf of Tonkin and left a blood-stained raft with your US passport and other paraphernalia for your countrymen and the Vietnamese to find."

"But then why was I chased by Captain Dam?"

"For some reason he appears to be the only one that we weren't able to fool. But fear not, no one seems to be listening to what he had to say since there is no evidence of an interdiction having taken place in Cambodia. The incident we staged with the crashed spotter plane and the rescue of the downed pilot seems to have been effective in covering our tracks. The North Vietnamese appear to be discounting whatever happened in Cambodia as an unrelated incident."

"Wow, I had no idea that you had gone through so much trouble for me."

Sully wanted to crow to Russ that the agency had left nothing to chance, but then thought the better of tempting fate, especially in light of their spotty record on the subject. Instead, he simply moved to his next question for the Russian.

"Did you ever receive full payment from Pierce Cutler, even though you never kept your rendezvous with Jake Diamond and the getaway plane?"

"Yes, and all the monies are still there in the Swiss bank account. Please understand that what I did I did for my country, and I cannot in good conscience accept money for it. I know you think poorly of me because I killed the people I did, but I simply was doing what I had to do. As I have told you, if I had been Pierce Cutler, I would have had me killed after the assassination. In our business it simply is good practice. I wouldn't be surprised if at some point you decide to eliminate me."

"You have nothing to fear. We don't operate that way. Now tell me, did I hear correctly that Jake Diamond was a big fan of Mrs. Kennedy?"

"Yes."

"If that's so, did he ever indicate to you why he would want to assassinate her husband?"

"Yes, but quite frankly, I dismissed it as a lot of bullshit."

"What do you mean?"

"He tried to tell me that he was doing the president a favor by assassinating him."

"Why was he doing him a favor? What was the favor?"

"Apparently Jake Diamond knew a woman named Amy Russell who was dating one of the Crooked Nose guys that frequented his night club. One time, during a road trip to New Orleans, she and Jake got into an in-depth discussion about an affair she had been having with the president. She told him that notwithstanding all the public relations hype about how vigorous and athletic he was, he actually was not all that healthy and could become quite incapacitated at times and worried that his health was going to deteriorate rapidly as he aged. She intimated that their affair was a part of the president's effort to try and cram the experiences of a normal life span into the shorter remaining time of relatively good health that he thought he had left. She claimed to Jake Diamond that the president told her that she was the spice in his life."

"Not a bad line, if you can make it work, I guess," said Sully, as he rubbed his chin with the thumb and index finger of his right hand. "Look, John Kennedy had health issues, we all knew that, but I don't think they were as dire as she depicts. Mary and I were invited to the compound in Hyannis Port on one occasion, and I played touch football with the president and his family. I thought he held his own quite well. Oh, and one more thing. It was clear to Mary and me that day that Jackie, and only Jackie, was the true spice of his life."

"You're very protective of your friend the president, aren't you, John? Even in the Soviet Union, we knew that he had a roving eye for the women—much like our Viktor Martynova. But to continue, Amy Russell also indicated to Jake Diamond that the president had confided in her that he had premonitions about his own death ever since the 1960 attempt on his life at the Kennedy family home in Palm Beach, Florida, when he still was president-elect. She referred to the president as an American history buff, who seemed to take a special interest in the presidency and the assassination of Abraham Lincoln. According to her, he was fascinated by the question of whether or not Lincoln would've been as highly regarded a president if he hadn't been assassinated while in office and had been allowed to live out his life."

"An awful lot of pillow talk, wouldn't you say?" spoke up one of the CIA operatives in the room, in a somewhat sarcastic and exasperated tone.

"Please don't shoot the messenger. I'm only telling you what Jake Diamond told me. I already have told you up front that I thought he was full of shit," retorted Russ Pulton.

The same CIA operative sarcastically asked, "Did Jake Diamond ever indicate to you whether or not the president shared his conclusion on the subject with his alleged concubine?"

"He did, as a matter of fact. Jake Diamond said that the president told her that in his opinion, President Lincoln's two greatest accomplishments were saving the Union and freeing the slaves. While they both were hotly contested issues in their day, over time they had come to be seen as correct, even if only begrudgingly by some. Lincoln's assassination magnified and rendered more poignant the results, as his actions have been sanctified and etched into your nation's psyche by the personal sacrifice the president endured to make them a reality."

Persisting with this line of questioning, the same agency operative asked with a smirk, "Did Jake Diamond ever indicate if the president tied this discussion about President Lincoln into his own situation for his supposed mistress?"

"In a way, yes. He told her that his finest hour had been when he and Mr. Khrushchev had saved the world from nuclear annihilation by peacefully resolving the Cuban Missile Crisis in 1962. The president told her that if there was such a thing as a good time to die, that would have been the time for him to have been assassinated, because he doubted if anything else he accomplished as president could outdo that feat. Nevertheless, he told her that he wanted to finish the job that President Lincoln had begun in freeing the slaves by enacting comprehensive civil rights legislation. More specifically, he told her he was anxious to work with the vice-president as soon as they were reelected, to have this civil rights legislation passed—and that in his opinion, if he were to be assassinated, that legislation would probably be the reason for it."

"Tell me, did Jake Diamond ever indicate to you why assassinating the president before having a chance to pass his civil rights legislation was a help to him?" continued the CIA operative.

"Yes. Pierce Cutler had convinced Jake Diamond that Lyndon Johnson, as president, had a better chance of getting that controversial legislation successfully passed. Killing Kennedy would spare him that failure."

"Let me see if I have this straight," said Sully. "President Lincoln saved the Union and freed the slaves—two great accomplishments that were magnified by the personal sacrifice he had to endure in being assassinated for achieving them. President Kennedy, along with Mr. Khrushchev, saved the world from nuclear annihilation and was preparing to give the descendants of the slaves Mr. Lincoln had freed true equal rights for the first time—one great accomplishment and one great ambition that would be magnified by the personal sacrifice he was destined to endure by being assassinated. This, an assassination that met a premonition, and possibly a death wish on the part of the president, gave his civil rights legislation a better chance of being passed by his successor. Is that a fair assessment of Jake Diamond's rationalization for his heinous crime?"

"Yes."

"What a nut case this fellow Jake Diamond must be! President Kennedy was right when he described the Dallas of 1963 as 'nut country.' Is there anything else we should know about the so-called pillow talk between the president and Amy Russell that Jake Diamond told you?"

"Yes, there is one more thing. If you can believe Jake Diamond, he claimed that Amy Russell indicated that the president confided in her that he had a recurring dream in which he is assassinated in a place filled with yellow roses. In the dream he is riding in his Lincoln limousine without the bubble top, and the car door by him is slightly ajar when he is shot. As a result, he supposedly told her that he always was careful to make sure that door is tightly shut when he rides in the limousine."

"So?"

"When I shot President Kennedy, the car door by him and the governor was slightly ajar. The president couldn't see it because of where the governor was sitting, but I could see it in my gunsight. It sent a chill down my spine, and I don't normally pay any attention to that sort of thing."

The room had grown silent. This last bit of testimony brought the events of November 22, 1963, back into vivid focus and ever so slightly reopened the wounds of that day. No one was sure why. Perhaps it was because it was a detail that none of them had heard before.

Sensing this sudden change in mood, Sully deemed it an appropriate time to adjourn for the day. They would reconvene in the morning. He made another note to himself to check—and check he did. The car door had been ajar; the pictures told him so.

– 28 –

John Sullivan Sr. was chief of the agency's Soviet/East European or SE Division—the tip of the spear when it came to the geographic divisions of the directorate of operations and one of the most secret because it was charged with collecting intelligence and with running covert operations within the Soviet Union and the Communist countries of Eastern Europe (excluding the German Democratic Republic). He had been given control of Operation Excalibur because Russ Pulton was a Russian asset. He had been placed in charge of Operation Waccabuc because Russ Pulton had been the source of the information, but more importantly, because the president of the United States especially requested that he and Matt Kerr run the mission.

As chief of the SE Division, Sully's office was on the fifth floor of the Langley headquarters building. The two men returned there while they awaited the arrival of the van that would be taking Russ back to "the Farm," where he was being kept.

"The Farm" is the nickname given to Camp Peary, the CIA facility that is located near Colonial Williamsburg. It covers more than ten thousand acres and is bordered by Interstate 64 and the York River. The countryside is picturesque, with woods and fields that are teeming with wildlife and lakes and ponds that are rich with fish. Its appearance would lead one to believe that it is a military base, and the CIA still doesn't officially acknowledge that it even exists.

The house Russ was being kept in had barbed wire surrounding it and numerous spotlights. It made for a foreboding sight.

When the van arrived, the two men took the blue elevator in the southwest corner down to the lobby. As they exited the building, Russ stopped for a moment to gaze at the bronze statue of Nathan Hale that stands in front of the headquarters. Reading the inscription at the base of the statue of the American spy, Russ turned to Sully and said, "I, too, regret that I have but one life to lose for my country." The American simply nodded and helped the Russian into the van, then stood and watched for a moment as it pulled away. Finally he turned and entered the building to return to his office.

A war raged inside Sully that he was barely able to contain. It started earlier that day when Russ was talking about killing Galina and her relative. But Russ's comment comparing himself to Nathan Hale and regretting he has only one life to give for his country caused that struggle to grow in intensity within the ex-marine. It finally erupted out of control as Sully rode up the blue elevator on the way back to his office. He liked Russ and was grateful to him for the information he had provided on Operation Waccabuc that enabled the rescue of the American airman from the Chinese compound. His intuition told him that Russ was the genuine thing and not feeding him misinformation.

However, quite a few agents in the conference room thought that Russ was a plant to mislead us on the Soviet or Cuban involvement in the assassination. Their view was that the information on the American prisoner that the Russian had given us had been a throw-away to win our trust in him and have us lower our guard about what he had to say concerning Dallas.

Whether Russ was the real thing or not, Sully found himself troubled by the callous and cavalier manner in which the Russian had dealt with his so-called "loose ends." Galina Daluda had been his lover, going all the way back to his days in Paris, albeit on an on-and-off basis. And her relative had risked becoming an accessory to the assassination of an American president for him. Yet he'd had no compunction about killing them—even after making love to at least one if not both of them.

Gnawing at him was the voice in his head that at first had been a soft whisper and now had grown to an alarming cry, telling him that his daughter Kate may have been one of Russ Pulton's loose ends. The story the Russian told of the coincidental meeting of brother and sister, now at polar ends of an emotional civil conflict, was plausible. But how could he know for sure? The letters delivered by Danielle Fabre and the COLIAFAM member seemed to indicate that Russ had not known of Kate's fate, but then again that had proven to be a ploy. It was equally possible that Kate simply had become a loose end and Captain Dam had been dispatched to deal with her. He told himself it was time to find out once and for all. If he had to, he would beat it out of the bastard!

Reversing course, Sully, who had just sat down in his desk chair, called his wife Mary to tell her that he would be late, grabbed his things, stormed back out to the elevator and pounded the down button. Once outside and in his car, he sped to the Farm. When he arrived, he hurried into the home and down the stairs to the basement cell where Russ was being kept—knocking first, but unlocking and entering the cell without waiting for a response. Russ was quietly sitting in a chair. Framed by the door, the over-six-foot-tall ex-marine still made an imposing figure. Russ wasn't as tall, but nevertheless also was impressive in that he was a solid hulk of a man, built like the proverbial brick outhouse, as they say.

Russ bore a startled look on his face as the American picked him up from the chair with his left hand by grasping his shirt collar and lifting him. The metal kitchen style chair with a cheap plastic cushion fell away from the Russian as Sully raised him up. Smashing Russ with a right hook that sent the stunned man reeling backwards and crashing first into the fallen chair and then the floor, Sully barked, "My daughter Kate—she was one of your goddamned loose ends, wasn't she? You killed her the way you killed your girlfriend Galina and her relative because she was a loose end. You and your fuckin' loose ends can go to hell."

Russ didn't try to fight back. Rather, he picked himself up from the floor and with the back of his left hand wiped the blood from his bleeding lip. As he did, he replied, "Your daughter Kate was fair game, a shadow warrior playing in our sordid world, taking the same risks as the both of us, and you're as much to blame as any of us because you placed her there, and you know it."

"Come on, Russ, cut the shit!"

"We who serve in the dark underbelly of the world—the smelly armpits and groin regions of society—are brethren, whether we think we are on the side of right, as we all do, or on the wrong side, as we all think of our adversaries. We sacrifice so that the multitude can go about their lives blissfully unaware of the price being paid by a few so that they may live as they do. Your Kate was one of those few—and by your making."

"For Christ's sake, Russ, enough with the bullshit! I want a straight answer and I'll beat it out of you if I have to."

"As I told you, I didn't know that your daughter was a loose end. In my mind, all she would learn about me from my fingerprints was that I was an American named William Robert Duxbury. She was the victim of a chance encounter with a sick, long-lost brother, as I have told you previously. That's not to say that if I'd known what I had told her in my delirium that I wouldn't have come back and killed her; for I would've. Such is the nature of the beast, John."

"If you're so goddamned concerned about loose ends, why haven't you simply killed yourself?"

"Because I still have three loose ends to take care of: Jake Diamond, aka Jack Ruben; the railroad worker, Martino Gutierrez; and the Lee Harvey Oswald double. They're the three remaining people that can place me at the scene of the assassination on November 22, 1963. The good news is that one of them, if not all three of them, should be dead within the next forty-eight hours, on that I'm willing to bet you."

"What do you mean? Which one?"

"Jack Ruben."

"How can you be so sure?"

"I told you that after Mr. Khrushchev was removed from power, I learned from the files in our Mexico City embassy that Jake Diamond had been a double agent, given a new identity and relocated in Costa

Rica. I think you may have assumed that it was we who gave him that new identity. It was not. It was your agency. We knew of this because at the time we had a mole in your organization. The code name given to him in the file was Robert. That's all I was able to learn, because the file was closed in early 1964, after Robert allegedly died of cancer.

"In the conference room today, there were agents who knew of the Jake Diamond, aka Jack Ruben situation, of this I'm certain. They will now take action in light of my revelations. You'll see."

"Are you saying that my agency was involved in the assassination of John F. Kennedy and I know nothing about it? That is impossible, my friend. Impossible! Do you hear me?"

"I don't know whether or not your agency was involved in the assassination, although there is a great deal of speculation on that point, as you know. However, it would appear that it was involved in the cover-up."

"Cover-up? What cover-up?"

"Did you ever wonder why Jack Ruby didn't take the opportunity to kill Lee Harvey Oswald on Friday night, November 22, 1963, when he had the chance, but waited until Sunday afternoon, November 24, 1963, to murder him?"

"No, but I guess from your question, perhaps I should have?"

"According to our intelligence reports, on Saturday, November 23, 1963, your new president, Lyndon B. Johnson, was briefed by your agency and Mr. Hoover of the FBI. These briefings left your new president sitting uncomfortably on the horns of an alarming dilemma. There was clear evidence of lapses in security leading up to and surrounding the assassination of President Kennedy. These lapses may have been the result of incompetence, as you posit; or they may have been part of an intentional plot to kill the president. The answer was not clear. Embroidered on that uncertainty were two exacerbating circumstances. There was at least some evidence, albeit not conclusive, that a rogue element from what your President Eisenhower described as the 'military-industrial complex,' may have had a hand in what took place—for instance, my sponsor *Pierce Cutler* and company. There also appeared to be *falsified* evidence of a plot by us and the Cubans to kill your President Kennedy—falsified evidence generated by an Oswald impersonator, but also fueled in part by Lee Harvey Oswald's own actions."

"Wait a minute—that is your interpretation of the evidence? That it was *falsified* and not that of this agency or of the FBI? Is that correct?"

"Yes, what we understand your agency and the FBI to have told your new American president in that Saturday morning briefing, on November 23, 1963, is that they did not know for certain whether it was real or false, only that there was some evidence of Soviet or Cuban involvement, and that to open it up to inquiry would tear the country apart and possibly lead to a nuclear war with us—the Soviet Union—before the truth could be known with certainty."

"I see what you're saying. Please continue."

"President Johnson chose to resist the bait in the form of the falsified evidence against us and the Cubans and declined to start the nuclear war his predecessor had striven so hard to prevent during the Cuban Missile Crisis only a year earlier. He would not be so strong two years later when he would take the bait of falsified information against the North Vietnamese at the Gulf of Tonkin Incident and escalate the war in Vietnam."

"Don't you think *falsified* is a little strong, Russ? I will concede in retrospect that the Gulf of Tonkin could have had an element of provocation attached to it, but at least the first attack was real. As for the second, it could have been an honest mistake. Even the president gave the American sailors the benefit of doubt later in recognizing that they simply may have been a little jumpy."

"That's a fair point, John. Perhaps my choice of words was too strong, as you say. But getting back to Saturday, November 23, 1963, your new president also realized that the faith of your people in their government had been severely shaken by seeing on television the shocking assassination of their beloved president, and he did not want to further erode that confidence by embarrassing your agency, the FBI, and the Secret Service, among others, and air your dirty laundry in public. He felt it would be too painful and chose instead to spare all involved. There was too much to be lost and too little to be gained by putting your country through such a bloodletting.

"The only solution that would leave your country intact was to sweep the entire sordid mess under the rug, so to speak, and claim that the man Jackie Kennedy would later call a silly little Communist, Lee Harvey Oswald, with his second-rate Italian rifle—*alone*—had felled the great beloved American president who had dared your people to dream big dreams and shoot for the moon. The Warren Commission, made up of some of your best and brightest, would be charged—not with covering up, but with the patriotic act of putting the punctuation on that sentence."

"I'm a little confused. Earlier you confirmed for me that to the best of your knowledge Johnson wasn't involved. Are you now implying that he was in some way?"

"Theoretically he could've been without me knowing. But no, that isn't what I'm saying. What I'm saying is that when President Johnson decided for the good of your country to accept that Lee Harvey Oswald acted alone in killing John F. Kennedy, those that were trying to frame us and the Cubans realized that their bait wasn't going to be taken by the new president and that Oswald and his claim of being a patsy had become nothing but a liability for them. With that development, their efforts to use Oswald to blame us and the Cubans had no chance of success, but still had the potential to boomerang and implicate them if Lee Harvey Oswald were allowed to stand trial. He had become a loose end, and the secret had to be protected, so he was executed on national television by Jack Ruby. My point to you is that it had not been the case on Friday night, November 22, 1963, but had become the case by Sunday afternoon, November 24, 1963, as a result of the presidential decision taken on Saturday, November 23, 1963."

"I see what you're saying. The irony, of course, is that you indeed had been involved."

"Please be careful. I have gone to great pains to explain to you repeatedly that we were a small rogue group that had been acting without the official sanction of our government. If Nikita Khrushchev had known what we were doing, he would have had our heads."

"Oh, yes. I hear you loud and clear. What a wonderful thing plausible deniability is. I use it myself, every chance I get!"

"John, I'm telling you the truth. I wasn't acting with official sanction."

"I believe you, Russ. What I can't rule out is that you were aware of all who knew and approved of your actions. As you have noted, Viktor Martynova was the grand puppeteer, and Jake Diamond was known to him, but not to you, as a double agent involved in the assassination. We do work in a wilderness of mirrors, as my good friend Jim Angleton likes to say."

"I see what you are saying."

"Do you know if someone hired Jack Ruby, and if so, who it might have been?"

"I don't know whether Jack Ruby was acting alone or if he was hired by someone. If he was hired, presumably it was by Pierce Cutler or whoever was trying to blame us and the Cubans and use Oswald as a patsy."

"Are you saying that you think Pierce Cutler was behind Jack Ruby, too?"

"I have told you that I don't know. I only can speculate that he may have been."

"I see."

"Now that I've told you all that I know, my friend, you too are cursed, as I have been, and as your Warren Commission has been, with having to protect the secret at all costs."

"Wait a minute. Before we go there, you have to tell me what you know about Lee Harvey Oswald. You conveniently have left him out of the equation until now."

"I've told you that I met Oswald when he was in the Soviet Union, both in Minsk and in Kiev, and that he spoke fluent Russian. I also have told you that I was never told by Pierce Cutler, Jake Diamond, or anyone else other than Mr. Kostikov's aide or perhaps my friend Dick that he— or an impostor—might be involved, either ahead of time or afterward.

I cannot even place him at the scene of the assassination. What I can tell you for certain and I have already told you is that the man who got into the station wagon with me was not Oswald."

"Is it possible that Oswald was working for Castro and sought a cover for his activity the way you did, by being hired by Pierce Cutler?"

"The fact that there was an Oswald impersonator on the assassination team would seem to indicate that Pierce Cutler may have hired Oswald, if for no other reason than to be a patsy. However, it is hard for me to believe that if Oswald had been working for Castro and the Cubans, they could have kept it secret from Mr. Kostikov and our embassy staff in Mexico. The embassy records that I saw from Mexico gave no indication that Oswald had actually ever been hired by Mr. Castro. And the aide I spoke with in September of 1963, had been merely speculating that Castro might be foolish enough to hire Oswald to kill Kennedy if the Americans had taken his bait and hired the Cuban government minister who was a double agent to kill him or members of his Cuban regime."

"Isn't it possible that those records were altered or purged and that Castro got to Kennedy before Kennedy could get to him?"

"That is pure speculation, John, and you know it. Furthermore, if that were the case, you must admit that Oswald and his impersonator left a pretty sloppy trail. But yes, I guess it is possible."

"You have said that you were told not to shoot until you heard the shot from the Book Depository. Who did they tell you would be doing the shooting and what were you instructed to do if no shots were fired from the building?"

"Pierce Cutler told me that I didn't need to know who would be doing the firing from the building, and I wasn't told. As to the second part of your question, I planned to take my shot regardless of whether or not any shots were fired from the Book Depository. In the end, I was answering to Viktor Martynova and his group that initially charged me with the assassination. Pierce Cutler and the others merely were my cover. I was on my own mission."

"Tell me everything you know about Oswald in the Soviet Union."

"The files that I read showed that there was a split of opinion on him. Some thought he may have been planted by your agency to gather information on us and were leery of him. Others were enticed by his claims to knowing top secret information, especially about your U-2 airplane, and were prepared to take a chance on him. You must admit that it was quite a coincidence that we were able to shoot down your U-2 for the first time not long after he defected in 1959. I think I read that even the pilot of the plane that we shot down, a Mr. Gary Powers, raised the possibility that Oswald's information may have contributed to our success.

"Those who wanted to use Oswald cited this divulgence of highly sensitive information as the reason to take a chance on him. In short, if he was bait, the bait was worth taking because what he knew was too valuable not to take the risk. They could not resist sneaking a peek up your skirt, even if it meant that they might get caught in the act."

"Did your government train Lee Harvey Oswald to be an assassin or program him in any way to kill on demand?"

"The file on him states that we had him examined by psychiatrists, and they found him to be mentally unstable. We kept an eye on him but pretty much left him alone. When he married a Russian woman and subsequently left, the file indicates that we were glad to be rid of him. However, John, I must tell you that I'm suspicious of that official account. First, it is very unusual for us to allow an American, especially one with no cultural or ethnic ties to our country, to enter and stay. As I told you, I think we did it because we couldn't resist the temptation to learn about your U-2 plane. Second, allowing him to marry a young Russian woman whose family had ties to the Ministry of Internal Affairs and then leave the Soviet Union with her is consistent with trying to build his ties and loyalty to our country. I am not aware of any program we have that is capable of making someone 'kill on demand' as you put it, but I suspect that we did an effective job of indoctrinating him with anti-American sentiments and then allowed him to repatriate to the United States on assignment. That assignment very well may have involved being an assassin. However, I doubt that it would have been to assassinate such a high-value target as your president. More likely, it was to assassinate defectors or others such as myself. The assassination of an American president would have been entrusted only to someone like me. What we did as a rogue group isn't all that different than the way we would have gone about it with official sanction."

"I see," said Sully.

"I'm not sure that you do. I know that you have little regard for me because of the way I have dealt with Galina and her relative. But you forget that I gave up everything when I took on this assignment. My wife and my son went to their graves thinking that I was dishonorably discharged from my country's military rather than a decorated hero. Galina was my lover—she kept me warm at night and saved me from being lonely. Her relative gave me refuge. However, in the final analysis, they simply were a means to an end for me. I couldn't allow myself the luxury of thinking otherwise. I know that you don't understand and loathe me for it. So go ahead and finish the job you started earlier when you punched me. I no longer am of any use to you, for I've told you everything that I know. I'm now simply a loose end."

"Stop it Russ. Do you seriously expect me to accept that this trail of carnage that you have left in your wake is due to your altruistic desire to save the Soviet leaders in Moscow and their form of government? I've done my homework and researched your background, going back to intelligence reports gathered about you from your early years in Paris with Galina. You became a soldier because it offered you an opportunity for better advancement. Are you going to deny that what I'm saying is true?"

"No, you're right. I've always hated the educated elite assholes in Moscow. I hated them in Paris as well, for that matter. I became a hunter because they could not collectivize hunting the way they had farming. The people I sought to protect by preventing a first strike on my country were the peasants from towns and villages like mine, who had been required to toil all their lives to eke out a living from the land and had the scars and calluses on their weathered hands to show for it. They, who had never harmed anyone and would be among the first to die, were my concern. It was for them that I left behind my wife and son and the life I had. It is for them that I shot your president and now have devoted my life to protecting the secret. I do so because I don't want his death nor my life to have been in vain. If a few others must die to protect that secret and avoid a nuclear war, so be it. What you call a trail of carnage, I call the removal of loose ends. As I've said earlier, now you, too, must be responsible for the removal of loose ends and the protection of the secret."

"Why?"

"Because I awoke the ghosts of November 22, 1963, by my hallucinations in the presence of your daughter, and now they must be put back to sleep—permanently."

"Look, Russ, I'm the first to admit that mistakes were made on November 22, 1963, and that some of them may have arisen to the level of incompetency or negligence. But I don't buy into your notion of a cover-up. And I certainly have no plans to become a part of one."

"But you already are, my friend, you already are—a part of a cover-up. My guess is that Martino Gutierrez, the railroad worker, and the Oswald impersonator who got into the back seat also are living in Costa Rica under assumed identities. What I am about to tell you, I did not mention in the meeting today.

"While I was riding with those two in the green Rambler station wagon back to my apartment in Oak Cliff, they talked about more than the plane they had to meet in the river basin near Dallas that was to take them to safety in New Mexico. At one point, they switched from speaking in English to speaking to each other in Spanish, obviously not realizing that I could speak some Spanish. According to them, Jake Diamond was scheduled to be flown out of Dallas later that day—after he dropped them off at the river basin in the red Ford—on a DC-3 that was waiting for him and others at Red Bird Air Field in Dallas. Their mistake in assuming that I could not understand Spanish benefited me because it demonstrated to me that they had been told more than I was about the plans and reaffirmed in my mind the need for me to go into hiding and to get myself out of the United States on my own, which I did with the help of Galina and her relative."

"They said more than what you've told me, didn't they, Russ?"

"What makes you think that, John?"

"I've had my staff working around the clock doing some investigating. In November of 1963, there was a Martino Gutierrez working for the railroad, who was renting a room at a house on East Tenth Street near Patton Avenue. In addition, he worked part-time on weekends at Austin's Barbecue, located at 2321 West Illinois Avenue. Officer Tippit, who was shot by Oswald near where Gutierrez lived on East Tenth Street, also is said to have moonlighted as a security guard at Austin's Barbecue on Friday and Saturday nights."

"So you are saying that Martino Gutierrez and Officer Tippit may have known each other. That would explain it."

"Explain what?"

"It would explain the rest of what I heard Martino tell the Oswald impersonator in Spanish. Martino told him that he had to get me home quickly because the police would be coming to the neighborhood soon. On Jake's instructions, Martino had told a Dallas patrolman he worked with that he had overheard a patron at Austin's say that something big was going down on Friday and that the patron doing the talking lived by me near Twelfth and Maralis. I thought it was a strange coincidence, but I dismissed it without much thought at the time, because I had no plans to return to my apartment anyway, as I've said."

"Well Russ, it sheds light on Officer Tippit's actions on the day of the assassination. We have always suspected that he was looking for someone, and now I realize it must have been you."

"What do you mean?"

"Immediately after the assassination took place, he was observed parked in a gas station named the Good Luck Oil Company, located at 1502 North Zangs Boulevard, about a mile and a half from the Depository, watching cars coming over the Houston Street Viaduct from downtown Dallas. Then he raced down Lancaster toward your place near Twelfth and Maralis. Assuming that he went to your place and found it vacated, it would explain why he drove to the Top Ten Record Shop, located at 338 West Jefferson Boulevard, and probably tried to call Austin's Barbecue. Presumably, it was to speak with Martino. It's said that when he got no answer, he hung up, got back in his car, and drove away. He then reportedly stopped James A. Andrews going west on West Tenth Street to look in the back seat, probably because he was driving a car similar to Martino's. But as you have told me, Martino was not driving his own car. He was driving a green station wagon that you think belonged to a woman. He apparently then went to look for Martino where he lived on East Tenth Street near Patton Avenue. When he got there, he stumbled onto Oswald, and the rest is history."

"But why was Officer Tippit looking for me, John?"

"Russ, don't you see what you have been telling me? While you were using Pierce Cutler as a cover, he was doing the same to you. They were going to use you to blame the assassination on the Soviets and the Cubans. All the activities Oswald engaged in that led up to November 22, 1963, either in his own name or that of his alias Alek J. Hidell, or by his impersonator, were designed to give credibility to Oswald after the assassination, when his Soviet connection would be used to blow your cover and expose you. Oswald clearly was involved, but as I've said, I do not think he ever was made aware of the extent of the role they had in mind for him and only figured it out after the fact, when it was too late. The Oswald impersonator that you met probably did the shooting, not Oswald. But Oswald may have been duped into smuggling the rifle into the building and would have been forced to cooperate because he was at the scene and his prints were on the weapon."

"I guess it was a good thing that I never went back to my apartment."

"When you stepped out of that green station wagon on the afternoon of November 22, 1963, and vanished into thin air, they were forced to change their plans and use Oswald directly to blame the assassination on the Soviets and the Cubans. It was then that Oswald's role was expanded even further to make him the patsy."

"So you are saying that Oswald knowingly was involved in some way, but may not have been told the whole story. And he cooperated beforehand with building his image as a Communist sympathizer because he was being paid to do it."

"Yes, and I suspect he also may have been under the impression that he was acting as an informant for our side. The agency held a 201 person of interest file on him. So we were watching him."

"But why did Oswald shoot the Dallas patrolman?"

"As I've said, when he realized that he was being used as a patsy, he panicked. The files we have on him indicate that he was a meticulous planner and a well-organized person. Yet all his behavior after the assassination points to a disorganized and panicked individual. He leaves the Depository and catches a bus going in the wrong direction back toward the Depository. Then he grabs a cab, gets out a short distance away from his actual destination, and goes to his apartment to change and get his gun. Witnesses state that when he saw Officer Tippit's car approaching, he changed the direction in which he was walking, a suspicious act that easily would've drawn the patrolman's attention to him. You would think that a meticulous planner and well-organized person planning to assassinate a president would've had an exit strategy in place beforehand. He clearly didn't."

"So, John, do you still stand by the conclusion of your Warren Commission that Oswald acted alone, or have I made a believer out of you?"

"Well, let's just say that you've given me food for thought. But up to this point, it's your word against theirs."

"Well, we will have our answer soon enough, when our three musketeers—Jake Diamond, aka Jack Ruben; Martino Gutierrez the railroad worker; and the Oswald impersonator—show up dead or missing in Costa Rica. You'll see! The ghosts of November 22, 1963, will have been laid to rest—permanently. And the secret once again will be safe. But, my friend, the curse will then be with you to keep it that way."

"And what about you? What will become of you?"

"My fate will've then been sealed, as the final loose end."

"This is crazy talk. I have to get home and get some sleep. We can talk about this some more tomorrow."

With that, Sully prepared to leave by putting on his jacket. There was a piece of string that had stuck to it somehow, and Russ inconspicuously plucked it with the thumb and index finger of his right hand while bidding his friend good-bye. Giving it no thought, the CIA agent left, got into his car, and drove home. Mary already was asleep when Sully quietly crawled into bed beside her.

The next day, Wednesday, June 30, 1971, it was reported on Costa Rican radio and TV that Jack Ruben, a local plantation owner and renowned flower grower, whose flower plantation was known for its orchards, lilies, snapdragons, sunflowers, carnations, and tulips, but specialized in roses, particularly yellow roses, had been killed in an unfortunate accident when the car in which he was riding was T-boned by a tractor-trailer at a desolate intersection not far from his plantation in a rural part of Costa Rica. Also in the car and killed were his chauffeur and his body guard. The bodies were barely identifiable as a result of the fiery crash, and dental records had to be used to confirm the identity of the three victims.

In a bizarre twist of fate, the refrigerated truck that hit them had just left the plantation and was carrying yellow roses grown there to the airport for shipment internationally. In the company's brochure, this variety of rose was designated by the inventory number 103-833-2 and was named the Yellow Rose of Texas. The brochure picture was of a beautiful, smiling, dark-skinned woman with shiny jet black hair, holding a basket of yellow roses like the one in her hair. The caption under the picture read "You, too, can have one in your hair or on your table for a special occasion. Call now to order: (022) 342–3180."

The truck driver, Mario Herrero, locally born and a long-time employee of the Cloverdale International Trucking Company, headquartered in New York, with an office in San Jose, suffered minor cuts and bruises and declined medical attention. It took road crews several hours to salvage the precious cargo of roses and load them onto another refrigerated truck. Three yellow roses were left at the scene, as others like them had been on November 22, 1963, in memory of the dead.

The US papers and news networks didn't bother to carry the story. They didn't see it as newsworthy. How silly of them!

Sully received the news from the agency office in Costa Rica and decided to bring it to Russ personally. He felt he owed it to the Russian, who had been right after all about the fate of the three loose ends. The three musketeers were dead, and while their deaths would be ruled an accident, it sure was one hell of a coincidence, even for the veteran CIA agent. Unfortunately, he was too late.

When he arrived at the Farm, Sully learned that Russ had been found dead in his cell a short time earlier. It seemed he had hanged himself with his belt from the overhead pipe in what was deemed to have been an apparent suicide. Unnoticed by the others, but not lost on Sully, was the loose strand of string in Russ's hand. It was the strand the Russian had taken from Sully's jacket the night before, when he was leaving. The last loose end indeed had been taken care of, and the ghosts of 1963, awakened in 1969 at the orphanage in Vietnam, finally had been put to rest—permanently. The secret had been preserved, and the curse now was on John Sullivan Sr. to see that it stayed that way.

After investigation, Russ Pulton's death was confirmed to have been a suicide—that is, to the extent that anything can be confirmed in a wilderness of mirrors. Already thought to be dead by the Soviets, Russ was cremated, and his ashes were quietly buried on the Farm, where his spirit would be free to roam and hunt.

Since there was no way to corroborate Russ Pulton's story, the inquiry spawned by Operation Excalibur was closed. The secret once again was safe, and the findings of the Warren Commission *remain* unchallenged.

The silly little Communist, Lee Harvey Oswald— acting *alone* shooting his second-rate Italian rifle— assassinated the leader who dared America to reach for the moon, thereby returning the beloved president to the dust of the earth bringing down the curtain on Camelot forever.

History is delicate—more easily preserved than changed.

– 29 –

You already know that George's Icelandic flight from Europe was diverted to Boston because of thunderstorms and being low on fuel. As it sat mired in mud at Boston's Logan International Airport, its cabin became filled with the cries and protests of its panicked and angered passengers. One passenger, however, sat there quietly, his mind having drifted back to his final departure from Vietnam as he began to doze.

When Matt Kerr's plane landed in Saigon after the return trip from the *USS Midway*, all four men disembarked together. Jon Trueblood, Lieutenant Sullivan, and Captain Chrisandra were still wearing sailor uniforms. Matt Kerr was dressed in his trademark light tan suit, white open collar shirt, alligator shoes, and tan socks. The others kidded him that he looked like the Ugly American, with his straw hat and dark sunglasses. However, he was anything but ugly and still a handsome figure of a man. There now was a touch of gray around his temples, but the face still was remarkably wrinkle-free. His waist remained trim and his stomach firm as the result of a vigorous exercise regime that the aging Yalie followed religiously with the discipline instilled in him by the US Marine Corps.

As the four men exited the plane, they paused for a moment and looked at one another. There was an unusual and forlorn nature to their gaze. It reminded Captain Chrisandra of the look he had seen on a dying friend recently when he'd been saying good-bye to him. Unspoken was the realization that they may never see one another again. A brotherhood forged in the intensity of combat now was being put asunder by the peaceful return to civilian life.

Captain Chrisandra was the first to break the pregnant pause. Reaching into his pocket with his right hand, he pulled out a key—the key to the door of the bathroom for the winged goddesses on The Yellow Rose of Texas. He showed it to the others by holding it up in his right thumb and index finger by its pointed end so that it looked like a monument on top of a mountain. As he did, he proclaimed, "The self-designated North Vietnamese dragon has been returned from whence he claims to have come—the bottom of the South China Sea—by The Yellow Rose of Texas on her final mission. You know what I say to that. Don't tread on me!"

"Don't fuck with the airborne," added Jon Trueblood.

The marine and the ex-marine in unison simply said, *"Semper Fi."*

As Captain Chrisandra put the key back in his pocket, Matt asked, "What do you plan to do with that key?"

"I'm going to give it to Mr. and Mrs. Sullivan. I want them to know that the beast who massacred their two daughters and the thirteen girls they were helping raise at the orphanage will never do anyone any harm again!"

"Amen!" responded the others.

Just then Anne Herndon appeared at the door to the modified KC-135 and waved to encourage Captain Chrisandra along as she shouted, "Let's go, Captain; it's time to get out of Dodge."

Exchanging a farewell salute with the three men, Captain Chrisandra turned to head for the gray behemoth when Lieutenant Sullivan grabbed him by the arm to say, "You take care. You're still family, little bro, even though Claire is gone. You hear?"

"I hear," replied Captain Chrisandra, as the two former Eagles hugged, in a way that I know brought a smile to Sister Claire's face.

"And a blood brother," chimed in the Apache with an uncharacteristic tear in his eye, as the two Screaming Eagles also hugged.

"Take care of that old broad with the sheer blouse and the big set of knockers," chirped Captain Chrisandra with a wink as he was being squeezed by the bear hug of the Indian.

"We'll name our firstborn Running Eagle for you," retorted Jon Trueblood, now with a big, wide characteristic grin on his face.

As he once again turned to run, Captain Chrisandra gave his blood brother a thumbs-up sign and yelled back, "You do that!"

Then in a flash he was gone up the steps and into the belly of the beast—a beast named Stewball. And that is how the Vietnam War ended for the man Captain Dam had called the Devil Priest.

In George's dozing dream, Captain Chrisandra was turning at the door of Stewball to give a backward glance. It was then that George was abruptly pulled back from his thoughts and into the chaos of the Icelandic jetliner's cabin by the cries of his friends saying that the Boston Police had decided to let those who were willing to leave their checked bags behind get off.

"Come on—come on, George—wake up and let's get off before the Boston Police change their mind," yelled Gene and Genie, the Canadian exchange students two seats in front. "Yeah, come on, George, quit dreamin'" chimed in Shirley and Charlie, the two lovebirds from Minnesota in the two seats immediately in front of him.

"What? Go where? I must have dozed for a minute."

"Come on, let's get off! Hurry, it's time to go."

"I'm not going anywhere; I'm staying put. If the pilots are okay with flying this thing, so am I."

"Suit yourself, George!" Yelled the fearsome foursome from Canada and Minnesota, as they grabbed their things and scurried down the aisle and out the door, into the July 1971 night. Not far behind them was the group of NYU medical students in the three rows of seats behind him. One of the medical students, Glenna, who also was from Canada, made one last feeble attempt to get George to join them. But he refused.

When the mass exodus was over and the commotion settled, George looked to resume his napping, but it was not to be. As he sat back and began to doze, he was awakened by a Boston police officer who asked him if he was George B. Angelson.

He answered yes, and the police officer asked George to please come with him.

"Where are we going?" asked George. But the police officer didn't answer him. He simply repeated, this time in a firmer voice, "Please come with me."

George thought of continuing to resist, but reluctantly decided to obey, albeit apprehensively. Once they were off the plane and on the tarmac, the police officer escorted George to a waiting black and white with its lights still flashing. When George was settled in the back seat, the police officer got behind the wheel and began to drive away.

George was becoming increasingly worried. His mind ran through the possibilities as he looked through the car's rear window at the shrinking image of the Icelandic jet and wondered if he would ever see it again. His inner voice began to question if this was the "executive action" that he had feared might mark his fate.

He told himself that he easily could overpower the police officer, who had neglected to handcuff him. With his training, he could kill the man instantly and take over control of the slow-moving vehicle before anyone realized it had happened. After all, he had been trained with a special set of lethal skills—skills he recently had successfully used against much greater odds under far more dire circumstances. Fortunately, he hesitated for as time would reveal, it would not be necessary.

Looking out the front windshield of the police cruiser as it rounded a corner, he made out the distinct figure of John Sullivan Sr. The company man was standing bigger than life on the tarmac at the bottom of the steps to a private jet, parked in an obscure nook of the giant airport. At the top of the steps, in the plane's doorway to shelter her from the rain, stood Mrs. Sullivan. Still a handsome woman, it was clear to George from whence Claire's beauty had come. His racing heart began to slow, and his nerves started to calm themselves at the welcome sight of the Sullivans.

His thoughts changed from one form of terror to another—the need to make himself presentable for his almost-would-have-been future in-laws. His hair had that I-just-got-out-of-bed look, and his shirt was wrinkled and only partially tucked in, from trying to sleep in the pint-sized Icelandic seat. Cautious by training, he asked the driver if he could straighten up and promised no sudden moves. The grunt that came back sounded enough like a yes, or at least like "I don't give a shit" that he did.

When the black and white came to a stop with its lights still flashing, John Sullivan Sr. walked over and opened the door. Thanking the police officer, he extended the coverage of his open umbrella to include George, as George exited the police cruiser. The two men walked to the stairs, climbed, and entered the waiting plane. After John Sullivan Sr. paused in the doorway to shake and close the wet umbrella, the door was shut and the plane took off into the dark and still menacing night.

Both Mr. and Mrs. Sullivan were impeccably dressed; George was not. He was in a pair of jeans, with a blue and white striped collared shirt, penny loafers, and no socks. What's more, he was soaking wet.

Once they were airborne, Sully turned to George and said, "You must be wondering why we had your flight diverted to Boston?"

George, still somewhat confused by the unexpected event, and now taken back by the remark, answered with a question of his own.

"You had it diverted? I thought it was because of the thunderstorm and the plane being low on fuel; that's what they told us, anyway. Is it not true?"

"Let's just say that we have our ways."

"Have your ways, sir? I just want you to know, with all due respect, of course, that you nearly caused an all-out riot on that plane. The poor crew and Boston police had all they could do to keep it under control."

"Nothing they can't handle, I'm sure. In any event, it was for good reason. What do you say we get down to business?"

"Yes, sir."

With that, Sully told George that Russ Pulton was dead of an apparent suicide, but not before they'd had the chance to thoroughly interrogate him. George was visibly disappointed, for he had been hoping to thank Russ personally for the scouting report on the

Chinese compound. Without that help, it was doubtful they would have succeeded. George was reassured by his CIA host that the efforts of Operation Excalibur to retrieve the Russian in Vietnam hadn't been in vain. Just the opposite, those efforts, along with the successful rescue of the navy pilot, had been most valuable and might provide the key to extricating America from involvement in Vietnam with honor.

"Speaking of keys, I have something for you," George told his host. He then reached into his pocket and removed the key to the makeshift lavatory on The Yellow Rose of Texas. Handing it to Sully, he said, "I couldn't save Claire and Mary Bernadette or any of the other girls, but with this key, you can be assured that the monster who did so much harm to them and to Kate will harm no more. He now is safely locked in a lavatory on a C-47 at the bottom of the South China Sea. I was so damn mad I wanted to rip his head off with my bare hands, but thought the better of it. Instead, I simply gave him a taste of his own medicine—a fitting burial at sea."

"I see," said Sully.

Just then, Mrs. Sullivan, who earlier had excused herself to use the private jet's powder room, came back to her seat. She turned to George and told him that she had come with her husband so that she could meet the young man who had meant so much to her daughter—so much that she had decided not to become a nun. Her actual words were; "I had to meet the man who stole the key to my daughter's heart."

Both men looked at each other and fought unsuccessfully to hold back their smiles at her choice of words. Sensing something but not knowing what, Mary Sullivan asked, "What is it?"

"Nothing," replied Sully. "It simply was your choice of words. A private joke so to speak."

"Men can be so silly at times," she commented and let the issue drop, with a hint of a playful twinkle in her eye. The two men breathed a sigh of relief at having been let off the hook and not having been made to explain themselves.

She then continued, "I can see why Claire was smitten by you, young man. And I just want you to know that we very much would've been pleased to have you become a part of our family."

"Yes," added Sully, "it would have made us very happy to welcome you to the Sullivan clan."

"Thank you, I can't tell you how much that means to me," replied George, somewhat awkwardly. He mustered the strength to continue. "It will be a long time, if ever, before I can stop living in the past and start living again. I don't know if I ever will be able to get over Claire. She took a piece of my heart with her."

"She took a piece of ours too, son," replied the Sullivans.

"I hope you don't mind, but I have no one else that I can share my grief with."

"Please, speak your mind. It's good for us as well," whispered Mary Sullivan, as she gently encouraged George on.

"We were so in love and wanted to marry. I should've known that this was more than I had a right to ask for. She was special and marked by God for Himself—too beautiful a soul to have her time squandered in this life—she was summoned early."

Mary Sullivan, in tears that already had started to mess the eye makeup she recently had made perfect in the jet's powder room, said softly, "That was very beautifully put, son."

But George appeared to be in a trance of sorts and didn't really even hear her as he continued to speak—as if he was talking to himself more than to them, "I guess she now is truly at home—at home with God. I know I should be happy for her, and I suppose somewhere deep inside me, I am; but I don't know where. All my feelings are shrouded in grief and loss, and while my memories offer some welcome consolation, they are overwhelmed by my profound sense of separation from her. I just miss her so very much."

When George finally fell silent, there was an extended quiet—broken only by sobs, as all on board tried to regain their composure. After a time, Sully reached over and patted George on the knee as he muttered, "We share your pain, son."

The three grieving souls continued to console one another as the private jet sped toward the nation's capital in the dark of the night. Mary Sullivan's tears were at epic proportions and her makeup a lost cause when the pilot announced that they soon would be beginning their approach into National and would be on the ground in a few minutes. The two men were not faring much better than Mrs. Sullivan was. But it had been good for all of them to take the time together to share their sorrow.

When the jet set down in Washington, all three exited the plane together. Mrs. Sullivan bid farewell to George by squeezing his hand in hers and giving him a kiss on the cheek as she said, "Good-bye, son, and Godspeed to you." She then got into one of two nondescript government-issued cars that were waiting there and was driven away. Mrs. Sullivan and George would not see each other again for eleven years, not until May of 1982, when George would come to Stockton, California, in my namesake, Mary Bernadette, the 1979 Mercedes-Benz 450 SL, to visit Sister Claire's grave and return the red and silver scarf she had given him at the gate to the convent in Paris.

The two men then walked and got into the other waiting car. As they drove away, George turned to Sully and asked where they were going. The answer he got was not very helpful and totally unexpected. "You'll see soon enough."

As the car made a right onto Pennsylvania Avenue, Sully leaned forward and asked the driver to please pull over to the curb. He then turned to George and suggested that they walk for a stretch. George somewhat hesitantly and without much choice, nodded his agreement.

Once the two men were out of the car and walking together alone, with the car and driver following behind at a discreet distance, Sully turned to George and began to speak in a serious and businesslike tone.

"Do you recall the doctor we had you see when you were being trained for this mission?"

"Yes."

"Do you remember that he gave you several shots to protect you from many of the diseases you might be expected to encounter in Vietnam?"

"Yes."

"Well, one of those shots was a top secret state-of-the-art mind-altering drug that mimics a mild form of dementia. Memory gathered after the time of the shot will not stick with you in the same way that memories normally do. Think of a heavily traveled road with a built-up film of grease on it from all the traffic and what happens when it first begins to rain. The grease prevents the water from being properly absorbed, creating a slippery surface. In a similar way, your mind is made smooth and slippery and the memory has a hard time being absorbed. It will stick with you while it still is fresh, but it will bead and roll off in time when your environment changes and there are no new experiences to remind you of the earlier ones.

"Shortly, when you board the jet for the trip back to Boston, a doctor will come on board before you leave and give you two more shots. The first shot is designed to accelerate the process and wipe out any memory that hasn't been completely absorbed, and the second shot is to restore your memory process to its normal function, as it was before we altered it."

Handing George a package he was carrying, Sully told him, "These are slides taken of your trip throughout Europe. Some were taken by you, and others were taken by us. When you get them developed, please review them thoroughly, and they will restore your memory of Europe. Also, the package contains your diary, some of which was written by you and some by us. Reading it carefully also will help bring back your memory of Europe. It is important that you do this sooner rather than later because the more time that goes by, the less effective the retrieval of the memory will be. Within a few weeks or possibly even a couple of months, most of your memories of Vietnam should be completely gone.

"All slides of Claire as well as all references to her in your diary have been removed. That is not to say that you will not remember her. You will, since she is associated with and very much a part of your memories of Europe. I am concerned, however, that because you met her and shared a part of your European experience with her, there is a chance that this treatment will not be totally effective. You may retain some memories of

Vietnam, especially of your time there with her. It is important that you *never admit having such memories.* If you do, you could invite an unwanted response, such as an *executive action*. I probably shouldn't tell you this, but there were some within the agency that raised a concern about letting you return alive. There was talk about having you disappear and be reported missing in Europe. However, Matt and I were able to put that to rest quickly. But we will not be there forever.

"This treatment is your ticket to reentry into society and a chance at a normal rest of your life. You will be tested when you least expect it, sometime this summer. It is alright that you remember Claire and your time together in Europe, as well as the fact that she subsequently was killed in Vietnam. However, if you acknowledge ever having been to Vietnam, you could well be signing your death sentence. Do you understand?"

"Yes," replied George quietly, as his mind tried to digest all that it was being told.

Sully continued. "There is an outside danger, albeit small, that the agent sent to test you will be overzealous and claim that he had to kill you because you broke silence, even if you didn't. We have had one or two suspected cases of this happening that are under investigation. Although it is highly unlikely, I can't rule it out completely. The stakes are high because it would be your word against his or hers, and you most likely wouldn't be in any position to speak, if you know what I mean. So I've decided to leave nothing to chance and have called in a favor from a good friend of mine who is my counterpart in Israeli intelligence. Two of his top agents will be protecting you, as needed, over the course of this summer.

"I could lose my job, or even worse, my life because of what I'm doing and telling you. But I feel I owe it to you, having gotten you into this mess in the first place. Furthermore, Mary and I are very appreciative of what you have done for Claire and our family; and I'm under strict orders from her to protect you. All things being equal, I'd rather take my chances with the agency than a Sullivan woman. You have no idea what you would've been in for, son!"

"Oh, don't worry. I think I got a small taste of it in the short time I knew Claire. But seriously, why do I need to be protected? I can take care of myself."

"These two women are experts at this sort of thing and will leave no trace of their activity, should they need to prevent overzealous behavior."

"Are you telling me that you have hired two Israeli agents and given them the authorization to kill a CIA agent?"

"Only if that agent oversteps his or her bounds, is no longer acting with the authorization of the agency, and needs to be stopped. Then yes, I am. I don't want to lose you the way I have lost Kate and Claire. Enough is enough!"

"How will I know these two agents?"

"If everything goes according to plan, you may never know who they are."

"Okay, I guess," said a somewhat perplexed and confused George.

"Have faith, son, and trust in me. I know what I'm doing."

"Yes, sir."

The White House came into view, and Sully turned to George and said, "Now I can tell you the reason we are here is that Lieutenant Broderick is the first lady's nephew, and she and the president have asked to meet you."

"What, are you kidding me?"

"No, I couldn't be more serious."

"No way. Come on, Mr. Sullivan, this isn't funny!"

"You're right, it isn't funny. It's serious stuff, and I have only a few minutes left to brief you before we have to go in. So can we please get on with it?"

"Yes, sir."

"The mission to rescue Lieutenant Broderick from the Chinese has been designated as Operation Waccabuc by Matt Kerr and me. Because the president knew about Operation Excalibur, but the first lady did not, only he knows that you were a part of it and that it was through the interrogation of the Russian retrieved in that operation that we learned of Lieutenant Broderick's status as a prisoner of the Chinese. The first lady has been told that you were part of an elite, clandestine retrieval team designed to rescue high-profile targets and that it was your team that rescued her nephew. She also knows that it was a North Vietnamese officer named Captain Dam who turned her nephew over to the Chinese and that he subsequently was killed as a part of your rescue mission.

"I know that you think you jeopardized Operation Excalibur by sneaking back into Vietnam without authorization and with the personal ulterior motive of tracking down and killing Captain Dam. But what you don't realize is that we were aware of your every move and sanctioned each and every action while retaining plausible deniability for the agency and our country. It was Matt who manipulated the situation that resulted in Anne Herndon coming to retrieve you and who paved the way behind the scenes for you and my son, John, and Jon Trueblood to accomplish what you did. In short, as a result of the time constraints, we had no choice but to reactivate the Operation Excalibur team and use you to attempt the rescue of Lieutenant Broderick. At the same time, because of the risks involved, we had to be able to deny involvement. We had to let you think you were acting unilaterally."

"Wow, you had us fooled! We thought you only found out of our plans when Anne gave you the note we left behind with her."

"The bottom line is that you were part of an elite team sent to rescue Lieutenant Broderick in Operation Waccabuc, and Captain Dam was killed in connection with that operation—plain and simple. Do you understand?"

"Loud and clear, sir!"

"Any questions?"

"Am I Captain Chrisandra, purportedly missing in action, or am I George B. Angelson, about-to-be law student?"

"You should meet them as Captain Chrisandra. They know that Captain Chrisandra has gone missing and assume this was to allow you the flexibility to go underground and perform clandestine operations such as Operation Waccabuc. They also know that Captain Chrisandra is not your real name, but they haven't asked to know your true identity, and I haven't told them. They do know that you are returning to civilian life and starting law school soon."

"Thanks, that is helpful to know."

"Anything else?"

"What is the significance of the name Waccabuc, may I ask?"

"The first lady's brother-in-law grew up in Waccabuc, New York, and apparently was champion of the Waccabuc Country Club tennis team when he was younger. Matt Kerr coached tennis there one summer while he was in college at Yale and I guess knew him from that time. It was Matt who came up with the idea for the name, and the first lady really liked it, so we went with it. Is that it?"

"Well, I do have one last question, if I may?"

"Shoot!"

"You said earlier that the president plans to use what we accomplished in Vietnam and China to help end the war, or at least our involvement in it. Can you explain to me how he intends to do that?"

"Yes, I was afraid you might ask me that. I think you have earned the right to know. The president has been following a policy that I believe a professor you had in political science at Boston College, a Professor Brooks, has helped him formulate. The president likes to call it his *Madman Theory*, designed to convince the North Vietnamese that he is just about crazy enough, especially when provoked, to resort to almost any measure, no matter how extreme, to obtain peace with honor. While he has been reducing our troop counts, he has been bombing and spraying the hell out of Vietnam, destroying the canopy on their forests and the small amount of infrastructure they have. But they have remained intransigent and appear to be willing to sustain the loss of millions of their people and unimaginable damage to their land rather than capitulate. He is resigning himself to the fact that we may have no choice but to up the ante. However, some of the more extreme options under consideration run the risk of provoking the Soviets or the Chinese. Since you have a crypto clearance, I can tell you in strict confidence that the National Security Advisor is engaged in secret negotiations to have the president visit China early next year, in 1972, in an attempt to normalize relations. This is part of the reason why Operation Waccabuc was so risky at this time. In any event, the president then hopes to visit the Soviet Union later that same year to place pressure on them to reduce their support for the North Vietnamese effort. If he is successful in improving relations with the Chinese and the Soviets, Vietnam will become of less strategic significance, and our withdrawal from there, especially in the context of a peace with honor, will be of less concern.

"Russ's revelations will be an embarrassment to the Soviets, as will Lieutenant Broderick's episode be a source of shame for the Chinese. The plan is to use both events to extract concessions from the two Communist powers. The president will be seeking, among other things, their acquiescence to the mining of Haiphong harbor and to an aggressive increase in our bombing of more high-value industrial targets in North Vietnam that might put some of their nationals at risk. He also will be looking for their assistance in pressing for the North Vietnamese to negotiate with us in earnest for a peace that allows us to withdraw with honor and turn the war effort over to the South Vietnamese."

"With all due respect, sir, from what I have seen over there, the South couldn't last long enough on their own to give us the time we need for an orderly withdrawal. The Vietcong and their allies in the North would be on us in a heartbeat."

"If the president gets his way, the Soviets and the Chinese will persuade the North Vietnamese to give us a wide berth and allow a sufficient amount of time to pass after we are gone, before they enter Saigon, to allow us to claim that Vietnamization worked and that we obtained peace with honor."

"I see."

"Now, is that it with the questions?"

"Yep."

"Well then, let's go meet the president and the first lady," said Sully as he turned and signaled the driver to drive up to them. When the driver did, the two men got in, and the car proceeded to pull up to the gate. After the usual security check, the gate was opened and they were waved on in. The black, nondescript government-issued car drove up to the portico where the car door was opened for them.

As they started to walk up the stairs, George could not help but notice the young marine standing guard. Captain Chrisandra's instinct was to salute, but George caught himself in the process of raising his hand and simply gestured hello. The transition back to civilian life would not be easy, he told himself, and he would have to be especially careful in the coming weeks and months to work at it.

Their visit was unofficial and would not be documented in the White House records. They were escorted to the private quarters, where the president and the first lady met them. Both were dressed in their bathrobes and pajamas, so George didn't feel as bad about his appearance as he had earlier in the evening. It was late into the night, and they clearly had been waiting up to meet them. There was a tray with a pot of coffee, a kettle of hot water, canisters filled with tea bags, sugar and cream, and a plate with finger sandwiches and cookies.

The president spoke first.

"Sully, thank you so much for coming. I know it is such an inconvenient time. The first lady and I are most appreciative."

Sully smiled and answered, "No problem, I am happy to do it."

The president then turned to George and said, "You must be Captain Chrisandra. I understand that you are an Episcopal chaplain."

"Yes, sir, that is correct."

"I must say that you have a unique way of saving souls for the Lord," laughed the president as he held out his hand to shake George's.

"Yes, I have been trained with a very special set of retrieval skills," and before George could finish his sentence, Sully finished it for him by saying, "and he is very good at what he does."

"Well, we are most fortunate to have young men like you."

At that moment, the first lady put her teacup down and stepped forward in front of her husband, the president. Taking George's right hand into both of hers, now warm from the teacup she had been holding, she said, "Yes, indeed, we certainly are. I cannot tell you how grateful I am to you and your team for rescuing Scott. He is due to become a father in October, and if it were not for you and the others, his daughters may never have known their father."

"I know how difficult that might have been. My best friend from high school was recently killed in Vietnam, and his widow is pregnant with their first child. I'm very glad that we were able to successfully return your nephew to you and his wife and spare you that fate."

"I assume that you have studied Chinese and can speak it. Which dialect did you study?"

"No, ma'am, neither I nor any other team member has studied Chinese, nor do any of us speak it."

The president seemed somewhat surprised. Turning to George, he said, "You mean that you went into China, and none of you can speak a word of Chinese?"

"With all due respect, sir, we didn't go there to talk."

The president was silent for a moment and then began to smile as he looked at Sully, who was doing all that he could to contain his pride and not burst out laughing at the response.

The president simply turned back to George and in a low voice said, "No, I suppose you didn't. God bless you, son. Lord knows we could use more like you."

"Thank you, sir."

At that point, Sully stepped forward to say, "We had better get going, sir. We have an international flight sitting idle on the tarmac in Boston."

"Yes, of course," replied the president.

The first lady, once again taking George's hand, said, "I understand that you will be starting law school in September. I wish you the very best for a long and healthy life. The law has been very good to my husband, and I hope it is as good to you."

"Thank you, ma'am."

Turning to her husband, the president, while still holding George's hand, she said, "Get this young man home to his family safe and sound, so he can have the long and fruitful life he deserves. If anything happens to him, you will have me to answer to. Do you understand?" She emphasized the last sentence, as she patted George's hand and grinned at her husband.

The president looked at Sully and with a smile said, "You heard the first lady, didn't you?"

"*Loud and clear*," replied a smiling Sully.

The president then turned to George and with a wink said, "Good luck, son,"

George nodded, turned, and began to leave. When he got to the door of the room, he turned around to face the president, the first lady, and John Sullivan Sr. He stood ramrod straight and saluted them. This would be the last time he would have the privilege of giving a military salute, and it meant a great deal to him to have it be given to his commander in chief, the first lady, and his almost-to-be father-in-law. The president and John Sullivan Sr. returned the salute, and the first lady nodded her head and gave him a warm smile.

Not long thereafter, the two men were again in the back seat of the black, nondescript government-issued car on their way to the airport and the waiting private jet. This time it was George who asked if they could get out and walk for a short stretch. Sully agreed, and the driver once again pulled over to the curb to let the men out.

When they were walking, George turned to Sully and said, "With all this security about me and Operation Excalibur, what will happen to the others? Will they be okay?"

"The short answer is yes. The only people still alive who know the entire story, Christian Carter and Bo Hicket now being deceased, are you, me, Matt Kerr, the Reverend Pratt, and my son, John Jr. With the exception of you, we are all company people with clearance to know. Jon Trueblood, Anne Herndon, and her crew know that Captain Chrisandra is not really missing in action and presumed dead. However, they do not know the real reason for hunting down and capturing Russ Pulton. The rest have no reason to doubt that Captain Chrisandra is MIA. As long as it stays that way, everyone's fine."

"That's wonderful. However, you should know that Anne

Herndon—but not the rest of the crew—and Jon Trueblood know that my true identity is George B. Angelson. They were told when Claire and the girls were massacred. Anne had to come find me in Italy and bring me back, and we had to recruit Jon to fly the China mission."

"It's not a problem. As I told you, Matt manipulated that situation and acquiesced in my son John and you doing what you did. We're in the process of recruiting Jon and Anne full-time for the agency. As long as the rest of Anne's crew doesn't know, I'm not worried."

"Great. And is it alright for me to go see the Reverend Pratt when I get back home?"

"Yes, but I don't think he knows that Lieutenant Broderick's rescue was a sanctioned operation. So, I would let him continue to think that you were acting without authorization."

"Okay. By the way, were you surprised by what the first lady had to say at the end, about the agency having to answer to her and the president should any harm come to me?"

"You picked up on that, didn't you? You should be very pleased. Tonight the first lady raised the stakes for the agency by putting us on notice in that way and holding us accountable to the president. While it is not a guarantee, it puts a real damper on any overzealous activity and provides you with extra insurance against such overreaching. Knowing that any executive action will be scrutinized in that way will make even the most ambitious agent think twice before acting—especially without clear evidence and advance approval. You should be fine, but I still plan to provide you with the protection we discussed."

"Thanks. It does give me more peace of mind. I guess that's all that I had to discuss."

"Then we can get back in the car now," said Sully as he waved to the driver to bring the car forward to them. "But before we do, please understand one thing. The stakes remain high, even now, almost eight years since the assassination. If the American public were to learn that the Soviets, even a rogue faction of them, killed our president and now were making things difficult for us in Vietnam, all hell could break loose—not what JFK would have wanted!"

"I understand. I only wish we had a way of getting back at the Russians for what they have done to us in Vietnam."

"Don't worry. What goes around comes around."

With that the two men got back in the car that now had come up next to them. When they finally arrived at the airport and George got out of the vehicle to board the private jet, he turned to Sully and with a wink said, "Take good care of that key I gave you. It took a bit of an effort to get it for you."

"I'll guard it with my life; you can count on it. Furthermore, I know it's bothering you that you got your hands dirty in this operation. But you must keep in mind that by you doing so, America has been able to keep hers clean, something that is very important."

"Yes, sir."

"Finally, can I count on you in the future, should the agency have a need for your services?"

"Sorry, sir, but I made a promise to myself and more importantly to your daughter never to bear arms again, and while I may have broken it in my most recent escapade, henceforth I plan to honor it—for the rest of my life."

"Alright," smiled Sully, "but please make sure you heed everything I told you, and for God's sake make something of yourself as a lawyer. Remember, I'm on the hook with the first lady because of you."

"I will," said George, as he waved to his CIA host, turned, and walked into the private jet.

On board the plane waiting for him, as promised, was the doctor to give him his "forget everything" and "back to normal" injections. When he was done, the doctor—a small mousy-looking man—scurried off the plane with his little black bag of magic. And the crew prepared to take off from National for the flight to Boston and the still waiting Icelandic Super DC-8.

Alone with his thoughts in the cabin of the private jet, he sat in a seat easily twice the size of the ones on the Super DC-8 that swiveled and had real armrests. The rain had stopped and the sky had begun to clear as George looked out the window. A silver fringe was beginning to show on one of the few remaining clouds, telling him that the moon was soon to appear. A good omen, he was sure. Then it did. Slowly, it began to reveal its bright face. It was Claire, to tell him that her mother had liked and approved of him, but that now it was time to move on. There was a future waiting out there for him, a future without her, and he should make the most of it. But he knew in his heart that she would have to coax him many more times before he would get to that place—a future without Claire.

Not long thereafter, he was on board the Super DC-8, once again strapped into his pint-sized seat and heading for New York City—the city that never sleeps. (But it does.)

The cavernous plane now was virtually empty, except for a bevy of empty water bottles and soda cans, some now rolling in the aisles as the plane taxied, lots of discarded candy wrappers stuffed into the backs of empty seats, and a bunch of sloppily folded magazines and some half-eaten sandwiches spread about on the empty seats. Just George and a handful of sleeping passengers had stayed with the pilots for the final leg of the trip to New York. The rest of the passengers were still wandering around Beantown without their luggage, which remained safely tucked away in the cargo bays beneath George's feet.

Spoiled by the private jet, George decided to spread out once they were airborne and the seat belt sign had been turned off. It would be a short-lived freedom as they soon would be starting their descent, and he would be commanded to once again get into his seat-belted cage. He smiled to himself. *Was this any way to treat the man who had apprehended the second gunman who had assassinated John F. Kennedy from the grassy knoll on November 22, 1963? You bet!* he told himself. *Everybody knows the president had been shot by a silly little Communist acting alone with his second-rate Italian rifle. The Warren Commission said it was so!* The president—the man now dead, had become the president—the legend. And now an *airport* with his name that required George to fasten his seat belt for landing. As Jackie had noted, he'd much rather be a man!

When they arrived at John F. Kennedy airport, you may recall, it was deserted. (The city does sleep.) George found a bus that was heading into Manhattan and grabbed it. The only other passenger was the young soldier Bill Fisher, coming home on leave for the Fourth of July weekend after having completed basic training and before being sent to Vietnam. You also may recall that when the bus got to Grand Central Station, George and Bill joined forces and took turns napping while they waited for the city to wake up and morning transportation to take them home. What you don't know, because George neglected to tell you, is what happened in Grand Central Station that night.

When they found a spot with an unobstructed 180-degree view and with a solid wall behind them, they settled in for the wait until morning. Bill Fisher said he would take the first watch because he wasn't tired, and he encouraged George to nap. George gladly agreed.

In preparation, George stood up and then got into a kneeling position. His left knee was bent and on the ground; his right foot was planted on the ground and the leg was bent at the knee in a ninety-degree angle. He pulled up his right jean leg to reveal the combat knife strapped to him—a knife that last had killed a Chinese guard distracted by pictures of naked ladies. It was one of two vestiges of Captain Chrisandra still left with him—the other being the collar he planned to return to Reverend Pratt.

When Bill Fisher saw the knife, he was taken back and asked, "Where did you get that?"

"My uncle gave it to me for my trip to Europe. He was in the 82nd Airborne during World War II and was awarded a Bronze Star and Purple Heart for capturing a house full of Germans."

"Shit, man, that's one serious piece of cutlery. Can I see it?"

"Sure," said George as he handed it to him.

"This is some fuckin' weapon. Did he show you how to use it?"

"No, I figured just flashing it around would do the job of scaring any gypsy pick-pockets away."

"Seriously, dude, I see your point—no pun intended," laughed Bill Fisher.

George sat back down on the floor with his back to the wall. The knife was in his right hand that was now resting on the ground beside him. He told Bill Fisher he was going to try and get a little shut-eye.

"Go for it, dude. I'll watch your back for you."

Still very much in combat mode, George slept a shallow, watchful sleep—with the proverbial "one eye open," as they say. It was a good thing that he did.

Growing bored and restless in the lonely, quiet, empty space of the deserted station, Bill Fisher decided to stand and stretch his legs. He didn't walk far away at first, but then wandering further, he went to see a poster that extolled the wonders of Bali. The poster next to it spoke of walking a mile for a Camel. The power of suggestion made him reach into his pocket, pull out his pack of Camels, and light up. He hadn't taken more than one puff when three men came out of nowhere, their faces obscured by ski masks. The angle of their approach to Bill Fisher, who had his back to them, didn't afford them a view of George sitting against the wall. Engrossed in the exotic images on the Bali poster, Bill didn't see or hear the masked men coming at him, but George did. That extra sense that men who have known combat develop was still fresh in George and woke him.

George hesitated for a moment, conflicted in his decision about what to do. His instincts screamed for him to help a brother in uniform. But his subconscious reminded him of the still very fresh admonishments of John Sullivan Sr. He knew that if he killed with that knife, he very well could bring unwanted attention upon himself and his recent whereabouts. He was torn—so very torn—because he knew from the bus ride that Bill Fisher was carrying everything he had earned during basic training in cash to buy his girlfriend an engagement ring. He planned to pop the question at a Fourth of July picnic that now was only two days away. Throwing caution to the wind, George (rather, Captain Chrisandra) followed his instincts into action.

All three masked men were sporting knives, but nothing like the one George had. One grabbed Bill from behind and stuck the sharp side of the knife's blade tightly up against the young soldier's neck. Bill Fisher instinctively stretched his neck upward, adding as many inches to it as he could, as he tried avoiding the blade's sharp edge now pressing against it.

"Keep quiet and you won't get hurt, soldier boy," the second masked man barked as the third rummaged through Bill's pockets, finding the wad of cash. Busy admiring their find, they didn't see George coming from behind and to their side. They felt comfortable that they had the situation under control, but they couldn't have been more wrong.

George had decided to bank on the fact that the first masked man, the one holding the knife to Bill's neck, would be startled by his (George's) approach, would remove the knife from its position on the soldier's neck, and would swing it around to protect himself. He was right.

The second and third masked men were the first to see George coming. But they had been overconfident and put their two knives down to count the money. Seeing the force, speed, and determination with which George was attacking, and the sight of the business end of the combat knife he was wielding, they knew to take flight and not stay and fight. Their reaction caused the first man to spin around, whipping his knife with him. It was too little too late, and he knew it immediately. Dropping the knife, he shouted, "Stop, stop, wait! I give up!"

George tried to pull up, but his momentum continued to carry him. His knife grazed the masked man, starting at the top of his abdomen, just below the rib cage, and continuing up to the neck and puncturing the lower jaw just shy of an inch deep. If the man had fallen forward, the knife would have gone up into his brain, killing him instantly. If George hadn't tried to abate his attack, the knife would have gutted the thief like a slaughtered pig and left him to die almost instantly. But Bill Fisher's attacker fell backwards, landing on his back, and pushed himself further away with his hands before standing up and fleeing. His wounds were minor, but enough to convince him to join his two comrades in taking flight.

A shocked Bill Fisher picked up the now disheveled wad of cash and his other belongings that were strewn along the ground, left behind by the thieves in their haste to leave.

Turning to George, he said, "That's not your uncle's knife, is it?"

"What do you mean, Bill?"

"That's your knife, isn't it? And you're no stranger to using it, are you?"

"What makes you think that?"

"You were loaded for bear, dude. Your eyes were like crazed!"

"My eyes were crazed? What are you talking about?"

"It was your eyes, dude—scared the shit out of them; was like you was a crazed madman—the dammed things scared the shit out of me!"

"I really don't know what you're talking about. You're not making any sense."

"When you were attacking, your eyes—they made your whole face look different, dude. I turned around when my attacker pulled his knife away, so I could see what was going on, and I saw them for myself."

"What did you see?"

"Rage, dude—savage rage, dude; like you got a lot of shit built up in you. Like you had no hesitation about killing; that's what I saw, dude. You've killed before, like close up and brutal, I mean like in combat, haven't you, dude? You've been there; you've been an animal—and real recently, haven't you? They told us about this in basic!"

"You're talking nonsense. What scared them was seeing the business end of that blade coming at them. Nothing more, nothing less. I never had to use it on any gypsies in Europe, but the net effect always was the same regardless of the venue. They were two-bit punks with pocket knives, and the sight of that monster blade sent them packing. It's that simple."

"I don't know who you really are, but I sure am glad I ran into you."

"Hate to disappoint you, but I've already told you who I am. I'm between college and law school and on my way back from a seven week trip through Europe."

"Well, I feel like you're my guardian angel, dude."

"Let's not get carried away, now!"

"I'm serious. I think those guys would've killed me if it were not for you. At the very least they would have gotten the ring money. I feel like a piece of shit, dude! I just finished basic, and I'm 'Nam bound, and

I let myself get jumped by some thugs in New York City. What a sorry mother-fuckin' soldier I'm gonna make."

"Take it easy. You're going to do just fine over in Vietnam."

"How do you know? You've never been there, have you?"

"No, but I have two friends that I sold Fords to who have been, and they came home alive and in one piece. If they could, so will you."

"I hope you're right!"

"Come on and get some sleep, Bill. You need to save your strength for your fiancée-to-be. What did you say her name is? Antonella?"

"Yes."

"It's my turn to stand watch."

"Okay"

Not too much later, Bill was sound asleep. George sat there looking at him and thinking about what he had said—about he (George) being a guardian angel. He wondered if he had saved his friend for a worse fate in Vietnam. He hoped not, but only time would tell. At least Antonella would have her boyfriend (alive and in one piece) for the Fourth of July of 1971; long enough to experience the joy of becoming his fiancée and glowing with the pride of showing off her new engagement ring—two lovebirds savoring every precious moment together, the way he and Claire had done during those final few blissful days at the orphanage. After that, they would be on their own; even a guardian angel could do only so much. At least that is what George tried to tell himself, but I'm not sure if he really believed it. I think if he could, he would have tried to do more.

Soon it was time for the first train to Connecticut, and George awakened his friend.

"Come on, Bill, wake up. It is time for your train. Let's get you over to track 13."

The two newly-minted buddies walked over together. As they did, Bill Fisher asked George, "Did your two Ford friends have any advice for someone like me when I get to 'Nam?"

"Are you going over as part of a unit, or will you be an individual replacement?"

"Individual replacement."

"Make sure the other guys get to know your name and that you get to know theirs. My two friends told me that doing so is very important. Your life will depend on them and theirs on you. I think it was the three musketeers that liked to say 'one for all and all for one.' You want to become like Shakespeare's 'band of brothers.' At least, that is what I've been told."

"Okay. Thanks."

"Good luck with popping the big question to Antonella this weekend."

"I'm not worried. I've got my guardian angel looking out for me."

George smiled, turned, and walked away. The guardian angel reference hit closer to home than George was willing to admit, even to himself. In his mind he had failed Bo, Christian, Sammy, Claire, and the thirteen of us. But he had saved the Russian—at least for a time—and Scott Broderick and Bill Fisher. He told himself that three saves and seventeen losses was not much of a record for a guardian angel, but it was. And he still had one more save in him. He didn't know it yet, but he would save Christian's son.

Not long thereafter, George would walk out of Grand Central Station and meet his parents on what promised to be a beautiful sunny day in New York. On the way, he would kneel once again, remove the combat knife that last had killed in China and almost had killed in New York, along with its holster, and toss them into a nearby trash can. The sign on the can read Property of the New York City Department of Sanitation. He had rendered to Caesar that which was Caesar's. He should have done it sooner, but he was glad he had not. Shortly, he would visit the Reverend Pratt to return his collar and render to the Lord that which is the Lord's and thereby be done with the last remaining two vestiges of Captain Chrisandra.

―――

In the late spring and early summer of 1971, the secret negotiations between the National Security Advisor and the Chinese were at an impasse. Neither side wanted to concede that they had been the one to initiate the meeting being arranged. A confidential call was made by the president to Chairman Mao Zedong, who shortly thereafter instructed his negotiators to drop the issue. It was not important who had asked whom. There is no official record of that call or of what was discussed on it. But on July 15, 1971, the president held a press conference to announce that he would visit China in early 1972 on a "journey of peace."

In February of 1972, the president and the first lady visited China. The president met with Chairman Mao, Premier Zhou Enlai, and others, while the first lady publicly toured industrial facilities, hospitals, and schools and privately visited an old, abandoned airfield used by the United States during World War II. In May of that year, the president visited the Soviet Union. In a private meeting with Viktor Martynova, he gave the visibly shocked Russian Russ Pulton's set of cuff links inscribed with the words Dallas Moon as he suggested that the time had come for an improvement in relations. As these visits took place, the North Vietnamese were forced to stand by and watch the pomp and circumstance, while they continued to be bombed and pressured to negotiate.

In November of 1972, the president won reelection in a landslide, and on January 27, 1973, an agreement was signed in Paris by the United States, the North and South Vietnamese, and the Vietcong that brought peace with honor. On March 29, 1973, the last American troops departed from Vietnam except for a small contingent of marine guards and military attachés, and by the next month, in April of 1973, the last American POWs had been released.

Notwithstanding the foregoing, the North Vietnamese did not seize control of Saigon for two more years. They waited until April of 1975, almost a year after the president had resigned from office as a result of Watergate, to make their move. Were they giving this president time to argue that Vietnamization had been a success and peace indeed had been obtained with honor? One can only speculate why the North Vietnamese gave such great deference to this one US president, the one with the Madman Theory, the one who opened the door to China and a thaw in relations with the Soviet Union. Then again, maybe this US president had the help of another US president, one who had been slain in office. One who was able to do through the ghosts of his assassination, the ghosts of November 22, 1963, what he had not been given the chance to do in life—end American involvement in Vietnam.

– 30 –

George has told you that immediately upon his return home, he went to see Michelle Carter, who now was living in that dark place we call *widowhood*. Life had changed for her in a flash, turning her world upside down and sending it spinning out of control. George already was under a severe strain himself—the strain of having to adjust to a return to civilian life that no one even knew he had left. At the same time, he was forced to deal with the knowledge that he would be tested in a potentially life-threatening manner by the very agency that had so altered his life.

He'd found it nearly impossible not to be able to tell Michelle that he'd been with Christian when Christian had been killed; that he'd served with him and also put his life on the line; and he'd not hidden behind money and connections as she thought. The situation was exacerbated for George by the realization that so many of those who'd been able to avoid service seemed to have little appreciation for the sacrifices of those, like Christian, who'd served, and for the ones they'd left behind, such as Michelle. If anything, there seemed to be a degree of contempt and disrespect for those who'd heeded their country's call to duty.

As you also know, with a little help from George, Michelle remained true to her deeply held convictions and *chose* to continue her pregnancy, giving birth to Christian Richard Carter on October 30, 1971. George was there at the hospital that day with Michelle and two weeks later when his godson was christened by Father Collins. Michelle remarried in 1978, and George attended her wedding to Daniel Dawson. He also was with Michelle and Daniel Dawson and their daughter Corinne (Christian's little sister) twenty years later, when Christian Richard Carter, named after two marines, his father and his great uncle, graduated from the United States Naval Academy in Annapolis, Maryland.

The day Christian Richard Carter graduated, he wore his father's marine tiepin, the one his father had given to his godfather for safekeeping so many years before. The time was now right for him to have it, and George had given it to him. Christian also wore something else of note that day, although no one could see it. He wore a madras shirt under his uniform. Christian knew from what his godfather had told him that he was fulfilling a promise his father had made to his godfather. What he didn't know was that the promise had been made while his father lay dying in his godfather's arms on a helicopter named Screaming Eagle a half a world away and a lifetime ago. His godfather, too, had kept a promise made to his father in that noisy vibrating machine so long ago and far away and had seen his godson to manhood—a fine manhood. The shirt marked that passage and the fulfillment of that obligation—the guardian angel now had one more save, a big one that was some twenty years in the making, but in his mind it still didn't make up for the seventeen losses. (And never would.)

There were several persons of note in attendance that day. There were Matt Kerr and his new wife (and soul mate), the former Sister Katherine Quinn, John Sullivan Sr. and his wife (and soul mate) Mary, their son John Sullivan Jr., and Anne Herndon. There was the senator from Arizona, the Honorable Jonathan Trueblood (the Screaming Eagle who had been piloting the helicopter of the same name that day long ago and far away), and his wife (who still was eleven years the Senator's senior and teaching him a thing or two in her trademark sheer blouses). Also there in spirit were Christian Carter, Bo Hicket, Samuel Lerner, Joaquin Arango and Sisters Kate and Claire. The guardian angel had *not* done it alone. He had help from his band of brothers and two Franciscan sisters.

– 31 –

On Thursday, July 8, 1971, George got into the GTO and headed up Route 95, also known as the Connecticut Turnpike, to New Haven. There he had a 10:30 a.m. appointment to meet with the Reverend Lewis Pratt in the reverend's office at Yale University. When he arrived, Livie, his assistant, was at her desk outside his office and very happy to see George.

She asked, "Where have you been, stranger? I don't think I've seen you since the beginning of May."

"I've been traveling around Europe and having a great old time."

"That sounds wonderful. You will have to tell me all about it. But you had better go in now. The reverend is ready to see you."

"Thanks," said George, as he knocked on the open door (out of courtesy) and walked in.

Lewis Pratt was thrilled to see his prize student and already had been putting together a curriculum for the young priest to resume his studies. George was an ordained priest, but Lewis Pratt was anxious to further hone the young man's skills as a preacher. He had big plans for George, none of which would come to pass.

The Yale mentor was shocked and disappointed when his returning student told him that he would be giving back his collar because he no longer was worthy of it.

"What happened to bring this on? You were so enthusiastic. This has taken me completely by surprise! You know I had big plans for you.

I was working on a curriculum for you earlier—just before you arrived. I was hoping to make a preacher out of you."

"Please, sir, don't make today any harder on me than it already is. This is one of the most difficult things I've ever had to do—turning my back on a lifelong dream, one I'd all but given up on when it came true thanks to you and Father Phillips."

"I can see this is serious—very serious. Please give me a moment to speak with Livie and have her clear my calendar through lunch. I think we can do that; I don't believe I have anything pressing scheduled. Please sit down while I check. Then I'll be all yours!"

"Thank you, sir."

The reverend picked up the phone and spoke in a hushed, serious, confidential tone of voice to his assistant. He fidgeted with the letter opener on his desk while he waited with the phone held snugly between his ear and his shoulder. George watched patiently but nervously, much like a field goal kicker awaiting the end of a time-out to kick the game-winning score. Finally, after what seemed an interminable amount of time, the reverend smiled and said, "Great," and hung up the phone.

Walking back around his desk and sitting down next to George, Lewis Pratt said, "I'm all yours, son. Now tell me what this is about. You can speak openly. This room is safe," as he encouraged George by patting him on the knee.

George began to speak.

"I met a young woman on my flight to Europe and instantly fell in love with her. It turned out she was a nun who was on her way to Paris and then to Vietnam to take over the operation of a girl's orphanage that her sister, also a nun, had been running when she was executed by a North Vietnamese officer. Naturally, when I got to Vietnam, I went to see her."

"Stop, don't tell me that we are talking about Kate and Claire Sullivan, the daughters of John and Mary Sullivan!"

"One and the same, I'm afraid."

"Oh my God. Please, go on."

"I was flown to Vietnam on a plane that had an all-female crew. This led the same demented North Vietnamese officer that had killed Kate to think that I was a Devil Priest that prophecy told him would be transported by 'winged goddesses' to Vietnam to further colonize and subjugate his country. This North Vietnamese officer, named Captain Ton That Dam, thought that he was the reincarnation of a dragon from the sea, which had been slain by a warrior who had tricked the dragon by disguising himself as a priest. I was his chance at a rematch—one that would change history and allow the dragon to slay the Devil Priest and bring to an end the colonization and exploitation of his country.

"Because I had spent time at the orphanage, this demented beast came looking for me there after Operation Excalibur was over and I had left Vietnam. When he did not find me and none of them could tell him where I was—because they didn't know—he raped, tortured, and murdered Claire and buried the orphans alive.

"I didn't turn the other cheek, nor did I forgive and pray for him. Rather, I went back into Vietnam and with premeditation, I murdered him in cold blood. More specifically, I buried him alive at sea so he could have a taste of his own medicine. Hardly the priestly thing to do, I think you would agree?"

"I see," said Reverend Pratt. "Because of this, you no longer feel that you are worthy of wearing the collar, is that right?"

"Yes. The priests who have worn this collar before me have worn it as disciples of peace. Some have even died as martyrs in peacefully resisting injustice. Not me. I chose to take up the sword and seek vengeance. I decided to avenge their deaths by killing him myself—not the priestly thing to do. Consequently, I feel that if I were to continue to wear this collar, I would be desecrating it as well as everything that it stands for."

"Look, son, we have our superstars, like Pope John XXIII and Mother Theresa; but we also have our share of human frailty in the religious life. You're about to start law school as I recall, is that right?"

"Yes, in the fall. But what does that have to do with it?"

"Well, let's just say that you've made a very persuasive and convincing case for the prosecution. Should the prosecution now be prepared to rest, I would like to make the case for the defense, if I may."

"Go ahead if you like, sir. I must warn you that I have given this matter a great deal of thought, and I doubt anything you say is going to change my mind."

Undaunted, the Reverend Pratt proceeded.

"I would like to call Captain Chrisandra as my first witness."

"Okay."

"Captain Chrisandra, you are to assume that you are under oath and must tell the truth, the whole truth, and nothing but the truth, regardless of any security restrictions."

"Understood."

"Is it true that after your mission was successfully completed—a mission of grave importance to your nation—a mission for which your country spent a great deal of time and money training you and others—a mission in which some of your fellow soldiers gave their lives so that it could be a success, you seriously jeopardized that success by going back into Vietnam without authorization?"

"Yes, sir, that was my state of mind."

"Do you think that is something a highly trained professional who is thinking clearly would have done?"

"No, sir."

"Is it possible that you were blinded by an overwhelming sense of guilt—guilt that these innocent people, who you loved dearly, died horrible deaths solely because they were close to you—and that if they had never met you, they still would be alive?"

"Yes, sir, it is more than possible. That is exactly how I felt."

"Is it true that there was no system of justice available that was capable or willing to bring this man to justice?"

"None, sir. The North Vietnamese were not going to punish him, and the South Vietnamese were too busy with more pressing issues to take any interest."

"So what you did was resort to what is commonly termed *frontier justice* and took matters into your own hands, is that correct?"

"Yes, I guess you can look at it that way. But I am about to start law school because I believe in working through the system. I'm not a vigilante."

"That is precisely my point. If something like this had happened here in the States, you would have let the justice system prosecute him, wouldn't you have?"

"Yes, of course, and what is more, I would have been prepared to live with the verdict regardless of outcome, because I have faith in our system of justice—for better or for worse."

"The defense rests."

"But what is the verdict?"

"Look, George, I am not going to tell you that what you did wasn't wrong; it *was* wrong. There are those who will argue that this war, or even any war, is wrong. To say that *war is hell* is to resort to an old and tired expression—perhaps even a cliché. But there is a good reason why it is old and tired, and that is because it is true. War is hell. It forces humans to face decisions they never should have to face; it raises them to great acts of valor and personal sacrifice; but it also lowers them to horrific acts of inhumanity.

"You are a good person, with a great deal to give. I have seen these qualities in you since we first met. It is the reason I have made so many exceptions in your case to see you become a priest. With this collar you can do a lot of good. It would be a shame to compound one mistake with another. We believe in a religion of forgiveness and in a God of redemption. You are deeply and genuinely sorry for what you did in Vietnam, and I have no doubt that if there had been a legal system under which your Captain Dam could have been brought to justice, you would have availed yourself of it. I am equally confident that if anything remotely like that were to happen here, you would work through our system of justice. You yourself have told me so. When we plucked you from civilian life, you were a peace-loving soul. You had never owned or fired a weapon, and I doubt you ever would have."

"I don't know, sir; I'm very confused right now. I'm not sure what to think."

"I will tell you what we are going to do. I'll accept this collar from you now and keep it in my top desk drawer," he said as he took the collar from George, got up, walked around to the front of his desk, and placed it in the left-hand side of his top middle drawer (a messy place where Livie kept his paper clips, note pads, pens and pencils, Scotch tape, staples, and more). "Should you change your mind and want it back, which I sincerely hope you will, you will know where to come for it."

"Fair enough," said George as he stood up and prepared to shake Reverend Pratt's hand and leave. But the reverend would hear none of it and insisted on taking George into New Haven for lunch. He knew a very nice French bistro that prepared exquisite cordon beau. So off the two went for a pleasant lunch at the bistro. It would be the last time they would break bread together.

After lunch, the two walked back to the Yale campus, where Reverend Pratt saw George to his car in the parking lot. As George was backing the GTO out of its parking space, Reverend Pratt walked over, leaned in the open window, and whispered to George, "Don't be a stranger."

"I won't," smiled George as he drove away. But he *would* be a stranger—it simply would prove too painful to do otherwise.

George never would return for his collar. It still would be where Reverend Pratt had placed it on the left-hand side of his top middle desk drawer, mixed in with the paper clips, staples, and the like, three years later when Reverend Pratt died suddenly of an unexpected heart attack. George would attend the funeral along with Matt Kerr, John Sullivan Sr., and Father Phillips.

It had been left to Livie to pack up the reverend's things and clean out his office. When she finally got around to making a start, a week had passed since the highly emotional funeral. As she sat for a moment in the great man's desk chair, she hardly could believe he was gone, and her mind began to journey back over the years they had worked together. Had it really been almost eleven years since he had hired her, when she had moved back East from Texas? No, it had been almost thirteen. The time had flown by.

First she did an inventory of all the books and boxed them, which took her the better part of a week. Any book with an inscription or special meaning went to the Pratt family, and the rest would be sent to the Yale library, to be kept or disposed of as they saw fit. One book she planned to keep. It contained a picture of her handing Lewis Pratt some papers at the very desk at which she now was sitting. (It had been the photographer's idea, which she had unsuccessfully fought—because her hair had gotten frizzy from the rain that morning.) Now she was glad to have it for the memory it provided her of the wonderful man who had circled her image in the picture and written "Frizzy Livie, still so pretty!"

Next she undertook the daunting task of cataloging the memorabilia, furniture, and other personal effects. The furniture went quickly since it was almost entirely university property, except for a rocking chair President Kennedy had given the reverend (as the result of a lost bet on a Yale versus Harvard game of some kind), and the chair in which she was sitting, which had been the reverend's father's, when the senior Pratt had been a Federal Appellate Court Judge. She marked the two chairs for shipment to the family and tagged the rest of the furniture for the university to take.

The memorabilia and other personal effects were a different story. She had been present at many of the underlying events (although she had been invisible to all eyes but those of the reverend, who looked to her for cues on names, titles, and other background information that he never could remember), and this caused her to reminisce and sometimes even to break down and have to regain her composure, as she slowly worked through the lifetime of achievements that these memorabilia and other effects represented.

Then she went through all the correspondence, unpublished materials, and other papers, some still in boxes the way the reverend had left them. Almost another two weeks passed by the time these tasks were finished, and the university was growing impatient with the time it was taking her to finish up.

The next day was Saturday, and all that was left for her to do was to empty out the big, old desk. Feeling rushed, she decided to come in on that Saturday morning to tackle the task. Starting with the top middle drawer, and not knowing the significance of the collar she found, but assuming it had been one of the reverend's many spares, she tossed it into the trash along with some unused paper clips, a partially empty box of staples, a heavily worn eraser, and some stubby number two pencils—the entire remaining contents of the drawer.

And that is how the priesthood ended for the man who was called Captain John Joseph Chrisandra, a chaplain assigned to the 101st Airborne Division of the United States Army in Vietnam.

> "War is hell."
> —Reverend Lewis Pratt
> Yale Divinity School
> July 8, 1971

He may not have been the first to say it, and he certainly will not be the last; but he is the one who first said it to George.

– 32 –

The next day, Friday, July 9, 1971, George set out for the Hamptons. The events of the previous day had left him emotionally drained, and he was looking forward to some very much needed rest and relaxation. He remained well aware of the warning he had received from John Sullivan Sr., but to date, he had seen no evidence of being tested or of being protected by his Israeli guardians, and he certainly was not expecting any such encounters to take place in the Hamptons.

When he arrived at the house on Elm Street, he turned the GTO into the gravel driveway. The car's tires made a crunching sound as they slowly rolled over the pebbles and came to a stop in the old, familiar parking space. It was music to George's ears.

When he climbed the front steps to the covered porch and approached the front door, he could see Mr. Billingsly through the living room window, sitting in his usual armchair.

"It's open, come on in," Mr. Billingsly cried out, hardly taking his eyes off the tennis match on the television.

George nodded to Mr. Billingsly, who got up to greet him but then got pulled back into the tennis match when he heard the roar of the crowd coming from the television.

"You know where everything is; make yourself at home. There are two exchange students in the double bedroom, so you will be sharing the bathroom as usual. They're females, so please remember to put the seat down. You know how bent out of shape they get over that stuff.

If you can't get in there, you always are welcome to come down and use mine."

"Thanks, I'll be fine," replied George as he started up the stairs to the right of the front door.

It was a charming old Victorian house where Mr. Billingsly now lived alone and rented the rooms to help make ends meet. Mrs. Billingsly had died several years earlier, and George never met her. The inside of the house and its furnishings were dated but warm and comfortable. George suspected that Mrs. Billingsly had been the same way, warm and comfortable to be with.

When he entered the single room, it looked the same as it always had. It'd been only a year since he was there last summer, but it felt like a lifetime. At least it had been for Captain John J. Chrisandra.

The single bedroom was painted a pale blue, and the bed had a white lace bedspread. Next to the bed was a dark wood nightstand with an old porcelain lamp. The only other furnishing in the room was a dresser that matched the nightstand. The floor was dark wood with a small white rug by the bed. There was a window that looked out on the front lawn and the tree-lined street below. The view was partially obstructed by a branch on the big, old elm that shaded the covered front porch below.

George placed his suitcase on the bed, as he'd done so many times before, and had sat down next to it to take in all the old familiar sounds and smells when one of the women from the room next door knocked on the open door.

"Hi, I'm Naomi Auerback, and I'm here with my sister, Fran. We're foreign exchange students from Israel and will be attending Columbia University in September."

"It's nice to meet you. I'm George Angelson, and I'll be studying law at Boston College Law School in the fall."

George had never met Sam Lerner's mother, and Sam had never had reason to mention her maiden name to him, so the name Auerback meant nothing to George. Naomi and Fran were distant cousins of Sam Lerner, but neither George nor they knew it.

"This is our first time to the Hamptons, and we thought you might have some suggestions for us."

"Well sure, but most people have very different interests. I come here mainly to relax, do the bar scene at night, and sun on the beach during the day."

"What bars do you recommend, and which is your favorite beach?"

"I like to hang out at Bobby Van's in Bridgehampton. He plays the piano from time to time, and the place always seems to be filled with interesting people. But nothing starts happening before nine to nine-thirty at night."

"What do you do before that?"

"I like to go over to the War Memorial here in Southampton. There is a pond behind it, and I like to sit and read while watching the ducks glide through the water as they go about their business. It's the quiet interlude before the bar scene storm, if you know what I mean."

"I do, and it sounds like fun. Maybe we'll see you over there."

"Great."

"By the way, what is the flashlight for?"

"I use it to read if it starts to get too dark before I finish a chapter. I can be a little anal in that regard, or so my friends tell me."

"I see. Say, could I borrow it for a minute? I'll bring it right back."

"Sure. Here, take it."

At this point Fran came out of the double bedroom to ask her sister for the keys to their VW bus. Naomi introduced her to George, who had noticed the bus when he was parking and asked about all the stickers on the windows.

"We bought it used. The prior owners were two guys who travelled around the United States in it and collected stickers form everywhere they'd been."

"Oh, I see. I noticed the airborne sticker on it and was wondering about it."

"Yeah, one of the guys had been in the airborne, but I don't know any of the details."

With that, the sisters went back into their room, and George decided to lie down on the bed and take a short nap. As he removed the suitcase from the bed so that he could lie down, he told himself the two sisters were extremely fit and most attractive. But it never occurred to him that they might be the Israeli agents John Sullivan Sr. had arranged to protect him, nor did he stop to think that their questions had been to learn of his plans and likely whereabouts.

– 33 –

When George awakened an hour later, the sisters appeared to be gone but had returned the flashlight and placed it on the dresser. At least he had the bathroom to himself, he thought, as he washed up and prepared to drive over to see his fine feathered friends and read by the pond. He just had started *Catch-22* by Joseph Heller and was anxious to read more. He still had one half of a peanut butter and jelly sandwich that his mother had made for him, which he planned to share with the ducks.

When George first arrived at the pond, he read his book. But as time went on, his mind began to wander, and he found himself once again thinking of Claire. He had left the radio playing in the GTO, and as dusk moved in, the ducks had come over to investigate. He could not resist and began to feed them morsels of bread from the sandwich. The song "There's a Moon out Tonight" came on the radio, as the moon rose and became brighter and more beautiful with the darkening of the sky. His memory went back to the night he and Claire had made love by the orphanage under that same moon and the stars and her words to him that wherever the future might take them, they always would be able to look up at that moon and talk to each other. Overwhelmed by his emotions, he mindlessly continued to feed the ducks until Officer Debrowski took pity on George and let him go without a ticket after questioning him about Sister Claire and Vietnam.

George once again had failed to realize the true nature of the situation and had been oblivious to the fact that he was being tested by Officer Debrowski, who was more than a former marine, Korean War veteran, and sleepy town police officer. He was a company man on assignment. George's life was far more scripted than he had realized, and even the Hamptons did not provide a total refuge from the shadows of his past.

You may have noticed that I said George "once again" had failed to notice that he was being tested. That is because he already had been tested once before by John Sullivan Sr. himself, who wanted to be certain not to leave anything to chance. Bill Fisher and his would-be muggers had not been who they had seemed to be. They in fact were elite Navy SEALs on assignment for John Sullivan Sr.—a favor arranged for him by his old friend Admiral William McCreery.

The report back to John Sullivan Sr. from Admiral McCreery read

> Your man stayed true and never revealed his past in Vietnam. However, he was flying a little close to the sun and almost got his wings singed by still having and brandishing his "uncle's" combat knife. I am told he was pretty good with it for someone who was supposed to be a chaplain. Not sure I'd want to have to confess my sins to him, if you know what I mean. He may be retired from your service, but he definitely can still be extremely dangerous.

Neither George nor Officer Debrowski had noticed the VW bus parked down the road, alongside the pond, with its lights off. Behind its blackened windows were two Israeli agents, one manning a listening device that was picking up and recording the conversation between the two men (the bug that had been placed in the flashlight was working perfectly), and the other with her high-powered rifle trained on the Southampton police officer should he draw his gun before George made any admission about Vietnam.

George never acknowledged that he had been in Vietnam. Officer

Debrowski never had reason to draw his weapon. And the two Israeli agents never had any cause to act. All went their separate ways, none the worse for it. As George has told you, later that night he drove to Bobby Van's in Bridgehampton. There he met the Israeli exchange students and bought them a drink, never realizing—of course—how much he really owed them. And he never would.

Eventually he would chase the moon down Sagg Main Street in Sagaponack and speak with Sister Claire one last time as he momentarily was suspended in time and space over Sagg Main Beach in his moon rocket—the GTO—before it came crashing back to earth. He would sleep on the beach atop his spacecraft until morning, when a friendly farmer would come to his aid. They would have coffee together, and then George would return to his room on Elm Street to pack his things and head for home. There to greet him in the living room window was Bubba, Mr. Billingsly's old cat, along with his new buddies, two kittens named Sam and Harley. The two kittens were too busy playing with wooden chips that Mr. Billingsly called "bull chips," to pay any attention to George. But old Bubba came and rubbed against George's leg.

Scarred forever by the sword of Excalibur and the loss of Claire, George not long thereafter got into his GTO and with hardly a notice drove west on Route 27, out of the Hamptons, and into the hot July afternoon.

And so it *really* was in the summer of 1971.

It was a time when the sage words of Robert Frost in the time honored poem, "The Road Not Taken," rang true for George. He had taken the road less traveled, and it had made a profound difference in his young life.

Oh, by the way ...

George kept his trusted friend, the 1967 GTO, for almost thirteen years, long after he had become a successful lawyer. That is, until he would buy the car of a little girl's dreams—my dreams. You remember, don't you? The car I had told him on a Saigon Street long ago I was going to buy when I came to America and became a famous movie star—the silver Mercedes-Benz SL with the red interior.

It would be a brand new 1979, the year I would have turned sixteen and been able to drive—had I lived. And he would name it Mary Bernadette, after me. The forget-everything injection the mousy doctor with the little black bag of magic had given him had not been so magical after all—he had not forgotten. (And they say men don't listen!)

In the words of Sister Kate, he is Hesperidean in his protection of that car.

— *Book Four:* —
THE AFTERMATH

– 1 –

The war didn't end for the others when it ended for Captain Chrisandra. They would be required to finish their tours of duty before being allowed to return home.

After the completion of Operation Excalibur, one of the two helicopters, Screaming Eagle, was retired and reassigned. The other, Headhunter, received a consolidated crew, consisting of Jon Trueblood and Nadim Haddad as pilots and Joaquin Arango as gunner.

On Wednesday, October 6, 1971, they were responding to a request for emergency medical help from a small village near Pleiku when the unthinkable happened. On board the helicopter that day, in addition to the crew, was a full complement of passengers: a top army surgeon and two of his best nurses as well as six soldiers to provide protection for them while they were in the village. They were high-profile passengers, and Joaquin was more nervous than usual about protecting them. He, Jon, and Nadim had been operating without sleep for more than twenty-four hours.

As Headhunter came in to set down, a young Vietnamese boy, no more than eight years old, came running toward the craft, yelling, "Candy, candy, candy—please candy." Joaquin thought he noticed something strange about the boy's shirt. It was fuller and tighter on him than it should be. He screamed to Jon and Nadim to abort, but they were busy concentrating on the landing, now made more difficult by their concerns that the boy would be decapitated by Headhunter's spinning blades. With only a split second to decide, he opened fire on the child. When the bullets ripped into their mark, the child exploded like a mortar shell, causing Headhunter to crash land and splattering human remains on the helicopter and its door gunner.

The six soldiers on board the helicopter became enraged to think that the people they'd been trying to help were Vietcong sympathizers trying to trick and kill them and lost it. Rushing from the helicopter, they began to indiscriminately massacre old men, women, and children, demanding to have the Vietcong among them be identified. Finally, a woman pointed to what appeared to be a man in his twenties and three teenage boys and said they were the Vietcong.

The soldiers then shot the man and his three younger companions. Joaquin had no way of knowing if the woman was being truthful, but her actions did end the killing spree. When it was over, twenty villagers were dead—twenty-one, if you include the young boy Joaquin had killed. But some forty or sixty had been spared.

Headhunter eventually made it back to base with all on board unharmed—at least not physically harmed. Joaquin was distraught and visibly shaken. He kept hoping it was a bad dream and he would wake up from it. But it wasn't; and he never again would be the same.

The press didn't pick up the story for some reason. So it went unreported, lost in the background noise of the war.

Not long thereafter, the three airborne soldiers would complete their tours of duty and be sent home. Their helicopters, Screaming Eagle and Headhunter, would not enjoy the same fate. They would never leave Vietnam.

Jon Trueblood returned to the reservation, where he was welcomed as a returning warrior and hero. Once the many tribal ceremonies and rituals of renewal and restoration were over, he finally prevailed upon that teacher of his, the one that was eleven years his senior, to marry him—Donna was her name. I guess Lieutenant Sullivan and Captain Chrisandra were wrong. For in the end, he did know what to do with her. After all, they had a son, who Jon sometimes called Running Eagle. Jon promised the boy he would tell him how he came to have that name when he was older. But he never would find the time. He was too busy in the CIA and then later championing the cause of his people as the senior Senator from Arizona.

———

Nadim Haddad returned to Brooklyn, where he, too, was welcomed back into his Syrian community and took over his father's taxicab business. His father had always insisted that his cabs have an American flag stickered to their rear windows. It was his way of recognizing the country that had given him so much. When Nadim joined the airborne, he added another sticker below the one of the American flag to honor his son. It was a black horizontal sticker with the word *airborne* arched and framed in yellow print. Every red and white cab of his had to have one.

Nadim Haddad would never forget his debt to Samuel Lerner for saving his life. After Jeanette Lerner's sister, Frances, died of cancer in 1978 and was buried in Sharon Gardens in Valhalla, New York, he regularly would drive Mrs. Lerner to visit her sister's gave. Four times a year an Arab and Jew together in a red and white cab, with an American flag and an airborne insignia stickered to its rear window, would make the journey there and back. When Mrs. Lerner died on July 26, 1986, and was buried beside her sister, the routine would change.

Five times a year, an Arab alone in a red and white cab, with an American flag and an airborne insignia stickered to its rear window, would make the journey there and back. The extra trip always was on Mother's Day, to put a single yellow rose on her grave for the son who could not do it—the one who had saved his life.

> For, in the final analysis,
> our most basic common link
> is that we all inhabit this small
> planet. We all breathe the same air.
> We all cherish our children's future.
> And we are all mortal.
> —John F. Kennedy

– 2 –

Unfortunately, Joaquin did not fare as well as his two brethren. He never would be able to get the sight of that little Vietnamese boy out of his mind. Even though the boy had been booby-trapped, it bothered him that he'd been willing to pull the trigger before he knew for sure.

He had difficulties keeping a job, and his relationship with his wife, Lucy, was a troubled one. The final straw came when he refused to have any children. He was petrified that any child of his would be punished for what he had done to the little boy yelling, "Candy, candy, candy—please candy." It kept him up at night!

Lucy told him that if he didn't get help, and soon, she would leave him. She even went so far as to find him a doctor who specialized in treating Vietnam War veterans. Joaquin knew that he couldn't afford to lose Lucy. He needed her too much, so he agreed to go and see the doctor. As fate would have it, the doctor was away on sabbatical by the time Joaquin finally agreed to seek help. Not wanting to see either of the doctor's partners, Joaquin chose instead to visit with his parish priest.

Father Rodriquez was a gentle and well-meaning man, who was adored by his congregation. But he was young, had been a priest for only a few years and was still somewhat naive and idealistic. He had never experienced guerrilla warfare and didn't have an understanding of the problems or an appreciation for the complexities presented by such situations. He would take a simplistic view, refusing to believe

Joaquin could have killed a young child, telling him that if he did, he was at risk of excommunication and eternal damnation. Joaquin tried in vain to explain that he hadn't taken part in the massacre, but only in the shooting of the booby-trapped boy. The boy's fate already had been determined by those who had strapped the explosives on him. The only question remaining was how many others were going to die with him.

Joaquin argued that what he'd done was in self-defense. He was defending himself and the others on the helicopter, as he'd been charged with doing. But Father Rodriquez saw it differently. He felt that as highly trained professionals, they should've anticipated something like that and been prepared in advance with a plan for aborting the landing, should the situation arise. He argued that Joaquin could've fired in front of the boy or over his head to discourage him, or maybe he could've wounded him in the leg to thwart his progress. All the good Father's arguments were valid to one extent or another, but not in the split second sleep-deprived world in which Joaquin had to decide. He had used his best judgment in that lonely moment of crisis and now would have to live with the consequences.

Unable to find the help and understanding that he needed or the forgiveness he so desperately sought, the former airborne soldier went home, sat on his bed, removed his revolver from the nightstand, and ended his own life, as he had that of the little Vietnamese boy a year earlier. In the words of Buck Jones, he had "wasted" himself. Then again, perhaps Father Rodriquez would see it differently and say that it was we who had failed and "wasted" such a promising young life by not having anticipated the problems of our returning veterans and been prepared in advance with a plan of action.

American society was still thirty years away from truly understanding and experiencing guerrilla warfare up close and dirty. That education would come on a beautiful, clear, and sunny Tuesday September morning—September 11, 2001—when a senseless terrorist act would kill more than three thousand innocent Americans in New York City on live national television.

On that beautiful, clear, and sunny Tuesday September morning,

American fighter jets would be scrambled, and their pilots would be made aware that they might be called upon to shoot down commercial airliners with innocent men, women, and children on board. More fortunate than Joaquin, they were spared having to pull the trigger—and live with the memory that he did. But I am sure if they had been required to pull that trigger, that no one would have called them "baby killers," not even Father Rodriquez.

– 3 –

The Winged Goddesses were disbanded in the fall of 1971, never to fly together again. They all would melt back into civilian life, except Anne Herndon, who joined the CIA. They had been ahead of their time and had paid the price for it. As a parting gift, Matt Kerr gave each of them an aviator jacket with their name on the front. On the back was sewn "Winged Goddesses," and under it the caption "First and Always." It was more than they had expected and all the thanks that they needed.

Stewball and Coney Island Baby, the two modified KC-135 planes that they flew, now sit motionless in the airplane boneyard located in the desert outside of Tucson, Arizona. Their markings have become worn and faded by the blistering sun and countless sandstorms, and some of their parts have been removed over time for one reason or another. But they have remained true—two loose ends perhaps, but then again perhaps not—for they never will reveal their secrets.

Also protecting her secret is The Yellow Rose of Texas. Her lavatory remains occupied and out of order, as she sits on the bottom of the South China Sea, marking the spot over which the *Midway* was steaming on that June day in 1971.

Matt Kerr would be one of the last to leave Vietnam in April of 1975. He refused to depart until all of his people had been evacuated. He was a company man to the end.

Mary Sullivan had been right after all, and her sister, Sister Katherine Quinn, would have her prayers answered, but not in the way she had expected. I guess the Lord had other plans for her, for she would leave the Franciscan order of nuns to marry Matt Kerr—her soul mate.

As for the Sullivans, John Sullivan Sr. would finally retire and get his beach house in Baja, California. But it would not be the same without Sister Kate and Sister Claire to share it with. John Sullivan Jr. would follow in his father's footsteps and, after a decorated career in the US Marine Corps, would join the CIA.

Captain Dam's real name was Van Le. He'd changed it when he went to the North so that no one would know who his mother was. In the end, it really didn't matter.

Frenchie has a new identity. He lives with his wife, Gloria, and their daughter, Jackie, named for the lady in pink, on John's Island near Charleston, South Carolina, Bo's old hunting grounds.

―――

Well, now you know what really happened in Dallas in November of 1963, and in Vietnam and China during seven weeks in the late spring of 1971. This story having been told, it is time for me to go.

I hope the truth will set you free—it has for me.

—Mary Bernadette, July 1, 2012

―――

> The wave of the future is not the conquest of the world by a single dogmatic creed but the liberation of the diverse energies of free nations and free men.
> —John F. Kennedy

Made in the USA
Columbia, SC
20 April 2022